David Yallop has established a reputation as an investigative writer without equal, a 'seeker of justice'. He is author of *To Encourage the Others*, *The Day the Laughter Stopped*, *Beyond Reasonable Doubt?*, *Deliver Us from Evil* and *In God's Name*, which has been translated into forty languages and has sold over six million copies worldwide. *Unholy Alliance* is his first work of fiction.

UNHOLY ALLIANCE

David Yallop

BANTAM PRESS

LONDON · NEW YORK · TORONTO · SYDNEY · AUCKLAND

TRANSWORLD PUBLISHERS LTD
61–63 Uxbridge Road, London W5 5SA

TRANSWORLD PUBLISHERS c/o RANDOM HOUSE
AUSTRALIA PTY LTD
20 Alfred Street, Milsons Point, NSW 2061, Australia

TRANSWORLD PUBLISHERS c/o RANDOM HOUSE NEW ZEALAND
18 Poland Road, Glenfield, Auckland, New Zealand

Published 1999 by Bantam Press
a division of Transworld Publishers Ltd
Copyright © by © Poetic Products Ltd 1999

The right of David Yallop to be identified
as the author of this work has been asserted in accordance
with sections 77 and 78 of the Copyright Designs and
Patents Act 1988.

A catalogue record for this book
is available from the British Library.

ISBN 0593 028848 (cased edition)
0593 044274 (trade p/b edition)

Typeset in 11½/13pt Ehrhardt by
Hewer Text Ltd, Edinburgh

Printed in Great Britain by
Clays Ltd, St Ives plc

To all those currently engaged in fighting
on the losing side in the Third World War.

'Religion is the opium of the people.'

KARL MARX

A contribution to the *Critique of Hegel's Philosophy of Right* (1843–4) introduction.

'Opium is the religion of the people.'

ANDREW SINCLAIR

A contribution to Yallop's *Unholy Alliance* (1999) chapter one.

'Fiction reveals truths that reality obscures.'
JESSAMYN WEST

A contribution to *The Book of Unusual Quotations* (1959) ed. Rudolf Flesch.

PROLOGUE

EVEN ON VERY COLD DAYS RICHARD NIXON HAD A TENDENCY TO sweat.

The newly elected President of the United States had learned painfully, from 1960, how awful it looked on television. It had cost him the debates against the ever cool Jack Kennedy. Ever since then, he had left nothing to chance, and, as he read over his speech for the ceremony, he dabbed repeatedly at his made-up face with a handkerchief sprayed with ammonium chloride.

The content of the speech was easy and familiar . . . peace with honour in Vietnam . . . sacrifice in a great cause . . . as President, expressing pride of the nation in an American hero . . . But he struggled, as usual, to remember the dead hero's name. He tried it over and over again, encouraged by Mr Haldeman and Mr Ehrlichman. 'Private Stanley Kubieski.'

The late private's name was indeed of importance. It represented a major reason why the President of the United States was greeting his coffin at the windswept Air Force base: his name and his congressional district. The President had decided, at very short notice, to repay a campaign debt from 1968. The congressman had delivered an impressive number of votes to Mr Nixon, enough to win his state over Hubert Humphrey and wipe out the memory of Illinois in 1960. Now, in almost the first public ceremony since his inauguration, the new President would be honouring a dead soldier from the congressman's district. Private Kubieski was chosen from a short-list of three candidates, at the request of the congressman's staff, because he was white and bore a Polish name.

The choice had caused some embarrassment to the authorities responsible for flying home the remains of Private Kubieski. They had been forced at the last minute to transfer his coffin from an unmarked CIA Air America aircraft into a regular Air Force jet with a presidential seal. There was no time to remove the yellow labels with the sign 'Do Not Open! Danger! Typhus!', and these had been covered with the American flag.

For one last time the President rehearsed the name 'Kubieski', and glanced round at other participants in the ceremony. At eleven in the morning, the congressman was thoroughly fortified with bourbon. His staff were plying him with black coffee: the strongest of them hovered at his right shoulder, ready to grab him should he sway too far from the vertical. Cardinal Cody, a fat-faced, piggy-eyed man, who looked as though he might have given good service to the Borgias, plunged into conversation with Messrs Haldeman and Ehrlichman. He, too, was anxious for repayment of a campaign debt, and he reminded the two presidential aides of the powerful sermon he had preached on the last Sunday before the election. The deputy chiefs of staff for each service circled each other suspiciously. They had not let each other out of sight for a single second, and in consequence none of the three men had managed to secure a private audience with the President or to convince him that his service held the secret of winning the war in Vietnam.

More important than any of the military brass was the anonymous, dark-suited civilian, blinking behind his thick glasses. William Colby of the CIA was responsible for the 'pacification' of Vietnam. As such, he directed a series of covert programmes that would have attracted severe criminal penalties if carried out in the United States. Mr Colby was prepared to make use of corruption, racketeering, narcotics and even first degree murder, all with an unshakeable belief that the end justified the means. By nature charming and gentle, he alone of all the high and mighty dignitaries had had the good manners to talk to Private Kubieski's family.

Mr Kubieski was a retired steelworker on disability, Mrs Kubieski a tired, mousy woman who was a cashier in a supermarket. They were mystified by the summons to honour their dead elder son: in all honesty they had been glad when he shipped out to Vietnam after a lifetime of uninterrupted trouble. Their surviving son was far more promising: bright, dutiful and an altar boy at St Saviour's. They were delighted when the congressman and the cardinal and the President had pulled him to the centre of their official photographs, and had some vague idea that these might be profitable to him later in his career.

The President was a big disappointment to all three of them. He was awkward and had mumbled their name. He had no glamour, and they were amazed that he was made-up like an actor, almost a clown, and smelt distinctly of ammonia.

The jet landed, and the flag-draped coffin descended slowly to the tarmac, carried by expert pallbearers. The band struck up the national anthem and the President crossed his right hand over to his heart.

His speech passed off very well indeed, except that he referred to the hero throughout as 'Stanley Kowalski', the Marlon Brando role in *A Streetcar Named Desire*. Television would edit out the mistake, and make the President refer to him simply as 'Stanley', giving a spurious impression of warmth and intimacy.

The mourners adjourned to the mess of the Air Force base, while the coffin was taken to a small side chapel where a most curious scene took place. Two men, one in an army colonel's uniform, the other in a civilian suit, made themselves known to the captain of the honour guard. They produced a paper signed by Mr William Colby and asked to take possession of the coffin. The captain pointed out, reasonably, that the coffin had just been honoured by the President of the United States and was now due for release to its occupant's family.

The colonel and the civilian at this point indicated that a mistake had been made: the President had honoured the wrong coffin. They drew attention to the signs warning of 'Typhus' that meant that this particular coffin could not be released until further medical tests had been carried out. The two men then pointed out to the captain the benefits to his career of accepting the order and of keeping his mouth shut. The captain directed the honour guard to release the coffin to a team of soldiers in white coats, who returned some minutes later with a second flag-draped coffin identical to that of Private Kubieski but without Typhus labels. The honour guard reformed, unaware of the substitution.

Private Stanley Kubieski, a high-school dropout, had never expected to be worth four million dollars when he died, still less to be honoured by his congressman, his cardinal and his President. He had not enlisted in the Army for the sake of wealth or distinction but because even Vietnam was better than home. When the mortar shell hit him, on his first patrol in the Central Highlands, he was beginning to change his mind. The shell tore away most of his upper body and his identifying dog tags.

The remaining parts of him were collected and delivered to a section of Tan Son Nhut airbase that was off-limits to all but a small staff of CIA personnel. They were buried in a silver aluminium coffin, with packets of heroin totalling fifteen kilos in weight. The coffin was plastered with yellow labels stating 'Do Not Open! Danger! Typhus!' and loaded into an unmarked CIA Air America aircraft.

The arrangement proved entirely satisfactory to all concerned, especially President Richard Nixon, who never discovered that he had saluted a consignment of narcotics.

CHAPTER ONE

PROPOSAL

'BROTHERS AND SISTERS, DO YOU WANT TO BE LOVED?'

'Yes!'

'Do you want to be loved by Jesus Christ?'

'Yes!'

'Do you want to be saved?'

'Yes!'

'Do you want to be saved by Jesus Christ?'

'Yes!'

'Then tell the Lord!'

'Yes!'

'The Lord can't hear you! He can hear your lips but not your heart! So tell the Lord with your heart!'

'Yes! Yes! YES!'

The evangelist joined their roar, and threw both arms upwards. He was six feet tall and the gesture emphasized his big chest and his athletic body. The searchlights picked out his face – immaculate teeth, wide mouth, deep-set eyes, high forehead – then followed his upraised arms. Their beams made the sign of the Cross on the dark sky. The orchestra and the choir delivered a mighty chord of E major. The huge congregation, still yelling 'Yes!', leaped to their feet and reached for heaven.

Adam Fraser flicked his remote control, and extinguished heaven and earth. The mighty chord gave way to the distant horn of a London taxi.

He was almost a match for the departed evangelist – a fit six-footer who might have been fifty but might also have been thirty-five. They both had strong jaws and regular features. But where the preacher's face was pleasant, Adam's was dramatically handsome, like a matinée idol, saved from vacuity by the lines around the eyes.

'The Reverend Patrick Collins,' he said, to the other man in the viewing room. 'Eight million followers in the United States alone. His own cable channel, and a network TV show. Runs a billion dollar business, merchandising the Lord.'

'What makes you think you can create not one, but two, ninety-minute-long documentaries about him? And why should the network spend money on them?'

Adam looked at his old friend and patron. Mitch was wearing his usual jacket, which would not button over the paunch and had never been fashionable or elegant even before it acquired the burn marks and the patina of nicotine. He represented the sole evidence of intelligent life among the executives of Network Enterprise Television.

'You have just watched forty-five minutes of Patrick Collins, unedited, without smoking a cigarette.'

In a tiny room in the giant football stadium, two men and a woman watched the ecstatic congregation. The men wore business suits and security badges. The woman wore a short white dress, which showed off her legs and her shoulders and suggested everything in between. When she stood up, it moved with her, sculpting her marvellous body like the sea falling on soft sand.

She was twenty-two, but already a veteran of movies. Her

16

best work was seen on the Internet, after many passwords. The screen revealed her conventional beauty, but live she was a force of nature, who could turn not only heads but minds, a stripper of souls.

She planted a long kiss on the Reverend Patrick Collins, until his screen image disappeared.

'You'll be meeting the real thing in about an hour. We should be moving,' said one of the men.

'Do you want to be saved, sister?' said his companion.

'Yes, yes, yes!'

'And is he really without sin?' said Mitch.

'Unless you count hypocrisy,' said Adam. 'He preaches the virtues of poverty from a pulpit in his Florida estate, which is worth fourteen million dollars. He talks about how difficult it is for a rich man to enter heaven before flying to Boston and entering a little bit of heaven in Brookline worth another six million. He proclaims "Blessed are the meek", and makes world leaders grovel for a slot on his TV show. Remember last year, he gave the prime minister second place behind a ventriloquist?'

'That will do for Pride. Now give me Lust.'

It took nearly two hours before the last worshipper allowed Pat Collins to reach his hotel suite. The woman in the white dress had arranged herself on his couch, giving full value to her legs and offering a glimpse of black panties. She was reading the Gideon Bible.

He switched on the light and jumped. He stood in the doorway, frowning. She put down the Bible. 'I want to be saved, Reverend.'

He smiled for a second. 'I do not do private redemptions. But the church is open all night and no one who wishes to be saved and who truly repents their sins is turned away.'

She lay back on the couch and stretched. 'But I have so many sins, Reverend. I cannot go to a church with these sins upon my soul. I need to tell you my sins, Reverend.' He sidestepped towards the telephone. 'Aren't you interested in my sins, Reverend? I have more sins than the Bible. I've been in porno movies; I have let men express their sickest fantasies through me. Make me clean again, bless me. Bless me and heal my soul, put your hands upon me. I want you to baptize me.'

He picked up the telephone. 'This is Pat Collins, give me Mr Podesta.'

She rose from the couch, and threw herself at his feet. 'I want to wash your feet like Mary Magdalene. But I bet she didn't do foot massage. I can do foot massage you wouldn't believe and not just on feet . . .' She fiddled unsuccessfully with the double knots in his lace-up shoes and then turned her attention to higher things.

'If you don't want my soul, Reverend, what about my body?' She rose and stood in front of him. 'Why do you think God made me? And why did He make you? You're fifty-three, but why did God give you the body of a thirty-year-old? Why did He make you turn on women like an electric light? I need you, Pat, I want you.' She grabbed his hands but he instantly broke free and spoke into the telephone.

'Jack, would you and Chuck come here right away?'

'This isn't a set up. There is no hidden camera. There are no bugs on me. Feel for yourself. Take me anywhere you want. Give me one night, one hour. Your wife is two thousand miles away with the flu. She won't know, cross my heart and may I go to hell . . . Don't deny yourself, Pat. Listen to the message inside you . . .'

'There is a bug in this room, because I asked for it. I am now telling the bug that I did not ask you to come here and you are not going to stay here. Security personnel will shortly escort you from this hotel. If you wish, they will take you to the church. I shall now recite the Lord's Prayer until they arrive: I recommend that you join me. Our Father who art in heaven . . .'

Jack Podesta and Chuck Talbot arrived, with excellent timing, on 'Lead us not into temptation'. The woman left with them quietly, showing no sign of recognition. They did not stop at the church, but dropped her at a black limousine and gave her a large brown envelope. The men returned to the hotel, and examined some photographs of their recent companion naked in a sauna with a well-known archbishop engaged in an unusual version of the baptism ceremony.

'Married to Teresa for twenty-eight years, with two grown-up children. Not a rumour, not a hint that he's ever looked at anyone else and I'm not surprised: she's a beautiful woman and she's said to be smart. She's written three self-help manuals and has a syndicated advice column: she seems happy to travel with him, walk on the platform and hold hands. She missed her first crusade last year with a virus, he nearly cancelled. He wrote a hymn in her honour; it went platinum . . .'

'Enough already.' Mitch finally smoked a cigarette. 'So where's the dark side, the inner truth, the trademark of an Adam Fraser documentary?'

The patient arrived in an ambulance and was delivered to Jack and Chuck's hotel suite, on a stretcher, swathed in bandages, with a large document envelope, which they opened and checked quickly. They put up the DO NOT DISTURB sign and made the patient comfortable. They woke him early and took him to a place in the woods not far from the hotel.

Pat Collins's heart skipped a beat when he heard footsteps behind him on his early morning run. He looked round and relaxed when he saw that the pursuer was a teenage boy. 'Reverend, wait up!'

Collins jogged on the spot until the boy caught up with him. He was slim and had floppy fair hair, and was wearing shorts and a tee-shirt. The face showed no signs of hair or spots, and was quite beautiful. He was fifteen and already a veteran of movies. His best work was also seen on the Internet.

'Gee, you're fast, Reverend! I chased you all the way from the hotel. The TV said you were a runner. I waited up for you all night.' He pulled off the tee-shirt to mop his face, and loosened his shorts, revealing a glimpse of black underpants.

Collins stopped jogging. 'We better get you home, son.'

'No! I ran away! I ain't got a home, just the institute. Don't make me go back there. They make me . . . do things.' The boy looked away and blushed. 'Turn tricks. You've no idea of the tricks.' He looked appealingly at Collins. 'I watched you on TV. I waited and waited until you came to the city. I want to be with you, Reverend. I wouldn't be any bother, I'd do anything for you.'

'What's your name, son?'

'Tommy.'

'Tommy, I can't look after you, but the Church will. We care for thousands of children who run away, and they stay with us until we're sure that they'll be safe and loved somewhere else. What I want you to do now is to run back to the hotel while I make some calls on my mobile phone. Go to the front desk and wait for a Mrs Erzen, she'll show you ID, she's our children's officer and she'll take care of you.'

'I . . . think I hurt my leg. Would you look at my leg, Reverend?' The boy rubbed his thigh and looked over his shoulder at Collins.

'The best thing for cramp is to run it off,' said Collins firmly and he pulled out a mobile telephone from his tracksuit. 'The front desk. Mrs Erzen.'

Tommy put his top back on and loped away towards the hotel. But he did not go to the front desk or meet Mrs Erzen. He turned away to a back road, where Jack and Chuck were waiting for him in a hired car. They gave him some clothes and a brown envelope. They dropped him close to the Greyhound bus station and said something that made him turn pale. Then they left him.

They studied more slowly the contents of the envelope the boy had brought with him. One photograph was fuzzy, but the other five showed a naked Tommy sitting on the lap of a completely bald man. Even without his trademark black wig, he could be identified clearly and unmistakably as the man tipped by many to be the future Speaker of the United States House of Representatives.

*   *   *

20

'Now, I want you to think of those beautiful children of yours, Mr Sherborne. What you have to believe is that unless you spend just a few dollars a week on these encyclopaedias, your kids could die mentally. Their minds would have nothing to eat . . .'

Twenty years gone, and Andrew Sinclair could remember his first sale. Encyclopaedias. Door-to-door. The supreme assault course of selling. He had survived it, and tasted power and exhilaration.

He had learned how to make people value an acquisition, make them feel that they could not live without it. The discovery had financed his escape from a working-class home in Memphis, Tennessee, and the mother who drank herself into a blind rage and the father and brothers who hid from her.

He sold enough encyclopaedias to pay his way through Stanford University. Then he sold the university. It gave him a job as a fund-raiser. He took rich alumni out to lunch. 'They're creating an illuminated list of honour called The Special Friends of Stanford. The entrance fee is rather high . . .'

A fee of half a million dollars for something less valuable than an encyclopaedia. But the principle was the same: make the buyer value the acquisition, make him feel that his life would be incomplete without his name on an illuminated list.

One Special Friend of Stanford made a further acquisition: he bought Andrew Sinclair. He gave Sinclair a highly paid job in his management consultancy. A few years later he made him a junior partner. Less than a year after that, the junior partner took away his best staff and ten of his biggest accounts: the former Special Friend was now in a mental institution.

Andrew Sinclair had retained his boyish looks and helpful, eager-to-please manner into his late forties and through over a decade of power and wealth. He was now chief executive of the most powerful management consultancy in the United States. It did not even style itself a consultancy any more, but proclaimed itself, arrogantly but truthfully, Corporate America. It not only advised but nurtured and restructured the great, blue-chip companies of the United States. Sinclair thought nothing of persuading his clients to make billion-dollar plus acquisitions – but his sales techniques relied on precisely the same principle as that first sale of the encyclopaedias.

Today Sinclair had to persuade his most important client to make a serious acquisition. The client was not well known to the public, but he took up far more of Sinclair's time than any other. The acquisition was extremely well known, a household-name enterprise with an international reputation. It would represent the largest transfer of assets in human history. As he waited for his client, Sinclair saw the face of Mr Sherborne.

Adam Fraser left Mitch's office. He paused to take a deep breath, and then gave a long victory punch. Twenty-one films in twenty-five years and still the buzz, in his late forties, when the new film went through its first green light.

He hurried down the corridor to his office, otherwise known as the phone box. As he entered, three heads turned and stared silently at him.

'Green light. Assuming the preacher man gives us full co-operation.'

Susanna, his researcher/PA, clapped. Leon, his cameraman, and Barry, the sound recordist, struck the most dramatic poses the cramped walls would allow.

Leon, arms wide, demanded, 'Do you want to be saved?'

Barry, on one knee, replied with a fervent 'I do.'

'My son, you can be saved today.'

'Tell me how, Reverend, please tell me how.'

'Take out your wallet, open it wide and repeat after me, "Help yourself." '

Susanna joined in the game. 'Stop being bad boys, or the preacher man will throw Adam out of the Garden of Eden.'

Adam watched the three. He would not make this film without them, or any other film. In Hanoi in 1979, before Susanna, Barry had saved them from jail when he bribed a Customs official with a fake Rolex watch. In Beirut in 1989, after Susanna, Leon had saved them when he gave a member of

Hezbollah who had been intent on kidnapping them his Manchester United shirt. Long live the consumer society. And Susanna loved him . . .

She ended the kidding with a serious question. 'Is there any reason why we shouldn't get full co-operation?'

Adam replied, straight-faced, 'Only an act of God.'

'I am obliged to you, Andrew, for coming to meet me in advance of the main board.' Victor Rodriguez swivelled in his chair as Sinclair was admitted to his office. By comparison to Sinclair's office high in the World Trade Center, this room was small and drab, as indeed was its occupant compared to Sinclair himself.

But it was Rodriguez who had the power – the power to buy what Sinclair had determined Rodriguez should buy. He was in no hurry. Sinclair listened patiently to an account of the bird sanctuary Rodriguez was building, and the rigorous measures he had taken to exclude poachers and chemicals. He listened, equally patiently, to a long-familiar account of his host's children's lives through Harvard, Yale and Princeton, their excellent marriages, their careers in law, accountancy and fine arts.

'Your fax was encouraging, but its content as always had to be opaque.' Holding the fax close to his face, Rodriguez read it aloud. 'The product's reputation is excellent and unblemished. It is a clear leader in a crowded market. Recently the product was tested in extreme conditions against reagents of opposite types. The product displayed no adverse reaction.' Rodriguez placed the single sheet of paper on his desk. 'Could you describe these tests more fully?'

'Our security people working for Collins supplied him with an exceptionally alluring – and expensive – young woman. He declined her offer and had her removed without fuss or attention. They then supplied him with a beautiful – and even more expensive – boy. Again, removed with no difficulties. For the record, he was more interested in the woman than the boy. I could arrange other tests, but I am confident that if I went right

23

through the animal kingdom he will lack the potential for a sexual scandal. Collins is smart. He'd actually bugged his own hotel suite. After the second test he fired both of our security people, and he now never stays in a hotel when he's away from home, always with a Church member, with loyal witnesses to his behaviour on hand.'

Sinclair studied Victor's impassive face for a moment, then continued. 'Our people have looked over his business. It's run competently and with total honesty. He's got a very proficient team headed by his good buddy John Reilly. Collins pays his taxes, declares every last cent and none of the money from the collection plate sticks to his fingers.'

Sinclair's voice rose very slightly. His pace quickened just a trifle. 'He's never used any cheap tricks to raise money, he doesn't promise miracles or cures or salvation. He does not brainwash people into signing their money away. Victor, we are not dealing with Elmer Gantry. Or Oral Roberts, or Jimmy Bakker, or Jimmy Swaggert, some cheap salesman . . . This is an American of exceptional quality. He has the power to change the millennium for good. This is our man, Victor.'

Victor Rodriguez stirred faintly in his chair. Andrew Sinclair saw the movement and drew breath. He was close to the euphoric, climactic moment of a sale: years fell away from him as he switched on the smile that had charmed so many Special Friends of Stanford. 'And he was your idea, Victor. You said, "Find me the man who will save our market." This is him.'

'But why will he listen to us? This is a man of God.'

'Exactly so, Victor. That is the beauty of it. God would never let him spoil the market. Any other man might, one day, see reason. But this man will always follow God – and save the market.'

Remembering that Victor Rodriguez was himself a devout man, Sinclair hurried on to another argument. 'We also, of course, have a powerful insurance. Everyone has something he cannot explain or excuse. We have found it for Patrick Collins – and kept it for ourselves. If he should ever threaten the market we can destroy him and we have something to control his successor.'

Rodriguez thoughtfully kneaded his chin with a knuckle. 'My preference has always been for more conventional methods of control. They have brought us success with little cost and little risk. But you have taught us well, Andrew. Every business must be prepared to innovate. Businesses survive when they see the moment to change. This is the moment, Andrew. I will be putting your plan to the main board.'

'Christmas in Florida. Good enough for you?' Adam Fraser smiled at Susanna. He felt like a parent holding out an especially desired present.

'I'll pack my water-wings. But I still want you to hold me up every time I go into the water . . .' She rolled on top of him under the duvet and guided his hands into position. 'Breast stroke . . .' She moved along his body, giggling. Presently she said, 'Start in the shallows.' And a little later, 'Deeper. Take me deeper.'

They dived in rhythm through their imaginary sea, until they caught the same ultimate breaking wave and subsided, gasping, on to the sands.

They lay entwined for a while and then she said, 'You're somewhere else. With whom?'

The 'whom' made him ache with tenderness for her: to remember her grammar in the midst of love. She was a perfectionist. Since she had worked for him none of his documentaries had ever contained even a trivial error. She would stay up all night to weed out a single split infinitive. He gave her a long, roaming hug.

'You're still not with me.'

'I'm sorry. Just a touch of pre-production terror. Every documentary we've ever made together, I always felt there was an inner truth and if we worked hard enough we'd find it. But now I don't have that feeling . . . I actually think that the outer truth of Pat Collins and the inner truth are the same. There are things I dislike about him, especially the money and the merchandising, things where we can point the camera and the mike, but nothing that we didn't know when we first started. And that scares me stiff.'

El Gordo was watching over them.

The location for the two-day conference had been chosen with great care. For Victor Rodriguez it was, of course, convenient to use his own headquarters in Cúcuta, Colombia, and for his visitors it was convenient to cross the Venezuelan border, unremarked, from San Cristobal. But one factor made the location irresistible: the presence of El Gordo.

El Gordo, the fat one, was the pet name for a computer regarded by its creator as 'out of this world'. An apt description for a system based on NASA's computer network. No one made a phone call, sent a fax, used a computer, in either Cúcuta or San Cristobal, without 'sharing' the line with the fat one. No car arrived in or left the two cities without El Gordo knowing the owner. The fat one was linked to its brothers in Medellin, Cali, Bogotá, Caracas, Lima and La Paz. It had immediate access to every scrap of information contained on police and intelligence computers in Colombia and Venezuela, Peru and Bolivia: the criminal records, identification data, status of all criminal investigations.

Everything.

El Gordo explained the complete lack of curiosity in Cúcuta when a stranger appeared in town – particularly when Andino Incorporated, Latin America's most successful multinational, held its annual general meeting. Andino Incorporated represents all that is good about Latin American business. The non-drug side. Its core industry is construction. Andino does not merely build for others, it also builds for itself. In Italy it owns seventeen of the country's finest hotels, twenty-three major business centres and eleven industrial companies. In France Andino has built and leased a huge office block on the avenue des Champs Elysées, another in rue de Ponthieu and a third in rue de Berry. In Canada it owns three of the world's tallest skyscrapers – the Three Towers in Montreal, the Harbor

Tower, and a three-hundred-apartment block, plus a marina in Vancouver and a three-million-acre forest near Edmonton. In the United States it has five huge apartment blocks in Washington, including the Rutherford Hotel, and in New York a residential area of two hundred and fifty acres situated at Oyster Bay.

In Brazil in the Matto Grosso it owns an entire satellite city, Santa Maria. In Great Britain Andino has substantial holdings in Canary Wharf, Belgravia, Mayfair, Hampstead and the City. It has a piece of the Channel Tunnel, a piece of the Japanese high-speed rail network, a piece of Sydney's business centre, of two marinas in Auckland . . . The above list of holdings represents less than 20 per cent of Andino Incorporated's assets.

This multinational derives most of its wealth from just three basic assets: people, paper and product – illegal drugs. All three are inexhaustible. Endlessly available. The product, whether cocaine, opium, heroin, marijuana or the range of chemical drugs such as amphetamines, PCP, LSD, generates the paper, the dollars, euro-currencies, sterling and the many others that feed the machine, the people.

With every mile that the heroin, the cocaine, the marijuana move from their production areas to their market their prices leap. If the annual supply of cocaine were to be packed into 1.5 kilo bags, the size of a regular bag of flour, the amount supplied to the United States would, if the bags were stood on top of each other, be four times as high as Mount Everest. If the amount supplied to the entire world were similarly stacked it would be thirteen times as high as Everest, the amount of opium fifty-two times as high.

In the world of narcotics there is a hard centre. At street level it is represented by the dealer, hustling drugs for a small margin, and at Cartel of Cartels level it is controlled by the board of directors of Andino Incorporated. Between those two poles exist all others who inhabit this particular world, from the humble mules to the high profile players like the late Pablo Escobar, the Rodriguez-Orejuela brothers of Cali, President Assad's brother Rifaat, the Burmese warlord Khun Sa, the

Inzerillo and Spatola Sicilian Mafia families. These are known to the world's intelligence agencies. The members of the board, the Cartel of Cartels, if they are known at all by those same intelligence agencies, are regarded as fine, honest businessmen, dedicated to all that is good in this life.

Its global turnover of narcotics would make it, in terms of gross domestic product, the eleventh biggest national economy in the world, ahead of the Netherlands, Australia, Russia and India. One year's profit would be enough to buy the world's three largest public companies.

Over drinks and canapés the twelve board members greeted each other like a family reunion. Markov from Russia hugged Sullivan from the United States. Victor Rodriguez from Colombia laughed with Pietro Pecolli from Italy. Each of the four, like every other member of the board, was responsible for a specific part of the world, their primary task to ensure that Andino's business philosophies were implemented.

The simultaneous translation facilities included a bilingual sign-language interpreter for the board member from Brazil. A satellite link allowed not only contribution from senior Cartel members, but also live reports from the Golden Triangle – Burma, Laos and Thailand – the Golden Crescent of Afghanistan, Iran, Pakistan, the Bekaa Valley, Tashkent, Wall Street and the City of London. The satellite was the exclusive property of Andino. Launched in 1994, it was built in the United States by a consortium of leading communication companies on behalf of the Colombian government. Its stated purpose was to enhance business between Colombia and the rest of the world through vastly improved communication links.

Like the stock exchanges of the world, the industry operated a twenty-four-hour marketplace in a multitude of tongues. Its annual report was written in thirty-three languages, including Hebrew to accommodate the Israeli board member, Rabbi Goldberg.

Moving casually through the chatting groups before the opening of the first session was Andrew Sinclair, *consigliere* to the

Cartel of Cartels, the board. Although younger than most, he was greeted respectfully, almost deferentially. As the chief executive officer of a monumentally successful legitimate management consultancy business, Sinclair's opinions and his counselling had been a crucial factor in Andino's sustained growth.

Victor Rodriguez opened the formal meeting and summoned him to the podium. Most of Sinclair's annual report sounded no different from that of an ordinary, legitimate company. 'We now have one hundred and thirty tonnes of product one stockpiled in Europe. The warehouses are strategically located in Poland, the Netherlands and former Czechoslovakia. Forty-five tonnes of product two are also stored at these locations. These stockpiles over and above the year-on-year market demand and supply are the direct result of the new European Union legislation relaxing border controls . . . We would like to put on record our appreciation of the vigorous lobbying that has been done by Signor Pietro Pecolli in the corridors of government in Brussels. His continuing efforts with regard to a single European currency are on the brink of bringing to Andino tremendous trading advantages. In one stroke many of our banking problems will be eliminated and our profits will rise within the European market by a minimum of twenty per cent.'

The board members applauded their Italian colleague, who rose and bowed.

Despite the fact that Sinclair had personally supervised the electronic sweeping of the conference hall, pure force of habit ensured that he still spoke in partial code. Product one was cocaine. Product two was heroin. Product three marijuana. Banking problems were a reference to the difficulties of the drugs business in laundering its profits. (Andino has no banks in its massive portfolio of assets: the board believes that to own a bank directly would be to create a potential Achilles heel.)

'I draw the board's attention to two appendices. Appendix A gives details of the agreements reached with the Russian banking and business consortium concerning trade routes and banking.'

Sinclair looked up at those gathered in the room and, for a moment, a half-smile passed across his face. 'More than one hundred and fifty years ago, Karl Marx famously observed that religion was the opium of the people. In the light of the information contained in that appendix, today, opium has become the religion of the people. In Appendix B* you will note the contrasting experiences of Mexico and Panama. During the past year we have dealt with the attempts by the Chinese government to prevent our Burmese colleagues from moving product into the southwestern province of Yunan. Your board recommended the two or two solution.'

(The 'two or two solution' – '*plata o plomo*', 'silver or lead' – has been applied throughout Latin America by the cartels with virtually 100 per cent success. It consists of asking a border guard or customs official one simple question: 'Would you like two thousand dollars or two bullets?')

Sinclair took a sip of orange juice, freshly squeezed, from the fruit of trees owned by Victor Rodriguez, and guaranteed by him to be free of chemicals. He then proceeded to a detailed analysis of the industry's largest market. 'Gross turnover across the board on all products in the United States for the year ended September thirtieth is one hundred and seventy billion dollars.'

As spontaneous applause began to erupt, Sinclair slapped the podium angrily with his fist. 'There is no room for complacency. Sales of product one have plateaued at three hundred metric tonnes. Sales of product two have again failed to break into double figures and stand at nine tonnes. The number of hard-core users of both products has remained relatively unchanged since the late eighties and is failing to rise much above three million. Those among you who are in a mood for self-congratulation should compare that figure against the over seventy million who, according to US government official figures, have at one time or another sampled our products. There are therefore another sixty-seven million potential

* Verbatim copies of the Appendices appear at the end of the book

customers out there. Another sixty-seven million potential hard-core users. Your board wishes to see that potential become a reality. Your board wishes to see, for example, the price of product one rise again to its nineteen ninety high of two hundred dollars per gram and not languish as it currently does at below one hundred and fifty dollars per gram.'

Sinclair paused, allowing the points to sink home, and then defused the tension he had created. 'To move on to more positive aspects within the United States. Dealerships. There has been a significant increase at all levels. Premier, first, second and third divisions. For every premier-division dealer quote removed unquote from the market-place by government agencies, six would-be successors immediately appear, fighting to replace him.'

A premier-division dealer is an individual moving in excess of 200 kilos of cocaine per week.

Sinclair was about to move on, then checked himself to add a postscript. 'Perhaps the reason above all others that makes these dealerships so attractive is the knowledge that the United States government agencies are demoralized and in total disarray, which is inevitable, bearing in mind that all of them are chronically underfunded and their efforts are severely disjointed. There are at least five United States government agencies working against our industry and, very fortunately, the CIA, the DEA, the State Department, Customs and the Treasury appear to spend more time fighting each other than they do fighting us.

'However, within the past twelve months the United States has succeeded in bringing heavy sanctions to bear on our members from Cali. Their infrastructure, their assets, including their pharmaceutical chain Drogas La Rebaja, have all suffered from White House harassment. It is, therefore, a source of deep satisfaction for me to announce that despite these local difficulties their annual turnover is four times greater than that of General Motors. Perhaps that old maxim of what is good for General Motors should be rewritten – or

31

perhaps General Motors should also arrange for its board of directors to work from prison.'

Sinclair paused for the laughs, and then deliberately gave the room a few moments of silence to build the importance of his next remarks. 'However, the Cali experience leads me to believe that the activities of the United States government should become more predictable and more controlled. The chairman of the board will now present to you a proposal to achieve this.'

To warm applause, Rodriguez stood up. He made no move to the podium, thereby compelling all eyes to focus on him. Small, benign, in his early fifties, Rodriguez looked like someone's favourite uncle. At five feet six, he was of average Colombian height. He was beginning to lose man's middle-aged struggle with his waistline. Apart from a gold wedding ring and a gold and stainless steel Cartier watch, there were no outward signs of the extraordinary wealth he controlled. His only other piece of jewellery, a heavy gold crucifix, was hanging inside his Fifth Avenue shirt. Victor Rodriguez waited quietly, and bestowed a kindly smile upon the gathering. 'Our annual global turnover in the past year was five hundred billion dollars. Gentlemen, we have yet again hit the magic five.'

New applause broke out, but Rodriguez killed it instantly and his smile disappeared. 'Gentlemen, this is not a moment for complacency and congratulation. Businesses survive and grow only if they recognize the moment to change. This is such a moment. Our achievement should remind us of our responsibilities to our market.'

The stern sermon produced the desired effect. The faces before him were serious and intent.

'Our market is driven by the United States. It not only supplies the greatest part of our turnover but it maintains the price structure of our products in all other markets. Despite our success in dividing and weakening each individual agency of the American government, our American market faces a permanent threat of extinction. I believe that there is a solution to this threat. I have given this solution a name. A name that will not attract any undue attention, although I ask you to excuse a pun.

32

The Colombia Project. Its aim is to ensure that the board is not above the law but that it *becomes* the law.

'Gentlemen, I propose that we buy the United States of America.'

CHAPTER TWO

PARTNERSHIP

THE FIRST NATIONAL BANK ON LASALLE AT JACKSON IN CHICAGO was packed with customers. The lunchtime clientele shuffled slowly forward. The mood was light, the air full of fragmented chatter. With the weekend beckoning, groups were discussing their various plans. The one thing that the many planned activities had in common was the need to draw out a little cash. No one took any notice of a large package in the centre of the bank. No one knew who had left it there. A couple of office workers were still leaning on it when the pipe bomb blew up.

There had been no warning. Five hours later no one had claimed responsibility for the attack and the death toll stood at fifty-three and rising.

Homecoming from his New York office gave Andrew Sinclair the best moments of his life. Home was hundreds of miles and millions of dollars away from the childhood place in Memphis. It was big and gracious: Georgian colonial, in the model community of Hamilton-on-Hudson, in the model county of Westchester,

New York, with twelve acres of ground. His acres. With his private dock on the Hudson river, his tennis court, his swimming pool, his summer-house. His artificial lake. His rolling lawns, trees, shrubs and flower-beds (on which no pesticides were allowed). His aviary, a gift from Victor Rodriguez.

His cameras, which patrolled every inch of his perimeter.

Home to his beautiful children, endless delights and total security, and to Mary, his beautiful wife. Mary was the only thing he found in any way wrong with his beautiful home . . .

The thought of her made him pause on the path from the private dock. He swung away through the woods, to savour his homecoming a little longer. To postpone the moment when he had to speak to her.

He let himself into the beautiful house, with the self-mocking cry, 'Honey, I'm home!' But only the butler answered him. Beach was the real thing, English and stately: Sinclair's income was much higher than that of the Earl of Emsworth, and the wages he paid reflected that difference. 'Mrs Sinclair is in the summer-house, sir.'

'And the children?'

'In the basement, I believe, with Miss Keeble, sir.'

Left to himself, Sinclair might have headed straight to the basement but the butler's impassive face reminded him of the power of convention. He turned away to the summer-house.

It was still hot enough for her to be wearing a bikini, and her figure was good enough for the costume to be scanty. Even so, he was irritated that she was not dressed. He was certain that she had not dressed all day, or done anything with the children, or done anything except lie in the sun.

'Did you have a nice day at the office, dear?' she asked, with the same lazy, lopsided smile which had entranced him when he was young and susceptible.

Mary had been a surprise addition to a lunch at which Andrew Sinclair had been aiming to make her father a Special Friend of Stanford. He had found himself fluffing lines, missing cues. In his whole career, she was the only woman who had ever made him miss a sale.

35

Not content with sticking the hefty lunch bill on Sinclair, Daddy insisted he take her downtown in a taxi.

For once anger had made him sincere. 'I'm not selling Stanford for the rest of my life. I'm going to sell me, and nothing else but me, for a terrific amount of money, and then one day I'll stop and become a buyer.' She had said nothing but had slipped her hand under his waistband, under his boxer shorts, right there in the back seat of the taxi.

She still did that at unexpected times and places, and once it had turned him on, but lately he found it irritating.

In their marriage, he had done all the travelling and she had stayed still. Beautiful, gracious, an excellent hostess, popular with the wives of important clients, she sat on many committees and took many lessons, which never taught her anything he found remotely interesting.

'Well, did you have a nice day at the office, dear?'

He had missed her first question, which alarmed him: his autopilot had failed. 'A problem with US Cola.'

'That's too bad.'

Lately he had been glad that she took so little interest in his work. So much of his time was taken up with the Colombia Project for the Cartel of Cartels that he would have found it difficult to talk to her about any of the legitimate business in his management consultancy. The reference to US Cola had been a mistake for that problem was also tied to the Colombia Project. But to his relief she demanded no further explanation.

'I'm bushed,' she announced. 'I'd like to go to bed early.' She reached for his waistband, but he stepped away to pour himself an orange juice.

'Me too,' he said on autopilot.

'And I'd like to get up late tomorrow. The children are going to a picnic all day.'

'All day? With whom?' he said, with fierce interest.

'The McKays.'

'Oh.' He frowned. The McKays were old money: he found them overbred and feckless. They let their children eat all kinds of chemical junk.

36

'I would really love to get up late tomorrow,' he smiled, 'but I have to go to Omaha.'

'Of course you do.'

He shifted uncomfortably. He was not certain that he needed to go to Omaha, but she had made him commit himself. He would hardly see the children. He placed the untouched glass of orange juice on the table. 'I'm going to take the kids to the lake.'

'That'll be nice.'

He turned away, without meeting her lopsided smile.

The butler had been right. The children were in the basement rumpus room, which contained the biggest TV screen in the house. They were watching cartoons with Miss Keeble, stupid cartoons, badly drawn and violent. He felt a flash of fury at the expensive English governess, for letting this junk into his children's minds. But at least it wasn't a news programme. It was a rigid house rule. No newscasts in front of the children. He was determined to cocoon them from life's realities for as long as possible. He relaxed as they both dived into his arms, with squeals of 'Daddy!'

Peter was a tall ten and Kathy a short eight. They both took after their mother facially, but Kathy had her father's energy. He adored them so utterly, wanted them to know nothing but love and safety, the sort of childhood he had seen only on television. He was the architect and sentinel of their magic kingdom.

'It's too hot to be in here,' he declared, when the hugs had subsided. 'We should be at the lake.'

'All right!' said both children, but their eyes strayed to the television screen.

As Miss Keeble helped them change into their bathing suits, Sinclair took charge of the towels and the life-jackets, then smeared them with natural, organic insect-repellent. He led them towards the artificial lake.

'Is Mommy coming?' asked Peter.

'Maybe,' he said. 'She's busy with dinner.'

One section of the lake had been engineered into a swimming hole for the children, a dream place, full of things to swing in, jump off, float upon. 'Put your life-jackets on,' he said automatically. The rule was rigid, despite the careful design of the swimming hole and the expensive swimming lessons for the children. As usual, Kathy protested mildly but Peter had his jacket fastened before his father had finished the instruction. Sinclair felt it ought to be the other way round. He saw them grown-up, Kathy starting a new business, Peter living off his trust fund.

He watched the two sleek heads, bobbing up safely above the designer life-jackets, then slid into the water himself. Instantly the children abandoned their toys to jump off Daddy.

Looking out on the patio, Adam Fraser saw Laura at the centre of a group. It was ever thus. If Laura had been standing in the middle of the Gobi Desert, it would not be long before she was at the centre of a group. Almost as tall as him, upswept red hair, a generous figure, she was always easy to find, even at parties like this one, crammed with luvvies and liggers. The host was an actor, a client she had originally taken on out of pity but who had suddenly become fashionable and profitable.

She broke and pounced on Adam, lifted him off his feet, and gave him a very public hug and kiss. Their schedules had kept them apart for weeks, and the party was a rare opening in both their diaries. Making sure she still had an audience, she asked, 'How's my favourite husband?'

They had met at a similar kind of party twenty-five years before. He had just left drama school, she had just started as an agent. She had taught him much more than the drama school had – some poise and grace to go with the spectacular good looks, how to open his mind as well as his mouth. She had propelled him into the West End play in which he had become an overnight sensation.

They had had a much-publicized wedding, at which jealous guests whispered bitchily that he had only married her to keep her percentage of his earnings. The play ran for an eternity, making them rich enough to buy a large house in Camden Town. She worked hard and made them richer, finding him commercials and a hospital soap opera. Then she found the perfect movie vehicle for him. She discarded her other clients, and started to talk about children.

But then, out of the blue, in their comfortable house in Camden, he said, 'I want to make the world more real for people, not more of a fantasy.' He retired from acting. Instead of playing the lead in the romantic comedy film (later to gross $150 million) he announced his intention to direct a documentary film about shanty-towns in Brazil.

Since then, his work had won many awards, but it had also turned her into the main breadwinner. She had built up her agency again, and instead of mothering their children she mothered her actors, coping with tears, tantrums, and the terrors of failure and old age. She kept up the Camden house, polished his BAFTA awards and kept the garden looking nice, even when his films took him away for months on end.

Susanna had become part of his team and then his life, her flat more familiar to him than his house. But he remained married to Laura. She wanted it like that, and it was the least he could do for her, after taking away the rich actor who had been her husband.

'Take me out for the evening,' she ordered, 'before all your sins are absolved by the Reverend Patrick Collins.'

As she drove him away from the party, more carefully than usual, she pumped him about the new documentary, his success with Mitch, the amazing access promised by the preacher and his entourage, his plans to look beyond the obvious targets of Collins's money and commercialism to find the preacher's dark secret, his inner life . . .

She stopped the car abruptly. 'Adam, how many people believe in this man? You told me eight million, I see eighty million. These people do not want to lose Patrick Collins. They won't thank you for showing them the inner life, the dark secret. They'll think you're an agent of the devil . . . Adam, I want a husband. I have another career for you. I would like you to make nature films about cute furry animals.'

*   *   *

They swam until it grew dark, and then Andrew Sinclair overrode Miss Keeble's protests and took the children to dine with Mary and himself. The food was delicious and free of additives: Andrew Sinclair had bought the local grocery business that had supplied it.

He carried each child in turn to bed and read aloud from *The Wind in the Willows* for some time after each had fallen asleep. Finally he could postpone no longer the moment when he had to go to bed with his wife.

He had hoped that she might be asleep, but she grabbed him suddenly from behind and reached into his boxer shorts. 'My big rich lover man,' she said, as she worked around his groin. 'My big rich lover man, who treats me so good, makes me feel so good, who works so hard, so *hard, hard, hard*!'

She pulled him on top and propelled him into her, kneading his buttocks. As she created the rhythm, he murmured suitable words while his mind stayed with the Colombia Project. It had reached a critical stage. The next morning in his office he had to have two answers . . .

'Yes, *yes*!'

Sinclair woke up as usual at six a.m. without the help of an alarm. He slipped out of bed without waking Mary, showered and dressed, and then went to look at the children, beatifically asleep. After restoring two lost teddy bears he moved quietly downstairs to his usual breakfast of orange juice and whole-wheat toast.

For once as Sinclair walked to the dock, he failed to pause to savour his possessions. He stepped on to his power launch and put the Colombia Project out of his mind while the boat captain pulled away from the dock and Sinclair reached for his morning papers. For the first time the horrific bank bombing in Chicago impinged on his consciousness. It had occurred while his launch was heading homewards on the previous day. Looking at the gruesome images on the front pages confirmed yet again the wisdom of his news ban in the home.

The launch roared downriver, past Dobbs Ferry, past

Hastings-on-Hudson. Within twenty-five minutes, it tied up at Sinclair's other private mooring, directly opposite the World Trade Center in downtown Manhattan.

The security check was much easier on Saturday mornings. On weekdays the guard would telephone his receptionist on the one-hundredth floor, who would then send out a tannoy announcement throughout the office suite of Corporate America: 'The time is nine-oh-four and Andrew Sinclair has just entered the building.'

But on a Saturday that announcement was pointless. He forbade his employees to work in the office at weekends, unless at his personal request. He told them how important it was for them to relax, to maintain their personal and family lives – and come back full of new ideas on Monday mornings. They thought him an enlightened employer – and left him two days to enjoy all his wonderful office space on his own.

He had discovered much valuable information about his employees and his business by his solitary tours of the offices at the weekend, but that day he had no time for spying. Clare, his personal assistant and secretary, was waiting for him. After exchanging greetings, they discussed for a moment the shocking events at the First National in Chicago. Then he moved on into his inner office and, without pausing to enjoy the view across the river of the Staten Island skyline, sat at his desk.

He frowned and made a mental note to talk to Clare about the office cleaning staff. Someone new had been assigned to his office. He moved a desk diary two inches to the right. A small clock, showing a range of international times, was repositioned, as were some pens and the two wooden coasters. Content, he reached for a key from his inside pocket. In the top left-hand drawer was a private fax machine, to which not even Clare had access. With luck there should be a message on it from the only person in the world who knew the number: Victor Rodriguez.

Sinclair unlocked the drawer. Even though he was alone in his office and knew that Clare would not enter until summoned, his face was expressionless. He could have been reaching into the drawer for a paperclip. There was, indeed, a single sheet of paper on the machine. To the naked eye, all that could be seen on it was a random pattern of black dots, like a white page filled with tiny black worms. No text was visible.

Sinclair laid the fax message flat on his desk and then, reaching into the same drawer, pulled out a customized plastic sheet, which he laid on top of the paper. It was a decryption sheet, and as Sinclair carefully aligned it with the fax, the black and white dots moved and formed a brief, legible message. As he read it, Sinclair's face broke into a rare, spontaneous grin. It read, 'The Colombia Project is now activated beyond stage one to its ultimate conclusion. Your proposed participants are approved, subject to the contingency plan for those found to be unsuitable.'

Reaching for a fax pad Sinclair encrypted a message, tapped in the appropriate number and watched as the piece of paper transmitted its sequence of dots, not to Victor Rodriguez but to another member of the board of Andino, Signor Pietro Pecolli in Milan. He retrieved the sheet of paper, carefully folded it twice and put it in his wallet. Then he pressed a button on his desk, stood up and began to pace. Turning, he stared out across the Hudson, not at the far shore but way beyond. There was a knock on the door. He responded without turning. 'Come in, Clare.'

The keeper of the pass entered carrying a tray of freshly percolated decaff and orange juice. He turned, to confirm that he had closed and locked the fax drawer, as she placed them carefully on the two wooden coasters. He smiled at his secretary, one of the many assets he had stolen from his former partner seven years earlier. Not even Clare, who knew more than most, had an inkling that he acted as business consultant to the biggest multinational in the world.

She busied herself pouring coffee and juice.

'Clare, do we have in the US Cola files a home number for the chairman?'

'For Leonard Meredith? Yes. Would you like to speak to him?'

'Yes, please – and, Clare, depending on the outcome of that

phone call, I may be flying to Omaha today. Could you check flights and a hotel?'

A few minutes later the gravelly tones of the chairman of US Cola were pouring like strong cement into Sinclair's left ear. After the usual pleasantries had been exchanged, Sinclair made an unusual request. 'Leonard, I want to fax some material to you for your eyes only. Do you have a personal fax line?' He jotted down the number. 'I'm putting this down the line myself. I'll start transmitting within the next five minutes. I won't say any more now. I'll await your response.'

Fifteen minutes later the phone on Sinclair's desk rang. It was Leonard Meredith. 'Andrew, I've read the material. I have five questions to ask you. Care to be my guest for the rest of the weekend? That's not one of the questions.'

'My pleasure. I'll have my secretary book a flight, then I'll advise you what time I'll get into Omaha.'

Again the sound of concrete being poured. 'No need for that. I'll send a corporate jet for you. Pack your tennis gear and I'll give you a thrashing.'

With the final arrangements made and the call concluded, Clare reappeared. She was carrying a walk-on case and a sports bag with several tennis rackets protruding from it.

'Your boat captain just brought these up, Andrew.'

'Thanks. You can cancel those reservations. The chairman is sending his own plane for me. Call Mary and tell her I have to go to a crucial meeting in Nebraska. I'll be gone until Sunday evening. I'll call her while I'm away, but please offer my apologies and say how sorry I am not to be able to keep today's appointment.'

Clare took his instructions on board without any reaction. 'You must have been clairvoyant about the weekend. Bags already packed.'

'Oh, just in case, Clare. Just in case.'

Later that day Cola Three flew out of Kennedy with one passenger. Tammy, the stewardess, brought Sinclair some US Cola and magazines. She had no idea how much he hated US Cola – kept it away from his house and his children. With loathing he read the list of chemical ingredients, but the Colombia Project needed US Cola. He closed his eyes, thought of his mission and took a deep swallow.

Having served Sinclair, the tall blonde swayed back down the aisle with an exaggerated swing of the hips. From her galley she stole a look back at Sinclair. Her performance had been wasted: he was already reading a magazine. Leonard had cancelled his weekend with her to spend it with this man. Tammy shook her head. She would never understand men.

Sinclair grinned as he saw the front cover of *Time*. What an omen. There on the cover was the man who had been the subject of his fax to Meredith. The man who would also be the subject of his weekend discussions.

'What kind of creatures would carry out an attack like that, Andrew?'

'The kind that place no value on human life. The kind that believe they can make their point by destroying what they see as a soft target.'

Leonard Meredith and his guest were watching the early evening newscast. The reporter had begun to list the likely identity of those responsible for the Chicago carnage. The Libyans. The Iranians. Muslim fundamentalists. Militia from within the United States. The list was long. Meredith growled. 'My money's on the Libyans.'

'Careful, Leonard. Remember the Federal Building bombing in Oklahoma City. Long before the death toll stopped at a hundred and sixty-eight there was a crescendo of calls across the country to bomb Libya. Turned out it was a made-in-the-USA atrocity. What bemuses me is that no one's claimed responsibility again. What is the point of these attacks if whoever launches them won't acknowledge it?'

Meredith nodded. 'One thing's for sure, though. This serves to underline the importance of the project we're about to discuss.'

After dinner, Sinclair and Meredith settled down in the library. The drinks had been poured and the butler had gone.

Meredith unlocked a desk drawer and removed the sheaf of fax pages. Sinclair noted this with approval: he liked a man who remembered basic security. Standing at his desk, Meredith waggled the pages. 'A sixth question occurred to me later, Andrew, and it's the one I would like to begin with. I'm one of a number of people you're planning to approach with this proposition. You haven't indicated who the others are. But am I right in thinking I'm the first?'

Sinclair was looking entirely relaxed, someone enjoying an after-dinner brandy with a close friend, but in fact he was keyed to maximum alertness. 'Yes, Leonard,' he said, 'you're the first.'

Meredith, looking thoughtful as he walked over, handed the papers to Sinclair. 'Why?'

'Because you're chairman of US Cola. If I had to choose one product, that went to the very heart of this country, it would be US Cola. Look, Leonard, before this plan is implemented and brought to a successful conclusion, a majority of this country's major players will be brought on side. At this stage I want just four.'

Meredith nodded. 'I see. And which of the four am I to be?'

Sinclair had learned long ago to keep his mouth shut when in doubt. He waited. Meredith continued. 'Am I Summer, Autumn, Winter or Spring?'

Sinclair's response came without hesitation now. 'You're Winter, without which there can be no explosion of new life, of regeneration.'

Leonard Meredith had achieved many things in his life. An impregnable defence against flattery was not among them. He slapped his thigh and roared with laughter. Sinclair smiled. He knew now he had Meredith in the bag and the euphoria that swept through him was sublime.

There was also relief that Meredith was not a movie buff. The line about winter had been a steal from the Peter Sellers movie *Being There*.

He had closed another sale and the first piece of the puzzle was firmly in place. His initial reading of the situation had been perceptive.

Meredith refreshed their drinks. 'My second question, Andrew, concerns the very key to ultimate success. How can you be sure that you can persuade this man to do what you want him to do?' He was pointing at a pile of magazines on the small table between them. The one on top of the pile was the current edition of *Time* magazine. On the front cover was a photograph captioned 'America's Favourite Preacher'. It was televangelist Patrick Collins.

CHAPTER THREE

PARANOIA

ADAM CLIMBED THE STEPS FROM HAMBURG'S RAILWAY STATION at Eppendorfer Baum, and, realizing he was running early, decided to stroll alongside the Isebek Kanal. It was mid-afternoon and a pale sun glistened on the water just below. The Dolls' House was just a few minutes' walk away. Time to savour the memory of what, so far, had been a highly successful trip.

Before coming to Germany he had persuaded TV companies in both Australia and New Zealand to commit to his proposed documentaries on Patrick Collins. Now, after a meeting with Kurt at ZDF, the biggest network in Germany was definitely on board and the production package looked healthy. Next week, there would be a meeting with Bruce Clay at the Network Centre. With the German involvement now assured not even Bastard Bruce Clay – or BBC as he was known – was likely to be negative. Then, thought Adam, as he stood watching the ducks, he would make a pre-launch production attack on the big three networks in the United States, the Holy Grail of all TV filmmakers. He had vowed to Susanna that this time he would not wait until he had a fine cut. He was confident that, just this once, the networks would see the potential and grab him to make a deal. The quiet voice of realism within him kept murmuring that it wouldn't be that easy, but this was not a day for listening to murmurs unless, of course, they came from the man he was now on his way to see.

Adam turned away from the canal's edge and walked towards the Dolls' House through the park. During the Second World War this area had been spared the worst of the Allied bombing but, according to Oscar, it had not been by chance: he insisted that the wealthy middle classes, who occupied these fine large houses, included key personnel of the Krupp companies. Bomber Command had spared their beautiful Hanseatic mansions, and certain Krupp industrial complexes, as part of Allied post-war strategy. It sounded fanciful, as did so much that Oscar had told him over the years, but Adam knew that what Oscar said invariably turned out to be the truth. An unusual characteristic in a man who, for decades, had been widely considered to be the CIA's leading disinformation officer.

It had always seemed delightfully apt to Adam that one of Langley's finest spooks should live on Martini Street. He pressed the doorbell and waited.

'*Könnten Sie ein bisschen links zur Seite gehen?*'

Although he did not recognize the voice, Adam obliged.

'Thank you, Adam. Good to see you.'

This time the voice was unmistakably Oscar's. The metal door swung open and he entered a small courtyard. A few yards in front was another door. As the first closed behind him, the second swung open.

Once inside the second metal door, Adam stood in front of a conventional front door of wood and stained glass. The sound of a number of keys turning in locks gave further indication of an occupant who disliked surprise callers. The door opened.

Oscar Benjamin was enormously fat. He rolled out to shake Adam warmly by the hand. 'Come on through, Adam. Good trip?'

'Excellent, Oscar. Who was that asking me to move to the left?'

'Just me. You were partly out of shot on the remote.' Oscar pointed to a speaker panel on the wall. 'This little beauty does an automatic voice distort.' Next to the panel was a screen giving a high-angle view of the street. Oscar had first seen this system used in a maximum-security prison in Kentucky – as an unwilling guest of the management.

Oscar turned and bounced back into his hallway. He looked like a botched statue of Buddha. His clothes suggested a man at war with his tailor – buttons threatened to explode, a zip was several notches short of home, and there were creases everywhere except where they are normally found. Oscar's aura exuded constant late rising in permanently untidy bedrooms. He led the way along a circular corridor then out on to a patio. He put a finger to his lips, motioned Adam to a chair, then poured him some wine and refilled his own glass from an already opened bottle. Adam was struck that a man of Oscar's build moved so gracefully. Without a sound Oscar eased himself into his chair, picked up a pair of binoculars, scanned the garden, and tensed.

Adam spoke softly. 'If there's someone out there, Oscar, shouldn't we move indoors?'

The Buddha shook his head, then handed the binoculars to Adam. 'Just below the gutter on that hut. Right-hand corner.'

Adam trained his gaze on a hut at the bottom of the garden. As he looked, a swallow appeared to fly straight into the wooden wall. Refocusing, he spotted the small hole that the bird had entered. A moment later, it reappeared, then soared skywards. He turned to see Oscar grinning at him. 'Damnedest thing, Adam. Last October that swallow wouldn't migrate. I'd been watching them all summer. She'd laid four. Three took off for Africa in late September. The fourth was a dumb little bastard, just kept flying back into that nest.'

Adam stared at him, intrigued. 'What about the male bird?'

'He stayed with his mate,' said Oscar. 'I watched the three of them for weeks. Every time she tipped her offspring out of that hole he'd fly around for a few minutes, then make back for the shed.'

'How did they survive a German winter?'

Oscar grinned again. 'They didn't. I netted them, ringed them and had Lufthansa carry them to Nairobi. Three weeks ago the hen and her mate came back here to my garden to nest for the summer.' He refilled Adam's glass, then left the room.

Adam turned back to the garden. How ironic that a man who lived in a virtual prison should be so captivated by the birds that took up temporary residence in the half-acre garden, but there was much that was ironic about Oscar Benjamin, born David Guilderstein. In 1938, as a young Jew in Dachau, he had found himself competing with every Jewish child within the camp for one of the top one hundred academic scholarships that American Jewry were offering. The prize was a new life in the United States. He won. Eighteen members of his family died in the Nazi camps. Now, many decades later, he had built a different prison for himself in Hamburg to ensure that he continued to live.

'Shame on you, my son. Still nursing the same glass.'

Adam jumped. Oscar had returned silently, freshly showered and changed and carrying another bottle of wine.

'And what have you been up to lately?' Adam asked his friend, and switched on his tape-recorder. It was a habit long-established. Invariably during their meetings Oscar would offer information both on and off the record.

'Oh, spying on the French and the Japanese.'

'For the Company?'

'Of course for the Company,' said Oscar. 'Who else? I may be a whistle-blower, but I'm not a turncoat.'

'But what about that problem with your friends at Langley? All this protection – and all these precautions.'

Oscar spoke as if to a student. 'Adam, that is the European Desk. I'm now working for the Commercial Desk. This is industrial intelligence.' An element of mockery crept into his voice. 'The military don't believe they need first-class intelligence agents any more. They're wrong of course, just as the

European Desk is wrong. The trouble with them is that they're living in the past. They're just pissed off with me and others like me because they've run out of traditional enemies.'

The European Desk of the CIA had convinced Oscar that not only was he burnt, but they also wanted him fried, hence the Dolls' House. Its previous occupant had been a senior KGB officer and precisely how Oscar had come to acquire it was shrouded in mystery, but Adam could see its appeal for a paranoiac like Oscar: it had corridors that led nowhere and doors that opened on to blank walls.

Oscar gesticulated at the tape recorder, a signal that he would speak off the record, and Adam switched off the machine.

'Getting shy about pointing the finger at your own team, Oscar?'

'Not shy. Just prudent. I'm going to give you some Company names. Some who have conspired with the Soviets on disinformation. You know, all that bullshit about the US winning the Cold War really sticks in my craw. Nobody won the Cold War. They went bankrupt and we became the biggest debtor nation on the planet. And we're still running up the bills for the next generation to pay. Now, of course, the CIA justifies its annual budget by talking up the threat of terrorism. Absolute fabrication. Annual intelligence budget for the current year?' He pointed at the tape machine, waited a moment as Adam pushed the record button, then continued: 'The official budget in the last financial year in the US for the intelligence agencies was twenty-seven billion dollars. The real budget for the agencies was sixty-four billion dollars. A lot of that's off-the-books money for off-the-books operations. Like failing to eliminate Saddam Hussein, or Gaddafi or the Iranian mullahs, or Fidel Castro. In the past fifty years the Agency has only succeeded four times in that area of activity – Patrice Lumumba, President Allende, General Zia, and the Swedish Prime Minister, Olaf Palme.' He sighed in disgust.

'There was a time when working as a case-officer was easy, when your job was to subvert people, to lie, cheat, steal and murder for God and country. Work that required a deep sense

51

of personal integrity. Not any more. Now our job is to steal secrets, but which countries are enemies? Which are friends? The whole damn thing lacks moral leadership. These days accountants are running Langley. One thousand agents fired in the past six months, just to cut the payroll.'

Knowing that Oscar had embarked on one of his favourite subjects, Adam deflected him.

'So who are the new enemies?'

Oscar grinned. 'Not so much new enemies, more traditional ones newly promoted up the pecking order. Would make more sense if my Company salary came from Detroit rather than Langley – after all, I've spent the past five months infiltrating the French and Japanese motor industries.'

'Reached any conclusions?' asked Adam.

'Yes. Buy German. Something else. The Cold War isn't entirely over. The KGB may have changed its name to the Federal Security Service, but they're even more active in industrial espionage than we are.'

Oscar stood up. He picked up the bottle and his glass, then turned back to Adam. 'Let's spend a little time in my nerve centre before we go out for dinner.'

They went inside, strolled along the circular corridor, past the first two doors then through a third to be confronted with another corridor. This time Oscar turned left and led Adam into his inner sanctum. It served as his bedroom and his workplace: conventional bedroom furniture was sparse and most of the space was given over to an extensive range of electronic equipment including a bank of computers. If an Olympic Committee ever ratified computer hacking as a legitimate sport, Oscar would take the gold medal. With the aid of a massive database, a powerful filing and retrieval program, he could unlock even the security-screened top-secret intelligence databases of many countries.

As Oscar settled himself in front of the computer, Adam remembered another occasion in the inner sanctum, when Oscar had entertained him by abstracting $20 million from a CIA bank account, transferred it to earn overnight interest for the Audubon Bird Society, and returned it the next day. The sound of his stubby fingers giving the machine a series of commands pulled Adam back to the present. 'What's that, Oscar? Looks like Russian.'

'Intercept of communication between Foreign Ministry in Moscow and their embassy in Damascus.'

Oscar's hands moved over the keys again, and paused to reveal a stream of Japanese. 'That's the minutes of a board meeting at Mitsubishi being sent to their New York office.'

Oscar continued to throw tantalizing fragments on to the screen: a phone conversation between a Brussels-based British diplomat and his mistress in Holland; another between a senior aide to the German Chancellor and his cocaine supplier; technical details on the new Russian super-jet. While he tapped, he talked. 'This is all coming up courtesy of Echelon. It's a global electronic surveillance with a difference. This is fully automated and integrated with secret monitoring stations right around the world. The Echelon Dictionary computers hold lists of different categories of intercept available on the system, which are identified by code. The level of information made available to you is dependent on the code to which you have access. The really scary thing is it functions automatically. No clearance from a government minister or a secretary of state. This thing virtually has a life force of its own. It processes two million intercepted messages per hour and its operators have little idea exactly what raw information Echelon is sending out or to whom it's sending it. Thought you'd enjoy this.'

'Enjoy is not the word that comes to mind. You get off on this stuff, don't you?'

'Echelon certainly helps me to keep a sense of perspective about Langley.'

Oscar rummaged briefly in a drawer. He produced a series of pill bottles, removed two tablets from each and proceeded to swallow them with a gulp of his wine. He spent his life in the high-tech world of databases, but he had an unshakeable faith in the efficacy of homoeopathic remedies. He took Rhus tox for his swollen joints; Bryonia for his lower back pain. When he had pain that moved from place to place he took Pulsatilla; for his red and swollen joints he swallowed Apis mel. Every part of his body was assisted with some form of medicine. He took drugs to cut his cholesterol; he had been continuously on some form of diet for over twenty-five years; he was a world authority on afternoon slump, age spots, excessive flatulence, body odour and constipation. He had identified thirty-three specific allergies from which he suffered.

'Don't you think there's a slight contradiction in taking your medicines with red wine?' Adam asked.

'Adam, the red wine is part of the medicine. It definitely reduces the risk of heart-attacks. Pass me your glass, it's empty.'

Oscar knew why Adam had come to see him and he would get around to the purpose of the visit in due course. Adam had learned that it was counter-productive to hurry him. This man spent so much time in self-imposed solitary confinement that when he had company he liked to indulge himself.

Later, at Ristorante il Posto, Oscar's favourite Italian restaurant, they were well into the main course before he turned at last to business. 'I have had every possible check run on your behalf,' he said. 'I have the subject's CIA file, FBI file, his Pentagon dossier, everything. I'm worried.'

Adam leaned across the table eagerly. 'What have you got on him?'

'You mean the skeletons in the cupboard?'

'Of course.'

Oscar paused, then he said, 'Nothing.'

'Nothing?'

'Not a thing. Not even a traffic violation. *That*'s what worries me. It's simply not feasible that someone with his life history is that clean.'

'You're the super-spy, Oscar. So what *does* it mean?'

'One of two things. Either that someone at the highest level has got into those files and cleaned them up. It's possible, but unlikely.'

Adam had lost all interest in his food. So, for once, had Oscar.

'This highest level, Oscar. Be more specific.'

For a moment Oscar reflected. 'The director of General Intelligence, the head of the National Security Council and the President. That kind of level. You see, Adam, I'm not just talking about a cover-up or the suppression of a court verdict. That's run of the mill, happens frequently. But even when it does, certain files in the database continue to record the factual details on that individual. Kurt Waldheim is a case in point. The US, the Brits and the Soviets all knew the truth about his war record *before* Waldheim became secretary-general of the United Nations.'

'And everyone kept quiet believing they would be able to manipulate him?'

Oscar beamed. 'Exactly. My point is that the records on Waldheim were doctored for public consumption, but the CIA, the KGB and MI6 all retained the true facts.'

Adam steered him back to the main agenda. 'Is it possible that there are files that you've not been able to access?'

'It's possible, but I would still have been able to establish their existence. There are no other security files on your subject.'

Adam waited to see if he was going to elaborate, but he remained silent.

'What's the other possibility, then?'

Oscar looked up. 'That this man you're so interested in is a unique human being. That Patrick Collins is a living saint.'

CHAPTER FOUR

PRESIDENTIAL PROSPECT (1)

VICTOR RODRIGUEZ WAS A CREATURE OF HABIT. HAD HE BEEN IN any other profession he would have risen at precisely the same time each morning and followed a set daily routine. One of the sacrifices he made for his work, however, was to be regularly irregular. During weekdays the Rodriguez family and its entourage occupied a suite of rooms at the Tequendama Hotel, in Bogotá. Victor, the patriarch, insisted that they all breakfasted together. Every morning this first meal of the day would be taken in a different location within the hotel, chosen by him only minutes beforehand.

On his way to work, he would customarily go to church for a few minutes of prayer but not even his driver Ernesto would know at which one until Rodriguez was sitting in the car. The route from the church to his Bogotá offices at Centro Internacional would only be revealed after he had emerged from his morning conversation with God. Frequently he augmented Ernesto with perhaps up to three other drivers, and would stop one car suddenly to get into another. He had taught his family to celebrate birthdays on the wrong days. Special holidays such as Christmas were collectively enjoyed either weeks before or weeks after the date. Apart from the suite of rooms at the Tequendama, he also maintained hotel suites at five other locations in Bogotá. He was deeply grateful for God's protection but felt that in these troubled times He should be given a little assistance.

Within the narcotics industry, it was almost as though he did not exist. No warrants, extradition orders or surveillance operations had been placed on the life of the quietly spoken Colombian. When Pablo Escobar had declared war on the government in seeking political power, Rodriguez had known long before the first bomb went off that it would end in tears for the Escobar family: the secret of success in the narcotics industry lay in *manipulating* political power. When the Cali clan declared war on the Medellin cartel, the chairman had both groups temporarily suspended from the Cartel of Cartels. Rodriguez believed that all publicity for the narcotics industry was bad publicity: he was so clean that police records, intelligence files, DEA files and CIA records had no incriminating evidence on him. On official Colombian records, Victor Rodriguez was merely a successful businessman, heading an equally successful financial and industrial conglomerate, a supporter of wildlife and environmental protection.

Every other director of the board was similarly a citizen above suspicion and led a blameless life: the Italian was a highly respected industrialist, the Russian a key adviser to his country's Central Bank; but Rodriguez differed from them in one remarkable respect: for over a decade he had apparently led a crusade against narcotics and was a prime target for many within the trade who regarded him as a deadly enemy. *Time* had front-covered Rodriguez twice as the man who represented all that was good about Colombia.

In Colombia, where tax evasion is a way of life, the accounts of Andino Incorporated were a model of clarity: there was no fiscal fudging, no creative accounting. Rodriguez was a student of history as well as of men: he knew that yesterday's mistakes if not remembered today would be repeated tomorrow. He was aware that Al Capone had gone to prison not because of the numerous murders for which he was responsible, but because of tax evasion. He shared the late Meyer Lansky's view that money had not been laundered until it had been subjected to taxation by government agencies.

It was the image of corporate legitimacy that had so appealed to Andrew Sinclair when he first had been approached by Rodriguez. Before accepting the offer to act as counsellor to the Cartel of Cartels – a position that would place him second in power and influence to Rodriguez himself – Sinclair had asked many questions and requested access to a huge range of data. In essence, he behaved exactly as he would if the products had been legal and the company law-abiding. He had been impressed by the sound business practices that Rodriguez had brought to the narcotics industry, at least at the highest executive level. The central government of the Cartel of Cartels was an object lesson in moral and ethical rectitude. If it acted outside the law, there was always a cut-out. Rodriguez, Sinclair and their fellow board members kept a fire-break between them and the inferno.

On this particular Friday morning Rodriguez had chosen the church of San Ignacio for his morning prayers. He sat quietly at the back as the priest concluded the rites of the eight o'clock Mass. This was one of Victor's favourite places of worship: exquisite stained glass, carved mahogany, and three exits.

Having given God some thirty minutes of his time, Rodriguez headed for the Bogotá offices of Andino Incorporated. Once inside the heavily fortified building, he could safely embrace his need of ritual. His working mornings always began with a stroll through the dealing room, which represented in a scaled-down form all that an investor would find on Wall Street, the City of London or Tokyo exchanges. It was computer- and phone-linked to all three, and to the stock markets of another fifteen countries. There was one vital difference between the dealing room in Bogotá and the global stock exchange: it functioned on behalf of just one customer,

Andino Incorporated. Through Andino's president, Victor Rodriguez, the company had access to cartel funds that gave unlimited and open-ended credit lines: when an Andino dealing room employee talked to someone in a foreign exchange they expected and got Rolls Royce service. No one messed with a billion-dollar trading company.

Having reviewed the opening prices in New York, the closing ones in Tokyo and the latest in London, Rodriguez received from his senior dealer a fax from a DEA source in New York: it gave that day's street price for cocaine in New York, Washington, Chicago and Miami. He studied it, then watched the dealer as he punched the information into a computer performance chart. Two parallel lines ran across the middle of the graph. Rodriguez smiled as he noted that the data did not move the price graph through either line.

If the price had gone through the upper graph it would have indicated a shortage of product in America, a scarcity of dollars in Colombia and it was a good time to sell the dollar. Had the price moved through the bottom line, which indicated a major new source of product on the streets, he would have issued two instructions: first, with dollars flooding back into the country, buy them cheaply; second, locate and destroy the major new source.

Yet whatever misery it might have brought to the consumer countries, the sale of Rodriguez's number-one product had produced benign effects for Colombia and other Latin American suppliers: in twenty years Colombia's legal economy had grown at double the rate of non-supplying South American countries and unemployment in some areas had fallen dramatically. It had been officially accepted by Colombia's Central Bank that cocaine had prevented the collapse of the balance of payments but the price of economic stability had been high. At least 30 per cent of the best farming land in the country was now cartel-owned and planted only with coca, poppy and marijuana. A largely agrarian society that had grown the crops of basic survival had turned overnight to cash crops that would sustain and feed no one. And the products extorted another price: every twenty minutes someone died violently in Colombia, now the most violent country on earth.

Content that all was as it should be on the financial front, Rodriguez went to his office where the view was of the dealing room he had just left. It was sparsely decorated, with photographs – of birds, of Victor Rodriguez receiving an award from the Prince of Wales, and of weddings and university graduations of his children and those of his brothers, Alberto and José. No Rodriguez children had ever touched the products of their fathers. They dared not. In any case, to abstain was good for business while to indulge was probably a mortal sin.

Sitting behind his desk, Rodriguez flicked his intercom. A moment later his secretary entered. In one hand she held a cup of coffee, in the other the daily printout from El Gordo. He leaned back, sipped his coffee and began to study the transcripts of all the phone calls from and to the US Embassy in Bogotá, those made and received by the President's office or the heads of the various intelligence agencies, the police and the armed forces. Rodriguez knew and understood the power of information. Men are frequently killed for what they know. Rodriguez, like Oscar Benjamin, continued to stay alive *because of* what he knew.

Rodriguez chuckled to note that yet again the Americans were preoccupied with establishing the corruption of Colombia's president. When, he wondered, would they understand that it was only because of his venality that he was allowed to continue in office? The cartels had 'invested' eight million dollars in ensuring that 'their candidate' won the election, and Victor Rodriguez knew, courtesy of El Gordo, that the US Embassy were aware of that and that they had threatened the President with economic sanctions if he did not co-operate in their high-profile fight against the cartels.

Rodriguez placed the printout in his out tray and began to study the overnight surveillance reports. One in particular caused him to frown and shake his head. He read it again, then unlocked the drawer that contained his fax encoder.

*   *   *

Less than five minutes later Andrew Sinclair left his office and took an elevator to the public concourse at ground level of the World Trade Center where he walked towards the public telephones.

'Good morning, Victor.'

'Good morning, Andrew. We have a problem.'

Sinclair listened as Rodriguez elaborated, choosing his words with care. Only Rodriguez knew with what painstaking attention to detail Leonard Meredith, the chairman of US Cola, had been chosen to join the Colombia Project. Only he therefore could appreciate the self-control Sinclair demonstrated as he pronounced the death sentence. 'My recommendation, Victor, is that you close the deal.'

'On both of them?'

'Yes.'

'On a brighter note, Andrew, I understand the items that you ordered from our colleague in Italy await your collection. Shall I arrange for them to be forwarded to the six addresses?'

'Yes, and please thank our colleague for his prompt response.'

Rodriguez made two further calls, placed the mobile phone in a plastic bag for destruction and buzzed once on his intercom. It was nearly ten o'clock and the receiving hour was at hand. The door opened and Carlotta, his secretary, showed in the first visitor, Deputy Vasquez.

Vasquez, slim, in his mid-thirties, looked as if he had just danced an exhibition tango at the dance Olympics. Elected with a massive majority and newly appointed deputy attorney general, he now faced a serious career problem. He was accompanied by a member of the Cali clan, Fernando Salazar, a squat, barrel-chested man whose bow legs gave a clue to his profession: 'mule man', or transport director.

'Victor, Deputy Vasquez is in need of your help. He feels that you are the only one who can save him to ensure that his important work for the country continues.'

The mule man explained that the deputy's mistress, Maria Elba, was a woman who made heavy demands both in and out of the bedroom. She was obsessed with becoming wealthy in her own right and, although her lover would undoubtedly be powerful and wealthy one day, that was in the future. Maria Elba was concerned with the present. She had devised a form of private enterprise: she had planned to smuggle a quantity of cocaine into Great Britain and sell it. Just like that.

Scoring a little coca in Colombia was no problem, but Maria Elba was a greedy woman. If she had been less greedy she would probably have got away with it. She was also particular about what she swallowed. 'I am not swallowing condoms full of coca,' she had said to Vasquez. 'What do you think I am? A common tart?'

Thus the uncommon tart went first class and the ten kilos of cocaine went Gucci. Neither got past Heathrow. When sentenced to ten years Maria Elba had remained silent. Now word had reached Deputy Vasquez that unless he arranged her removal from Holloway prison and her immediate return to Bogotá, she would talk to Scotland Yard. She would give names and places. She had made tape-recordings that implicated him and several members of the Cali cartel.

Rodriguez stared at him. 'Why have you come to me, Señor?'

The deputy fluttered his hands, and stuttered, 'It is well known that you are a man of great influence, sir. The President values you highly – that, too, is common knowledge. I beg you to intercede on my behalf.'

Rodriguez rubbed his chin thoughtfully. 'But surely the President also values you highly? Within the past year he has made you deputy attorney general. Surely you yourself could ask him to have a quiet word with the British.'

Again the hands flailed, and the deputy swallowed hard. 'I was not the President's appointment. A faction, small but growing all the time within the Party, forced my rise to the cabinet.'

Rodriguez's eyes moved to the mule man, who gave a barely perceptible nod. Inwardly Rodriguez kicked himself: it was impossible that this arrangement had not been recorded by El Gordo – he must have missed it on the transcripts.

He stood up and extended his hand. 'Thank you for coming to see me, Señor. Let me consider how I can best help you.'

He hadn't buzzed, but Carlotta was standing at the open door to escort the deputy out. The mule man remained. Rodriguez sat down again and indicated that he should do the same.

'Does the deputy have what is needed to become president?'

Salazar grinned, showing an impressive line-up of gold fillings that garishly contrasted with his unshaven cheeks. 'If you decide to help him he does.'

Despite himself Rodriguez roared with laughter. Salazar was such a delightful cynic. Yes, given that the deputy was compromised and indebted to the cartel he indeed had what was needed to reach the presidential palace. 'One thing, Fernando. Assuming I am able to persuade the President and he in turn is able to persuade the British, when Maria Elba returns to Bogotá take steps to ensure that we acquire all copies of her little tape-recordings. Then have her killed.'

Though the receiving hour had only just begun, Rodriguez lingered with Salazar. He envied the mule man, who by the nature of his expertise remained close to the product and the action. The largely desk-bound Rodriguez pined for the late 1970s before the narcotics industry had exploded into multinational proportions. He yearned for the field trips to the savannah to check on the plants, the jungle laboratories of Guaviare and the putrid smell of the coca leaves fermenting in petrol – the first stage in cocaine production – the sweating excitement of illegal border crossings into Venezuela, Ecuador and Peru. Like many who have risen through the ranks to the very top of their professions, Victor Rodriguez retained a warm, nostalgic vision of his early days.

'So how are the mules, Fernando?'

'Still working hard for their two-hundred-dollar carrots. The Polish mules cost a little extra, but more of them get through. One woman in Kraków has made over fifty trips to London and New York – she prefers the New York run, gets upset when we use other mules.'

'Why New York?'

'All those extra air miles. She's clocked up enough to give six members of her family a free trip to the States.'

'The Nigerians?'

'No shortage. The arrest rate is rising all the time, but many are getting through at Heathrow and the other European airports. The US is tighter, but the margin, of course, is always with us.'

Fernando's job was to ensure a continuous supply of mules for the Cali cartel. It was work that brought him much job satisfaction. Many women in the prisons of Europe and the United States could testify to that. On Sundays in Cali and in Medellin and in many other cities it was the custom for the people to walk to the parks, to the fountains, to the central squares. Among those abroad in Cali would be Fernando and his team. One particular Sunday, one of the young women approached was Mónica.

Salazar saw her sitting on a bench in the square, beautiful, but obviously deeply troubled. 'Why do you look so sad?'

'I have many problems.'

'How can a beautiful young woman like you have problems?'

Mónica explained that her husband had vanished eighteen months ago. She did not know if he was dead or alive. She, her mother, her father and her daughter were struggling, there was not enough to eat, there was no money for clothes. Fernando had opened the flood-gates. He waited for Mónica to finish, then he said, 'Look, it's a lovely day. I hate to see young beauty so troubled. I'll lend you some money. Here's a hundred dollars. Pay your debts. Buy food, clothes. Give some to your parents.'

Mónica was stunned and overwhelmed. Never in her life had she been shown such kindness. She vowed to go directly to church and offer her thanks to God.

The cynic within Salazar stirred. 'No, my child, don't do that. To do so would be to occupy a place for someone less fortunate. Someone who cannot get God to listen. Just give me your address, then run home to your family.'

Three days later, at six in the morning, he came calling on Mónica. 'I've come for the money you owe me.'

She was distraught. 'But I've done as you said. I gave some to my parents. I paid our debts. I've bought food and clothes for my family. There are only a few dollars left. Señor, you never said you would require repayment so quickly.'

'Unfortunately I must call in the debt now. I am on my way to arrange the shipment of certain items of value. If you were to agree to take these items to England for me, I'll waive the debt. Who knows? I might even give you a little more money. Perhaps another hundred dollars.'

Later that week, and again at six in the morning, Salazar reappeared with dozens of little packages and a large quantity of surgical gloves. He cut off the fingers, filled them with cocaine, tied up the ends, dipped them in oil and Mónica began to swallow them. After she had swallowed twenty-six she threw up five. When she refused to swallow them again, Salazar produced a gun and pointed it at her. 'Swallow them, all of them.'

Before seeing her through Customs he had told her that she would be met at Heathrow by a Spanish-speaking person. She was. A bilingual Customs officer. The cabin crew always pass on to Customs the identity of passengers from drug-producing countries who neither eat nor drink on a flight.

In Holloway prison the staff were deeply concerned about Mónica, now serving seven years' imprisonment: the close-knit, loving family of which she had told Salazar on their first meeting had proved non-existent. When Mónica was two her mother had died. She had never known her father. She had been brought up by an elderly aunt who saw her as nothing more than another unwelcome burden until, when Mónica was ten, an 'uncle' appeared. Money changed hands between him and the aunt, and she went to live with him. He raped her on their first day together. He continued to rape her until she was sixteen, when she ran away. Within weeks she met and married a man little better than the 'uncle', who took to the hills long before that meeting by the fountain. When she met the charming Salazar, her daughter was twelve. Mónica saw the child's future clearly – and could not bear to live with it.

Her days in prison were made worse by the taunting from the next-door cell, the constant boasts about Maria Elba's 'powerful friends', the daily litany that 'I won't be in here much longer. My friends have already taken steps to get me out of here and back to Colombia.'

Rodriguez had read Mónica's all-too-familiar story the last time he had studied the cartel file on Salazar. He was fully acquainted with the mule man's sexual activities and made no judgement, merely a mental note.

The 'items from Italy' that Rodriguez had mentioned during his conversation with Sinclair were in their hotel suite in Washington. Their leader had just returned from a briefing that had been organized after a sequence of phone calls by different contacts. These had been triggered by the call Rodriguez had made on behalf of Sinclair. That was how the system worked. So many cut-outs that it would be impossible to trace the chain of command back to the chairman of the board. The items – three middle-aged men – listened as Roberto gave an account of his recent meeting.

'Perhaps these people think that only the law-abiding are allowed to take a professional pride in their work? The man who asked us to undertake this task, our good friend in Palermo, assured me that this was probably the most important job in my career. Can you imagine that? Do you know what they want? They want us to break into an office in Gary, Indiana; into a garage in Berkeley, California; a cellar in San Francisco.' Roberto stopped reading from the list in his hand and tossed it on the floor. 'I will call our friend in Palermo and tell him we're coming home. These Americans are crazy. You do not ask a Formula One Ferrari to stop by the supermarket and bring home the weekend groceries.'

Eventually Rodriguez bade farewell to Fernando Salazar, a man who evidently relished his work. Then he stood up and gazed unseeingly at the scene below in the dealing room of Andino Incorporated. It seemed to those below that he was gazing intently at their activities so each began to work just that little bit harder. In fact, Rodriguez was calculating the size and power of his unique organization. Annual turnover for the past four years had held steady at five hundred billion dollars. The Cartel of Cartels had over the previous decade become so powerful that it could no longer be dismantled – or, at least, thought Rodriguez, as he walked moodily back to his desk, not by democratically elected governments. With one exception, only the members within the organization had the power to threaten the industry.

The exception did not know that he posed a threat to the cartels. He was about to die in that blissfully ignorant state.

As Cola One climbed into the skies above Shannon airport and headed for La Guardia, the timer attached to the bomb showed six minutes. In the executive passenger cabin Leonard Meredith reviewed with his colleagues a highly successful week in Dublin. The European sales conference had concluded with a standing ovation for Meredith. He'd never been on better form, vibrant, positive, painting a picture of even greater sales for 'America's favourite'.

Leonard smiled appreciatively as the stewardess swayed towards him with a tray of the ubiquitous Cola. He was looking forward to getting between the pair of superb legs that were gliding towards him. He looked up at her.

'Why, thank you, Tammy. And how are you today?'

'I'm just fine, Mr Meredith. Really looking forward to the weekend.'

His face betrayed nothing. 'I'll drink to that.'

Meredith raised his glass of US Cola to toast the forthcoming delights he would soon be sharing with Tammy. His fellow executives followed suit.

'To the weekend, gentlemen.'

The glasses were still in mid-air when the Semtex bomb exploded.

The fragments of Cola One first rose, then fell inexorably into the Atlantic. The timing had been meticulous. The Syrians who had made the bomb had learned much from the bomb they had planted on Pan Am 103. Then a delayed flight resulted in an overland detonation, with the wreckage falling on Lockerbie. Recoverable wreckage. The Syrians impressed on Victor's surveillance team that the later the timer was activated before take-off the more accurately the moment of destruction could be predicted.

Sinclair read the Press Association story of the explosion as it came over the wire service. 'No survivors. Recovery of either the victims, the black box flight recorder or parts of the plane unlikely in such deep waters, experts say.'

The press picked up a curious coincidence. The plane had blown up on Friday, 28 May; the First National Bank in Chicago had been blown up exactly two weeks earlier on Friday, 14 May. No one had claimed responsibility for either the bank or the plane. The media saw a pattern. Big business was under attack. Friday was significant to the bombers. The press had a label. The Friday Bombers. Neither Rodriguez nor Sinclair felt inclined to argue the point. If the newspapers wanted to link a contract with a bank bombing that was their business.

As management consultant to US Cola, Sinclair moved as soon as he had read the story. He contacted those board members who had not attended the sales conference and offered them a concise business strategy to ensure that the damage to US Cola stock was limited. He offered recommendations on new board appointments and a press release that mixed measured elegy with bullish forecast. By the end of that day's trading the stock price of US Cola had actually closed a dollar higher than on Thursday. Then he turned to address the self-same task on behalf of the Colombia Project. 'Paul, I want to fax some material to you for your eyes only. Do you have a personal fax line?'

US Cola was about to be replaced by ATZ Oil.

*   *   *

Rodriguez had just one more visitor to see during his receiving hour. He flicked his intercom and Carlotta showed Alberto Ortega into the room.

Victor looked sadly at the pleasant young man as he gestured him to a chair. He had had such high hopes for Alberto, had regarded him almost as a son. He had nurtured his career, proudly watching him rising through the ranks on the dealing floor to become the heir apparent to the senior dealer – until the arrival of the report that lay on his desk. Victor looked unblinkingly across the desk at his protégé. 'The last report on you is positive.'

Alberto made a slight gentle gesture of resignation. 'I won't insult either you or the laboratory by insisting they've made a mistake.'

'I'm glad to hear that,' Victor said.

'Well, sir, wouldn't be much point, would there? I've read the data on those tests. The same methods have been applied to a lock of hair taken from the British poet, Keats. One hundred and seventy years after his death they established opium traces in the hair.'

Victor listened without reaction. He too had read the research data on the tests; he had personally introduced them at Andino. Periodic testing of all senior personnel to ensure that they had not picked up the habit.

'And as well as using you have, of course, been selling.'

That was something Alberto had not been expecting. 'But how . . . ?'

'How did we know? Come, Alberto.' Rodriguez sighed and tapped the reports he had been reading earlier. 'El Gordo. Your phone calls, your credit-card transactions. The little visits to the *ventanillas siniestras*.'

This last remark, a reference to the 'left-handed windows' that had been introduced in banks throughout Colombia, caused Alberto to pale. It was where one went to exchange coca dollars for bolivars.

Rodriguez was not enjoying the interview at all. He hated any form of waste, particularly of talent. 'Why, Alberto?'

'The tests are random, everyone knows that. I was gambling that I wouldn't be tested for a while.'

Rodriguez shook his head. 'No, no. I mean, why take it in the first place?'

'I have it under control, sir. I do really. It's just something that I like. It's not a problem. You know most of the dealers we do business with in London, New York and the other exchanges, they all snort. It's how we kill time.'

Victor flushed with anger. 'Killing time. No man kills time, Alberto. Time kills us all.'

'I'm sorry, sir. Really I am. As for the dealing, there are young boys out on the street shipping twenty kilos and becoming instant millionaires. I wanted to be one of them.'

As Alberto cleared out his desk under the watchful eye of company security and was escorted from the building he felt enormous relief. He had thought the old man was going to give him a far rougher time. Threaten him perhaps. Thank goodness Rodriguez had a soft spot for him.

That evening Alberto Ortega left his bachelor apartment in Bogotá for a dinner date with his fiancée. He slipped a cassette of salsa into the car radio and flicked on the ignition. He did not live long enough to hear even the opening bar. Yet another of those anonymous car bombs.

Fifteen minutes after Alberto died, Rodriguez, still at his desk, was quietly reading his way through the Medellin dossier when he heard the whirring of a fax machine coming from a locked drawer.

He removed a single sheet of paper from the fax receiver and placed the decoding skin over the random dots and squiggles: 'A new WINTER has joined Spring and Summer.'

Victor grinned. So Sinclair had three of his seasons back in place. It was to be hoped that the three were more discreet in bed than Meredith had been with his air stewardess.

All in all, Victor thought, it's been a satisfactory day.

CHAPTER FIVE

POKER

UNDERNEATH HIS SIX-FOOT-FOUR FRAME, HIS BLUFF, NO-bullshit manner, his heavy fake Australian accent and copious swearing Bastard Bruce Clay was a coward, with a bureaucrat's ink not blood in his veins. Never having made a documentary in his life, he was secretly terrified of his responsibility as head of documentary purchasing at Network Centre, London. His terror had overflowed when Mitch, his subordinate, had given Adam Fraser his green light for two ninety-minute documentaries on an American preacher. The proposed budget was nightmare enough, but three whole hours? The Network might even have to cancel a game-show to make room for it.

Curious how he always thought of Stanford as home. He was now thirty miles north of the university and heading through the city towards the Golden Gate Bridge.

Sinclair's destination was Mill Valley, the home of his fourth season. With luck, Autumn might come in June, thought Sinclair, as he glanced from the bridge to the bay beyond.

It was a lovely San Francisco day, clear blue sky, temperature already in the mid-sixties before nine in the morning. It was unusual for Sinclair to acknowledge something as trivial as this but he considered this city a special place. And he was on a roll.

Three in the bag. Paul McCall, chairman of ATZ Oil. Rupert Turner, chairman of the multi-media conglomerate Network International, and Rick Forrest, chairman and majority stockholder of Forrest Computers.

Sinclair was about to breakfast with number four.

Turning from Highway 101, he stopped the car outside a pair of large iron gates. A metallic voice said, 'State your name and if applicable your rank and number.'

'Andrew Sinclair joining Edgar Lee Stratford for breakfast.'

Like all men afraid of decisions, Bastard Bruce Clay had called a meeting. Adam and Mitch listened to him slag off a fashionable director for nearly an hour. '*The Times* said that Dean Cooper's work is like that of a young Orson Welles. Tunbridge Wells, more like. Suburban, middle-class and spiritually dead.'

Adam and Mitch indicated assent. 'Now, come on, you two,' Clay said sharply, 'we're not here to gossip. Adam, why *two* programmes on this Patrick Collins? For that I can get a whole year of cute animals fucking.'

'We have a lot of facets to cover. Family background. His family's role models during the fifties when he was a young boy included General Franco and Joe McCarthy. Are they still an influence? College – turns down a glittering prize, a place at Harvard. He's a devout Catholic and opts for more Jesuit training at Boston College. Unlike many of his generation, although he had a watertight legal deferment from the draft, he actually volunteered for Vietnam. He fights godless Communism, loses two close friends but saves another, John Reilly, who is now his number two. When he returns he leaves the Catholic Church and studies instead at a small Bible college . . .'

'All right, Adam, a fascinating life. Now take a taxi home and tell it to the driver. Tell him why, after a hard day of shit work driving people through this arsehole city, he should care a monkey's toss about a multi-millionaire chat-show preacher who survived Vietnam?'

The gates swung open and Sinclair was confronted by a pristine white guardhouse and a sixty-foot flagpole with the Stars and Stripes fluttering. To its left were eight kennels. Several glossy black Dobermans studied Sinclair with interest as an armed guard emerged from the guardhouse.

'Good morning, Mr Sinclair. The escort is on its way.'

Sinclair half raised a hand. 'Oh, no need for that, I know the route up to the house.'

'Just a precaution, sir. Here they are.'

Two uniformed guards on motorbikes swept down the drive, swung round and positioned themselves fore and aft of Sinclair's car. The security man saluted and the convoy moved up the drive. The journey from the front gates to the main house was a pleasant meander of exactly a mile.

Edgar Lee Stratford, president of Global Systems, the engineering and construction giant, high on the Forbes Four Hundred list of America's richest, had put himself through university by playing poker. Throughout his career he had always known the precise value of a poker hand or a company's shares – and when to throw them in. His luck was not confined to poker and the stock market. His wife had once asked him to buy a fashion magazine, so he purchased the publishing empire that owned it. Later he sold it on, making a net profit of twenty million dollars. Reserved and shy, Stratford bought trousers in a number of sizes to avoid trying them on in the store. Sinclair was one of less than two dozen people in the country who knew Stratford's home telephone number.

The group broke through the avenue of trees and saw in front of them an exact replica of the White House. Standing on the steps, grinning from ear to ear, was all five feet one inch of Edgar Lee Stratford.

Clay liked nothing better than goading people, particularly those who needed something that was within his gift. Having exhausted the 'how will this play to the tired taxi driver' argument, he had turned to the film's length.

Adam went in quickly, smashing that particular lob and winning a point. 'Look, Bruce, we've been discussing these two docos for three hours this afternoon. The subject will hold up for three hours on screen. Particularly when I replace your contribution with one from Collins.' Mitch developed a coughing fit.

Clay raised an eyebrow. He knew that people like him were expected to admire those who stood up to them and he also knew when to stop needling.

'If I green-light these programmes,' he said, 'when am I going to see the finished product?'

'Within twelve months.'

'Hm, that would mean we could use them as part of a major launch in the fall?'

Adam sensed a breakthrough. 'Yes, autumn delivery. No trouble.'

'Let me sleep on it. I'll let you know by the end of the week. You sure you can get to Patrick Collins?'

Adam saw Mitch looking at him anxiously. He reached into a folder and produced a letter.

Clay attempted to seem unimpressed by its content, but failed. 'Full facilities. Unlimited access to myself or any member of my staff. Would be delighted if you and your crew would be my guests either in Boston or Florida.'

Adam felt he could relax now. It must be in the bag. Typical Clay – he always wanted to prolong the agony.

In the orangery, Edgar Stratford replaced his cup and saucer on the white linen tablecloth. 'Andrew, I have given your proposition careful consideration. I have weighed it painstakingly. I have decided not to take up your offer to participate in the Colombia Project. I think the idea, the plan, call it what you will, has great merit and is brilliantly conceived. It is, however, not for me.'

Sinclair had been planning it since long before that day in

Cúcuta on the Colombian-Venezuelan border when Rodriguez shared the plan with the other cartel board members. This Californian Napoleon was jeopardizing five years' work, which had involved large sums of money, commitment and dedication. However, he continued to stare calmly into his host's grey eyes. Then he said, almost gently, 'I want to thank you, Edgar, for giving it such careful consideration. I'm very grateful for the time you've devoted to it. I respect your decision and, of course, I accept it. I would like to take with me the faxed material I sent you earlier. Your assurance that you have not made copies would also be appreciated.' He gave no hint of anger or frustration, just continued to gaze across the table. It was not every day that he had a close-range view of one of the most powerful men in the country totally stupefied.

Edgar Stratford's jaw had dropped. 'I don't understand.'

'What is it you don't understand, Edgar?'

His head swung from side to side in disbelief. 'Just like that? Thank you and goodbye?'

'Absolutely. Look, Edgar, it must be obvious that the Colombia Project will succeed only if every one of the key players is committed. What's the point of me attempting to persuade you to change your mind? Six months on, you might change it again.'

Edgar studied his napkin ring. 'So I was not indispensable to your plan?'

'Edgar, you were vital.'

Suddenly Stratford grinned. 'Good.'

'I'm sorry?'

'I'm in, Andrew. I was in as soon as I'd read your fax. Come on, now, I'm supposed to be one of the best poker players around. I wanted to know how you'd respond if I tossed it all in the trash can. If I'd really been prepared to reject your proposal and then gone public on your plan, it would have been destroyed before you could move on to phase two. Yet you remained so composed. I'll tell you this, I'm deeply impressed. That's the kind of control that's going to ensure this project of yours succeeds. Before today I just *thought* it was a winner. Now I *know* it is.'

Laura loved preparing parties, especially parties that showed off her husband in their home. For the party celebrating Adam's victory over Bastard Bruce Clay, the food and drink bill was high and the guest list selective. No celebrities, no journos unless they were friends. Mitch, of course, and his wife, Barry without his wife, Leon with his boyfriend. And Susanna, whom Laura respected so much and was so happy to introduce as Adam's brilliant assistant . . .

Clay had been true to his word. His letter had been delivered by motorcycle courier on the Friday when Adam was on the phone, inviting a few more people to the party. Laura came in waving the envelope.

'From the Network, Adam.'

He tore open the envelope. Inside was a single page.

'He's rejected it, Laura. "Deep consideration. Regret I have concluded the idea and its central subject are without relevance to a British audience. Bastard Bruce Clay." '

Laura gripped his arm. 'Dirty little shit! I'd cut his balls off if I could find them. What about the real BBC?'

Adam laughed derisively. 'They turned it down for the same reason. Lack of relevance to their audience's interests. Fuck it.'

Laura put her hand on his shoulder. 'We'll cancel the party.'

'No, we won't, Laura. It's bad enough that the Bastard's got a victory he knows about. We're not giving him another – even over something as small as a party. Never give your enemies unknown victories.'

Adam and Laura invited more guests, bought more drink and food. On Saturday, after their third raid on the wine stores of Camden, they called in at their bank. Adam checked his balance. 'Wonderful! None of the cheques for this party have hit our account yet.' She didn't reply, but picked up a leaflet about the bank's facilities, then sent him off for yet more champagne.

What had originally been planned as a dinner party for half a dozen had become a gathering of over fifty, planned to start at six. By five everything was ready, the host and hostess had showered and dressed, were relaxing with their first drink of the day, and had reached that moment familiar to many who have thrown a party.

'I wish no one was coming, you look good enough to eat.'

Laura laughed and recrossed her long, elegant, black-nylon-clad legs. Adam stirred in his seat, then raised his glass. 'To the man who invented slit dresses.'

Laura giggled, sipped her wine, then glanced back at him. 'Now, then. No brooding.'

'Sorry, love. Just running it all through my mind again.'

Laura got up and moved to an armchair close to him. She ran a finger gently down his face. 'Are you trying to find a way out?'

'Yes, I suppose I am.'

'And?'

He patted her knee in an abstracted way. 'I can't find one. Without a UK slot I can't make the pieces fit. No UK slot, no fifty per cent of my budget. No show.'

He ran his finger moodily around the rim of his glass until it began to squeak. 'There's no point in my asking any of the foreign co-producers for more cash. I've already got the maximum from them. I'll call them on Monday, tell them it's off. No, I won't. Can't let Bastard Bruce Clay win this one. I'm going to call Kurt. Perhaps I can persuade ZDF to come up with the whole budget.'

He left the room in a rush, adrenalin pumping as he geared himself for another attempt to kick-start the project. Laura had been here before, lots of times. It seemed to her that it required more creative energy to get the commitment than it did to make the film. When he came back she looked at him questioningly. 'He's out. Back in two hours. His wife says she'll get him to call me. Come on, give me your glass.'

She pulled it away from his outstretched hand. 'Plenty of time for that. Tell me why this project is so important to you.'

'Thought I had.'

Laura shook her head slightly. 'You know very well you

haven't. I've heard all the stuff you've pitched to Mitch and Clay. What I haven't heard is the bottom line. The real reason. What is it that you want to go looking for?'

Adam walked out on to their small balcony. It was a lovely early summer's evening with a gentle breeze. He turned and looked back to where she was sitting, placed his drink on a table, and began to pace into the room and out on to the balcony, making swift movements in the air with his hands – karate chops and sweeps followed by gentle rippling tai-chi movements. Laura had seen him do this many times when he was struggling to find the right words or correct response.

Finally he said, 'I feel sure that Collins is not one of those what-you-see-is-what-you-get men. He wields enormous power and influence. What makes him unique is that there doesn't appear to be an angle. If you asked *him* what the bottom line was I'm sure he'd say eternal salvation.'

'Do I hear just a touch of cynicism?' asked Laura.

'Everyone has their dark side. I want to find the element of his personality that he keeps hidden from his faithful congregation and his adoring TV audience. There's going to be an angle, there always is. If there is no dark side, no angle, then great. Collins is what I've been looking for since I was sixteen.'

Laura looked bemused.

'My faith,' said Adam.

The party was a cracker. It got off to a flying start when Susanna, Barry and Leon all arrived half-cut, and by seven-thirty quite a number of the other guests were well on the way to catching up with them. The house was big enough to offer a variety of moods: in one room the more energetically inclined were dancing, in another people were eating, in a third they were chatting quietly, while in a fourth a game of snooker was in progress. Elsewhere some were gathering for the first of two weekly rituals.

'I know what I'd do if I won the lottery,' Laura slurred. 'I don't want a lot. Just enough for a thatched cottage in the country, no more than an hour's drive from London. Roses around the door, a few acres, tennis court, swimming pool and

. . .' She looked around for Adam but he had disappeared. '. . . and I'd give Adam the money he needs to make his docos on Patrick Collins.'

The phone interrupted her daydream. She spoke for a while, then said, 'Very well, I'll tell him,' and hung up.

At that moment, Adam bounced in. 'Well, my love, have you won the lottery?'

Laura was abruptly sober. 'No. You have. I had Kurt on the telephone. Subject to board approval, which he's pretty certain he can get, he will put up the entire budget for the two documentaries.'

Mitch gasped. 'Why the hell will he do that, Adam? He'll never recoup from foreign sales.'

Laura wheeled. 'He has faith in Adam, Mitch, and perhaps you don't!' Then she broke the tension. 'I want everyone to grab the person nearest to them and repeat after me, "We're off to see the Wizard, the Wonderful Wizard of Oz!" Now, follow the yellow-brick road!' She grabbed Adam and led the entire company Scarecrow-dancing out into the street. As they danced, they indulged in the second of the weekly rituals: throwing their losing lottery tickets away.

It still made little sense. Roberto had spent a long time on the phone talking to their friend in Palermo. Subsequently there had been another meeting in Washington with the contact who had briefed him. Everyone was anxious to reassure the sensitive Italian and his colleagues that this was indeed an operation of supreme importance. To indicate just how important, the fee for the work had been quadrupled.

Roberto and his team began to take the operation far more seriously after they had arrived in Indiana. He had been advised that they would be safe-housed in Gary, not far from the first target, in fifth-floor offices belonging to a company called Cyber World. The safe-house impressed Roberto: it had everything a prima donna might want, including a Roman chef. An hour after they had enjoyed their first *saltimbocca alla Romana* a couriered package had arrived, containing instructions on how they could enter and leave the office block without, as the unsigned note said, 'disturbing the tranquillity of the security staff'. Roberto gave a theatrical shrug. The Americans were still crazy but they seemed to appreciate that they were dealing with professionals. He began to study the plans of the office block.

The last guests had been flushed out, including the one asleep in the bath. The house was a shambles. Adam felt a stab of guilt: his visits were rare enough without wrecking the home she kept so neat for him. He picked up a butt-filled glass, but she seized it from him. 'Don't do that. We're going to bed now.'

They explored each other for a long time, like children who have been away from home.

'I love you, Adam Fraser, what you were, what you are. I want more of you but more of the same. Now go to America and make me a sensational documentary about your preacher.'

He sat up. 'Jesus! I must phone Kurt!'

'Forget him, Adam. He phoned to turn you down. I took the call. But there was no need to spoil the party. You've got the money.'

'How?'

'I mortgaged the house.'

Andrew Sinclair stood up from the breakfast table and carried his coffee out on to the lawn. As he strolled across the grass towards the Hudson river, he savoured the memory of his meeting with Edgar Stratford.

With the last of the four key players in position, Sinclair was now confident that lords of the media, like Rupert Murdoch, Bill Gates, Ted Turner and Michael Eisner, would all come on board, and captains of industry like the Rockefellers, the Du Ponts, George Soros and the Mellon family. Now he could focus on the vital factor that had to be brought on side. The one element that, unlike the presumptuous Stratford, was indispensable and, at the moment, lacking: the agreement of Patrick Collins to commit to the project. Without him, the Colombia Project would come to nothing. Sinclair's adrenalin surged as he anticipated his meeting with the evangelist. It would be the most important pitch he had ever made.

Once more he felt amused at Stratford's conceit and his belief that he could have wrecked it. Like Meredith and the others, he had been under twenty-four-hour surveillance long before being contacted by Sinclair. His telephones had been tapped, his homes and his offices bugged. Sinclair had demanded of Rodriguez that, if any of the four were to show less than complete commitment, they would be murdered. It was a demand with which Rodriguez had been happy to comply. The surveillance team assigned to Meredith had learned of his bedtime conversations about the Colombia Project with the stewardess and Meredith had paid dearly for his indiscretion. Sinclair had made the same demand concerning Collins: if he declined his offer, he too would be a dead man.

'Coming, kids!' he called to his children, who were waiting for him to take them to the swimming hole.

CHAPTER SIX

PREACHER

'HOLY FATHER, WE THANK YOU FOR BRINGING OUR FRIENDS Adam, Susanna, Barry and Leon safely to our table. We ask that you watch over and protect them as they go about their work. May their labours be pleasing in your eyes. Bless them and their families, and all who are gathered at this table. Thank you, Lord, for this food and for your continuing bountiful gifts. Praise be to Jesus Christ, your only Son. Amen.'

Patrick Collins opened his eyes, lifted his head and looked around the table.

'Teresa and I are delighted you're here. For the duration of your stay, our home is your home.' The preacher looked young, even without makeup. He darted a glance at his wife. She was petite and sharp-featured, with coal-black hair and a pale complexion. Adam sensed an acute mind, and noticed that her dress, although simple and unthreatening to Collins's flock, was beautifully cut and expensive. He already knew wheelchair-bound John Reilly, Collins's number two and chief executive of his business empire.

The Collins magic was effective and Adam watched as Collins switched effortlessly between dynamic evangelist and urbane talk-show host. But he was only half engaged in what was going on: his latest conversation with Oscar Benjamin kept replaying in his mind.

'The man you're catching a plane to see.'

'Yes, Oscar?'

'My friends at head office who ran the checks on him for you have been in touch again and I thought you should know that someone else has been running precisely the same profile searches on him.'

Adam had been doodling while he listened. Now his hand froze, along with the rest of his body.

'Adam? You still there?'

'Yes, I'm still here, Oscar. Who's been running checks on the man?'

'I dunno.'

'Oh come on, Oscar. Head office must know.'

'Oh, yeah. Sure they do. They just won't share that information with me. All I can get out of them is that whoever made the request has clearance at Level One. You remember, we discussed the possibility of someone organizing a secret clean-up of your subject's files? Well, the answer to your question is one of the same possibilities. Just watch your back while you're in the States, my son.'

'But, as Pilate said, "What is truth?" '

Adam realized that Collins was talking to him. 'I'm sorry, Pat. Touch of jet-lag. As for Pontius Pilate, I've been trying to answer his question for most of my life. "And ye shall know the truth and the truth shall make ye free" is a lot easier said than achieved.' There was silence. John Reilly, Collins and Teresa were staring intently at him.

'Oh, I'm sorry. I suppose quoting the Bible at the dinner table of the most famous preacher in the United States is a bit presumptuous.'

Collins beamed. 'Not at all, Adam. I'm delighted to hear you quoting St John. That just happens to be one of my favourite lines from the Bible.' He continued, with deep conviction, 'If the Son of God sets you free, then you will be really free.'

Adam decided to pursue the theme. Someone else was looking for the preacher's dark side. It might pay to throw a little bread upon the waters. 'Each of my films is a search for a particular truth,' he said.

'How do you know when you've found it?' asked Teresa Collins.

'Sometimes it's obvious. Specific facts. Particular evidence.' Adam looked ruefully at her. 'Other times it's less tangible and I just hope and pray that I've discovered what I've been looking for.'

'When you discover whatever truth you're looking for in this film, do let me know, Adam,' Collins said.

'I promise you, Pat. You'll be the first to know.' He caught the glance that passed between Collins and his wife.

Teresa Collins was demure, soft-spoken, but, Adam thought, vigilant. It could not be easy sharing your husband with millions of others. Had anyone caused him to stray? Adam thought back again over all he knew of the man.

Five years earlier, when Adam's first Vietnam documentary had been shown, John Reilly had seen it and had been overwhelmed. He had written an effusive letter to Adam, and had shown a video of the programme to Collins. Both men, survivors of the war, had been deeply moved. They had rejected the film's central thesis that the United States had had no place in Vietnam, but fully acknowledged that some things done in the name of democracy were as evil as the ideology they had fought to destroy. An exchange of letters had been followed by a meeting between the three in London during Collins's last evangelical mission to Europe. Collins had questioned Adam closely about the MIA issue – the 2,393 servicemen who were listed as missing in action in South East Asia.

'There are no torture camps, no slave labourers,' Adam told him. 'But a considerable number of former American servicemen went AWOL during the war. They've married Vietnamese women, they're happy, and they don't want to go back to the States.' He then revealed to the evangelist that he had met a number of these missing servicemen always on the strict understanding of total confidentiality. 'They don't want to cause even more distress to their kin in the States than they already have. Yes, it would indeed have made for a sensational film, but some things in life are a bit more important than that.'

They had met several times since and when Adam had told John Reilly he wanted to make a factual, in-depth film about Collins's life and work, Collins himself had cabled: 'I will be delighted to give you full co-operation.' Whether he would remain delighted was another matter: many of Adam's subjects had felt differently when viewing the finished work.

Collins dabbed at his mouth with a napkin. 'And tell me, Adam, how is your relationship with God?'

As a conversation stopper that took some beating. None of the diners could even take refuge by concentrating on their meal, which had reached an interval between courses. Susanna gave a laugh which she quickly choked into a cough.

'My word, Pat. I need notice of a question like that. It's not an easy one to answer.'

'Good.'

Adam looked at Collins, slightly bemused. 'I'm sorry?'

As the preacher responded, his hands rose and his arms parted. Christ of the Andes had come to dinner in Naples, Florida. 'Anyone who tells me his relationship with the Almighty is perfect or who gives me a quick glib answer worries me. How can they be that sure? How can any one of us be that sure? All we can do is to keep talking to Him, hope that He's listening and hope that we understand His responses.' His hands descended again and rested on the tablecloth.

Adam was momentarily moved to total candour. 'Yes, that's probably part of my problem. I don't talk to God as often as you do. When I was a child I prayed every day. But then . . .' He tailed off uncertainly.

'You put away your childish things?' Johnny proffered.

'No, Johnny. I just stopped getting down on my knees and saying "Bless me, Father, for I have sinned".'

'I see that you're starting to film on Monday. You'll be coming to the Sunday service, won't you?' Collins asked Adam.

'Of course.'

After dinner Adam strolled through the gardens that stretched from the main house to the Gulf of Mexico several miles away. The crew had gone to bed early, leaving him to gather his thoughts. Collins's Florida estate was like a state within a State, with its nine-hole golf course, six tennis courts, outdoor swimming pools, guest bungalows, and beyond it was an even bigger piece of real estate. Collinsville contained a vast shopping mall, the Patrick Collins Business Center, his Church of the Evangelist, a service station and a bank. Collins was a man who offered his congregation a wide range of services. Ostentatious wealth didn't square with Adam's view of priests, but at least it had given him a working title: 'Eye of a Needle?'

Again his thoughts returned to the huge uncut gem that Oscar had placed in his hands. Who within the American government was running every conceivable check on America's favourite preacher? Why? What had they discovered about Collins?

'Get rid of him, Patrick. He's sharp.'

'Of course he's sharp, honey. You don't get all the awards he's won by having clean shoes and a bright smile.'

The evangelist and his wife were also out, enjoying the cool late evening, and they had seen Adam Fraser strolling in the grounds below the main house.

'Just remember he has an agenda. There's no percentage for him in making a two-part documentary that does nothing but praise the preacher.'

Collins put an arm around her protectively. 'Teresa, what on earth have I to fear? I have nothing to hide.'

The sun was setting over the Gulf of Mexico and Adam looked up at the beautiful blood red-spattered sky as he walked towards his guest bungalow.

When he opened the door the lights were already on. The bed had been turned back, his suitcases unpacked. The bedside radio was tuned to a classical channel. Susanna had been here.

He missed her acutely. For once they were not sharing a bed as well as a project. He was certain that the Reverend Pat Collins would not open up to a man committing a sin in his house. And, in any case, it did not seem right when his wife had financed the documentary.

'Try it both ways, Leon. Slow pan along the front line. Close up on that lead tenor, then pull out wide to show the entire thousand members of the choir.'

It was Sunday morning and the service at the Church of the Evangelist was in full swing. The choir were rocking up a storm with 'Praise be, He loves me'. For Patrick Collins and his congregation this was an hour set aside for God. For Adam and his crew it was a technical rehearsal.

The singing seemed to end and Adam was about to sit but someone in the choir sang, 'He cares for me.' The congregation responded, then the mass choir and all around him people were rocking back and forth in rhythm. Adam found himself moving in tempo, while the congregation jumped about, proclaiming their faith, their need, their love. He had to struggle to remain detached from it. He was here to make a documentary, for God's sake, not to be converted.

Eventually the lead tenor sang, 'Amen,' and brought in the congregation on that last triumphant note. A moment later there was silence. Adam glanced at his watch. The hymn had run exactly fifteen minutes.

As if from nowhere Patrick Collins appeared.

Leon hissed, 'He moved in slowly during the last amen, stayed hidden just behind the band.'

Adam smiled. Leon never missed a trick.

'Praise be to God,' said Collins. He held a Bible in his right hand. 'If we have faith in God, we stand on the threshold of everything we desire, everything we need. Praise be to God.'

As Collins developed his sermon, Adam's concentration

drifted from his words to the TV crew covering it for Collins's cable channel. It would be good to get some of that show-within-a-show element into the film. He was just about to whisper an instruction to Susanna when his attention was drawn back to Collins. 'And this friend of mine, he's probably one of the best documentary-makers in the world with a truly glittering track record. You may have seen some of his work. He made three films on the Vietnam war. They all won prizes.'

Adam sat transfixed as Collins told the congregation about his films, on the Brazilian shanty-towns, El Salvador and Chile. Of his two-parter on the drug cartels of Latin America. He turned to Susanna. 'Can you make the ground open up and swallow me, please?'

All he got by way of sympathy was a terse 'Sssh.'

'This friend of mine feels passionately about his work. What he calls his obsession to get to the truth, the heart of the matter. Imagine a man seeking truth every minute of his working waking life! What commitment that must take. My friend believes in the biblical injunction "And ye shall know the truth and the truth shall make ye free." Amen to that.'

The congregation echoed, 'Amen.' For one wonderful moment Adam thought the sermon was over. But Collins continued, 'Some time ago this man asked me if I would co-operate with a documentary he wanted to make. The central subject, the man whose life would be examined in minute detail seeking the flaws as well as any virtues, the bad along with the good, is quite well known to me. His name is Patrick Collins.'

From around the church there was considerable applause, a burst of 'Praise the Lord' – and from immediately behind where the crew were sitting a loud 'Well, I'll be damned!'

By now Adam felt sure he knew what was coming. He hoped to God he was wrong.

'After some reflection and prayer I agreed to co-operate and I am truly delighted to tell you all that this man is among us today. He is here from London, England, and his film crew are with him. Adam – Adam Fraser, please stand up and let the people see you. And your crew. Susanna, Leon and Barry.'

Every camera in the church swung round and focused on them as the four shuffled to their feet and acknowledged the ovation they were receiving. Again came the voice from behind. 'Well, I'll be damned!' They sat down again, cheeks burning. A camera remained on Adam.

Collins told his congregation, and the part of the nation that was tuned to the televised service, of Adam's struggle to get the documentaries financed. 'But God moves in mysterious ways, my friends. The day after that rejection he sat and considered what seemed to be an insurmountable problem. All the work in preparation for these documentaries had been in vain. Many men would have given up at that stage. Would have thrown in the towel. Adam Fraser is made of stronger material. He has faith, my friends, that if you truly believe that something you want to happen is going to happen, then, why, it does. He got busy on the telephone and before the day was through he had persuaded a foreign TV station to pick up the cost of the entire budget. He had faith. Oh, I tell you, my friends, faith can move mountains. Let us praise the Lord.'

The organ swelled. The orchestra joined in. The choir stood, then the congregation. Adam was stunned and angry. Then he heard the voice behind him again. 'Excuse me, Mr Fraser.' He turned to see a small black boy, eyes like saucers. 'Can I be in your movie?'

Adam winked at him. 'Yes, of course you can.'

'Well, I'll be damned!'

Andrew Sinclair was in his den watching *The Patrick Collins Hour*. There was a big close-up of Adam on the screen as Mary came in wearing a dressing gown and carrying a tray of coffee. She paused and stared at the screen. Then, almost instinctively, she pushed a bare leg provocatively out through the sheer silk of the robe. The movement was lost on her husband. 'I thought we might take these back to bed, Andrew,' she said.

He turned, smiling. 'What? Oh, yes. Great idea.'

'Perhaps I should have a look at that church programme you've been watching. Why so happy?'

'Oh, a problem I had has just been solved. It's true, you know, Mary. God indeed moves in mysterious ways.'

'Look, Susanna, all I'm saying is that you might have checked with me before you sent my entire CV to Johnny Reilly.'

'As I remember, Adam, you'd gone walkabout in Hamburg when he phoned. He needed it faxed there and then because Collins had raised some queries.'

'You mean he wanted to see how much mileage he could make out of me for one of his sermons. You any idea how that felt?'

'Oh, come on now. Is this the man who always fronts his own documentaries, who's a legend in the field of self-promotion?'

'Bitch!'

'Bastard!'

'Not secretly working for Bastard Bruce Clay, are you, Susanna? It's not enough that my personal history is bandied about in Collins's church, it has to be on cable TV as well.'

Susanna shook her head. 'You really should get an award for double standards. Every film you make exposes someone to the public – and they're practically stripped naked. Collins hasn't hurt you like that.'

'You should still have cleared it with me before sending that CV.'

'Adam, what would you have said if I *had* got hold of you in Germany?'

'I'd have said yes!' he shouted.

'So what the fuck are you getting so excited about?'

'Because I would have known that he had it!' His voice went up an octave. 'And why the hell did you tell him about the German deal?'

'Why not?'

Because there is no German deal, thought Adam. Because my wife came through with the money. And because I have not told you or the others that, and now I feel like a cheat and a traitor after millions of people have been told I'm a hero of faith. He slammed out of the bungalow.

*　　*　　*

Working quickly, Leon changed the film magazine and nodded to Adam. Barry made an adjustment to the sound level and Susanna held the clapper board in front of the camera. A moment later Adam turned back to John Reilly.

'Where are we, Johnny?'

'This is the third floor of the Corporate Institution, the headquarters of the Patrick Collins Evangelistic Association. The heart of the Crusade.'

Dozens of women were sitting at rows of desks, all talking into telephones. Leon, camera on his shoulder, with Barry crouched beside and just below holding a mike, was moving slowly along a line of desks pausing to pick up fragments of conversation.

'Your cheque should be made out to the Association. Mr Collins does not accept donations made to him personally.'

'Yes, American Express will do nicely, sir. What is your card number?'

Adam waited while Leon worked his way down the room. It would make an excellent montage of corporate Christianity. Then he turned back to Reilly. 'It obviously costs money to run. How many people are on the payroll? Give me some of the infrastructure, Johnny.'

'Here at headquarters we employ seven hundred and thirty-one people. Worldwide we have a further eleven hundred on permanent staff. That number can easily quadruple when Pat is on tour. Our annual budget is running at seventy-three million dollars. The helpers on this floor are entirely engaged in soliciting donations. The first floor deals with incoming mail, which averages three and a half million letters per year.'

Adam had researched all of this information before leaving England, but his expression of stunned surprise was impressive.

'That's a *lot* of letters.'

'Immediately after a televised crusade we get at least two hundred thousand a day for several days afterwards. The mail is scanned into the master computer, then separated electronically into two categories, donors and non-donors.'

'What's the ratio?'

'Around seventy-seven per cent donors, average donation twelve dollars thirty cents.'

'That's going to bring you in about thirty-three million dollars per year. Where do you get the balance of your budget – the other forty million – from?'

They had been strolling along the vast open-plan office and had arrived at a large section given over entirely to rows of computers.

Johnny gestured towards them. 'In a variety of ways, Adam. For example, in here we hold the master mailing list. Any contact that anyone makes with the Patrick Collins Evangelistic Association for whatever reason is entered on to it. From this we send out a hundred million pieces of mail each year.'

'All asking for donations?'

'Yes. For example, if you write in for some of our free books or pamphlets we will, of course, send them to you no charge, but we would ask you to consider making a donation to the Crusade.'

'And most people do?'

'Yes, thank the Lord, they do.'

As they roamed over the building Adam assembled an image of an organization that ran like a Swiss watch, and was geared to perform just one function, as Reilly succinctly put it.

'What we are doing here, Adam, is supplying the world's greatest product to the greatest number of people as cheaply as possible.'

They filmed the morning prayer services that were compulsory for all staff, with each group's particular pleas to the Almighty. 'O Lord, help your humble servants, the computer operators, to perform good accurate work. May our efforts and our computers bring ever greater reward for this ministry.'

They filmed on the first floor where the daily Niagara of mail was received, where each clerk prayed, 'Let my eyes find every potential for donations in the letters I read today, O Lord.'

Reilly explained how the letters were answered: 'We underline key words like "financial worries" or "lonely", "drink", "sex", "delinquency" and so on, which helps us to label the problem troubling the writer. Then, from the computer coding we give each letter, another department sends out to each writer the appropriate tape.'

They filmed a computer automatically printing out an 'appropriate' letter to go with a tape. The letters came out with Patrick Collins's signature already on them. It was impossible to tell that the preacher had not personally penned the letter. Along with the tape and the letter went 'appropriate' verses from the Scriptures, also automatically chosen. If the writer had indicated a preoccupation with lack of money, Ecclesiastes would comfort him: 'The sleep of the labouring man is sweet, whether he eat little or much: but the abundance of the rich will not allow him to sleep.'

As Reilly told Adam proudly: 'We can pull out the computer data on any individual who has ever written in and give you their entire spiritual history.'

After two days' filming at the business centre, Adam and the crew moved location to inside the church. They filmed Reilly and other members of staff demonstrating the state-of-the-art master control centre that operated sound, cameras, music, lights and special effects. They filmed the press room: Patrick Collins had long ago realized his message needed the media. Whenever he was on a crusade he never failed to call on, dine out or spend time with the major reporters in every city the mission visited. As Reilly observed: 'It ain't no good having the best soap in town if the people in need of a wash don't know you've got it.'

Throughout all this Adam was struck forcibly by one constant element: the material made available to him was entirely uncritical of Collins and his organization. It asked no hard questions, either of Collins or his colleagues. It was apparent that scarcely a harsh word had been spoken by the United States media of him.

When he asked Reilly about this on film, the other man responded pleasantly, 'When you conduct your series of interviews with him I suggest you raise this point.'

Adam had allocated an entire day's filming at the store but there was just so much to catch that it ran on into a second day.

The evangelist had named it 'His Store', and it contained a cornucopia of faith from many different sources, including the diet, book entitled *Less of You. More of Jesus*, to one on finance *Jesus Works Here* subtitled 'Leading Christians in business talk about how you can walk with Christ through stress, change and other challenges in the workplace', and in the novelty section there were Bible Bingo, neckties covered in crucifixes, Scripture Fresh Scents and car stickers announcing 'Jesus is my Rock' and 'Oh Magnify the Lord'. The cash registers flagged each transaction with 'Thank you and God bless you.'

Adam and his crew came out with Johnny's final words ringing in their ears: 'Two days ago, Adam, we received a truly wonderful tribute. It hasn't been made public yet, but Pat has cleared it for use in your documentary. *Fortune* magazine has just rated the Patrick Collins Association the most efficiently run organization in the United States of America. Praise the Lord!'

Back at the guest bungalow, a message was waiting for Adam. 'Please call Oscar.'

'Where are you phoning me from?' Oscar's irritation at having been woken up was plain.

'A guest bungalow on the Patrick Collins Estate.'

'Get yourself to a safe telephone.'

'Oscar, this—' There was a dialling tone. Adam shrugged. He went outside, got into his car and drove out of the Collins estate, then cruised slowly through Naples looking for a telephone booth. Eventually in the Edgewater Hotel, he resumed his conversation.

'My friends at Head Office have had another request at Level One, Adam.'

'Oh, yes? Who are they running checks on now?'

'On you, my friend.'

CHAPTER SEVEN

PROMISE

'SHOOT ABOUT HALF A MAG ON THE CONGREGATION GOING IN, Leon. I'll join you before the service begins.' Adam left his crew near the church doors and walked towards the parking lot. He had noticed Johnny Reilly arriving for the service and he wanted a word with him. 'Johnny, are you planning any surprises for me today?'

'Surprises?'

'Last week Pat did his own version of "This is your life, Adam Fraser." Are we going to get part two today?'

'Hey, wasn't that something?' Johnny laughed. 'You should have seen your face. Great publicity for your shows, though. We've had over ten thousand letters about you already. For a moment Adam looked bemused until Johnny elaborated. 'Wanting to order video copies of your documentaries on Pat when they're completed. I wasn't supposed to tell you that – he wants to tell you himself. Hey, and I promise, no surprises.'

'If you would just tell him I'm grateful for the exposure.'

'Our great pleasure, Adam. See you after the service.'

Collins believed that all the great religions in the world were variations on a theme, that there was only one God but many true faiths. His aphorism was frequently quoted. 'It doesn't matter what recipe you use. They all come from the same chef and you'll always come up with the same cake.'

The Collins version of the Faith believed in God's supernatural power. If you really believed, he preached, all things were indeed possible. The sick will be cured, the poor enriched, the lonely befriended, the homeless given shelter. If you want it, you can get it, with sufficient faith.

A service at the Church of the Evangelist was an extraordinary experience. Some spoke in tongues, others convulsed and crashed to the floor of the church. People threw away crutches, stepped out of wheelchairs and proclaimed that God had cured them.

Collins never claimed these miracles as his responsibility. He distanced himself and his Church from faith-healing activities. But the more that he declared that these events were as mysterious to him as they were to anyone else, the more people chose to believe the opposite. And because he declined to cash in, the money flowed into his Association.

Adam knew that others had tried to discover an ulterior motive in Collins's organization and that they had all failed. Instead they had all become converts. He was determined to hold out until he found that secret agenda. He paid careful attention to that day's sermon.

'It's no secret that I love the game of golf,' Collins declaimed. 'It's equally no secret that golf does not seem to love me. I've shot low nineties and high eighties on some of the most beautiful pieces of countryside in the world. I was playing at a course in Colorado a while ago. Charming spot, called Englewood. Much to my surprise, I was on to the first green in three. This is a par-five hole, folks. Probably the first time in my life I was pretty certain of making par and might, with a bit of luck, make one under. I had the ball lined up perfectly, about eight feet from the flag, dropping away slightly to the left. Now, what do you think happened?'

Collins had asked the question naturally, casually. A man in the front row responded – Adam had noticed that one of the TV cameras had been on him before the question had been asked. 'You missed,' the man said, to a roar of laughter in which Collins joined.

'You better believe it, sir. I certainly did. But do you know why?'

The prompt shook his head.

'I missed because just as I went to hit the ball a pair of panties exploded right out of the ground. A moment later, on another part of the green, a domestic freezer rose up before me.'

Collins had every single member of the congregation in the palm of his hand. There was not a sound, not a single movement.

'Apart from my golfing partner there must have been, oh, a dozen or more good souls keeping us company out there. I looked at them to make sure they could see what I could see. The freezer was about three feet out of the ground by now and still coming. I lined up on the ball again.'

His face broke into a grin. 'I mean, no one was offering an explanation and after all, I was on the green in three. And then, my friends, the hole, the flag, the caddie just vanished. Only things left in sight were a pair of panties and this white freezer.'

There were whoops of laughter.

'I tell you, we ran over, grabbed the caddie out of the earth and got the heck out of there.' He joined in the laughter again, then looked down and shook his head. The entire congregation was silenced.

'Turned out the golf course had been built on a huge mountain of garbage. It was a landfill course. On the surface, a thing of beauty – trees, woodland, lawns, lakes. Just beautiful. Underneath, a festering, ugly, rancid heap of garbage. Now does that sound familiar to you? Does that remind you of someone you know? Is it someone you know really well? Is it *you*, perhaps?'

Collins was building his rhythm now, talking faster.

'They're going to have to take that golf course apart at Englewood. They're going to have to either dig up that mountain of garbage and destroy it or find somewhere else to build their golf course. You know, a lot of people, I mean a lot of people, I mean thousands, no, hundreds of thousands, no, millions of people in this country are walking around and if you look at them, if you see them, why, they look so fine, so handsome, so beautiful. Good, clean-living people. But if you could just dig down a little way under the surface, you'd see garbage that would shock you, horrify you, *frighten* you. Maybe it's just as well that we can't see into the hearts and minds of those around us. But Christ can. Christ does. Christ sees inside everyone. Whether they want him to or not. He sees right inside, not just under the surface, but right down to the very deepest corner. To the dark side of the soul. The black side. It's there, you know, in every single one of us.'

The power of his words unsettled Adam. Collins had reached into his shadowy side and touched it. He was seized with a desire to shout out that he wanted forgiveness, that he wanted to witness publicly his own sins. He shook his head as he heard what for a moment in his panic he thought was himself shouting out, 'I have sinned. I have sinned.' A wave of relief coursed through his body at the realization that it was a member of the congregation shouting out. Then another, then another. Then a chorus of people proclaiming that they had done wrong, that they wanted forgiveness.

Adam had no explanation for the way he had been affected. Perhaps he had caught a piece of the collective hysteria that seemed to be such a feature of these services. All he knew for certain was that these were dangerous places to hang around in. People were going forward, pouring towards Collins, who stood with his head bowed in prayer. He lifted his eyes, then his hands rose. Adam glanced at Leon, who pointed the camera towards Collins whose hands were now stretched high above him.

'Whosoever therefore shall confess me before men, him will I confess also before my Father which is in Heaven. But whosoever shall deny me before men, him will I also deny before my Father which is in Heaven. Think not that I come to send peace on earth: I come not to send peace, but a sword.'

Adam suddenly realized he was sweating. He got up and hurried out of the church.

'I know that these checks on me began before Collins told the nation last Sunday who we are and what we're doing here.'

'Is this person having security checks run on me and the boys too?' asked Susanna.

'I've asked my friend to find out if he can.'

They were strolling through the grounds near the guest bungalows. 'Could be our host?' said Leon.

Adam shook his head. 'Someone's been checking him out too.'

Susanna stopped. 'The same someone?'

'Yes.'

They walked on past the deserted tennis courts. Adam reached up and looped a finger in the wire fence. 'There's something else. My source thinks it likely our bungalows are bugged and that the phones are tapped.'

Susanna's indignation was instant. 'Bloody charming! What are they planning to do? Release edited highlights of us cleaning our teeth?'

'Do you want to know if we're being bugged?' asked Barry.

Adam had to smile. Only Barry would ask such a question. 'Yes, but how do you propose we find out?'

'In England I've got a gizmo capable of detecting a change in the electrical level, even a few millivolts change.'

Leon snorted. 'Great, Barry. We'll all just hang around for a few days while you pop back home.'

Barry stared at him, then turned back to Adam. 'As I was about to say, I'm sure in somewhere like Miami it should be easy enough to find one.'

'It's a hell of a long way.'

Leon was already heading towards the parking lot.

'I'm getting an identical reading in every bungalow. The phones are all tapped and there are more bugs all over the place.'

It was Sunday evening, and it was conference-of-war time at the deserted third green on the Collins nine-hole course.

'Can you locate them, Barry?'

'I already have.'

The others waited as Adam paced up and down. Eventually he said, 'Tomorrow we're flying to Boston. We won't be coming back to Florida until early July. We do nothing about the bugs until then. If we take them out now, all we succeed in doing is alerting whoever put them in place, so just act normally.'

'Just a minute, what are we getting into here?' Leon asked. 'This isn't Vietnam in the late seventies or Lebanon in the eighties – we expected to be spied on in those places, but this is the US of A, Adam, and I want to know what's going on.'

There were murmurs of agreement from Susanna and Barry. Adam shared their unease. 'I wish I knew. All I'm suggesting is that we play along with it until we come back from Boston. Maybe we're not the targets. Perhaps someone's monitoring the Reverend and as we're here we qualify for the same treatment.'

Susanna squeezed his arm. 'I prefer life like it usually is, Adam, with us doing the investigating.'

As the plane levelled, Adam glanced across at Barry, who was fiddling with the sound equipment. He checked several dials, then looked happy. 'The background noise is within acceptable levels.'

Leon was on his knees on the seat behind Adam, shooting across a coffee table at which Patrick Collins was sitting facing him. Next to Adam, also out of shot, sat Susanna, armed with clipboards and a stopwatch. Collins was quietly observing the last-minute preparations of the film-crew. 'I hope the facilities are what you need, Adam.'

'They're superb, Pat. Regular studio in the sky.'

'Good. We had the plane modified to make it more media-friendly.'

They were just about to start filming when Collins raised a hand. 'I'd like a moment, please.' He joined his hands and closed his eyes. Adam indicated to both Barry and Leon that they should start recording.

'Holy Father, guide me towards an honesty of emotions, a clarity of thought and, above all, the truth as I respond to these questions. Amen.'

Collins opened his extraordinary sea-green eyes, and Adam wondered, not for the first time, if he wore coloured contact lenses.

'Tell me, Pat, do you begin every interview with a prayer?'

'Yes, I do. But then I try to begin every new activity in a day with a prayer. It helps to focus my mind on why I'm here.'

'And why are you here?'

'To serve God.'

Adam was in quickly. 'Yes, we'll be talking quite a bit about exactly how you serve God. But first tell me about those personal rules of yours.'

Collins grinned. 'Ah, what I call the gospel according to Elmer Gantry. It's just that I realized a long time ago that there are three traps that any would-be evangelist must avoid. First, money. I've spent a great deal of my life asking people for money and, as people opened their hearts to God, I'm happy to say that they opened their wallets and purses and bank accounts to me. Now, I have had to make sure that none of the money that passed through my hands got stuck there. So, to avoid any temptation, I set up the Patrick Collins Association. It's got a board of directors, the finances are made public and I hope you can confirm to me that a serious investigative reporter like you has been given every access to those records?'

Adam was impressed: to get your inquisitor to endorse you during the opening minute was clever. 'I'm happy to confirm that to date I have been given every piece of information I have asked for. What's the second trap?'

Collins looked serious. 'Sex. Morals. I vowed that, as far as was humanly possible, I would never be alone with any woman other than my mother or my wife. Take my secretary, for example. I've never been alone with her in a car or walking or at dinner.'

Adam nodded sympathetically. 'This is to avoid being tempted?'

Collins neatly avoided the ambush. 'This is to avoid being compromised. There have been attempts . . . two on my last crusade.'

'Are you saying you've never been tempted?'

The preacher shook his head. 'No, of course not. I'm as vulnerable as the next man, but temptations of the flesh, no. Never.'

'And the third trap to be avoided?'

'The third trap is the deadliest. Hubris. The sins of pride and arrogance.'

Adam caught something in the way that Collins had dealt so rapidly with it. Casually he asked, 'Why is pride the deadliest pit to be avoided?'

Collins looked directly at him. 'To stand as I have stood in Madison Square Garden, or the Shea Stadium, or in your own country, in Wembley Stadium, to speak, to preach, to maybe one hundred thousand people, to know that for a brief time you have control over those people.' His eyes moved to search the middle distance. Adam kept very still. 'To say to that vast gathering, "I want you to come forward and give witness", or "Now all of you with offering envelopes, hold them up," and to see a moment later a sea of white envelopes. Then to say to that same multitude, "Now hold up the dollars that you want to offer to the Lord" and to see a sea of green rippling and tumbling all the way across the stadium towards me. I become the audience and the audience becomes me. And when you have experienced that, God is indeed upon you. The power of God is coursing through your body. You are consumed by a religious ecstasy.'

Collins checked himself, and brought his luminescent eyes back to Adam.

'That is the moment of greatest danger for the evangelist. It would be easy, frighteningly easy, to believe after that kind of experience that you were someone really important, someone very special. That belief must be rejected utterly.'

No one spoke for what seemed a long time. Then Leon said quietly in Adam's ear, 'I need to change the mag.'

Adam declined the offer to stay at the Collins residence in Brookline. It was unlikely that the rooms he had booked at the Copley Plaza in Boston would be bugged or the telephones tapped.

Oscar took a different view. 'When will you learn to use a clean telephone?'

'Funny you should say that. Remember telling me the other day how if you were Pat Collins you'd make sure my phone was tapped?'

'Go on.'

'It is. And our rooms *are* bugged. We've left everything as it was. We've said nothing to Collins or his people. But my crew want to know if they've been screened too. If I modem you their details, can you find out?'

'Not for a month, but send the details. I'd also like as much technical data as possible on the bugs. It might throw up a lead. Are you licensed to carry a gun?'

'Oscar, I'm English.'

'What the hell does that mean?'

'We don't carry guns – well, most of us don't.'

'Christ, no wonder you lost your empire. Send me your itinerary with those details and watch your back.'

'Johnny, ever heard of a man called Andrew Sinclair? Chairman of Corporate America?'

The evangelist and John Reilly were sitting in the library of Collins's Boston home.

'If you read the *Wall Street Journal*, Pat, you wouldn't need to ask. He heads one of the biggest management consultancies in the country. Why?'

'He wants a meeting. Comes highly recommended.'

Reilly laughed. 'Perhaps he heard about that piece *Fortune*'s running on us, most efficiently run organization in the United States. Maybe he wants your advice.'

'Maybe. Before I get back to him I'd like him checked out. Pentagon, Langley, our friends in Washington.'

'Thought you said he came highly recommended.'

'He does. No harm in running our own checks on him, is there?'

' "Now, hold up the dollars that you want to offer to the Lord, and to see a sea of green . . .'

Andrew Sinclair sat in the stern of his boat listening to Patrick Collins talking to Adam Fraser. The quality was excellent. The plane was indeed media-friendly.

Sinclair pressed the pause button and finished reading a document Roberto copied during his recent out-of-hours visit to the research and development section of a small company based in Amarillo, Texas. His team had yet to hit the jackpot. As Sinclair weighed the problem, a possible solution occurred to him. He made a mental note to send a coded fax to Philip Hyde, the Andino board member based in London. At the last annual general meeting he had talked of a young man in Glasgow who could hack into any computer system in the world, especially the Pentagon's.

Sinclair wondered if Fraser had grasped the real significance of this section of his interviews with the evangelist. The tapes covering the film-crew's time in Boston had not revealed any cause for concern, Sinclair mused. Except one thing. Who was Oscar?

'You had a BA from Boston College. You were about to go to Boston Law School. Triple Eagle, the whole thing, but you put it all to one side at a time when thousands of your generation were ducking the draft, when you would have got an automatic deferment to enable you to study law. You actually volunteered to go to Vietnam. Why?'

They were filming on the patio of the Collins residence now.

Collins reflected for a moment then spoke rhetorically. 'Why did I go to Vietnam? There's no quick answer to that. I felt it was my duty to go. As an American and as a Catholic. I felt that if the Vietnam war was about anything, it was about rolling back Communism. I was twenty years of age. It was the mid-nineteen sixties. Times were different, values were different. If there was one bottom line reason, I suppose it was John Murphy's death.'

Collins paused. Adam's expression asked, 'Who was John Murphy?'

'John Murphy was a young man I greatly admired. He was a year ahead of me at college. He was that rare combination of top scholar, top athlete. John came from Charlestown which, as you may know, is a tight little Irish-American community. A whole group of them volunteered for the draft the year before I went out. The day I got my degree I heard that John Murphy's platoon had been wiped out by the Vietcong. Five were from Boston. I volunteered the same day.'

As Collins talked of life and death, of the madness of war, he was hesitant, almost unsure. 'Yes, my Roman Catholic faith was strong when I went to South East Asia and, no, it did not remain so for very long. My experiences in Vietnam caused me to ask some urgent questions. What was God trying to establish in Vietnam? Was He trying to prove that mankind could be cruel, bestial, vicious?'

Adam thought of potential visual images to which he could cut here. The naked napalm girl, the gun-to-the-head execution, My Lai . . . 'My Lai.' With a start he realized that Collins was still speaking. He watched him lean forward, hands in a praying position, and listened to him narrate the story of the My Lai massacre. Unarmed Vietnamese, old people, women, children, babies, clubbed, burned, gunned down by Calley's platoon. 'He was sentenced to life imprisonment with hard labour. President Nixon intervened. Calley was confined for just three years, most of the time under house arrest in his apartment at Fort Benning, with visitation rights for his girlfriend.' There had been a bitter, angry edge to his voice as he spoke. Now Adam's tone was light, indifferent.

'We've all had our My Lais in one way or another . . . With a thoughtless word, an arrogant act, or a selfish deed.'

With some difficulty Collins kept his voice calm and level. 'That's probably the most unChristian statement I've ever heard in my life. You don't seriously believe that, do you?'

'No, that's what Billy Graham believes. That's how he justified and dismissed My Lai.'

Collins looked stunned. 'Are you sure, Adam?'

'Oh, yes, I'm quite sure. You'll find his original quote in the *Charlotte Observer*.'

Collins attempted to backtrack. 'Well, Billy must have had his reasons for saying that, I suppose.'

Adam persisted, anxious to get him more firmly snared. 'But you'd agree that it's an unChristian, amoral view.'

Collins knew that for once he'd been caught. There was no escape. 'Yes, I would.' For a moment he became reflective. 'I met Billy Graham in Vietnam. General Westmorland invited him over Christmas nineteen sixty-six. I attended a service he held on Christmas Eve at An Khe in the central highlands. There were about ten thousand of us. I remember one of his group singing "I Heard the Bells on Christmas Day". Speaking for myself, I heard the Vietcong firing at me on Christmas Day.'

Adam referred to his notes. 'I'd like to ask you now about what happened near Khe Sanh during the Tet offensive of nineteen sixty-eight.'

Without warning, Collins got up and walked across the patio to where Johnny Reilly was sitting. He knelt down. 'Are you sure about this, Johnny?'

Reilly was calm. 'Yes, I'm quite sure, Pat. Go on.' He gripped the evangelist's hand, then Collins stood up, came back across the patio and sat down again.

'I'm sorry about that, Adam.'

'Not at all.'

Collins eyed him for a moment, then, breathing deeply as if to gather himself, he began to talk, with no trace of the pulpit performer, just someone struggling with terrible memories.

'I was in charge of a jungle patrol on a recce at Khe Sanh. Five thousand marines were trapped under siege by twenty-five thousand North Vietnamese soldiers. Mine was an intelligence-gathering mission. The trouble was that the intelligence we had been given about the precise positions of the enemy was wrong. We ran straight into an ambush. There were ten of us. Difficult to say how many of them. Later estimates suggested twenty-five to forty. There were at least eighteen. That's how many we killed.' He was striving for composure.

'They killed eight of my men. I was wounded, bullets in chest and legs. The only person uninjured and in one piece was Johnny Reilly. It was only a matter of time before the VC came back with more. I ordered Johnny to return to base. He told me he was prepared to obey that order as long as I went along too. I couldn't walk. Now, I'm six feet two inches and at that time I weighed one hundred and eighty pounds. As for John, well, you know how big he is. Five nine and at that time he weighed, oh, fifty pounds less than me. He picked me up, put me across his shoulders and began to head south. We were about three miles from our pick-up point. He'd made nearly two miles before the VC caught up with us. As he bent down to put me on the ground he got hit. Didn't make a lot of noise. Just a grunt. We sat up back to back. That must have really thrown Charlie. No matter how they came at us we were always facing them. By the time the team from the chopper located us and drove off what was left of the Vietcong, John and I had killed a further twenty-seven men.'

Tears were streaming down his face. He called across the patio. 'John, come here, please. Come on.'

Reilly hesitated, then spun the wheels of his chair and glided across the patio. Collins reached out and placed an arm round his friend's shoulders. ' "Greater love hath no man than this, that a man lay down his life for his friends." The bullet John took in his back cut his spinal cord and left him paralysed from the waist down. That night in the jungles of Khe Sanh there were three of us in that little clearing. I know for a certainty that God was with us. I know that God was there when somehow John picked me up and began to walk not just a few yards with one hundred and eighty pounds on his back but almost two miles. I owe him my life. Maybe you should ask John about that.'

Adam looked at Reilly, who said, 'God was there all right. No doubt about that. I don't know where I got the strength from for that walk if I didn't get it from Him. What Pat hasn't told you is that, whatever I managed to do for him that night, he certainly saved my life. It's true that after I had been hit we sat back to back, but after a while I lost consciousness. Then Pat kept the Vietcong at bay until the chopper team located us. So I guess the bottom line is that we looked out for each other.'

Leon was making desperate signals. He was about to run out of film.

'And cut.'

Adam knew he now had a great Road to Damascus sequence for the film.

'I can't thank you enough,' he said to Collins and Reilly. 'It was moving and inspirational. It's early days yet, but I think you've just given me the very heart of the Patrick Collins story.'

'I'm glad to hear that.' Collins looked relieved. 'Now, if you'll excuse me, I must go and welcome a visitor.'

The crew began to stroll back to the bungalows. 'I think we've got some great reaction material on camera, if Susanna kept focus,' said Leon.

'Of course I didn't, Leon. Soon as you stopped watching I let it go soft on Johnny Reilly. The hands, Adam, watch Johnny's hands as Collins tells the story. I thought he was going to burst a couple of knuckles.'

Collins re-emerged with his guest on to the empty patio.

'Sorry about all this, Andrew. I've got a crew here filming a documentary.'

Andrew Sinclair hit the ground running. 'The Englishman, Adam Fraser. I saw you introduce him during your televised Sunday service last month.'

'Are you a regular viewer?'

'Certainly am, Pat. Have been for nearly three years.'

'That's good to hear. Now, we can talk here or perhaps you'd like to stroll around the grounds. Then we could take a drink in the gazebo. Got a clear view all the way to the Gulf from there.'

Sinclair looked around the patio, littered with cameras and sound booms. 'The gazebo sounds perfect.'

Sinclair's opening gambit was directly from the school of Machiavelli. 'Pat, I'd be most grateful if you would be kind enough to say a short prayer asking God to bless this meeting.'

The evangelist was delighted. He closed his eyes and bowed his head. 'Holy Father, we ask you to look kindly upon your servants gathered here today. May the fruit of your blessing be upon us. May this moment be of benefit to you. Amen.'

'Amen. Thank you so much.'

'I must tell you, Andrew, you come most highly recommended. When four of the most powerful men in this country sing your praises, I think it safe to say that you are a man to whom I should listen very carefully.'

'Did they tell you what I wanted to talk to you about?' Sinclair knew the answer to his question, but it was as good a way in as any.

'No, they didn't, and I must tell you I pressed them hard. All I know is that you wish to put a proposition to me and that I should give it very careful consideration.'

Sinclair took a deep breath and dismissed every rule he knew about selling. He'd come straight to the point. 'I think you should run for President of the United States.' He glanced at Collins, saw his eyes flicker, and hurried on, 'I have no doubt that if you do run you'll win. This country is in desperate need of your leadership, your vision, talents, faith and integrity. The office of President will give you a pulpit on a scale never given to any preacher in history. You would be not only leader of this nation but leader of the only superpower in the world. Your congregation would be the entire planet.'

Collins sat very still, his face expressionless. Only his eyes betrayed his shock, amazement and growing interest.

'Just for a few minutes, Pat, let us consider the state of a few parts of this world. Our closest ally, Great Britain, no longer great, with a pseudo-socialist government in office and in deep trouble. The Prime Minister has Thatcher's arrogance but none of her luck. She squandered five billion pounds' worth of national assets on vote-catching policies and was never found out. Now the country is drowning in debt and the current occupant at Number Ten has been stuck with the tab. The moral climate in Britain is about as putrid as ours. One former Royal lies prematurely in her grave having been murdered to prevent an Anglo-Arab scandal. Another is hosting her own chat show. The future king has an in-house mistress . . .' Sinclair raced on through the corrupt, crisis-haunted French and Spanish, the disintegrating European Union. 'Russia? Despite all the billions of dollars we've poured in, it's got another dictator who's carving up Europe with the Germans. Seems like nineteen thirty-nine all over again. The Chinese are going to invade Taiwan sooner or later, and if the wrong man gets into the White House next year it will be sooner. And just look at the way they're behaving in Hong Kong. It's run by a combination of the Triads and corrupt politicos from Beijing. The law of supply and demand points to China embarking on even more colonialism. They can only continue to feed twenty-two per cent of the world's population from seven per cent of the world's arable land for just so long. Elsewhere? Christian refugees fleeing from Muslim fundamentalists and refugees knocking at our doors in their thousands, from former Yugo-slavia, Algeria, Turkey, the Middle East, the Gulf States.

'And while the rest of the world is going to hell in a handcart, what's going on here in God's own country? The First National Bank in Chicago is bombed and eighty-seven people die. The chairman of US Cola, Leonard Meredith – a fine man, a good man, a man I was proud to call my friend – is blown to eternity along with half of his board. No one has admitted to per-petrating these dreadful acts and much more to the point, no one has been arrested.

'We've got over one and a half million people locked up in prison and people live in their own maximum security forts. Intolerance stalks the land and pollutes the airwaves. We have white Nazi disc jockeys who call blacks mutant and savages, and self-appointed black racist leaders like Farrakhan who hate Jews and admire Hitler. These are the people preparing America for the moment, in the lifetime of my children, when whites will become a minority in this country. Filth!'

Sinclair punched an open palm with a clenched fist. 'And what do we have in the White House? A living monument to venality. A nobody.' He stood up and crossed to a side table to refill his glass, giving Collins an opportunity to digest what had just been laid before him and respond.

'What makes you think I can provide the moral leadership this country needs?'

'Pat, I don't claim to know everything about you, but I've had every possible check run on you. There's no Chappaquid-dick in your past. No pot-smoking at Oxford. No links with the Mob. No undocumented immigrants working in your kitchen. No well-endowed young woman on a weekend boat trip. You've never even drunk alcohol – with one exception that is, two bottles of beer behind the bike shed at Boston High, with, if I am correctly informed, Tom O'Riley.'

Collins looked startled. 'Any minute now you'll be telling me the name of my first girlfriend.'

'She was tall, dark and beautiful. She was also very shy. Her name was Kathleen Jacobs. First week of term in the fall of 1960 you walked her home every evening. She had pale blue eyes . . .'

Collins held up a hand to stop him. 'Right, but why did you go to such lengths?'

'Because if you run for president, those are the lengths to which your opponents may well go. I wanted to establish that there was nothing in your past that could damage your future.'

'I assume you're here today because you've found no pre-vious convictions?'

'What I found, Reverend, was the next President of the United States.'

The evangelist looked like a boxer trying to recapture his senses after a heavy blow to the skull. 'How can you be so sure that there's nothing in my past that will come back to haunt me?'

'Reverend, I'm quite prepared to share what's in those files with you. School records, military records, everything.'

Looking troubled, Collins went to refill his cup.

Again Sinclair found encouragement in the trivial. His dossier on the health of Collins included the observation, 'Tendency to over-caffeinate when under acute stress.'

'Andrew, leaving aside every other consideration, and there are a great many, it costs a huge amount of money to run for president.'

'Maybe eighty million dollars.'

'And you're proposing that I should raise eighty million dollars?'

'Not at all, Pat. I'm proposing to raise it for you.'

'What, all on your own?'

'Of course not. The four men I've talked to about this meeting will be helping me, and we will raise at least one hundred and fifty million dollars, all of it to be spent, if necessary, on your presidential campaign. That is my promise. As God is my witness.'

Collins turned to stare across his lawns, past the orangery, the undulating acres. Then he walked to the edge of the gazebo and stared out to the shimmering waters in the Gulf. ' "And the devil, taking him up into a high mountain, shewed him all the kingdoms of the world in a moment in time.

' "And the devil said unto him, All this power will I give thee, and the glory of them; for that is delivered unto me; and to whomsoever will I give it.

' "If thou therefore wilt worship me, all shall be thine. And Jesus answered and said unto him, Get thee behind me, Satan; for it is written, Thou shalt worship the Lord thy God, and him only shalt thou serve." '

Sinclair was at his shoulder. 'But I'm not asking you to renounce God for the devil. I'm asking you to denounce the devil for God. There was never a time when the United States had greater need of a president who could lead the fight against evil. Because of these acts of terrorism, the bank bombing, the destruction of Cola One, a climate of fear stalks the land. The people are returning to their churches. Quite frankly, I think you can win the White House at this time precisely because we are so threatened by the enemy within. Patrick, I'm convinced your time has come.'

Collins began to pace. 'You're right to speak of evil, Andrew, but it's become unfashionable to do so. Psychiatrists have replaced priests and brought with them a modern jargon. We're now told, for example, that drug pushers are not evil, merely sociopaths.'

In his eagerness, Sinclair gripped Collins's arm. 'It's crucial for the future of our country that, when you are elected, you immediately declare all-out war on the problem of drugs. The marijuana, cocaine, heroin, amphetamines and the other filth pouring into the United States must be stopped. It's time for the Third World War. The enemy has been clearly identified. I have no desire that you run a single-issue campaign, but if there is one issue that the next president must address, it is the desperate need to halt this flood of drugs contaminating the soul of America.'

CHAPTER EIGHT

PRISTINE

'ONE HUNDRED AND FIFTY MILLION DOLLARS IN MY HAND, Johnny. That's what the man said. No need for fund-raising dinners. No need to spend two or three hours of every day on the phone chasing the fat cats. No need to ask the government. That's what the man said.'

Sinclair had gone, leaving Collins with an injunction. 'At this stage, Pat, until you commit, I would ask that you confine your conversations on this proposal to just your wife and John Reilly. Any leakage could prove highly counter-productive, if not fatal, to the entire plan.'

Collins had accepted the restriction, thus ensuring that the Victor Rodriguez' contract on his life was not activated. He had returned to the gazebo and remained there for a few minutes, lost in thought. Then he went to find Reilly, and they had settled down on the patio.

'Are you going to run, Pat?' Reilly looked at him intently, leaning forward in his wheelchair.

'Too soon, Johnny. Ask me when you and I have finished

talking. Ask me when Teresa and I have finished talking. Ever since Dallas every potential candidate's wife has held the right to a veto.'

'It's tempting, Pat. Very tempting. Look how well Perot did as an independent candidate in ninety-two. The polls showed him running at over thirty per cent in that midsummer before he pulled out. But how does Sinclair plan to get this one hundred and fifty million? How long is it going to take? Who's in on the scheme?'

Collins put up a restraining hand. 'Easy, Johnny! At this stage Sinclair's keeping his cards close to his chest until I give him my decision. All I know is that Paul McCall, Rupert Turner, Rick Forrest, Edgar Lee Stratford and Sinclair have each put a million dollars on the table. If I say yes, that five million is mine. As a gift. Then with you overseeing and approving their plans, to ensure that everything is above board, they plan to invest that five million on my behalf.'

'Hey, Pat. I'm from Missouri, the show-me state. When a farmer in my home state sells a cow, the guy buying counts the legs. If you ran as an independent candidate you'd have to declare by the middle of next year at the latest. That gives them exactly a year to turn five million into a hundred and fifty million. That would be a modern miracle of the loaves and fishes.'

Collins smiled. 'John, just look at the calibre of these men. McCall and the others. We're talking *Fortune* Five Hundred. Chairman of ATZ Oil. Head of Multimedia. Head of Forrest Computers, and Stratford's head of so many things that only he and his accountant know which. If anyone can raise that kind of money, they can. I don't know if I want to run, but I do know that with serious money behind me I could put up one hell of a fight.'

'Pat, there's one major problem above all others that has to be faced.'

'I know. But Sinclair insists he's had every kind of check run on me.'

'And?'

'Nothing.'

'Ask him to show you the files.'

'He's already offered.'

'Good. Take him up on it. I find it difficult to believe that there's nothing on the problem in those files.'

'So do I.'

Sinclair swung the Cadillac into the motel parking space. He carried a small suitcase and his briefcase to the reception area.

'Good afternoon, sir, and welcome to the Miami Airways Imperial Lodge.'

Sinclair put down the cases. 'My name is Richard Whiteacre. I have a reservation.'

The receptionist ran his pen down the booking page. 'Ah yes, for one night. Can I tempt you to make that two nights, sir?'

Sinclair stared hard at the receptionist. 'I beg your pardon?'

'Three per cent discount if you stay for two nights, escalating to twelve per cent if you stay for nine days.'

Sinclair barely repressed a shudder. 'Do you actually have people who stay for nine days at an airways motel?'

'Certainly do, sir.'

'My God, where is their connecting flight to? The moon?'

'No, sir. They use the motel as a vacation base.' Sinclair gaped. He had reached another world.

The receptionist rummaged in a drawer, then placed two towels, a bar of soap and a glass on the counter. Sinclair stared at them bleakly. 'It eliminates the cost of a maid,' the receptionist explained. 'If you should change your mind and stay for longer than one night, we'll exchange the towels and give you a new bar of soap. Could you bring them back to Reception when you leave, please? Now, how would you like to pay? We take all the regular cards.'

'Cash.'

'That'll be forty-three dollars.'

'I'd also like some clothes pressed. I hope that's possible.'

The receptionist looked doubtful. 'Not usually, I'm afraid.'

Sinclair pushed a fifty-dollar bill across the counter and waved an expansive hand over it.

'But I should be able to take care of that for you, sir.'

'Good.' Sinclair produced the items from his case. 'Be sure you put creases in.'

'The shirt, sir?'

'No, the boxer shorts.'

It was the receptionist's turn to stare hard at Sinclair.

Clutching his towels, soap and glass, Sinclair picked up his cases and headed for his 'nice quiet single away from the pool area but adjacent to the cafeteria'. It was small. Sinclair imagined spending nine days in it and repressed another shudder. As he showered, he reflected on his meeting with Patrick Collins. The evangelist could listen as well as he could talk, and Sinclair was confident that his pitch had been well received. Collins had asked him for details on how the four men had been persuaded to take part in the project, and had obviously liked what he had heard.

'I reminded them that you were untainted by Washington. You're not in the Beltway. You haven't manipulated the system. We all know that Patrick Collins is what this country is crying out for. I said that a man of your calibre leading this country was crucial to our future, but that this was not going to happen unless people like them with access to capital not only approved the idea but made sure it happened.'

Collins had been fascinated when Sinclair recounted how he had demonstrated to the four how he was modelling his own plan on the kitchen cabinet that had raised money for Reagan and persuaded him to run for governor in California. 'Reagan's second term as governor was an excellent demonstration of making your money work in the polling booth. The Democrat that Reagan was fighting was Jesse Unruh who spent forty-two cents a vote. Reagan spent more than double, ninety-eight cents per vote. Reagan won. Now if Reagan could do that with a kitchen cabinet, just imagine what Patrick Collins will do with a corporate cabinet made up of the cream of American business . . .' There was no doubt that Collins had been riveted.

Collins and Reilly clearly had a special relationship, thought Sinclair. The evangelist never took an important decision without running it past Reilly. To tell him that he wanted a commitment from Reilly to the plan was a masterstroke, but it was high-risk. Reilly had a mind of his own and had never been a yes man for Collins. Sinclair wondered if he had made a tactical error in not pitching to both men. Too late now.

The voice of Patrick Collins, with its trace of a Boston accent, floated up out of the cold-box to two totally absorbed listeners.

Earlier Collins had phoned Adam Fraser as he sat in the guest bungalow putting the final touches to the questions he planned to ask him that afternoon.

'Adam, I'm sorry, something has come up that requires my attention. I'm afraid I'm going to be tied up for some time. Can we shoot the second session on another day?'

Adam had reassured Collins graciously and continued to work on his script. Several hours later he heard a gentle tap on the window-pane and saw Barry, index finger to his lips, motioning him outside. 'I want you to come for a ride with me.' Barry glanced around the grounds. 'Don't ask why. Just come.' He studied the horizon. 'I'll meet you by the hire car in five minutes. I'll get Leon to tell Susanna that we've gone out for a while.'

It was only when they were on the beach near the Edgewater Hotel and had walked about a mile that Barry relaxed and sat down on the sea wall. 'After we'd shot the Vietnam material this morning, I thought it would be a good opportunity to do a wild-track recording. There's birdsong and background ambient sound on the Collins estate and it was there throughout the recording, and I felt we should have a reel of it for matching sound purposes.'

Adam nodded. It was standard procedure for Barry.

'I'd put on a tape when we broke this morning and you forgot to tell us that Collins had cancelled the afternoon session. I've only just retrieved it.'

Barry took the lid off the cold-box, which contained two beers and a tape recorder. He handed a can to Adam and opened his own. 'I thought it best no one saw me leave the Collins place with a tape-recorder.' He pushed Start. They sat on the warm white sand and listened as Collins and Reilly discussed Sinclair's proposition.

Adam made him stop the tape, then asked, 'Before we began recording this morning, did you sweep the patio area with that detector thing you picked up in Miami?'

'Yes, I did. It was clean.'

'So this is the only recording of this conversation?'

'Absolutely. If anyone had gone out and planted a bug we'd have heard them doing it on this tape.'

'Let's hear the rest of it, then.'

'Can I speak to Mr Whiteacre, please?'

'Speaking.'

'Which Mr Whiteacre do I have?'

'This is Richard Whiteacre.'

'*Bueno.*'

Rodriguez's voice was so clear he might have been in the room, but Sinclair knew that he was out walking in his fields at the ranch in Sevilla. He reduced his two-hour meeting with Collins to two sentences.

'So far so good. But maximum vigilance should be maintained until the target buys the concept.'

'Of course, Richard, and the contracts will remain in place until close of sale.'

'I'd like to reactivate the R and D locations. Three and five should be paid a second visit.'

'Certainly, Richard. I'll have Roberto contacted. Goodbye, and well done.'

Sinclair hung up. Using the British computer hacker had been a rewarding brainwave. He looked at his watch and made another telephone call, one he never missed on the road. When it was answered he pulled a book out of his case and read his children a bedtime story. Yesterday, he had finished *The Wind in the Willows*. Today he moved on to *The Lion, the Witch and the Wardrobe*.

Adam and Barry had not moved even though the tape had finished sharing its secrets.

Adam's mind was whirling. 'That is gold,' he said, as Barry stared out to sea. 'If Collins agrees to run, it'll be sensational. Even if he decides against it, it's brilliant material. The major problem they're discussing near the end, that's what I've been looking for, Barry. Every sinner should have a future because it's a certainty that every saint has a past. That's . . .'

Barry stiffened. 'Stop, Adam. No, don't turn round.' He rubbed his chin thoughtfully. 'That gave me quite a nasty shock. Do you want the good news or the bad news first?'

'I doubt that any good news could better what I've already had today.'

'The good news is that it's not a rifle. The bad news is that it's a rifle mike. Pointing out of the front passenger window of a red Buick parked at the end of the dunes.'

Adam continued to look seawards as he spoke. 'Right. I suggest we stroll towards the Edgewater and get back to the bungalows, and while we walk I'm going to tell you what happened when I dated Sharon Stone.'

Barry put the lid back on the cold-box, put the carrying strap over his shoulder, and stood.

'I have heard that she cooks a great breakfast.'

Adam grinned. 'Let me tell you about it.'

Having received an encoded fax from the Miami police officer in charge of the surveillance operation at the Collins residence, Victor Rodriguez was personally sending a copy of the report with a covering encoded note. They were waiting inside the locked drawer of Sinclair's desk when he arrived at his World Trade Center headquarters the following day. Rodriguez's covering note read: 'Shall we activate contracts on film-crew?'

Sinclair put the note to one side and read the report from the Miami police officer. The film-crew knew they were being bugged – the surveillance team had been able to pick up enough of the conversation between Adam and Barry to establish that. More alarming, from Sinclair's point of view, was the revelation that Collins had unwittingly been taped while discussing Sinclair's proposal with John Reilly. His men had not been able to get close enough to monitor the entire conversation, but the fragmented phrases they had heard confirmed the existence of a tape-recording.

Sinclair stood up, crossed to the large window behind his desk and gazed out over the Hudson. Murdering four members of a film-crew while they were in the middle of making a documentary about Patrick Collins presented problems: they were guests in his house; Fraser, at least, was a friend not only of Reilly but of Collins. To authorize the four deaths would be to invite every muck-raking hack reporter to come armed with a shovel, and that was before Collins committed to run for the presidency.

Sinclair tried to put himself inside the mind of Adam Fraser. What would he do with the information that had fallen into his lap? If Sinclair could work that one out, then the decision as to whether Fraser and his crew should live or die would make itself.

'It looked like one of those self-powered directional microphones. They give you a range of, oh, about sixty DB at one kilometre.'

'You're the sound expert, Barry,' said Leon, 'but if it's self-powered, playing directly into a cassette recorder, the quality's going to be lousy.'

'First thing we have to do,' said Adam, 'is find out all we can about Andrew Sinclair and his four friends. Susanna, get busy on the phone, your Washington and New York contacts. I'll give you some names as well. Let's build a dossier on this guy.'

'Is that "get busy" on a bugged or unbugged phone?' asked Susanna.

'Unbugged. Let's not make it any easier for this bastard.

He'll be the one who's having us bugged. At least now we know why – protecting his potential investment.'

'I saw him after we broke from the morning filming, walking towards the gazebo with Pat Collins.'

Adam turned in the driving seat to look at his cameraman.

'No more than average height. Five feet nine. Brown hair, flecks of blond in it. Aged early fifties but a boyish look. Very sharp dresser. Fifth Avenue. Italian shoes. Wedding ring. Tanned. Slim, no, not slim, lean, no fat. Good muscle tone.'

'Pity you didn't get a good look at him,' Barry responded, deadpan.

'With or without his Italian shoes, I want to know all about him,' said Adam. 'Get me all you can, Susanna, and I'll take it to a man I know.'

'Sure, but what are you going to do about the information we already have? What about this tape? And the bugs?'

Sinclair was still staring unseeingly out of his window. It was now the best part of twenty-four hours since Fraser had learned of the plan to put Collins into the White House. There had been no news flashes, no breaking story. Sinclair reckoned he had decided to wait for Collins to make up his mind. And there was no doubt that the tape-recording would be well away from the Collins estate in Florida by now. Probably on its way to London. Concentrate on what you can change, thought Sinclair. Ignore what you can't.

Roberto and his team had already checked out the area in daylight. The precincts and surrounding area of Berkeley University presented no problems to a man as experienced as the Italian. On 20 January 1976 Roberto and his team had been invited to Beirut by the PLO. When they left, the British Bank of the Middle East had been relieved of over a hundred million dollars and Roberto's team had earned an entry in the *Guinness Book of Records* under 'Biggest Bank Robbery of All Time'. The Buick glided to a halt. The team picked up their equipment, as, almost apologetically, the best cracksman in Italy led his men towards a large double garage.

'Let me refill your glass, Andrew.' It was exactly a week since Collins and Sinclair had sat in the gazebo in Florida. A week of hard thinking and hard talking with both Teresa and John Reilly. Now they, and Teresa, were in Collins's drawing room in Brookline, Boston, with the genuine, much-admired eight-eenth-century fireplace.

When the staff had withdrawn after coffee had been served, Sinclair's heartbeat quickened as Collins began to talk. 'Of course it's enormously attractive to consider leading a religious revival or making a new covenant with the entire nation, but I asked myself, "Is that what the people want?" I have no doubt it's what they need. However, that's not quite the same thing.'

Sinclair looked at Teresa Collins. Perhaps her behaviour would offer a clue as to what Collins had decided, but she merely sat with her hands folded on her lap looking at her husband.

'I'll tell you, Andrew, more than anything else you said last week, there were two points that swayed my thinking. First, what you had to say about narcotics and how they're destroying the fabric of our society. Of how an entire generation of Americans are being stolen from us by their addiction to drugs. The contribution they would have made to our society has been irredeemably forfeited. It's one thing for a nation to lose the flower of a generation on a foreign soil in wartime but we are suffering the same loss right here on American soil in peace-time. You were absolutely right to say that it's time for the Third World War. The drugs trade is pure evil.' Collins slapped his open palm down on to the table. 'It has to be stopped. It is indeed the devil's work. Second, your comments about the bank bombing in Chicago and the destruction of that plane carrying Leonard Meredith. This terrorism demands a powerful response, by a real leader. I was deeply moved by your comments about Leonard. He was our friend too, Andrew.

'Those files that you have been kind enough to make

available to me since our last meeting. Thank you. It isn't everyone that gets a chance to see what the CIA, the FBI and the various other agencies have on them. How do I know that *all* the information these people have on me was made available to you?'

Sinclair had been anticipating this question. He produced a plain envelope and handed it to Collins. 'You'll find a number of covering letters in there. One from each of the heads of those agencies. They give a contents page to your file with a brief description. The bottom paragraph in each letter is what you're looking for. These files are pristine.'

The evangelist scanned the letters, then handed them to his wife. The hint of anxiety on her face disappeared as she read the final paragraph of one. 'I can confirm that there is no further material held in any shape or form by this agency on Patrick Collins.' Teresa looked across the table. 'You're a very resourceful man, Mr Sinclair,' she said, then glanced at her husband. If a silent message passed between them, it eluded Sinclair.

The preacher appeared about to speak, then he paused and suddenly put his hands together in prayer. 'Holy Father, I have asked you many times in the past few days and I ask you again now. Guide me. Guide my heart. Guide my mind. Guide me at this time to work for you as you wish me to.'

Head bowed, eyes closed, he sat immobile. After what seemed to be an eternity to Andrew Sinclair, Collins spoke. 'If you can indeed raise sufficient funds to ensure that I can run for president without placing a single dollar burden on the American people, and if you and your four friends can raise that sum in a manner that meets with the approval of John Reilly, then I'm your man. If this campaign goes ahead, I'll make mistakes and I ask your forgiveness before I make them, but it's only those who do nothing who do not make mistakes.'

Long after Teresa had retired they were still talking. There was at most a year before Collins would have to declare himself a candidate for the presidency.

Eventually Sinclair raised a subject that sent the preacher

into a state of high alarm. 'After my visit to your home you had a conversation out on the patio with John Reilly.'

'Indeed I did. I discussed your proposition . . . But how did you know that?'

'Your conversation was taped. Entirely by accident, I'm certain. Fraser's crew had left a tape running.'

Collins tried hard to hide the inner panic that rose instantly within him as he moved to the coffee trolley.

The following day Collins flew back to Florida in Evangelist One to take part in a further filming session of Adam Fraser's documentary. Before they began to record, he called the film-maker into his private study. 'Adam, I am aware that by accident you discovered the reasons why I had a visit here a week or so ago from a man called Andrew Sinclair.'

Adam was startled. 'Er . . . um, yes.'

'Do you have that tape still?'

'Yes, Pat, I do.'

Collins swung in his chair and looked directly at him. 'What were you planning to do with it?' he asked casually.

Adam delayed. 'I'm not sure. If you decide to run I thought a section of it where you and John Reilly are reviewing the state of the union might make a powerful counterpoint to some of the footage of affluent America that I plan to shoot.'

Collins remained relaxed. 'Excellent idea. Could I have a copy?'

'Of course you can, Pat.'

'I want you to know that I'm deeply impressed that you didn't go running to the media with the story.'

Adam shrugged. 'Not my style.'

'No, it isn't. Thank God. Adam, I've decided to run. Subject to certain conditions, that is.'

'Like whether Sinclair can raise the money?'

Collins laughed. 'That's one of them.' Reference to Sinclair reminded Collins of a suggestion that he had made. 'I'd like you to think about making another documentary as well as the two you're already working on. Suggested working title, "The making of a President?'' With a question mark, of course,' he added. 'Follow me around. Sit in on strategy meetings. Record tactics. Fly on the wall. Be an interesting subject, don't you think?'

'That's a marvellous idea.'

'You'll be given the same freedom as on these two films, although I'll need you to sign a confidentiality clause to cover the period before I go public.'

Later, after the filming session, Patrick Collins returned to his study, locked the door and put the tape cassette Adam had given him on a small portable machine. Framed moments of his life looked down on him from the walls: Nixon decorating both Collins and Reilly on the White House lawn; Brezhnev holding his arm; Margaret Thatcher looking up at him admiringly; his collection of theology prizes. He plugged in a headset to ensure that no one but he could hear the tape, and pressed the start button. As the tape played on and he listened to his conversation with Johnny Reilly, beads of sweat began to form on his forehead. Patrick Collins began to pray silently. When he heard himself and Reilly discussing 'the big problem' he began to shake, overwhelmed by an inner fear. Then, suddenly, the tape was silent. He rewound, then pressed Play again. Yes. It was all right. The soundman's tape had run out well before he had returned to the patio with Teresa. Thank God for British incompetence. Now his prayers were no longer internal. With the tape's continuing silence acting as balm to his soul, Collins spoke out loud: 'Holy Father, thank you for protecting your servant from himself. Thank you for restoring my peace of mind. Thank you for this sign that the path I am about to walk down is one chosen by you. Amen.'

'It happened over in your country. In London, during my first crusade. A lifetime ago.'

Pat Collins had lost no time in calling Adam in to talk to him about 'the problem'. 'We were staying at the Ambassador Hotel on Park Lane as guests of the British organizers of my tour. Teresa was back home in Boston looking after the kids. They were too young to bring on the trip. If she'd been in London there never would have been a problem. I came back from a late-night rally at Wembley Stadium, said goodnight to John and the rest of the team and went to my suite. I was bushed. Too tired even to face a snack, so I thought I'd freshen up with a shower and then call room service. I don't know how she got in, but when I came out of the shower back into my bedroom, there was a naked woman stretched out on my bed. I went to ring the desk, but before the phone was in my hand, a couple of guys were in the room with flash cameras. It all happened so fast. She'd wrapped her arms around me and tried to give me oral sex. I was pulling her off and going for these guys at the same time. Moments later they were gone.'

Adam waited for the preacher to continue, but he seemed to be lost in a distant memory. 'What was the objective, Pat? Did they want to blackmail you or destroy the crusade?'

'All I can tell you is what Ambassador Scott later told me. The only one of the crusade team I confided in was John, we contacted the embassy in Grosvenor Square and the ambassador handled the whole thing. I never even spoke to a police officer. They were caught three days later. Apparently they planned to score two home runs. Hit the Collins organization for a bundle of money, then the press for another payout . . . I never saw the photographs. Ambassador Scott assured me that the negatives had been destroyed. Since then I've been waiting for those photos to turn up.'

'Surely not, Pat. Not after so many years?'

'I get panic spasms from time to time, that's all. And the trick's been tried again. Twice on my last crusade . . .'

'So that's the real reason why you make sure you're never alone with a woman?'

'You better believe it, Adam, but I can hardly go public on that, can I?'

Adam and Susanna were checking the timings of the film segments when there was a knock on the door of his bungalow. Adam found Barry and Leon on his doorstep. He motioned them in. Since the discovery that their bungalows were bugged and the phones tapped, they had become adroit at conducting silent conversations augmented by notes. Adam poured drinks while Barry and Leon checked the room with two electronic scanners. They stripped the phones, then reassembled them.

'Damnedest thing.'

'Let me guess, Barry. All the bugs have gone?'

'Yes,' said Barry. 'How did you know?'

'Just an educated guess. I was finishing off these timings with Su before getting the crew together to organize a little celebration.'

'What are we celebrating, Adam?' asked Susanna.

'Oh, a little extra film we're going to make. Just the greatest scoop of our entire lives. Sinclair has no need to keep tabs on us now. We're part of the charmed inner circle.'

Victor Rodriguez had been sitting at his desk when he had heard the tone sound on his personal fax. Unlocking the drawer, he watched as a piece of paper with meaningless squiggles emerged from the machine. Using the decoding sheet he read the one-line message from Sinclair. He smiled. 'Habemus Praefectus.'

We have a President . . . As ever Sinclair was demonstrating his positive thinking. In reality they did not even have a candidate. That would only become a certainty when Sinclair and his four friends achieved a classic American Dream and transformed five million dollars into a hundred and fifty million. It would have to be clean, untainted money. A legally acquired fortune.

CHAPTER NINE

PAY DAY

IMMEDIATELY AFTER PAT COLLINS MADE HIS DECISION TO RUN, Andrew Sinclair caused important changes to the careers of four people who had been briefly associated with him.

The woman in the white dress landed the leading female role in a major studio movie release. Tommy, the rent-boy, was given a home with a childless couple, the first adults in his life who had ever loved him. Each was visited shortly after by a man in a black suit, and both agreed to his suggestion that they had never been asked to meet Pat Collins. Tommy's foster parents signed an affidavit on his behalf concerning his meeting with the multi-talented member of the House of Representatives, which the black-suited man took away with him. The police in Detroit showed little interest in the death of Jack Podesta in the fire that burned down a cheap hotel. The police in Miami equally showed little interest in a dead mugging victim called Chuck Talbot. Neither force discovered that the two men had briefly worked together in security for a recent Pat Collins crusade.

*   *   *

To soothe the sensibilities of four of the most powerful men in corporate America required remarkable tact and delicacy. To arrange a meeting that involved at least two men who still declined to phone Bill Gates on the basis that he should phone them first, was in its own way as formidable a task as the agenda they had met to discuss.

Sinclair waited for the servants to leave the imposing conference room in Edgar Lee Stratford's home. The host had assigned at least three members of his staff to each of his visitors: Sinclair was amused at this opening salvo in the hospitality war. This first meeting at Stratford's home in California was to be followed by a second at Paul McCall's home in Virginia, a third at Rick Forrest's ranch in Texas and a fourth at Rupert Turner's Long Island estate.

'Before you begin, Andrew,' said Stratford, 'I'd just like to say how delighted I am at the news that he has agreed to run.'

There were murmurs of agreement from the others.

'The fact that we've come this far is due entirely to the four of you. From the beginning this enterprise depended on your total commitment. All that stands in the way of his commitment reaching the same level is the question of our capability to fund the Collins campaign. We have promised him a hundred and fifty million dollars. We have a bare twelve months to deliver it. I have developed a strategy that will achieve this. It should realize a further billion dollars for distribution between the people in this room.'

For once Andrew Sinclair needed no eye-contact with his potential buyers. He could scent greed in the atmosphere. The four emperors of American capital were like children promised ice cream.

'Gentlemen. In the past you have each powerfully demonstrated to me your visionary gifts. In the future, as together we guide the destiny of our country, there will be many calls on our collective vision. The scheme I am about to share with you requires no such vision. Its potential is immediately apparent. We have an opportunity to own the twenty-first century's equivalent of the safety-pin.

'Microsoft, Sony, Hewlett Packard, Rick Forrest here and all the other leaders in the computer world are seeking to dominate the extraordinary potential that the Internet offers. All too often any expansion in the industry is sideways, buying up photographic archives, data banks, that kind of thing. What we have is a rare opportunity to expand dramatically forwards. Imagine, gentlemen, how much lies waiting for the individual who controls the ability to create a secure environment for anyone wishing to access the Internet. Imagine that someone had invented a "fire-wall" which kept out all but the bona fide caller, which gave unassailable security and protection from attack by hackers, cyber-warriors, cyber-terrorists, rival companies and rival countries.'

Rick Forrest rumbled, in a deep Texan drawl, 'You have any idea how much my laboratories have spent on R and D in this area?'

Sinclair merely replied, 'The whole industry is in pursuit of it.'

'And you say you've got it?' Stratford's eyes narrowed.

'No, Edgar, I said we have an opportunity to own it.'

Two weeks later Sinclair returned to San Francisco. He gunned the car over the Bay Bridge and on to Berkeley. Reaching the university, he drove from the campus to Solano Avenue. For a Stanford graduate the area abounded with memories but Sinclair was not sentimental. All that passed through his mind was a suggestion of self-congratulation that after all these years he had remembered the street-names so well.

He pushed open the swing-over door to the double garage. He knew the inside intimately though he had never before entered it. No room in here to park the smallest car because all available space was occupied by computer equipment, some of it stripped down to bare frame, some of it fully functioning. Two young men glanced up as Sinclair entered and approached. Paul and Bobby Carson looked at him with open curiosity as they shook his hand. Paul, the older twin by forty-five minutes, had evidently been elected main spokesman. He said, 'We're very flattered that you should come all the way from New York to see us, Mr Sinclair. What is it we can do for you?'

'I want to talk to you both about what I can do for you. I want to make you an irresistible offer. First, I know what you're working on, how close you are and what problems you have yet to overcome. You need money. Quite a lot of money. Maybe if you went into Silicon Valley you could get some high-tech seed money but would it be enough? How dear will it come? You need fresh input into the project you're working on. You might get a sprinkling of cash from Bill Gates or Paul Allen, but what you won't get from them is their time and commitment. You're close, but on the other side of the bay there's a guy working on his own who is just a little bit closer. He's funded by a company that doesn't appreciate him. When you learn how close he is to solving the problem you're all working on, I'm sure you'll appreciate him a great deal. With money you could lure him away from the opposition. Now, if I could persuade someone like Rick Forrest to go on your board, we could take you public and very, very quickly the Carson twins will be millionaires. I've got five million dollars. I want to buy seventy per cent of your company. We'll bring in the guy from the other side of the bay. We'll get Morgan Grenfell to handle the flotation. What do you say?'

Victor Rodriguez enjoyed Sinclair's account of how he had acquired the controlling interest in Cybersafe. He shook his head in admiration as a manservant appeared on the verandah with a tray of drinks.

'Will you join me in a bottle of Dom Perignon? I insist.'

'It'll be a pleasure. After my teetotal sessions with the preacher, it's a relief to sit with someone who enjoys a drink.'

Victor Rodriguez had never seen Sinclair so relaxed. He picked up two glasses of champagne and handed one to Sinclair. 'The White House.'

'The White House.'

'Roberto and his friends. Were they of any use?'

'Research and development *par excellence*. Their contribution was vital. I'd been quietly trawling through my contacts for some time. Investment banks, venture-capital brokers. I knew that whoever came up with a method of ensuring security on the Internet would have another Klondike on his hands. It was clear that none of the major players was close to the answer. My efforts sourced eight possibles, all young unknowns, all under-funded, just like the Carson twins. The problem was, which of these unknowns was making real headway? They were all guarding their development projects with great care. By the time Roberto had finished I knew exactly who the likely winners were. Then, thanks to the talents of a young British hacker *extraordinaire*, I had a final shortlist of three. The fact that he could still access their files demonstrated that all three had some way to go. The solution then was to buy control of one of them, and through that buy control of the rivals who would enhance what the Carsons were doing.'

Rodriguez moved to refill Sinclair's glass. Sinclair placed a hand over it.

'And Rick Forrest?' asked Rodriguez.

'Was delighted at the chance to be on the board. We've also acquired the bright young man on the other side of the bay and two other smart guys.'

Victor sipped his drink. 'And the research for the computer firc-wall. Now you have to test it?'

'That's been done. We have all the facilities at companies owned by my executive cabinet – McCall's ATZ, Turner's Network International, Forrest Computers, of course, and Stratford's bank. We also ran extensive tests at the Patrick Collins Association.'

'Most satisfactory, Andrew. If this Cybersafe comes through that kind of field testing, the endorsements will enhance the share value. What stage are you at with the tests?'

Sinclair held up his glass to the sun and studied it. 'We've got it. The Carson boys and the rest of the team finished three days ago. Results, one hundred per cent.' He looked at Rodriguez and grinned. 'Two days ago I insisted on the ultimate test.

Without telling the Carson twins and their colleagues, I arranged for the young man in Britain to hack into their central computer. Fourteen hours later he admitted defeat. No matter what he did, Cybersafe repelled every strategy. The ultimate green light. The planted stories in the financial papers will start mid-August. Morgan Grenfell will take the company public one week before Thanksgiving Day. Everyone involved is going to make a huge amount of money. After the appropriate statutory period the five million dollars' investment that has been made on behalf of Patrick Collins will be worth well in excess of two hundred million dollars.'

'Andrew, I congratulate you. Extraordinary. I take it your colleagues have all piled in?'

'Oh, yes,' said Sinclair. His face gave away nothing as he continued, 'I've also brought Stratford's bank into the flotation.'

Rodriguez began to laugh. His entire body shook. He gasped for air, tears ran down his cheeks, and Sinclair became fearful that the chairman of the board might excite himself into a heart-attack. Finally he controlled himself enough to say, 'You've done it, Andrew. Let's lunch, then walk in the fields.'

Victor Rodriguez's habitual prudence might seem to have been dispensed with at his ranch at Sevilla in the Valle del Cauca, but Sinclair knew the reality. All roads in and out of the region were owned by Rodriguez, all were subject to twenty-four-hour surveillance and there was enough heavy weaponry on the estate, including Stinger missiles, to thwart even aerial attacks.

The swimming pool, the parabolic dishes and the other paraphernalia that advertise significant wealth in Colombia were, like everything else about the chairman's estate, discreet. The only unusual feature was a large bird sanctuary with a clinic, fully equipped and staffed. As usual, it was Rodriguez's first stop with his visitor. He was greeted, effusively, by Professor Cardona, one of the finest avian veterinarians in the world, and certainly the best paid. Rodriguez talked to him rapidly and expertly, then showed Sinclair a small red bird with dull eyes. 'A victim of chemical poisoning. Defoliant,' explained Rodriguez. 'It's a vile thing. When is your government going to stamp on the chemical trade?'

They walked on, then Rodriguez took Sinclair to his Land Rover. They bumped over the rough terrain until they reached the road, then, accelerating, Rodriguez drove through the nearby village of Sevilla.

'This Oscar, the documentary-maker's friend. I need more information to get a location on him. Fraser only phones him from public phone booths.' Rodriguez took his eyes off the road for a moment. 'Believe me, Andrew, if Fraser ever phones his friend from Colombia or Venezuela, that will present no problem. We will be able to trace this man. El Gordo listens to everything. But in the States . . . Perhaps one day, but not yet.'

'Not to worry, Victor, I think we've got under control any long-term problems that Fraser might pose.'

The car swung off the main road. On either side sugar-cane reached high above them until suddenly they were out in the open. Rodriguez stopped and gestured at the fields in front of them. 'Bet you've never seen a crop like that before.'

Sinclair took off his sunglasses. 'Are they what I think they are?'

Rodriguez failed to respond, his attention on the cigarette he was rolling. He lit up and inhaled deeply. 'Two weeks ago I had a visit from one of our most senior DEA sources in Miami. I'd been expecting him for some time. He was due to bring us a large consignment of sniffer bags from his source in England.'

Sinclair put up a hand. 'I'm sorry, you're losing me.'

'Sniffer bags were perfected by the forensics people in Scotland Yard. They're used by the British government when they want something to come through Customs without the sniffer dogs picking it up.'

'Did he bring the bags?'

'Oh, yes – invaluable for moving product into Britain. But he brought something of even greater value. Information that the DEA, in collaboration with our own government, was planning to crop-spray this entire region to contaminate the cocaine harvest and the poppy crop. The spraying was scheduled to take place a week after his visit. The following day, small aircraft began to make runs over these fields. Our people thought that either our contact in Miami had got it wrong or, worse, had been compromised. The planes made run after run. They didn't spray the crops, they dropped thousands of packets of condoms. Here, look, here's one of the packets.'

Rodriguez held one up. Written on it was a message. 'A gift from the World Health Organization. Use wisely.'

'So,' he said, 'our people took their advice. What keeps sperm in is going to keep DDT out.'

The two men gazed across the fields. Each young plant as far as the eye could see was sheathed in a condom.

Sinclair gazed at the scene fascinated. 'Best example of cross-fertilization I've ever seen.'

Rodriguez laughed. 'Now, let us discuss the seating arrangements for the Thanksgiving dinner. I've invited Roberto and his colleagues, but they won't need seats.'

Before the dinner Sinclair was very busy.

August. The *Wall Street Journal* was the first to run a major story on the Carson twins. The article told how 'substantial finance' had been made available to them to bring their 'significant research in the field of computer software' to a 'potentially ground-breaking threshold' with 'global implications for the industry'. While advising its readers that the twins had established a 'clear lead in their hunt for one of the industry's Holy Grails' the newspaper neglected to reveal that the clear lead had largely been created by buying up their nearest rivals. Indicating that this particular Holy Grail had Internet implications, the article was a masterly mix of circumspection and eager anticipation. Media interest was immediate. The twins remained elusive and ducked all requests for interviews but this merely fuelled interest. During the next fortnight in-depth profiles appeared in the *New York Times*, the *Washington Post* and *Time* magazine: 'The Reclusive Geniuses Across The Bay'; 'Better Open The Gates, Bill. Your

Successors Are On Their Way', 'Two Minds With But A Single Thought'.

September. A *Fortune* magazine exclusive revealed that the twins had Rick Forrest on their board. The presence of a man widely acknowledged as one of the shrewdest minds in the computer industry sent business interest in Cybersafe sky high. In an enigmatic press release, Forrest hinted at a public flotation.

October. Morgan Grenfell announced that they would be handling the public flotation of Cybersafe. That was followed by carefully placed leaks indicating that the corporate subscriptions for shares were outstripping potential availability by a ratio of fifteen to one. On 14 October, Morgan Grenfell unveiled exactly what it was that the market was falling over itself to buy: an electronic fire-wall that offered impregnable security against any hacker or would-be criminal. The implications not only for the computer industry but for any user of the security system were stunning. The *New York Times* editorial was ecstatic:

> We have today entered a new age. With the announcement of this breakthrough historians will in the future talk of BC, Before Cybersafe, and AC, After Cybersafe. Its implications for commerce are awesome. Mr and Mrs America can now order any product they wish on the Internet market safe in the knowledge that their credit details will remain inviolate. Cyber-currency has come of age. A truly globalized economy has become a reality. Its implications for national security are equally staggering. In 1997 General Marsh reported to the President that cyber-terrorists could sabotage nuclear-weapons systems, power, water, air-traffic control, and emergency services. Cybersafe, used correctly, will end this threat. It will protect our nation's essential secrets.

Fortune magazine was more concerned with the private sector:

> In recent years financial institutions have been plagued by cyber-terrorists who have amassed billions of dollars by

extortion. Banks, broking firms, investment houses here in America and in many countries around the world have secretly paid out colossal ransoms to prevent catastrophic computer meltdown and a total collapse of confidence among their customers.

The cyber-terrorists have penetrated the most sophisticated systems using logic bombs, coded devices that can be remotely detonated. The deal was simple: 'Pay up or we will destroy your computers.' Now, thanks to the Carson twins, there will be no more pay days for these criminals.

Interest became so intense that Morgan Grenfell had to announce that the planned flotation for mid-December was being brought forward to 28 October. On the due date, shares in Cybersafe opened at thirty-five dollars and closed at sixty-one dollars. Only 20 per cent of the company had been available to the general public, the remaining 80 per cent remaining under the control and ownership of a small handful of people that included Patrick Collins. At close of business Collins was on paper a hundred million dollars richer. If the gurus in the market-place were correct with their predictions, that figure was set to double at least during the statutory period of one hundred and eighty days that had to pass before disposal of stock could take place.

'Almighty God, we thank you for the gifts that have so recently been bestowed upon your humble servant. The riches that have showered upon me fill me with deep wonder and inexpressible gratitude. We thank you for this food and drink, which we are delighted to share with all of those gathered here today, old friends and new ones. On this day of all days, O Lord, we give thanks to you. In the autumn of 1621 the pilgrims celebrated their survival after a time of terrible deprivation, disease and death. They gave thanks for their survival and for a bountiful harvest just as we, in this autumn, give thanks. May we show the same courage and fortitude as we confront the tasks that lie ahead of us in the coming year as those first settlers showed. Amen.'

Leon began to pull out, widen his shot, as Collins turned and, with a slight gesture of his hand towards his seated wife, looked around those assembled at the table. 'Teresa and I wish you all a very happy Thanksgiving Day. Twelve months from now we will know if the shared hopes, dreams and aspirations of those gathered here today are to be fulfilled.'

Collins paused, then looked slowly round the table. 'I believe that there have been three defining moments in the history of the United States. The American Revolution in the seventeen eighties. The Reconstruction in the eighteen sixties and the New Deal in the nineteen thirties. I also believe that, if we can triumph over our opponents and the forces arrayed against us in the coming months, it is possible that we may see the birth of a fourth American republic.'

Leon panned along the rapt group seated at the dinner table. For a moment it seemed that Collins was about to launch into a policy speech. Instead, with a gesture towards the food, he defused the mood. 'But before we get to the fourth republic, there's a turkey waiting to be eaten. Enjoy.'

In the run-up to the dinner, Sinclair had been obliged to soothe the nerves of some of the dinner guests.

'Edgar, I promise you I have had this English film-maker vetted. He's one hundred per cent clean. Pat is allowing him to make a documentary on the Collins-for-President campaign. Nothing, but nothing, will go to air until long after Collins has declared and, indeed, has either won or lost. By which time who's going to care a damn about some documentary?'

Two days before the dinner Sinclair had flown down from New York to run his personal slide-rule over the final arrangements. He'd suggested to Adam Fraser that they had lunch 'to finalize the scenario'.

Although he knew he was being schmoozed, Adam felt himself warming to Sinclair as he fought to save his access. 'You see, Andrew, I finished this part of the shooting schedule weeks ago. I've just kept the crew hanging on here in Florida to film the dinner. After that we head for home. Won't be back until next year for the run-in to the Reverend going public.'

Sinclair explained a little about the Four Seasons and their role in persuading Collins to run. 'Further down the line I guarantee you access to all four. At the moment a couple of them are paranoid about any kind of publicity. When Pat has declared he's running, it'll be fine.'

Adam decided it was better to give in gracefully now and keep Sinclair as an ally. 'Tell you what, Andrew, how about I film Pat's prayer before dinner and any opening remarks of welcome he might make? At that point we'll stop filming and go out for a meal along the beach somewhere.'

Sinclair extended a hand. 'Thank you so much. I won't forget this.'

Adam knew that Sinclair could have excluded the film-crew from the dinner, but Sinclair had reason to be pleased: what they had agreed upon was precisely what he had planned they would agree upon.

The film-crew took their equipment out of the room and the dinner got under way. At one end of the long table that had been set up in what was normally a conference room, Sinclair observed the scene with quiet satisfaction: his plans had come together well. He was curious to watch and listen to Teresa Collins. As she chatted to Rick Forrest and Paul McCall, Sinclair became convinced that the American public would adore such a first lady – elegant and beautiful but unthreatening, devoted to her husband and family, surprisingly liberal on some issues but a fierce opponent of drugs.

Next to her, Patrick Collins was in deep conversation with Ricardo Semper, a Colombian businessman whose empire included insurance brokerage and travel agencies. Next to him sat the Colombian industrialist, Alberto Cornejo, in animated conversation with Edgar Lee Stratford and Rupert Turner. Sinclair turned to the man sitting quietly in the next chair. 'Victor, this is the first opportunity you've had to meet our candidate. Reaction?'

'His commitment to declare war on the narcotics industry is impressive. I doubt that we could have found a better man in the entire country.'

His opinion was clearly shared by every other guest at the table. As the group relaxed between courses, Sinclair was intrigued to note how such all-powerful men like McCall, Turner and the others hung on Collins's every word. The little side conversations faded as the preacher, without even wishing to, held the attention of everyone else in the room.

'You know, I've wondered many times what would have happened if Ross Perot had stayed the course in 'ninety-two. Wondered if an independent could go all the way. Now I'm going to find out. With Teresa's and your help I'm determined to give it my very best shot.

'I don't want to get into a deep examination of potential policies tonight other than to observe how delighted I am finally to meet and talk with our friends from Colombia. It's good to get this opportunity to thank you for the support you have given my crusades over the years. I'm certainly not going to run a one-issue campaign, but the war against narcotics will undoubtedly be an important plank in my platform.'

He reached for a carafe of water and refilled his glass before continuing. 'We have much to discuss in the months ahead, not least my hopes that the informal, unofficial corporate cabinet seated around this table will exercise their minds with regard to certain states. Just consider, Paul, you have power bases in Virginia and Illinois. Rupert in New York State. Rick in Texas and Edgar in California. There's one hundred and fifty-four electoral votes wrapped up in your home territories. That brings me to the reason for our Colombian friends being at this table. The Hispanic vote. Victor. Ricardo. Alberto. I look to the three of you to give me what will be vital help in this area. In the last seven presidential elections the Hispanic voting turnout has averaged under thirty per cent. Less than half the white vote, nearly less than half the black vote. In Texas, California and Florida the Hispanic impact will play a vital part in deciding who takes those states.' Collins tapped loudly on the table to emphasize his point. 'Just those three states, Victor. Deliver me those and you'll be delivering me one hundred and eleven electoral votes. One of the aspects that I would like each of you to consider is how we can neutralize the power of the various governors within those states, and indeed, all of the other governors. One way or another they are tied to a system and to a political philosophy that has failed the people of this country. I'm talking about both Republicans and Democrats. You know, in the first two hundred years of our independence, successive governments ran up a collective National Debt of a trillion dollars. In the next eight years, the Reagan years, that debt became four trillion dollars, and those years are looked back on now by both major parties as a time of unparalleled success.'

The film-crew was preoccupied with more prosaic financial matters.

'Trouble is,' said Adam, 'I can't go through the usual Wall Street shuffle, knocking on doors making a pitch and holding out my hat.'

'Not to finance this one, you can't,' said Susanna. 'Until he declares he's running, it's a bloody state secret.'

She glanced at Leon, who hadn't spoken since they'd entered the restaurant. 'You all right, Leon? Something worrying you?'

Leon had been doodling on a paper napkin. He stopped. 'I keep wondering who the man on the roof was.'

As a conversation stopper it was most effective.

'What man on what roof?' said Adam.

'Roof of the Collins conference centre where we've just been filming. There was a man up there.'

Barry waved a hand dismissively. 'It was probably one of those security people. They were crawling about all over the place.'

'Why was he taking photographs, then? If he was security, he'd have done that at ground level when the visitors were arriving. He wouldn't climb up on a roof in the middle of the evening and stick a camera through a skylight.'

Adam was intrigued. 'How did you see him?'

'Before we started to film I tilted the camera and went around in front of it to clean the lens as I always do. I saw the guy above me, in the reflection. He was pointing a camera directly down towards the dinner table. After that I kept an eye in that direction. From time to time I saw him taking shots. He didn't want to be seen.'

It had been worth flying home to London via Hamburg if only to see Oscar's reaction. He sat in the very heart of his Dolls' House staring into space. His mouth opened and closed, like a goldfish, but no sound came out. Adam had given him a full account of the Thanksgiving dinner and its roof-top photographer. He had played Barry's tape-recording of the patio conversation between Collins and Reilly, and he had run a video of the section of the dinner he had been allowed to film.

'Now tell me, Oscar, can Collins win the presidency?'

'For sure he can. The sheer genius in selecting him is that, once the idea is put to you, you think, why didn't someone persuade him to run before now? Then, of course, there's Sinclair's ace in the hole. Somehow he's persuaded four men of enormous power and influence to back Collins. They're bound to pull in a basketful of other players from big business.'

Oscar padded silently up and down. 'Then they trump the ace with a piece of brilliance. Not a dime needed from the good ol' American public. Collins will be using his own money.'

'But where has all this money come from? Fine, Sinclair put up five million dollars in July. How has that become at least a hundred and fifty million by November?'

'Cybersafe.'

'What, the Carson twins and their Internet invention?'

'The Carson twins and Rick Forrest. I think you'll find that the Collins five million went to buy a piece of that action. Another stroke of genius. A one hundred per cent legitimate business. And there's our boy Collins helping to foster the American Dream, not just for the Carson twins, but for anyone else lucky enough to get their hands on Cybersafe shares. Adam, run me that video again, please.'

Leon's camera began to pan along the table. Oscar turned to Adam. 'Mind if I take some shots from this?'

Adam hesitated. 'I've given a written undertaking to Collins that none of it will see the light of day until after the presidential election.'

'No problem. My eyes only.' Oscar froze-frame on Victor Rodriguez and pressed Print on a small machine attached to his video-recorder. There was a whir then a bleep, and Rodriguez's face emerged from the bottom of the copier. Oscar moved the videotape back and forth until he had a colour still of everyone at the dinner.

He laid them on a tabletop, carefully reconstructing the Thanksgiving seating plan.

'Why are you doing that?'

Oscar glanced up. 'I don't suppose you know who arranged the positions?'

Adam shook his head. 'I remember there was a very British fuss about who was sitting where. The to-ing and fro-ing seemed to go on for ever. I remember that clearly because we were waiting to turn over.'

Oscar stared hard at him. 'Adam, for Christ's sake.'

'I was too focused on getting as much as I could on film. Checking on the lighting, discussing shots with Leon, timings with Susanna and sound with Barry. I'm making a documentary, remember?'

'And I'm trying to help you stay alive long enough to finish it.' Oscar stabbed a pudgy finger angrily at one of the photographs. 'Just tell me why this guy is tucked away right at one end of the table instead of being next to Collins or at least right in the middle of the four wise monkeys?'

'Which guy?'

Oscar held up the photograph. 'Victor Ramirez Rodriguez. President of Andino Incorporated.' Oscar waggled the photograph. 'Jesus College, Cambridge. Three years ago. I attended a six-day symposium there. So did Victor.' He moved to the coffee percolator, poured two cups and handed one to Adam. 'It was the thirteenth international Symposium on Economic Crime. One of the subjects under discussion was money-laundering. Rodriguez made an exceptional speech. I'll give

144

you a copy before you fly back to the States. It's a country-by-country analysis of just how far organized crime has infiltrated into the legitimate world. Of just how much black money has been made white. Of the global corruption.' Oscar paused, lost in recollection. 'One figure that Rodriguez quoted still haunts me. He estimated that the size of the global underground economy per annum was at least a trillion dollars. He finances a monthly magazine called the *Laundry Report*. It's definitive.'

Oscar rummaged in a drawer and tossed a copy to Adam. 'A continuously updated assessment of the narcotics industry and its laundering techniques. Small wonder that the cartels have made attempts to kill Rodriguez. If I have one hero in this life it's this man. So why was he placed so far below the salt?'

Adam shrugged. 'Perhaps he's shy. Perhaps Pat Collins, or whoever did the seating arrangements, was badly briefed?'

Oscar turned back to his picture montage and removed all of the photographs except for the one of Rodriguez. 'Or perhaps someone wanted to make sure they could get a good clear shot of him. If you put out a contract on someone it's useful to give the trigger man a photograph of the target.'

Adam frowned. 'Like everyone else at the table, Rodriguez was there by special invitation. The security around the house that evening had to be seen to be believed. You'd think Collins was already president.'

'So the man on the roof must have been there by invitation too, eh?' Oscar resumed pacing. 'I'm not talking about someone trying to kill Rodriguez at the dinner, Adam, but maybe a month, a year later. Collins is committed to making the war on narcotics a major political issue. He, or someone, invites Rodriguez, one of the world's leading authorities on the drugs war, to break bread, then he's seated almost in the next room.' He sighed. 'Maybe it's nothing. I want to run the shots of these two through the machine. Apart from Mrs Collins, I already have a file on everyone at the dinner except these two. I've never seen them before. What are their names?'

'The one with the mouthful of gold teeth is Ricardo Semper.

The other guy is Alberto Cornejo. They're businessmen from Bogotá, active in fighting the narco trade.'

'Mind if I put them through my CFR?'

'No problem. All I know about them is what I picked up when everyone was being introduced before dinner.'

Oscar pushed the photo of Semper into a metal box the size of a small photocopier. He took the receiver from a phone attached to the box, laid it on the desk and rapidly dialled a number. The Computerized Face Recognition unit was not readily available. Oscar had somehow acquired one for 'field testing'. The system has been introduced secretly at sensitive locations throughout the world. When locked to a camera it is capable of scanning a crowd at the rate of twenty faces a second and matching the images against a database of up to a million photographs. Oscar's model was linked to several databases, including two in Langley.

'That'll take a few minutes. Now, Adam, those bugs that were used in your bungalow. Funny, you know, things keep leading back one way or another to the narco business.'

'How do you mean?'

'That equipment is made under exclusive US government licence. The only people who have them are the DEA.'

'Why would they be interested in a film-crew?'

Oscar shook his head. 'Not necessarily the DEA, Adam. Just someone with a good connection to them.'

'Like who?'

'Dunno. Sinclair, maybe. He seems to be running this entire Collins-for-President operation. If Collins had been responsible for bugging your rooms, why would he wait over a week before getting you on-side with the tempting morsel of an exclusive film on his campaign? How did Collins know about the patio tape? Maybe because Sinclair's people heard enough of your conversation on the beach with Barry. So Andrew Sinclair tips off Collins and probably suggests the extra documentary. It ties you up neatly. Stops you going public too soon. Wouldn't be in your interests, would it?'

'That's just hypothesis, Oscar.'

'Of course.'

'Oscar. You've heard the tape. His conversation with Reilly out on the patio. Those references to some major problem. They obviously felt it would show up on file in Washington or Langley. It hasn't.'

'Your only chance is to identify whoever authorized a clean-up of the files on Patrick Collins. If there was a clean-up.'

'This incident in London, the naked woman and the photographers. Surely that would have been put on file particularly as he contacted the American ambassador?'

'You're right, Adam. So someone has definitely cleaned the Collins files. Can you trace the ambassador? All these years later he just might talk and tell you what he placed on State Department records.'

'Ambassador Scott died three years ago.'

The CFR clicked into life and a single slip of paper emerged. Oscar studied it, then clipped it to the two photographs. 'Nothing known on either man. That's another wild idea down the pan.'

Adam looked at him questioningly, but Oscar, as if swatting a passing fly, dismissed the idea from his mind without a word. Then he snapped his fingers. 'Olaf. If anyone knows anything about Ricardo Semper and Alberto Cornejo, it'll be him.' He stretched across the desk and pulled an unusually large telephone towards him. It had curious switches, a meter with a dial and three glass indicator lamps protruding from the base. As he picked up the phone and flicked a switch, the three indicator lamps lit up red. Satisfied that the scrambler was working, he rapidly punched in a long series of numbers. He listened. Suddenly all three lights went out and Oscar slammed down the phone. 'I rang him on his scrambled line, the one he keeps locked in his desk. It was intercepted. Sounded like a police officer. Now how would a police officer get access to Olaf's locked phone?'

'Try his normal home number. Isabella or Lucas will tell us what's going on.'

Oscar punched in another series of numbers. A moment later

all the lights went out and he smashed the phone down, hard and quick.

'Same son-of-a-bitch. Don't like it, Adam.

'Not much we can do to help this far away. You keep trying all his numbers and I'll do the same. Come on, Oscar, I'll buy you dinner. Let's get some fresh air. How was it that you never put me on to this Victor Rodriguez when I was making my two-parter on narcotics?'

'Because you were only interested in the bad guys, if you remember. Victor is one of the good guys. He'd hardly have fitted into your journey by mule from Peru to Colombia, or your crazy trips round Cali and Medellin. I'll give you a confidential dossier on Rodriguez before you go. Makes fascinating reading.'

Oscar had demolished an avocado salad, a plate of pâté and was waiting for his third appetizer before he pointed a stubby finger at Adam's cassette indicating he wanted to talk. 'I want to tell you why Victor Rodriguez is my hero. I've told you about my first tour of duty in Vietnam in 1970, working for Colby on the Phoenix Program. I've never told you about my second tour or my introduction into the narcotics business.'

'*Into* the business, Oscar? You've always been passionately opposed to drugs.'

'Not always. Not at the time of my second tour in Vietnam. When I got out there in March 'seventy-two, the ambassador and head of CIA operations, William Colby, had been running the long silver train for nearly five years. The Montagnards and the Meo – two tribes the CIA got to fight for South Vietnam – strongly objected to using M16 American-issue rifles. They were carrying out missions for us in the central highlands and on the Ho Chi Minh Trail. These people were a first-class fighting machine and Colby and the other CIA executives were anxious to keep them on-side. The M16 jammed frequently, while the Russian Kalashnikov functioned perfectly even when smothered with sand or mud.'

Obviously the United States could not go on the open market

and buy Russian guns, nor could any US government money be allocated for such purchases. William Colby had devised a bizarre solution: the long silver train.

'Colby arranged for the remains of American servicemen to be brought to an off-limits section of Tan Son Nhut airbase. This section was entirely staffed by CIA personnel. The cadavers were opened up, their vital organs removed and replaced with packets of processed heroin, fifteen kilos per body.'

Oscar dipped some bread into his minestrone, then popped it into his mouth. 'There would always be unidentified bodies. No dog-tags. The bodies would have been blown to pieces. So you've got a regular body, call it Bernie.' Oscar paused to take in more minestrone.

'Bernie's body goes into a lime pit. The pieces of the guy taking Bernie's place plus fifteen kilos of heroin are placed in a silver aluminium coffin. Yellow labels stating "Do Not Open! Danger! Typhus!" are stuck to it.'

Adam had long ago lost all appetite. His steak sat untouched on the plate. Oscar stared over at it as he pushed the empty soup bowl to one side. 'You gonna eat that?'

Adam shook his head. Oscar reached out and began covering the meat with tomato sauce. 'Then these selected bodies were loaded on to Air America and sent to selected funeral parlours in the States, ones run or controlled by the Mafia.'

The Buddha again paused between mouthfuls. 'Hoover was in on this scam. In fact he had black agents collecting the heroin from the funeral parlours, then moving it into black communities. Hoover figured you could handle the whole problem of Civil Rights by getting the black population so hooked they'd be spaced out most of the time and politically impotent.'

Oscar told him how the heroin was grown in specially designated and protected regions in Laos, and processed in laboratories also within the Golden Triangle. He added the names of men who went on after their Vietnam tour to high office both in the diplomatic service and also the DEA.

He described how the money had found its way back to

Saigon inside heavy plant and military equipment. Again the CIA's own personal airline, Air America, had been utilized. 'A T16 generator, for example, would come in with a red label attached that said "Additional parts must be added".' Oscar's eyes glistened as he recalled the amount of money that arrived on Air America.

'There was a room in the Rex Hotel on Leloi Boulevard about thirty by twenty. If you had clearance you could go in there, sign a chit and take whatever money you'd been authorized. In 1972 alone we spent more than eight hundred million dollars on weapons procurement. I'm talking just about money stored in the back of the Rex Club.'

'Did you use a cut-out to procure the weapons?'

'A third party? Sure. That was set up in Pakistan, run by an army officer called General Zia Ul Haq, later President Zia. When he began to blackmail us, he was knocked off.'

'Twenty years ago, Oscar, I made a documentary about Vietnam that tried to nail once and for all the myth about the MIAs, American servicemen who are still listed as missing in action. What you've just told me could account for . . . how many?'

'Minimum of twenty a month.'

Adam exploded. 'Good God, man, that's twelve hundred bodies over the five years Colby was running this operation.' He stared hard at the man spread out opposite. 'There are still one thousand seven hundred-odd servicemen listed as missing in Vietnam. You've just accounted for nearly all of them.' His anger erupted. 'I don't want to stay at your place tonight, Oscar. I need a shower. I'll find a hotel. I'll come and collect my things tomorrow.'

Oscar reached out a hand. 'Adam. Don't judge, please. It's because of what happened in 'Nam that a man like Victor Rodriguez is my hero.'

Adam leaned towards him. 'Don't you understand, Oscar? It's because of what you and your friends did in 'Nam that your country needs men like Rodriguez. It's because of all that shit you sent back inside those bodies that your country got fucking hooked in the first place.'

Adam punched the tabletop. 'In 1965, there were only fifty-seven thousand known addicts in the entire USA and most of them were comfortably out of sight in black urban ghettos. By late 1969, courtesy of your friends in the CIA, that number had jumped to over three hundred thousand. By 1971, nearly six hundred thousand, with at least fifteen per cent of the GIs in Vietnam on heroin. And instead of giving you a prison sentence, they gave you a chestful of medals and ribbons for your contribution to the war effort.'

Oscar reached out and gripped his arm, but Adam snatched it free and left him to his table of empty plates.

Oscar watched his retreating figure, then spoke softly to himself. 'I know.'

Adam stood in his hotel room, staring out across the Alster lake at a city still pulsating with energy and life. He needed a stiff drink and a friendly voice that would not talk of silver coffins.

He was wondering about flight times to London and Laura when the phone rang.

'How did you know where I was?'

'I suppose I should claim I planted a monitoring device in your left shoe. In fact, the restaurant doorman heard you give the cab driver an address. I brought your stuff round. Figured you might need it.'

Just for a moment, Adam paused. 'Order two large ones. I'll be right down.'

Oscar looked contrite. 'Look, I know what I did was a wicked, disgusting crime. Those were disgusting times.'

He was right. Vietnam had tainted many.

'Brought you some documents that might be interesting.' Oscar looked like a small boy hoping for forgiveness. He reached into a briefcase. 'That's a secret report from one of *my* friends in the Treasury. Bottom line? If the drug cartels were to pull out all the narco money that they currently have invested in government bonds, T-bonds, gilt-edged securities and other Western government stock, there would be a global economic collapse that would make the thirties depression and the crash of 'eighty-seven look mild.'

Another clip of papers came across the table. This one was a report that had been compiled by the German secret service for the chancellor.

'You're getting that four days before the chancellor,' said Oscar laconically. 'It confirms what the US Treasury report says, then it goes further. Top of page five, Adam.'

Adam turned to the respective page and read:

> The cartels therefore have as a working base capital amounts of money that exceed the costs of weaponry systems for nuclear armament globally . . . In this context the drug dealers' aim is to get the industrial companies deep in debit by using the immense financial resources at their disposal to buy, for example, government bonds, which will make central government heavily reliant on such investment to finance budget deficits . . .

Like a demented conjuror, Oscar pulled out sheaf after sheaf of papers – top-secret reports, highly classified briefing papers and 'for your eyes only' documents. How Western governments depended on the drug cartels to fund their budget deficits . . . how the Triads were running Hong Kong . . . how Saddam Hussein bought a piece of CNN before he started the Gulf war . . .

Adam knew that he was trying to buy forgiveness for being part of the long silver train, but he had neither the power nor the will to absolve him.

Finally, he handed Adam an envelope and got up. 'You'll find those photos of your Thanksgiving dinner in the envelope. You could do a lot worse than ask Olaf about Golden Mouth and his buddy. If you need to contact me over the next few weeks I'll be on the Amsterdam number.'

They kissed, then held each other, oblivious of others scurrying by with trolleys and suitcases.

'I've missed you, darling.'

'It's good to be home.'

They had begun to move out of the terminal. Adam checked just inside the revolving door. 'Did Hollywood call?' It was his standard line whenever he returned from a foreign location.

Laura looked at him. 'No, but the Venezuelan ambassador did. Three times.'

'That's a happy coincidence. He was on my list to call. I'm having trouble locating Olaf Nilsson.'

He had first met Olaf Nilsson at the Venezuelan embassy in London, at a meeting arranged by the ambassador, who had believed that the two men shared a common interest in the illegal drugs trade.

Over lunch Olaf had explained that he had been appointed by President Perez to head an internationally co-ordinated anti-drug campaign. The appointment carried the rank of ambassador and underlined Venezuela's determination to fight the narcotics industry. Olaf had seen Adam's two-part documentary on the drugs business and wanted to exchange intelligence information. It was the beginning of a friendship that had strengthened over time as they realized they had several mutual friends, including Oscar Benjamin.

'. . . I was planning to call you today anyway. I'm having trouble locating Olaf and I wondered if you knew where he was?'

Ambassador Da Costa's English accent was flawless. 'Yes, I do. Adam, could you join me for lunch in the usual restaurant?'

'Today? But I've only just arrived home.'

'Yes, I'm aware of that. I would not normally impose . . .'

Adam was fully aware that the ambassador worked on the assumption that all of his calls were bugged by the government in Caracas.

'I would be delighted. One o'clock?'

The ambassador was already seated at a table for two tucked in the corner of the Kensington restaurant. When they were free of the maître d's attention he came straight to the point.

'Our friend Olaf is in great danger. His family are desperate for help. I can do little officially, but I know they would be as grateful as I will if you can do anything. I don't know who else to turn to.'

'But what's the problem?'

'Olaf was arrested six days ago. He is being held at a secret location. I have no details other than that soon he will be facing some serious charges. I can arrange, unofficially, for a complimentary return ticket to Caracas. I know you have just come back home from the States and that you're looking forward to being with your wife, but—'

Adam interrupted, 'What time's the flight?'

CHAPTER TEN

PRISON (1)

'WE'VE BEEN VISITING THE POLICE STATION EVERY DAY. THE police say he's not there. That he's being held in prison.'

'Which prison, Lucas?'

'They won't say.'

He was driving into Caracas from the international airport, with Olaf Nilsson's son, Lucas. He had hoped against hope that this would prove to have been a wasted journey, that Olaf would be at the airport to greet him and tell him all about his wrongful arrest – it was now more than a week since armed police officers had arrived at his office and bundled him into a car.

'Lucas, what was Olaf working on when he disappeared?'

The young man hesitated.

'If you want me to help your family, you have to trust me. Look, I know he's investigating cartel activity in Venezuela. We share information.'

'Yes, I know. It's just that I would be happier if I could first obtain Daddy's permission.'

Despite the situation Adam found it endearing that a son in his mid-twenties could still refer to his father as Daddy.

As they entered the city, Lucas turned off the motorway and headed for San Bernardino and the family home.

'He was investigating the activities of four of the biggest banks in the country. Acquiring evidence on money-laundering activities by the Medellin and Cali cartels.' He drove slowly through his home suburb and then turned into the street where the family lived.

Normally a quiet backwater, it had become a three-ring circus. While Lucas had sat at the airport, his father had been transformed into the country's public-enemy number one. He had been accused of being the mastermind behind a terrorist group. During the previous month there had been a series of car bombs in Caracas. In Venezuela, trembling on the brink of destabilization, such outrages usually heralded only one thing: a coup. The police holding Olaf were controlling the game, and he was about to be moved from Central Police Headquarters. The entire national media had certainly been tipped off.

Having drained Olaf's transfer to the last drop, including interviews with the chief of police Ramón Silva, the press, television and radio pack had moved on to the Nilsson residence and, while a group of grinning police officers looked on, were laying siege to the house.

Adam restrained Lucas from rushing out into the middle of it. 'I won't stay with you. I'll book into the Hotel Avila. Tell this mob that the family will hold a press conference tomorrow evening at eight p.m. at the Hilton. I'll be here tomorrow morning at nine. We have a lot to do, Lucas.'

El Gordo responded to the computer entry at the Hotel Avila just as it had responded earlier to Adam Fraser's recorded arrival at Caracas International Airport. Part of El Gordo's program had been designed by the same intelligence experts who, many years ago, had installed in the north of England the automatic computer monitoring of all phone calls to the United States. If certain key words were spoken, the computer activated and recorded. Within days of his arrival with his film-crew at the home of Patrick Collins, Adam Fraser's name had been entered as a key word on El Gordo.

'The chief of police Ramón Silva is either corrupt or stupid. There can be no other explanation for his conduct.'

Adam's statement at the Nilsson family press conference was a study in how to electrify a room of Venezuelan reporters. He spoke Spanish fluently, but he had chosen to work the press conference at the Hilton with Lucas acting as his interpreter, which gave him twice as long to consider any question.

What had been scheduled as a one-hour meeting with the press continued for over four hours. In a country where government censorship of the news media, like political cor-ruption, is a way of life, the following twenty-four hours were going to be crucial. Adam was gripped by a terrible fear: what he had learned from the Nilssons had convinced him that Olaf had been framed by the bankers he had been close to exposing, and that he was to be murdered. He was being held in the maximum-security prison Reten de Catia, known throughout the country as Sucursal de Infierno de Caracas – 'Hell's chartered branch in Caracas'. Nilsson, the anti-drugs tsar, was being held in a cell with twenty-seven other men. All had been charged with either drug-trafficking or money-laundering offences.

Lucas had visited his father with a list of questions from Adam. Now, playing the media with great care, Adam began to drop some of Nilsson's answers into the interviews: ex-Pre-sident Sanchez and the banker Antonio Perez, the richest and most powerful men in Venezuela, were the biggest names on Olaf's list.

By the following day, with a couple of notable exceptions, the press were giving huge exposure to the Englishman who had come to Venezuela to help a friend and had stunned the country with his allegations of narco-corruption. The exceptions were a TV and radio channel and a newspaper owned by Antonio Perez.

The round of interviews continued. The first wave of news reporters had been replaced by the leader writers and political analysts. One of their number showed Adam an afternoon paper that carried an interview with the minister of justice, Fermin Marmol Alvarez, who had been asked to respond to Fraser's allegation that Nilsson's life was at risk within Catia prison. He had said, 'We all know how dangerous and unstable are the conditions within Catia. I cannot guarantee the life of Nilsson.'

Adam boiled over with a mixture of rage and fear.

'The minister of justice is giving a public invitation to those in this country who wish to silence Olaf Nilsson for ever. It is an invitation to murder. There are men inside Catia who will murder for a packet of cigarettes.' He was certain that the only way he could keep his friend alive was to make such an uproar that it would be impossible to have him murdered. Nothing connected to this matter would stay quiet while he was in town.

The mule man Fernando Salazar had been on his way to play with a friend when he heard a news report on his car radio from the channel's Venezuelan reporter in Caracas. Hearing Adam Fraser's name, Salazar pulled over and listened carefully to the detailed account of the controversy swirling around the documentary-maker.

Salazar knew that this Englishman represented a potential threat to the long-term aims and aspirations of Victor Rodriguez. Now it seemed that fate had given him an ideal opportunity to take care of the man. He pulled his car out into the Saturday evening traffic in Cali and headed back to his office.

The queue seemed never to move forward. They stood immobile in the filth, mud and deep puddles caused by the previous night's ferocious storm. Neither Adam nor Lucas had any idea if he would be allowed in. This was not England with its visiting orders on white slips of paper. It was not the United States where in many places you can pick up a phone, dial a number and talk to an inmate serving life.

On this Sunday morning what passed for officialdom in Catia still declined to stir itself at the prison entrance. Adam studied the people around him. Most were from the shanties that ringed the city. Some were mothers or wives, others, who looked more than capable of committing effortless murder, were quite likely visiting men who had done just that. Eventually the line began to shuffle slowly forward.

At the guard-post, Adam watched the procedure. The woman in front of him handed over her identity card, and her wrist was stamped with a government seal. Lucas told the guard whom they had come to visit. As Adam handed over his passport and the guard conferred in muttered tones with a colleague, he experienced momentary panic. The second prison officer was reading *El Nuevo Pais*. On the front page, under the banner headline, '*Adam Fraser garantiza la inocencia de Nilsson y acusa a gente ligada a bancos y aseguradoras*' was a large photograph of him. A moment later he and Lucas had been waved into a world unlike any other.

The section of the prison they were visiting was clearly being run by the inmates. Not a prison warder was in sight. Lucas approached a man with two prominent knife scars on his face and an expression that indicated he was still looking for the man who had put them there. A muttered conversation took place then a bundle of money changed hands. Scarface turned to a man a good foot taller than himself, said something and the giant took off.

Other supplicants were asking for prisoners. If they had money, Scarface listened, then sent one of his team to collect the man. If they didn't, he swatted them away like gnats. An inmate in his twenties shouted at Adam in an incomprehensible patois. Scarface strode towards the youth and brought down his forehead sharply into the other's face. He slumped to the floor and was dragged away by two of Scarface's assistants.

Adam was shocked at his friend's appearance. Olaf's face had a sickly pallor and his eyes were full of exhaustion. Instinctively, Adam put his arms around him and hugged him tightly. Olaf groaned. 'Sorry, Adam. They've broken some of my ribs.'

More money passed from Lucas to Scarface, who led them to a landing, then departed. Son and father embraced gingerly. Then the three men stood in the open and talked. Above them another fight had broken out. Below a man was pissing against the wall and swearing at invisible demons.

Olaf spoke quietly, pitching his voice below the noise. 'The day you arrived in Caracas a group from another part of the prison entered this wing. They went into cell 407 and killed two prisoners. I'm in cell 417. They realized their mistake the next day. I'm told they were planning to come back that night. Thank God you stood up and said what you did.' He laughed, then winced. He had just seen that Adam was holding a small tape-recorder inside his jacket. 'How the hell did you get that in here?'

'No problem. Just talk into it. Anything you want me to make public.'

'It doesn't matter, they'll still come and beat me up. They went ape yesterday after you attacked the minister of justice.'

'Do you want me to stop?'

Olaf coughed weakly. 'No, of course not. I can handle the beatings. You stick it to them good. You're my insurance, Adam. The more shit you throw, the better my chance of seeing Christmas.' He began to talk quietly into the tape-recorder. Names, dates, bank-account numbers. Complex movements of cash through correspondent accounts – based on his investigations, the Colombian cartels were using a large part of the Venezuelan banking and insurance industries as a vast laundry. Of how he had been lured back from New York for a meeting with a contact in Banco Latino, one of the corrupt banks. And of how, the following day, he had received a 'polite invitation' to go to police headquarters. He talked of what awaited him if he continued to resist Police Chief Silva's demands for a full confession. 'I haven't been charged with anything. Two reasons for that. They are still trying to force me to confess and they are still shopping around for a corrupt judge. That last titbit you'd better keep to yourself for a while. Right now you're all I have, Adam. Lucas told me you tried to phone me from Hamburg. How is Oscar?'

At that, Adam remembered the photographs he was carrying. He produced the stills Oscar had created in Hamburg.

'Just something I'm working on, Olaf. Nothing to do with what we're talking about, but Oscar thought you just might recognize these guys. The one with the gold teeth is called Ricardo Semper. The other man is Alberto Cornejo. Businessmen from Bogotá.'

Olaf stared at the photographs. 'No, Adam. You're wrong.'

'Sorry?'

'This guy with the gold teeth is Fernando Salazar, mule man to the Cali cartel. The other is the chief accountant of the Medellin cartel, Alberto Pastrana. How did you get these photos? I've never seen these two men in the same room, let alone at the same table.'

'It's a long story. Are you sure of this, Olaf?'

'Oh, I'm sure. I'm investigating them. They're up to their necks in the Venezuelan laundries. I've had both of them pointed out to me by Colombian intelligence.' Olaf raised a cautioning hand. 'There's no documentary proof. Not a shred. No one has ever lived to testify against either of these guys. Be careful, Adam. What I've just told you comes from both civil and military intelligence. Nothing has ever been said in the open simply because there isn't any proof. Don't mention their names here in Caracas or we'll both be dead men. Now, put that tape back on. I've just remembered something else about Antonio Perez.'

Back in his room, Adam paced the floor. He wanted to talk to Oscar, share a little of what he had just learned, particularly the information about Salazar and Pastrana. At virtually the same time that he had been sitting in the Dolls' House discussing the pair, Olaf, who had been investigating them, was being arrested and framed by the Venezuelan police. The two Colombians, senior members of drug cartels, had sat down for dinner with a group of America's most powerful men, all brought together with one ambition: to place Patrick Collins in the White House as the next president.

Adam glanced at his watch and made a decision. He left the hotel, headed down the street and eventually found a phone booth. He dialled the code for Amsterdam.

'Hotel Beethoven.'

'I'd like to speak to one of your guests, please, Oscar—' He just stopped himself from asking for Oscar Benjamin. Outside Germany Oscar used a different name. 'Oscar Montague.'

'Mr Montague is out at the moment. Would you care to leave a message?'

'Please tell him that Adam Fraser called from Caracas and will call back later.'

As he turned back into the hotel, Adam congratulated himself on not having phoned through its switchboard where calls were monitored by local police officers. He had no way of knowing that it had been a wasted effort. El Gordo was already relaying details of his brief call to Holland to its central control in Bogotá.

'Olaf. This man Ramiro Helmeyer has accused you. He says that you and he planned and carried out the car bombings together.'

'Right now, Adam, I'm in the same cell as Helmeyer along with another twenty-two people. We have to take it in turns to let a couple of men stretch out on the floor for a while. Helmeyer's been doing a lot of talking: before he confessed, he was repeatedly tortured. Before he accused me he was tortured again.'

'What kind of torture?'

'Electrodes to the genitals, then they got a bucket of gas . . .'

'Gas? What kind of gas?'

'Petroleum. Petrol. They held it over his head. A policeman said, "Now are you going to tell us that Nilsson was involved in the car bombs?" The poor son of a bitch had no choice.'

Adam stabbed the off button.

The press reporters at this particular conference included some from the Perez-owned media. One of their number in particular affected total indifference at the evidence that Adam was producing. 'Why did you insult our chief of police?'

Adam stared at her. 'You can ask a question like that after what you've just heard? Who do you think authorized the torture sessions? Go and ask your chief of police how he can afford a wardrobe full of two-thousand-dollar suits on his government pay.'

Afterwards Lucas took Adam to meet with more reporters in Caracas who wanted further information. He returned to the Hotel Avila at three in the morning, and threw clothes in a suitcase. Lucas would call for him at six a.m., when they planned to drive to Valencia to meet a friend of his father's who might have information.

Soon after six a.m. they set off. They took the road to the interior and began to climb out of the valley. Suddenly they heard the wail of police sirens and two police cars were alongside them. Lucas was forced to the edge of the motorway, a police car back and front. Officers fanned out. One man in a black leather coat, gun cocked, stood close to the car and shouted at Lucas, who turned to Adam. 'They want you to get out of the car.'

'Why?'

'You must go with them to police headquarters.'

'Why?'

'They want to question you about the statements you've been making to the press and TV.'

'Lucas, please tell them that they have had four days to question me. Tell them we have a meeting in Valencia.'

Again the police began to shout.

'They say their orders are to bring you directly to police headquarters.'

'Ask them who gave the order.'

A moment later: 'The chief of police, Ramón Silva.'

'And if I refuse?'

'They will take you forcibly.'

'Please tell them their "invitation" is accepted, but make it clear that I am not going to get out of this car. I will go with them, but in this car and with you driving.'

Another *tête-à-tête* followed. Again Lucas turned to Adam. 'They want to know why you insist on going to police headquarters in this car rather than theirs.'

'I want to make sure that I don't get shot trying to escape.'

Fraser was supposed to be in London, not Venezuela. Victor Rodriguez sat absolutely still, deep in thought. Then, he leaned forward, flicked a switch and spoke into the intercom. 'Among the European disks there is a file on Oscar Montague, a.k.a. Benjamin, a.k.a. Guilderstern. A copy, please.'

Now that the Englishman's friend had a second name, lots of second names, Rodriguez remembered him. The Cambridge symposium on economic crime. They had had a long conversation and afterwards Rodriguez had made some discreet inquiries. His secretary came in carrying a sheaf of papers. 'Thank you, Carlotta. I would be grateful if you would check the monitoring reports to see if a Señor Adam Fraser made any calls after this one to Holland at three thirty-seven yesterday.'

'Of course.'

Rodriguez began to study Oscar's file. He paused over a psychiatrist's report written after the Korean war. Oscar had been concerned when he had experienced an orgasm after killing a North Korean. Rodriguez noted the doctor's observation: 'Reassured Captain Benjamin. Perfectly normal experience.' Oscar's various narcotics activities on behalf of the United States government were all detailed, also his involvement in the capture and subsequent killing of Che Guevara, his organization of the Swedish security group who carried out the murder of Olaf Palme, his part in the Phoenix Program in Vietnam that resulted in the killing of over twenty thousand Vietnamese, Operation Long Silver Train, the Aldo Moro kidnap and murder. Eventually he reached the section which confirmed the enduring bureaucratic inefficiency of the CIA: one section considered Oscar an asset, a second was actively seeking to kill him. Rodriguez snapped the file shut and reached for a phone.

*   *   *

Thirty minutes after his arrest Adam Fraser and Maria, a police translator, were sitting in an interrogation room in the basement of police headquarters. The exact location to which Nilsson had been brought when he had accepted a similar 'invitation'. Lucas had been dismissed.

Maria was painting her fingernails. Two plastic cups of surprisingly good coffee were brought in, then an officer in his early twenties joined them. He sat down and began to chat up the middle-aged Maria. She brightened and listened wide-eyed as he told her that Adam was the ring-leader in a plot to overthrow the government, destabilize the country and place the military in power.

Adam wondered who his fellow 'plotters' were – other than Olaf, of course. He watched the pair discussing him. They lit one cigarette after another, sent out for more coffee, chatted about the movies they had seen recently. It was obviously the beginning of something special.

Salazar picked thoughtfully at his gold teeth with a match. 'Excellent, Ramón. Might I suggest that after he makes a statement you transfer him from your police headquarters to Reten de Catia pending further investigations? Of course I know that Fraser's English. Look, I'm not talking about a long time. Just overnight. By the time the British ambassador stirs himself the matter will have been taken care of. Good.'

Fernando Salazar ran through a mental list of employees currently residing in Catia – so many to choose from, so many who would be eager to please.

Some three-quarters of an hour had passed when the young officer was replaced by another. Number two was less talkative. In fact, he said nothing at all, just stared unblinkingly at Adam. After a further fifteen minutes, number one reappeared. Chief of Police Ramón Silva wanted Señor Fraser to make a full statement, he said. Speaking through Maria, Adam told the man that he had said publicly all that he desired to say on the Nilsson case. However, he would make a statement on the *coup d'état* that was planned to take place shortly after the elections to be held in a few weeks' time. He was prepared to quote from intelligence sources.

'No further phone calls, Señor, but I thought you should see this.'

It was Carlotta, holding the daily computer printout. El Gordo's brother, in the border town of Cúcuta, had noted a series of messages from the police headquarters in Caracas. One was an arrest-and-apprehend-on-sight directive to all officers. The name on it was Adam Fraser. Rodriguez made a phone call to another part of Bogotá. He spoke for less than a minute. Seven minutes later a fax machine in his office sprang into life. Page after page began to spew out. He crossed to the machine and began to read. 'My word, Mr Fraser. You *have* been busy.'

One of the many benefits of having Andrew Sinclair as counsellor to the Cartel of Cartels was that Bogotá and New York were on the same time. Ever cautious, Rodriguez began by encoding just two words. '*Buenos dias.*' The reply came through instantly. 'Good morning.' Reassured that Sinclair was at his desk, he began to encode an edited account of what he had learned from his sources. As he finished each page it was transmitted. The last one had been sent only thirty seconds before when a one-page response came back from Sinclair.

Rodriguez put it under the decoding sheet and read: 'Subject must be protected at all costs. Arrange for his safe removal from your neighbour soonest. Regards.'

It had been precisely what Rodriguez had expected. Sinclair had concluded that not a breath of scandal should fall on Fraser's head. It was public knowledge that he was working on a documentary on the preacher. Any adverse publicity might be fatal to the campaign. That Fraser was making large waves wash over four major cartel laundries made imperative his removal from the eye of the storm he had created.

Rodriguez made a brief telephone call to another part of Bogotá. It was ten thirty-five a.m.

*   *   *

Having made a three-page statement outlining details of the planned Army coup, Adam and Maria were shown into the office of Ramón Silva. He was small, bald and portly, with wide-set eyes and a flat nose. His two-thousand-dollar grey-flannel suit shone in the muted light of his office. Silva gestured to two seats in front of his desk, then continued to read the statement that Adam had just made.

Silva looked up. 'These things that you have said about me in the press. Why?'

'If you've read them, you know why. What I want to know is why I've been forced to come here.'

Silva shrugged his shoulders. 'I needed to question you.'

In one of his documentaries, Adam had met a man who had had electric shocks to his genitals. The memory returned, acutely: the man had never looked up from the floor. Adam forced himself to stare directly into Silva's face. 'Olaf Nilsson is innocent. The only evidence you have against him was extracted by torture from the man responsible for the car bombs—' He was interrupted by one of the many phones on the police chief's desk. Silva snatched it up.

'Yes. He is here. Yes, I am interrogating him now. But I have much more I wish to ask him about. I'm sure he'll talk after a night in Catia.'

Silva's demeanour changed as he listened to the response. The bombast drained away. 'Yes, yes, I understand. No, you have my personal guarantee.'

He slammed down the phone and stared angrily at Adam, who struggled to keep poker-faced. Silva had clearly been warned off. The man who had been about to send Adam Fraser to Catia, to his death, was charm personified.

'I hope you have not been too inconvenienced, Señor Fraser. Can I have you driven to Valencia?'

'No, thank you.'

Silva extended his hand. Adam, with self-disgust welling up from within, shook hands.

*   *   *

Before the end of the day Victor Rodriguez, the man responsible for Adam Fraser's freedom, was reading a copy of his statement. A coup in Venezuela was likely. He wondered if Fraser's source was Oscar Benjamin. If it was, then the documentary-maker would soon be in need of a new informant. One entry in Oscar's dossier had suggested the value of his immediate death.

Like Victor Rodriguez, Oscar never took a cab all the way home. When abroad he took the same care. He paid off the driver on the corner of Beethovenstraat in Amsterdam and was on high alert as he approached the hotel. Two men were apparently window-shopping across the street: evidently an object of extraordinary interest had caught their attention in a display of industrial vacuum-cleaners. Timing his approach to coincide with a slow-moving tram, Oscar was well into the foyer before it had passed the front door. The two men were still staring into the shop window opposite.

'Ah, Mr Montague. A number of phone messages for you.'

Interesting: he had told only one person that he would be in Amsterdam.

'Mr Adam Fraser phoned you yesterday from Caracas. Said he'd phone back, but has not yet done so.'

That was the one person taken care of.

'A number of other calls. All local, asking when you would be back. No name given. I told them we had no idea.'

'Thank you, Jaap. I'm going to shower then vanish again for a couple of days. Please take any messages and keep my room for me. It's paid for until the end of the week. I'll be back before then.'

Forty-five minutes later the men who had been given the contract saw what they had been waiting for. Signs that the guest in room 317 had returned. The curtains were being pulled together. Crossing the road they calmly entered the hotel. The reception desk was temporarily unattended. They already knew the room number and, sure enough, the key was absent from its hook. Helping themselves to the master key, they chose the stairs rather than the lift. Pausing at the door they heard sounds of an unmistakable activity. They grinned at each other, then one opened the door and the other took aim.

Two bodies on the bed were noisily preoccupied. The silenced gun made far less sound as the entire clip was emptied into the writhing forms. Within minutes the two men were out of the hotel, in their car, and out of the city and on the A10 road to Schiphol airport. Indeed, they were out of the country long before the bodies of the hotel receptionist and his girlfriend were discovered. It had seemed to Jaap an opportunity too good to miss. He had grabbed Paula from her cleaning duties on the first floor and they had been inside Oscar's room only minutes after he had left the hotel quietly by the rear entrance and hurried across the sports park.

In the Hotel Avila Adam Fraser turned on the lunchtime news. The first item contained clips of film taken at the first press conference, then a montage of press pages followed by the newsreader declaring: 'The English film-maker and author Adam Fraser has been declared *persona non grata* by the President and expelled from Venezuela. The reasons for his expulsion were the continuing disrespect he showed to the President and the Venezuelan people during his recent visit. Fraser is now in Bogotá.'

The following morning Adam attempted to leave a country that, officially, he had already left. In the hotel foyer he met Lucas. Some other friends had come along for the ride – in four cars, from police headquarters. Their spokesman approached. 'Mr Fraser. My orders are to make sure that you are not troubled on your journey to the airport.'

'You really didn't need to go to all this trouble. I don't suppose we could stop off at Catia prison and pick up Olaf Nilsson?'

'I'm sorry, Mr Fraser, your friend is not mentioned in my orders. My instructions are to ensure that you leave our country safely.'

On the journey to the airport Adam mentally checked

through the long list of things to do that he and Lucas had compiled. People to contact, media to alert, senators and congressmen to be lobbied. Then he remembered someone else. 'Lucas, will you please call my wife, Laura, and tell her I'm coming home a little earlier than planned.'

He had been so focused on Olaf's dreadful predicament that he was long airborne before he recalled his friend's response to the photographs he had shown him. So Gold Teeth was Fernando Salazar, mule man to the Cali cartel, and the other was the chief accountant of the Medellin cartel, Alberto Pastrana. Olaf had identified them from intelligence sources, nothing known about them on the record.

Adam stared at the photographs. He opened the flight table on the seat next to his own. The plane was scarcely half full and he had a row to himself. He began to spread out the series of photographs just as Oscar had, recalling the old man's rage at not being able to find the reason for his hero having been placed way down the dinner table.

Adam moved the photographs around. Rodriguez had not been the target. Patrick Collins, the man who would be president, had been the main agenda for the photographer on the roof. Collins, and the two 'businessmen' from Bogotá sitting on either side of him.

Rodriguez read an apologetic report from the Frenchman who had placed the contract on his behalf. 'Without a current photograph there is always a risk of mistaken identity.' Quite how the two men had been able to mistake an athletic young man in his late twenties and his nubile girlfriend for Oscar Benjamin was not addressed. Next time, Rodriguez would personally select the hit team. He concluded that Benjamin would think it had been a CIA attempt.

Oscar thought nothing of the kind. The mere fact that Adam had attempted unsuccessfully to phone him from Venezuela had been enough to propel him out of the Beethoven. Unlike his English friend, Oscar knew all about El Gordo. He felt the paranoia rising as he travelled back to Hamburg and the safety of the Dolls' House. If they wanted him dead they felt threatened – but why? How could one old CIA agent represent a threat to anyone?

CHAPTER ELEVEN

PRISON (2)

THE DOOR OF NUMBER TEN OPENED. WITH OPINION-POLL ratings now in the low twenties, the Prime Minister had aged dramatically in the thirty months since his landslide victory. He looked grey and pouchy next to his guest, Patrick Collins. The waiting reporters on the other side of the street called for a brief statement and the two men walked over. Barry's mike was just a little closer than the others.

Adam Fraser seized the moment. 'Prime Minister, tomorrow you're facing a vote of confidence in the Commons. Today you're visited by the most famous preacher in the world. Any connection?'

'Oh, I don't think I need divine intervention to deal with the opposition. This has been an opportunity to step outside party politics and share thinking on global issues with a global leader.'

'*Another* global leader,' hissed the Prime Minister's spin doctor to his favoured sycophants in the British media.

'Mr Collins?' asked Adam.

'I thank the Prime Minister for his kind remarks. This is not a political visit. I'm here to learn, to help where I can, but before a man can help he has to learn.'

'That will make a great campaign commercial,' said John Reilly.

Teresa Collins slapped him on the back and laughed.

'And I bet that's exactly what his advisers are telling the Prime Minister.'

They were watching the BBC news coverage of the British section of the Collins global tour organized by Andrew Sinclair, part of a carefully orchestrated plan to gain the evangelist increased media coverage of a specific nature. They had yet to realize it, but the American public were watching a transformation: the preacher was becoming a politician. This was being achieved partly by visits to a number of heads of state and political leaders, which added gravitas and authority to an already charismatic figure.

After the global tour the Collins bi-weekly syndicated newspaper column would take on a distinctly more political tone. So would the chat-shows out of Boston and the church services from Florida. Then in April there was the USA tour to publicize the book that was now under discussion in their London hotel. Adam and his crew were setting up to film part of the strategy meeting on its launch. Apparently preoccupied with note-taking, Sinclair strolled over. 'Welcome back to civilization. Any news from Venezuela?'

After what he had learned about two of the men who had sat at the same dinner table as Sinclair, Adam had decided on a circumspect approach. 'Not good news. Olaf Nilsson's been charged on ten counts.' Then, on impulse, he confided, 'I'm going to ask Pat for help. I've pressed all the buttons I can reach in the United States and I'm sure that he would like to help a man who has dedicated his life to fighting the drug cartels.'

If he had expected any significant reaction he was disappointed. Sinclair responded calmly. 'That's an excellent idea, Adam, but as you know, it's crucial at the moment that Pat holds focus on this overseas trip. I think you should wait until he returns to the States. There will be a window in, say, two weeks. Meanwhile, I'm not without buttons myself but I can't do anything until we've completed the European section of this trip in three days' time.'

'I'll be very grateful, Andrew, for any help. Olaf's family are desperate.'

Susanna approached. 'We're ready when you are, Mr Sinclair.'

Adam felt relieved. Firstly he had just eliminated Andrew Sinclair from any conspiracy that might be gathering around the Collins-for-President campaign, and he was sure now that Sinclair, with his formidable army of connections, would be able to help Olaf Nilsson.

'Thanks very much, Andrew. It's deeply appreciated.'

'In three days' time. I'll see what I can do.'

Sinclair went to sit with the others and Susanna looked questioningly at Adam.

'I'll tell you later,' he said. 'Right, let's film.'

Moments later the camera rolled as Sinclair picked up a copy of Collins's manuscript.

'You have what amounts to an election manifesto wrapped up in one man's vision of what the future could be like. Title?'

Reilly had been rocking gently in his wheelchair as Sinclair had been speaking. He stopped and looked across at him. '*One Nation Under God*?'

There were murmurs of pleasure from Pat and Teresa Collins.

For a moment Sinclair's face was expressionless. Then an ever-broadening smile appeared. 'Beautiful, Johnny.' He wrote it on a small pad. Reilly did not see him add the words 'Test with focus groups'.

'The book tour,' said Sinclair. 'Coast to coast. North to south. Treat it like a full-scale rehearsal for the campaign.'

The ever-prudent Victor Rodriguez had celebrated New Year with family and friends on the twenty-ninth of December.

The previous year had been kind to him and his associates.

The cartels had once again grossed in excess of five hundred billion dollars. The three Ps – powder, people and paper – continued to be readily available. As long as that situation prevailed, he could view the coming year with serenity. The chairman of the board had much to be serene about.

Cartel penetration of the DEA, from high executive to coastguard patrol, continued to ensure that the agency's best efforts were constantly thwarted. In fact, every organization involved in the drugs war – the CIA, the FBI, Customs, Treasury, Justice, State – had been infiltrated. The departments of Defense, Agriculture and the Interior also contained cartel informants. Long before Sinclair's audacious plan had been unveiled, the cartel had had an impressive list of countries in its pocket. Now, the greatest prize of all was within touching distance. Rodriguez glanced at his watch. Precisely on cue he heard a knock at the door of his hotel suite. He crossed the living room and opened it. 'Andrew. Welcome. I thought the television coverage of his visit to the Prime Minister was most satisfactory. Drink?'

'No thanks, Victor. Before I give you a briefing on Collins's meeting with the Prime Minister, I think we should deal with a problem that Fraser has created. It requires immediate action.'

'Have I ever told you that being married to you is like not being married?'

'Laura, my love, it's very early in the day for a Zen lesson.'

'Hey, just because you get to take the piss out of the Prime Minister on the telly.'

'He's such an unctuous bastard. Couldn't resist it. Now, come on, do you want to go out for a meal this evening or not?'

'Course I do, but when my husband says, "Come out for a meal so that we can be on our own and have a quiet conversation," I feel like we're having an affair. You remember all those snatched meetings that always began with 'How long do we have?"'

'Of course. It's just that we never seem to have those quiet times any more. Either this place is full of people or I'm getting on a plane or you're going to some rep theatre in Middle England to look at the next Olivier. I'm flying out tomorrow evening to cover the next leg of Patrick Collins's tour and I'd like to take my best friend out for a meal.'

The telephone rang. Adam sighed.

It was Olaf. Released from prison in the middle of the night, he had taken the first flight out to Miami with his family. 'All charges dropped,' he said. 'Warrants for the arrest of Antonio Perez and seven of his colleagues, Police Chief Ramón Silva suspended, the trial date for former President Sanchez will be set soon. I owe you my life, Adam. The Nilssons are for ever in your debt.'

'You owe me nothing.'

They had chatted awkwardly, celebrating what they both knew was a miracle.

'Olaf, I'll be coming back to Florida in a few weeks. We must meet up soon.'

'Just call, my friend. I'll be there. All my love to Laura.'

After he had hung up, he was thoughtful. He mentally ran through a variety of possible plans, all involved high-risk strategies. When he told Laura, she reacted fiercely. 'Adam, you think you've seen two faces from the drug cartels. Who gave you those faces? Olaf. You saw what happened to Olaf. You know what nearly *happened* to him. I'd like a live husband. With a full set of testicles.'

'Put that way, you have a point. Come on, let's eat.'

They sat under the same tree in the Harrow churchyard where they had lain in 1971.

' "A jug of wine, a loaf of bread and thou . . ." '

'Not quite. Pink champagne, a picnic hamper from Fortnum and Mason, a couple of joints, and then thou.'

There had been a macabre symmetry to the conversation between Sinclair and Rodriguez. To one of Fraser's friends it had given back his life and his freedom. But it had also agreed that, if the opportunity presented itself, another friend should be killed.

Sinclair had anticipated that Rodriguez would agree with his analysis of the Nilsson problem. Now he told the chairman of the board why he had indicated to Fraser that it would be at least three days before he could possibly help.

'It ensures that if you are able to have this man freed, say in the next twenty-four hours, there is no connection between Fraser asking me for help and "good fortune" duly obliging. As Fraser may then regard me as a friend, he might confide in me if he ever stumbles on any aspect of the Project.'

Rodriguez continued to weigh the options. 'I assume you fear Fraser kicking up a major international protest if Nilsson is killed in prison?' he said.

'When you first told me he was in Venezuela I was alarmed. He was supposed to be here in London preparing for the Collins visit. I thought for a moment that somehow he had got an inkling of the Project. It transpired, of course, that he'd only gone there on a mercy mission. I want nothing to deflect from the Collins campaign. Just consider the uproar Fraser caused in Venezuela merely because Nilsson had been imprisoned. It's too dangerous. He's a loose cannon, a maverick. The one way to contain him is to keep him focused on the film he's making. I recognize the type – an obsessive personality.'

'We will have to write off four good laundries in Venezuela, Andrew – plus, of course, a number of excellent people. But you're right, the alternative would be to risk losing a far bigger prize. And Fraser's other friend, Oscar Benjamin?'

'No question, Victor. After what you've shown me in his dossier. Any opportunity you get. Close the deal.'

Since returning from Amsterdam, Oscar's already low-profile life had become subterranean. He read with interest the various Dutch press accounts of the police investigations into the double murder in the Hotel Beethoven. The police inquiry had established the presence of 'two men of Latin-American appearance' who had come calling for a visitor named Oscar Montague, and had concluded that the two deaths were due either to 'mistaken identity' or that the victims had been 'unfortunate witnesses to the forcible abduction of Oscar Montague'. The file was left open. What irked Oscar particularly was that he would have to change his false passports and that he had lost the use of an excellent hotel. He did not answer the phone in case Adam was calling yet again from Venezuela. There were other ways for him to make contact. Adam knew them.

Oscar glanced up at the line of clocks on the walls of his inner sanctum, each giving him the time in a different country. He needed to talk to someone, to shake off this recurring feeling of being always on the outside. But even deep throats, spooks, spies and agents take holidays and, in this first week of the new year, Langley was on automatic pilot. He accessed his computer file of special contacts – the nearest thing he had to a personal friends' file – and began to punch out the names. He stopped when he reached the contact numbers for Adam Fraser. His hand went to the phone, then rested on the receiver.

Maybe Adam was still in the States, working on his projects about the preacher. Maybe he was still going Latin. Or maybe he just didn't want to talk to a fat old man who had assisted in the mutilation of dead servicemen's bodies and helped pack heroin into them. Oscar switched off the computer and stood up. He knew where to go to enjoy the company of a fellow human being. A few minutes later he left the Dolls' House and headed for the bright lights of the Reeperbahn. At least the whores would still be working.

If you work in London in the week after New Year's Day you usually get an office to yourself. Adam was surprised to have company. 'Susanna. If I didn't know better I'd think you sleep here.'

'What makes you think you *do* know better?' she snapped back. 'Maybe here's a little more exciting right now. Don't worry, Adam. I'm still terribly proud to be part of your documentary crew. I'm double-checking I've got everything before we fly to Germany. What brings you in?'

'Just passing through.' He ran his finger along a shelf.

'What are you looking for?'

'The contacts files on the drugs two-parter.'

Susanna moved to another shelf and pulled out a file, which she handed to him.

'Brilliant.' Adam opened it and began to leaf through the contents.

'What are you looking for?'

'The woman who lives out in Hertfordshire. Venezuelan. Prison visitor to some people serving sentences for drug offences.'

Susanna snapped her fingers. 'Francesca Luisa Palaéz.'

Adam clapped his hands in delight. 'Well done.'

She picked up a card index from her desk. 'There we are. Shall I phone her?'

'No. It was just bugging me that I couldn't remember her name. Thanks, Su. I can forget about it now.'

Susanna got off the desk and sat opposite him in her own chair. 'Now, just a minute, what's going down here?'

'Nothing.'

'Come on, Adam. This is Susanna. I know you. You're following up a lead, aren't you?'

Adam leaned against the wall and took a deep breath. 'After Olaf was released and phoned me, I was talking over the whole situation with Laura. I told her that I was wondering how I might get some evidence on Salazar and Pastrana. She was alarmed at the prospect. She reminded me of my narcotics doco, which made me think of Francesca, only I couldn't remember her name. Where was I?'

'Laura's alarm.'

'Yeah, well, of course I reassured her. The idea of one man taking on the cartels is the stuff of fiction. I deal in facts. End of story.'

Susanna said nothing, but got up and brought out a bottle of gin, a couple of glasses and tonic water. Adam watched as she poured two stiff drinks.

'Su, it's nine forty-five in the morning.'

'So?' She passed a glass to him. He stared at her as she drank half of hers in one gulp, then refilled the glass. His was still untouched.

'Why?' Adam asked.

'Because it isn't every day I hear you say you've lost your balls, Adam. It's *because* you deal in facts, in reality, that you have to go after Salazar and Pastrana. It's because you, above all people, know how those shits screw up the planet.'

She finished her second drink in one swallow and again refilled her glass.

He reached out a hand to restrain her. 'Su, I can't talk to you about this if you're pissed and I'm sober.'

She knocked his hand away. 'Better start getting pissed then.'

'Why are you so angry with me?'

'I just told you. Because you've lost your balls. Because you and Laura sat and had a little *tête-à-tête* and decided that as you're obviously rushing towards your dotage you should settle for nice, cosy, safe little films and let all the fucking reality of this story go down the Swanee.' She finished her drink and put down the glass.

'So you're telling me that two senior members of the drug cartels sat down and had dinner with Patrick Collins, the man who's going to try and get himself elected president this year, and you're not going to do anything about it? Not even refer to it in your two-part doco on Collins the evangelist? Not mention it in your special *The Making of a President*?'

'I've no proof that Olaf is right about these men.'

'Then go out and *get* the fucking proof.'

'Why me? Why do *I* have to save the world, just because you say I should? I'm a middle-aged man who wants to live longer, who wants what other middle-aged men have. A bucket of money – no, a bathful. I'd like to go to a smart tailor. I'd like to own an Aston Martin. I'd like to own land—'

'And build Laura a house in the country?'

'Yes, a fucking big one! Get some coffee inside you, you stupid bitch.'

'If you lose your balls over this, Adam, then that's just what I am. A stupid workaholic bitch. I've given you and your documentaries some of the best years of my life. I haven't done that so that I can be here to watch the cop-out.'

'Then piss off. Get another job, another life. Get someone else.'

'If I did, with my luck it would probably be a Belgian ski instructor with a very small dick.'

Suddenly his anger was transformed to helpless laughter. Susanna joined in. Adam picked up his glass, drank, then looked at her. 'Now what about getting me that phone number?'

Francesca remembered him well. How could you forget working on a documentary entitled *Here's a Thousand Dollars. Stuff It Up Your Nose*? For a number of years she had been a prison visitor: her clientele was exclusively Latin-American women, mules who had failed in their bid to bring consignments of cocaine into Britain. She had opened a number of doors for Adam; now he wanted her to open some more.

'If what I've been told is true, Fran, then it's only right that you should be aware of the potential risk. Certainly your clients need to be made aware. It's very delicate. I don't want to alert anyone in Colombia, but this man, for example, appears not only to have a variety of names but a variety of professions. Sometimes he's a respectable businessman in Bogotá called Ricardo Semper, at others he's the mule man for the Cali cartel and his name is Fernando Salazar.'

Francesca studied the photograph. 'It's the old problem, isn't it? How to obtain information without giving any away.'

'Exactly.'

'This will take a little time. How long do I have?'

'Then you'll help me?'

'Of course. We can't beat the cartels, but that doesn't mean we shouldn't try. I owe that at least to the women I visit.'

'I'm flying to Germany this evening but I'll be back by the end of the week. This could be important, Fran – it could also be dangerous.'

Francesca laughed. 'For a little old lady living in her thatched cottage? Don't be silly. Leave it with me, Adam. Another coffee? It's best Colombian.'

Since the events in Venezuela Adam not only understood Oscar's paranoia, he had begun to feel it. When Oscar gave him a series of instructions which he would have mocked previously, he accepted them without question.

'Leave the hotel by the main entrance. Take a cab to St Michael's. Walk from there to the Bismarck monument. There's a kiosk nearby, get a copy of *Frankfurter Allgemeine*. Gaze at the monument for a few minutes, then go to the little coffee bar on Helgoländer, order a coffee and read your paper, minimum fifteen minutes. Stroll down the Reeperbahn. Do not accept any of the various offers that will be made to you. Then take a taxi—'

'To the Dolls' House?'

'No, you dumb English bastard. To your hotel. Then go directly back to your room and wait for my call.'

Adam returned to his room to find Oscar raiding the mini-bar.

'I lied about the call,' Oscar said, by way of greeting. 'That was just in case they also had your line on an external tap. They don't, and there are no bugs in the room.'

'Fine, so we have nothing to worry about.'

'We have everything to worry about, my friend. You were followed by a minimum team of four. You must do nothing to indicate I live in Hamburg. No sudden disappearances. No unusual behaviour. You are here to film the evangelist Patrick Collins meeting senior German personalities in Hamburg and the chancellor in Bonn. You are not here to help these motherfuckers kill me. Now I'll tell you what happened in Amsterdam, and you can tell me what happened in Venezuela.'

Thirty minutes later the mini-bar was empty, and both men were a little wiser, if perplexed.

'That's why I put photographs of Salazar and Pastrana

through the CFR. Olaf was right when he said there were no data on those two. Find out who invited them to that dinner. Come to think of it, find out who invited Victor Rodriguez.'

'You still think he's on the side of the angels, Oscar?'

'I know he is. It's rare in my business to meet someone you believe in. Somebody wanted to finger Rodriguez . . . Maybe that's why he stayed away at the end of the table . . .' Oscar punched an open palm. 'Too many questions. Who had you arrested? Who had you released before that police chief could put you into Catia?'

'Well, come to that, who tried to have you murdered in Amsterdam?'

'That one's easy. The cartels. They control El Gordo.'

'Are you sure about this El Gordo?'

'Yeah. Quite sure. The intelligence world knows it exists. The evidence for some form of computer monitoring by the cartels is overwhelming. No one knows where it's based – take my word for it. Never call me from anywhere in Latin America.'

'Why would they want you killed?'

Oscar got up and began to move slowly around the room. He stared at the carpet intently as if seeking from it the answer to Adam's question. Finally, he said, 'There has to be something that links me to whatever it is they're doing. In some way they regard me as a threat but I don't know what it is.'

There was a pause, then Adam said, 'I've been researching Patrick Collins for a long time. I've collated everything that's ever been written about him. On top of that, I've interviewed dozens of people, accessed a whole rack of documents, including, thanks to you, many classified ones. I think it's time you fed everything I've got into your computers and cross-referenced it against your own life – not just the bits you've told me about, the censored stuff as well. Let's see what you have in common with him, Oscar.'

Oscar grunted. 'Not a hell of a lot, but sure, have it sent to my post restante in Rome.' He walked towards the door. 'From here on, my friend, take extra care – oh, I've just had a thought.' He beamed. 'Something you might do when you and your crew get to Paris.'

Rodriguez read the report from the surveillance team with increasing frustration. Obviously Fraser's friend Oscar must be based in Paris and if those following Fraser had exercised just a little more expertise, Rodriguez would now have a precise location and that particular problem would have been eliminated. But the team had lost Fraser, which – since he was unaware that he was being followed all over Europe and the Middle East while he filmed the Collins trip – was little short of rank incompetence.

Now, the film-crew were back in London, preparing to return to Florida. The surveillance team would have to do better next time Fraser visited Paris.

The day before Adam and his crew were due to catch their flight to Miami, he had a phone call from Francesca, who wanted to see him. On the journey to north London she explained how she had approached the problem.

'First, I thought, if this man Salazar was involved with the Cali cartel mules, then that would be the best place to start and he would be the best bet. Pastrana, you said, was chief accountant of the Medellin cartel, unlikely to have come into contact with the women. Second, Señor Salazar has an impressive mouthful of gold. Easy enough to establish if any of the men responsible for using these mules had that many gold teeth, not something one would forget.'

Francesca had not shown the photographs to any of the prisoners, just made mental notes as the few who would talk described the men who had persuaded them to make 'just this one journey'. Some women's stories she had discounted because the man involved did not appear to match up to Fernando Salazar, and others because they were too frightened of what would happen to them, or their families in Colombia, if they talked.

They walked across the courtyard towards the visiting room.

Adam looked round at the modern buildings. He remembered the old prison that had stood here with its mock Warwick Castle front.

It helped that he spoke the prisoner's language and understood a little of her culture, but he left most of the talking to Francesca. It was clear that if this woman trusted anyone, she trusted Francesca.

'You must understand. This is not official. Adam is a film-maker. He is not a policeman.'

The woman nodded gravely then held out her hand. 'May I see the photograph, please?'

Adam watched her closely as it was pushed across the desk. He saw recognition in her eyes and a sad, sardonic smile.

'Yes, that's him,' she said. 'His name is Fernando Salazar.'

Adam's heart raced. In truth, part of him had been almost hoping for failure – the sensible part that valued the quiet, safe life.

'I know what you will want me to do. To make statements. Maybe to testify. To go public on this. I will do these things, but I want something from you.'

Adam and Francesca looked at her. She was still staring at the photograph, but she was far away.

She looked directly at Adam. 'I want you to go to Cali and find Carla, my daughter, and bring her to London. I want you to look after her until I get out of here. She is only twelve years old, but a good girl. Francesca tells me you are married, but that you have no children?'

Adam was open-mouthed. He managed a nod.

'Then, if you agree, you will have a little daughter for a while. But only a while, you understand?'

Francesca, too, had been unprepared for this. 'Mónica, I know how worried you are about Carla, but this idea of yours is impractical. Adam travels all over the world. Laura, his wife, has a full-time job. How does Adam get her out of Colombia? What of her schooling? Her friends? The language problem? The climate, the culture . . .' Francesca trailed off, over-whelmed at the problems she was putting to a woman who, one Sunday afternoon, had had the bad luck to sit by the fountain in the main square at Cali and meet the kindly Fernando Salazar.

While Francesca had been talking, Mónica had been doodling on a piece of paper. She continued to draw as Adam weighed in. 'Mónica, Francesca is right. Look, I'm sorry that you're in here. I'm equally sorry about your daughter, but this is a crazy scheme.'

'Sometimes people in Britain reach out to help others. Children from Bosnia have come here. Children from Somalia. From Nigeria. From lots of countries. I know – I've seen it on the TV in here.'

Adam tried another line of reasoning. 'Look, Mónica, apart from anything else, consider this. Suppose, just suppose, I agreed to your suggestion—'

Francesca interrupted. 'Adam, don't be crazy.'

'No, it's all right, Fran. Look, just suppose I said OK. Now suppose that somehow I persuade my wife that we should look after your daughter until you get out of prison. Right? Then suppose I'm able to get her out of Colombia.'

Mónica looked at him triumphantly. 'Then I will testify for you. Give evidence in public against this man.'

Adam leaned towards her. 'And his well paid defence lawyers will destroy you. They will accuse you of fabricating this story against their client, the respected Bogotá businessman who is in fact not some figment of your imagination called Fernando Salazar but Ricardo Semper. They will say that you have made up these wicked stories about him to get your daughter into Britain and close to you. What will you say to them then?'

'I will ask them how it is that their client wears a gold ring on the little finger of his right hand engraved with his initials, F interlocked with S. It looks like this.'

She pushed her doodle across the desk. It was a clear sketch of a ring with small flowers and the initials FS engraved on the face.

'Then I will draw two more rings for them. Different

designs. One with a series of small stars, the other with the letter F entwined with an L.'

Adam looked at the photograph of Salazar. It was impossible to tell if he was wearing any rings so the information had not come to Mónica by that route. He stared at her. 'That is an extraordinary amount of detail. It is unbelievable that you would have seen so much during a brief meeting in the square in Cali.'

Mónica began to cry quietly.

Ah, I've got her, thought Adam.

'You're right. Impossible to have seen all of that in the square. I didn't. I saw it as he prepared one hundred and five fingers of cocaine. I saw it as he kept pushing those condoms down my throat with his fingers. I saw it as he held the gun close to my skull and forced me to swallow the condoms I had vomited. That's when I saw the rings. That's when I saw what was on them.'

As Adam drove Francesca to her thatched cottage, she told him what she knew of Mónica's history. The childhood rapes from the age of ten, her overwhelming fear that her daughter now stood at risk of reliving her mother's experiences . . . including, perhaps, a chance meeting one Sunday by the fountain. 'Adam, a month before you first showed me those photographs, Mónica confided in me that one of the male prison officers in Holloway had raped her. He's done it a number of times since then. She won't let me go to the authorities. As she says, who are they going to believe, a drug smuggler or a prison officer? She says she can handle it. "After all," she told me, "it's what men have been doing to me since I was ten years old." '

Francesca turned in her seat, her big brown eyes unblinking. 'I know it's crazy. We both know all the reasons why you should walk away from this. But what's it going to be, Adam?'

Adam was so preoccupied – and deeply troubled – he had failed to pick up the large black car that was following him.

CHAPTER TWELVE

PRESIDENTIAL PROSPECT (2)

'TAKE THE STRAIN . . . AND UP. HOLD, TWO, THREE, DOWN. PAUSE. Take the strain . . . and up. Hold. Two, three, down . . .'

Since deciding to run for president, Pat Collins had had no time to run for fitness. He had substituted workouts with a personal trainer.

John Reilly waited for the man to leave before he brandished the newspapers. 'You've done it, Pat.'

Collins looked down at him. 'Still number one?'

'Still number one in the *New York Times* list and you've relegated the Pennsylvania primaries to a second-division story in every paper I've seen so far.'

The look of surprise on Collins's face was almost genuine. 'A book tour? The lead story?'

Reilly began to read aloud from the *New York Times*. ' "It is perhaps an eloquent but sad commentary on current politics when day after day a non-politician effort-lessly steals the headlines from the men who are fighting to get to the White House . . ." ' He handed the newspaper to Collins. 'Some reporters in the hotel lobby want a reaction to that.'

'Do I have time on the schedule?'

'Sure, I'll phone the TV breakfast show and get you on to a later slot. It won't be any problem, you're flavour of the month, Pat.'

'Wrong month, Johnny. I need to be the flavour of November.'

Reilly stared up at him. 'Just imagine, Pat. That first Sunday after your election. The entire nation as your congregation. Just imagine that.'

'I frequently do. Three hundred million faces. We have to love them all, Johnny. *One Nation Under God*.'

Andrew Sinclair flicked the intercom on his desk. 'Clare, I'm just going into the command centre. When the viewing figures on *The Rutherford Show* come through, bring them in to me, please.' He got up and walked to a side door. The command centre functioned as a temporary control headquarters for a campaign that did not yet officially exist. An electronic switching system had been built into the suite. This enabled Sinclair to watch any TV programme on any channel without leaving his office. There were wire services from every major news agency, computers that automatically logged and recorded any media reference made by or about pre-selected subjects, computer files on every potential candidate, on congressional records, senate hearings, every government publication for the past twenty years, and every public utterance made by President Clinton during his years in office. Sinclair knew the value of exhaustive research. He was living proof of how potent a weapon it could be in the right hands.

'Slight tendency to look away from the interviewer. Eliminate. Four times in five minutes rubbed chin thoughtfully. Once or twice, attractive. More, irritating.'

Sinclair switched off both his tape-recorder and the video-recording of the Rutherford interview. This had been one of the main reasons why Collins had been sent to Seattle. John

Rutherford's show was major league. Syndicated across the States, it attracted huge audiences. Sinclair had a list of the hundred key TV and radio programmes that largely formed public opinion in the United States. Added to this had been all the influential newspaper columnists.

One Nation Under God was published in mid-March (the title had tested well with Sinclair's focus groups). Since then, Collins and Reilly, a support team and the Fraser film-crew had been crossing and recrossing the country. Sinclair and his team had planned this tour with precision. Only a few hand-picked individuals knew that the author tour was a full-scale dress rehearsal for something bigger.

So far the two groups had worked together surprisingly well. Unified by a common purpose, they had succeeded in creating so much interest in Collins and his book that it went into the bestseller lists a week before it was published. Two days before the official publication date the publishers had announced they were reprinting.

Articles, reviews and interviews began to appear and it was at this stage that Sinclair and his team reaped a special bonus. Because of Collins's international reputation, his meetings at the beginning of the year with various heads of state had not been given a political spin by any of the domestic commentators. The trip had been seen as a fact-finding tour for America's favourite preacher. When his syndicated column and his Boston-based TV chat-show began to address themselves more and more to the issues of the day and to develop an interest in the forthcoming primaries, it seemed a natural progression in an election year. The show's ratings increased. TV critics, along with the public, liked what they were hearing.

So it was with the book. The fact that it was a campaign manifesto when there had been no declaration of a campaign did not strike reviewers as odd. After all, there was no candidate. When an international figure, a visionary preacher, looks to the future and tells his readers what he can see, there is no reason why they should consider that the author is making an election speech, even if he is.

Pat Collins habitually began his meetings with a specially composed prayer for the media. 'Dear God, please give those members of the press, radio and television who are present today the strength and will to carry out their vital work in helping to bring your word to all.' The prayer was answered. The initial media coverage of *One Nation Under God* was, without exception, positive. The media loved it, as they already loved its author.

He gave good copy. 'Welfare comes in many shapes and sizes, many colours and disguises,' he told *Face the Press*. 'If someone gets up at a convention shouting, "Take all welfare away from the single mothers," they get a standing ovation. I'd like to see that same "reformer" get up and condemn the kind of welfare that gets given out on a silver platter to the lawyers and lobbyists in this city.' He darted a quick off-camera smile at Teresa, who had written it.

No one commented on the curious coincidences that began to occur during the author's tour of the United States. When the Republican and Democratic primaries took place in Florida on the twelfth of March, Collins just happened to be in the state on his author tour. Consequently the media showed far more interest in the preacher than they did in the politics. It happened again in Illinois on the nineteenth and again in California on the twenty-sixth. What also happened was that politics and the preacher became increasingly linked.

Alongside the rival primaries, the Collins author tour became a third event to be discussed, commented upon and considered, and as March had given way to April, more and more space in the papers and air-time on TV and radio was devoted to Collins and less to the primaries. It was only a matter of time before the unspoken thought was voiced. Sinclair wanted very much to control the moment at which it happened. He checked Collins's schedule for the day in Seattle: breakfast TV was finished, he and Reilly would be on their way to a downtown radio station. He crossed to the printer tracking the latest from Wall Street and picked up a phone.

'John. And the top of the morning to you. How is the man?'
'In excellent shape and even better form.'

'Good. Stay on the line, Johnny, while I talk to Pat. Good morning, sir, and congratulations on yet another week in the number-one spot. How does it feel to be the most popular author in the United States?'

The preacher's voice came on the line, loud and clear. 'Just a little exhausting, Andrew, but it's an interesting experience. One becomes obsessed with showers, clean shirts and suits, and where the time is coming from to allow for a sandwich. How are things in New York?'

Sinclair checked the Wall Street prices again. 'Never better, Pat. I'm looking at the current price of Cybersafe shares. The price has gone through the roof so many times since we floated that I guess it won't come as a shock to you to learn that your personal investment is currently worth two hundred and seventeen million dollars.'

'Andy? This is John. I think you've rendered him speechless. Quite an achievement. Here he is.'

'Funny thing is, Andrew, I haven't given it a single thought on this tour so that news does shock me. Good Lord. So much money. I assume you and Johnboy here will want to start selling my stock soon?'

'We'll wait until you're both back on the East Coast. Then, Johnny, I think we should convene a meeting of the financial trust.'

'Tomorrow in L.A. is the last day of the tour.'

'Exactly,' said Sinclair. 'I want to keep the momentum. Hold as much focus on Pat as we can throughout May. The Cybersafe story should do that.'

Since the company launch, Cybersafe had proved the hottest share on Wall Street. Because only 20 per cent had been made available and each share was being chased by a herd of would-be buyers, the price, as Sinclair had observed, had indeed gone through the roof. From a first-day closing price of sixty-three dollars, the shares by late April were being quoted at well over a hundred. During the first week of May Sinclair orchestrated the revelation that the majority of the Cybersafe company was owned by his Four Seasons and Patrick Collins.

Within the Sinclair team the spin doctors who had ensured the initial success of the book were busy again. 'Sure, Walt. It's the American Dream and it couldn't happen to a nicer guy. Remember the Lee Iaccoca story? In some respects this is the new millennium version. Poor Boston boy makes good in spades. I'll fax the press pack to you as soon as I get off the phone.'

'You see, Bob? It's a definitive example of his vision. He had faith in the Carson twins at a time when no one else did. What's that? Right on. It certainly does say something about the power of prayer.'

'His initial investment. It was his own money, Jean. Look, you know as well as I do that there's no one financially cleaner in this entire country. You tell me one other person of the status of Pat Collins who makes his annual accounts available to the media. All right, so you want to know where the initial five million dollars came from. You'll have to wait on that. No, not long. Tell you what, you'll be one of the first to know. No, I promise.'

When Sinclair listened to a tape-recording of that conversation between one of his team and a senior reporter on the *Wall Street Journal*, he concluded that time was running out just a little faster than he had wanted it to. He had wanted to delay the next stage of the Project until the conventions were out of the way but, then, to bring that stage forward to mid-May would hopefully put both the Republicans and the Democrats on a pre-convention defensive. He studied his political calendar. Yes, the nineteenth of May looked excellent.

He looked up as his secretary entered.

'Clare, the four-day meeting scheduled for June, I'm going to bring the date forward. This may cause complications for those on the list. The sooner we establish if those difficulties are surmountable, the better. Bring me a copy of the list and we'll divide it up. I'll take the ones who may prove difficult. By the way, I'd like you to attend this conference. Is that going to be a problem?'

'When and where, Mr Sinclair?'

'May fourteenth through May eighteenth. Lake Winnipe-saukee.'

'Thank you, Clare. Would you please tell Mr Sinclair that we look forward to seeing him on May fourteenth.'

'Certainly, Mr Fraser. We'll fax you the precise itinerary in the next forty-eight hours.'

Adam hung up then walked to the window of his bungalow on the Collins estate and looked out across the miniature golf course. Time to make some decisions. He went to his dressing-table and picked up the contents of an air-freighted package that had arrived from London three days earlier. Once again he took out the photographs and the report from the forensics laboratory. He stared at them for a while, then dialled a number. 'Su, get the boys and we'll go to the Beach Café.'

Though constant electronic sweeps confirmed that the bugs had not been put back in the bungalows, Adam was alert to the need for vigilance. The best feature of the Beach Café was not the menu but the amount of space around it.

While Adam talked, Susanna, Barry and Leon sat listening quietly. He talked of the Thanksgiving dinner, omitted Oscar and Olaf, and picked up the thread with Mónica, her identi-fication of Salazar and the bargain she wanted to make. Sanctuary for a daughter in return for sworn testimony against the mule man.

Leon interjected, 'I remember his rings and the gold teeth. What I can't remember is if I shot any close-ups with his hands coming into frame.'

'You did,' said Susanna.

Adam looked at her. 'How would you remember something like that?'

'Because you pay me to. Because I log every single shot Leon shoots.'

Adam held up a hand placatingly. 'Easy, lady. What's the problem?'

'I seem to remember having a New Year's Day conversation that touched on this business.'

'It touched on the business of me contacting a lady in Hertfordshire, yes, what about it?'

'You must have seen this Mónica in early January.'

'Yes, I did.'

'It's now May. We're all involved in this too, Adam. Why didn't you tell us this earlier?'

'Until I knew what I wanted to do, there really wasn't anything to put to the rest of you.'

'Yes, but—'

Adam leapt in. 'Su, shut up.'

Leon and Barry exchanged a quick glance as Susanna bit back a retort.

Adam, breathing deeply, continued. 'I'm going to try to get this child of Mónica's out of Colombia and into England. I don't know what's going down between the Colombians and Patrick Collins, but for sure that man at the dinner is the mule man and for sure he used Mónica as one of his mules.'

'How can you be so certain?' asked Barry.

Adam picked up the package from the table and pulled out the contents. 'These photographs are taken directly from the footage you shot, Leon. A sequence that starts with a two-shot and ends with Salazar resting his chin on his hands. The next series are computer-enhanced images created at a forensics laboratory in England. Which is why, Susanna, it's taken from January until now before I had anything to say to all of you. You can't walk into these places and just ask for help. It's a government establishment. I had to wait until the right man was in the right place. Fortunately Leon adjusted and held perfect focus when Salazar brought his head down into the palm of his hands. The lab technicians kept enhancing the shot, twenty to one, a hundred to one. Here's what they ended up with.'

His crew stared at the image, then Leon said, 'Looks like I picked a good moment to hold focus, guv'nor.'

Adam grinned. 'Never better. It matches perfectly the drawing I saw Mónica make while she sat listening to me attempting to rubbish her story.'

'That would seem to prove a link between this guy and the lady in Holloway, but he could just be a low-level dealer,' Barry remarked. 'Colombia's full of these "one deal and I'll be a dollar millionaire" merchants.'

'The source that revealed Salazar as a senior member of the Cali cartel has never been wrong with his information on narcotics.'

'In that case,' Barry persisted, 'why hasn't Salazar been arrested before now?'

'Because before now no one was prepared to testify against him.'

Susanna said quietly, 'If she signs a statement she's signing her own death warrant.'

Adam replied to her, 'She wants her daughter out of Colombia, and I'm prepared to try to get her out.'

'What part of Colombia, Adam?' asked Leon.

'Cali.'

There was a collective intake of breath from the crew. Barry was the first to speak. 'Oh, that's all right then. As long as it isn't somewhere dangerous.'

Adam guffawed. 'I'm not asking anyone to go there with me or get involved in this any more than you already are. If any of you want to pull out of the documentaries, I'll understand.'

No one spoke for a moment. Then Barry said, 'We'll finish the job.'

Adam turned to Susanna. 'Could you give me a status report on our docos, please.'

'Right. The two on Collins the preacher. Your rough-cut assembly of the first is running at seventy-five minutes, and part two at sixty-eight. As for *The Making of the President*, including the footage recently shot covering his author tour, you have just over sixteen minutes in the can.'

Adam reflected, then tapped the table. 'I've decided to rationalize what we're making. Instead of three films, I'm going to make just one. We'll mix all the elements we already have with the campaign footage we have yet to shoot for one ninety-minute doco. It'll cover everything in one hit. Between now and the Collins pre-declaration meeting, we'll sit and pull apart everything we've done, put it together again, then plot the material to be shot between now and election day.'

The crew digested this information. Susanna, who had been making notes, looked up from her pad. 'We've got until early June before that Collins meeting. That gives us about a month.'

Adam shook his head. 'Sinclair's office just called me. The meeting has been brought forward to May the fourteenth. That gives us seven days. They've obviously decided to light the blue touch-paper a little earlier than planned. Apart from totally restructuring the doco within the next seven days, I want to see a lady in London. If anyone asks for me while I'm away, I'm in New York tracking down some research.'

The only difference since his last visit to Holloway was the prisoner-grown tulips in a well-tended bed. Useful survival aid, thought Adam. Just what a Colombian mule would need to know.

During the drive, Francesca had told Adam of her subsequent visits to Mónica. 'She has prayed nightly, Adam, hour after hour. She has invoked God, the Virgin, Jesus and his disciples and a choir of angels to intercede on her behalf and persuade you to fetch Carla.'

'If I'm her best hope she should keep praying.'

'You're her *only* hope.'

'In that case perhaps I'd better start praying too.'

In the visiting room Adam placed his overcoat on the table then looked squarely at Mónica.

'Mónica, I want you to tell me again. From the moment you met this man at the fountain in the central square in Cali. I want to hear everything and this time I want to see all three drawings.'

Mónica shrugged. 'But I've already told you.'

Adam persisted, 'Now tell me again. I want to see if it comes out the same second time around.'

She began to talk. When she had finished, Adam leaned over

the desk and gripped her hands. 'I'll try and get Carla for you,' he said.

'I knew you would help. You have such a kind face.'

'No, Mónica, what I have is a small brain, but if you're prepared to risk so much to help me then I believe it's only right that I should do what I can to help you.'

Just how much Mónica was risking soon became apparent. They were discussing the best way forward and Adam put forward a plan. 'I was wondering about the Colombian ambassador here in London. The Venezuelan ambassador is a friend of mine and I know that the Latin-American embassies work closely together here. What do you think?'

Both women reacted sharply, a verbal interchange between them that was far too fast for Adam to understand. It was followed by an explanation from Francesca. 'No, Adam. Under no circumstances. Mónica is adamant. She would rather have nothing done than go through the embassy. Five months ago I had a similar case with one of the women I visit at Styal. Another Colombian national with children back home but no husband. She wanted help. She had someone from the embassy come to see her. The woman told him that if the government in Bogotá would look after her children, see that they were fed and that they had a roof over their heads, she would co-operate.'

'By giving evidence against one of the cartels?'

'Exactly. The diplomat contacted the Bienestar Social, the welfare department in Bogotá. Two weeks later the woman's sixteen-year-old son, the breadwinner, was shot in the head. Her brother took in the remaining children. One month later he was executed. The woman in Styal withdrew her offer to testify while she still had some family alive.'

'What part of Colombia was this?'

The two women exchanged a look before Francesca replied, 'Cali.'

There was another interchange between them. Again Francesca explained to Adam, 'Also last year there was a woman in the next cell to Mónica. Her name was Maria Elba. Mónica has never talked of this before today. This woman was different from the rest of them. She was not a mule. She had set up in business on her own account. Same result. Seven years' imprisonment. Maria Elba used to boast to Mónica, how her lover was a deputy in Bogotá, how she knew senior members of the Cali cartel. How she would be going home soon, would never serve her sentence, a deal was being done. I remember this woman well. I never understood how it was arranged or who fixed it, but she was certainly well connected, someone close to the President, or perhaps the President himself, spoke to someone in the British government. She served only a few months. Then, suddenly, she was deported. Two weeks later she was shot in the head in her apartment in Bogotá.'

Speaking slowly, Mónica talked directly to Adam. 'They are everywhere, Señor Adam. Everywhere. They know everything. Which prisons we are in, our sentences, our prison numbers. They regularly visit our families. "Ah, so Mónica is in Holloway. Her prison number, it's 2754980, isn't it? She is serving seven years. Tell her we stopped by." I had that in a letter from my sister last year. The last letter she sent to me.'

'And despite that you still want me to try to get your daughter out of Cali?'

'Yes, I do. I will write a letter for you. Give it to my sister, she and her husband are caring for my Carla. They will be only too happy to get rid of her. My sister's letter was full of what a burden Carla was.'

'I think, Mónica, you should also write a letter to Carla, explaining who I am and telling her to trust me.'

Mónica put her hand to her throat and unclipped a small chain from around her neck. On it was a crucifix. She handed it to Adam. 'Carla cannot read, but give this to her. She will remember it. She used to sit on my lap cuddling me and playing with it.'

After they had left Mónica, they went for a drink in Islington.

'Fran, this stuff about the cartels knowing all about the mules in English prisons. Paranoia?'

'No.'

'But how do they get their information? Corrupt prison officers?'

'Corrupt prison officers, corrupt Home Office officials and good basic common-sense techniques. Look, each of these women, when they were mules, was expecting to be met. The Customs, the police, the drugs squad, none of them ever seem to think about that angle. So, if someone is waiting for a mule at Heathrow who doesn't show, when they get home they phone Cali or Medellin or wherever she was sent from. They get confirmation that she got on the plane. Next day the London-based dealer or one of his associates goes to Hillingdon Court, where most of these women are remanded. Day after day they check the lists of cases to be heard until sooner or later Mónica and the others appear. Now the London-based dealer knows what the mule looks like and soon he knows what sentence she's got. Are you getting the picture?'

Later that day Adam flew to America. He had not contacted Laura during his trip to England. Time enough for that later. She had not wanted him to continue his investigations into Salazar and Pastrana. He had agreed to drop them, then done the opposite. Now, if he got really lucky, his childless career-wife might just have a little Colombian girl to stay for the remainder of Mónica's time in prison. Only four years with remission.

Two days before the first campaign meeting the newspapers and television news were full of grim reminders that on the coming Sunday it would be exactly a year since the attack on the First National Bank in Chicago. No one had been arrested, every conceivable theory as to who had been behind the attack and the subsequent destruction of Cola One had been aired. The bombers did not wait for the anniversary. They struck again on the twelfth of May. Another Friday. This time their target was one of the most prestigious hotels in California, the Bel Air. At lunch-time three bombs made from fertilizer and fuel oil were detonated long-range. Simultaneous explosions occurred in the main restaurant, the cocktail room and reception. Yet again no warning had been given. Yet again no one claimed responsibility. Yet again the devastation was horrific. 117 dead, 41 seriously injured and much destroyed of a hotel that was synonymous with wealth, power and privilege.

The news media did not wait for official investigations: the following day the headline 'The Friday Bombers are Back' was on the front page of every newspaper in the country. When the President went on nationwide television vowing that, no matter how long it took, the perpetrators would be brought to justice, many political commentators were unimpressed. They pointed out that he had used precisely the same words a year earlier after the Chicago outrage. No evidence was discovered that linked any particular country or group to the attack. Everyone had a theory. No one had a clue.

Lake Winnipesaukee in New Hampshire had been chosen with Sinclair's customary obsession with detail. It is close to interstate highways and airfields giving easy access but he had taken no chances on unwelcome visitors: he had taken over Beaver Island for the duration of the meeting. A one-mile path circles the island; no one could come or go without his knowledge. Accommodation varied from the main lodge to small secluded cabins in the woods. In Sinclair's mind, this would bring back a frisson of frontier man to some of the guests, with the added benefit of mini-bars and central heating.

It was Sinclair's hope that being confined to a small private area like the island would help to focus everyone's attention. 'Any of the comings and goings, that's OK. Any of the meetings in the main lodge, that's open season too. Anything that's arranged for outdoors can be filmed. The only no-go areas I would ask you and your crew to respect are any private meetings in the cabins.'

Sinclair had arranged thoughtfully for Adam and his crew to be the first on Beaver Island. He wanted the arrivals, other than his own, to be filmed. 'I'm fully aware, Adam, that you have the opportunity here to make a truly historic and unique film. I want to give you every chance to do just that.'

'I hope the finished film lives up to your expectations. This is a brilliant location. The light is superb, going to make for some great filming.'

'Good. Here's a tip for you. Quite a number of the people coming here, members of my staff, for example, have no idea what's on the agenda. They probably think it's connected with the recent book tour that Pat's done. You might get some interesting audience reaction.'

Next thing, thought Adam, he'll be telling me to be sure and get a few close-ups of Collins. 'That's a great idea. Thanks.'

The most spectacular arrival was that of Rick Forrest, who flew in straight on to the lake. Sinclair was secretly amused. None of the other members of the executive cabinet could top that entrance.

Except one. 'Ladies and gentlemen. I am proud and privileged to be the first person to introduce you to the next president of the United States of America. Patrick Collins.'

Excluding Adam Fraser and his crew, sixteen people were seated around the large galleried lounge in the main lodge when Andrew Sinclair got casually to his feet and made his announcement. Adam, working a second-unit camera, could hardly suppress his laughter as he panned round the room. Johnny Reilly and the corporate cabinet of four were applauding vigorously. Others, such as Clare, Sinclair's personal assistant, sat open-mouthed.

Collins walked to a large open fireplace and surveyed those dotted around the room. He clasped his hands together, closed his eyes and bowed his head. 'Dear God, we ask you to bless this gathering. It begins. Here. Now. Today. At this moment we are less concerned with what we would do if elected to the White House. Our preoccupation is in getting there. We ask that you guide us in the tasks that lie ahead. Amen.' He lifted his head and looked at his audience. 'The odds against us reaching our objective are formidable. I take great heart from two earlier examples in this country's history. At least twice before men have been elected to the highest office in the land after being helped by amateur president-makers. One was Abraham Lincoln, the other was John F. Kennedy. Let me make it clear to all of you at the outset, in the very near future I will publicly declare that I am a candidate for the presidency. I would not be making that declaration if I did not believe deeply that I can win this election.

'My running-mate in this adventure will be the man with whom I have shared so much of my life. John Reilly. John, you care to tell the people what you said to me when I asked you to run for vice-president?'

Reilly grinned broadly at him. 'Pat, you know that I feel deeply honoured.'

'That isn't quite how you phrased it when I first asked you.'

Reilly looked round the room. 'This stays between these four walls. The opposition might have some fun with it. I just quoted to Pat what the first vice-president, John Adams, said after being elected. "My country has in its wisdom contrived for me the most insignificant office that ever the invention of man contrived or his imagination conceived." '

When the laughter and clapping died away, Collins continued, 'My campaign manager in this enterprise will be Andrew Sinclair. In view of the fact that he was largely responsible for persuading me to run, I think it appropriate that he should organize the race. In this room are the crucial elements of our team. They will, of course, be augmented as and when necessary, but I most devoutly believe that whether I win or lose will be determined by the talent, efforts and abilities of those gathered here today. It was only when I walked into this room that I realized a rather charming coincidence was in the making.

'In October nineteen fifty-nine, the Kennedy campaign team gathered for the first time at Hyannisport.' He grinned and opened his hands in an expansive gesture. 'There were sixteen of them too. Now, there's so much to do and so little time to do it in. Let's get to work.'

A wave of excitement surged through the room. It was more like a revival meeting than a policy session and Adam was shaken: he knew the preacher could move the masses, but to generate the same frenzy among these sixteen hard-headed professionals . . . He forced his mind back to business. 'Right. Su, Leon, Barry, the secret of these sessions is not to linger too long with any one group. They're going to be brainstorming for four days. Should make for a wonderful montage. Go for it.'

Leon and Barry moved quietly away from the seminar on drugs, conducted by an animated Andrew Sinclair, to find Patrick Collins out on the patio with a small group around him. 'I am deeply concerned about this Fortress America attitude that is beginning to take hold,' he was saying. 'Isolationism does not work, either in foreign policies or in our everyday lives.'

'I understand the reference to foreign policies, Pat, but everyday lives? How?'

'OK, Sam. You have two residential neighbourhoods. One is regular Main Street, USA, different kinds of people living in different kinds of houses and apartments. The neighbourhood reflects that mix. Some people have money, others don't. Some have work, others are on welfare. The neighbourhoods on either side are much the same. The whole area is an identifiable urban area. Now you have a second neighbourhood. Its streets, sidewalks, parks, the whole shebang is private. It has high walls around its perimeter. There's a security guard on the gate. Access either by car or on foot is controlled and monitored. This neighbourhood has its own codes, its own rules covering external appearance and maintenance of the properties. More and more people are rejecting the first neighbourhood and choosing the second. We are becoming a walled and gated society. We are no longer One Nation Under God but many nations under surveillance.'

Others having caught a fragment of this discussion drifted out on to the patio.

Sam Barnes, head of media relations at Sinclair's organization, had been chosen for the post of press secretary on the campaign team. He had worked as a newspaperman in California and had headed Senator Ruskin's press office before being head-hunted by Sinclair. Jesuit-trained, he enjoyed testing any strongly held view to its furthest limits. 'So people want to get away from the mugger, the rapist, the pusher. They don't want to be beaten up or burgled. They want to live free of fear. Seems reasonable.'

'Very reasonable. Welcome back to the Middle Ages, complete with moats and drawbridges. Your walled settlement is defensible. It's linked to other walled settlements by roads, fibre-optic cables and digital electromagnetic signals. You won't be meeting people on your way to work. Your work is on the other end of that PC in the den. The public commons have been replaced by private WalMarts. If we abandon our cities, our humanity, our compassion, our tolerance for each other will diminish. Carried to its logical conclusion, we'll have enclaves of militiamen and terminal paranoia. Why, look, it's happening here to all of us. We all know in our hearts what we're talking about now is what happened in Chicago last year.'

He paused, then, looking directly at Andrew Sinclair, continued, 'We are talking, too, about what happened to Cola One, to Leonard Meredith and his colleagues. And about what happened last Friday in California. We cannot, must not, allow the enemy, whoever they are, to bomb us into submission. We must not allow the climate of fear that they have created to prevail.'

Out of that interchange came a series of powerful TV commercials.

Adam was fascinated with the group dynamics. By the end of the third day it was beginning to seem as if an extended family had taken over Beaver Island. The bonding, the warmth, the camaraderie, that had developed produced a tightly-knit team who would go to the barricades for each other. More importantly, they believed they were a winning team.

Andrew Sinclair was equally impressed, and he was not relying only on his eyes and ears. No one had attempted to make a discreet indiscreet phone call. No one had shown the slightest hint of disloyalty to the common cause. Sinclair was sure of that. Before the official advance team had arrived, he had sent in his own security. They had bugged every room, every phone, and a fair proportion of the trees.

'Thought you might like to know how much we've shot,' Susanna said.

Having stepped out of the main lodge after dinner, Adam had strolled to the water's edge. He turned and looked at her.

She checked the notes on her clipboard. 'Twenty-three hours.'

He looked at her closely. 'You're joking.'

'I never joke about running times or what we've shot.'

'Twenty-three hours in the can and he hasn't declared yet. It's only the middle of May. Got to be more selective otherwise I'll be editing until next Easter.'

Susanna came and sat on the low brick wall. 'What's your deadline or is that another state secret?'

He bent his head towards her until their noses touched. 'You going moody again?'

'Oh, I just don't like these exclusion zones. We never had them before this project.'

'We've never had a project like this before.' He blinked and stood back a little. 'My deadline depends on who does what deal for what rights for what territory. Once it gets out what kind of exclusive deal I have with Sinclair and Collins everything is going to be negotiable. We'll see.'

He turned back and gazed across the lake. The sun was low in the sky now, and the entire water surface was a silver skin, wrinkling, then smoothing flat again. He stared at the shimmering image. 'That's entrancing. I want to dive in and cup all that silver and gold in my hands.'

Susanna moved closer to him and slid an arm inside his. 'I'll come in too but only if you cup me in your hands. But I think we should put cossies on. You wouldn't want to shock the preacher, would you?'

The possible future president was, in fact, otherwise engaged.

A group sat on the patio surrounding him. As they, too, enjoyed the last hour of sun on the lake, they were picking at the strands of foreign issues.

Edgar Lee Stratford, president of Global Systems, had been clasping his drink thoughtfully. 'Sure, we have to take a long hard look at the Russians and the Chinese, no doubt about that. I think an issue that requires even more urgent attention is the fact that much of the world is rapidly becoming dead, unproductive dust.'

Susanna returned wearing her black swimsuit, and a fluorescent life-jacket.

'Did you bring that with you?' said Adam, in surprise.

'No, it was in my hut.'

Adam felt chilled. No one else had been issued with a life-jacket and no one besides himself and his crew should have known that Susanna was terrified of water.

As they sprinted into the lake and he began yet another attempt to teach her to swim he put the thought out of his mind.

'If that hasn't frozen off my balls nothing ever will. Come on, quick.'

Susanna and Adam rose out of the cold lake, clambered over rocks and ran to the steaming jacuzzi by the woodland path. Shouting and laughing, they jumped into it. 'Now are you going to tell me who you went to see in London?' she said.

Adam pushed his back against the side of the tub. 'No, Su, I'm not.'

It was a wise decision. The jacuzzi had been the first area that Sinclair's security team had bugged.

On the nineteenth May, the day after the Beaver Island conference finished, the entire campaign team plus Fraser's film-crew were flown from a New Hampshire airfield to New York.

The press conference was called for four in the afternoon. Sinclair and Sam Barnes, who had masterminded it, had concluded that this gave everyone time to file their story and enjoy the hospitality that had been laid on.

At precisely four o'clock, Patrick Collins walked out on to an empty podium. 'Good afternoon, ladies and gentlemen. Thank you very much for coming here this afternoon. Those of you who have met me before will know that I usually begin occasions such as this with a short prayer. Today I am dispensing with that. I'll admit to having said a prayer before I stepped out here today but a short prayer before this meeting is not appropriate when I consider the condition that this country is in. We need prayers, lots of them. We also need action. I have been concerned for some time about the direction in which we are heading as we move into the new millennium. I wish to change that direction. Indeed, I believe that it is my duty to do so. As such I am today declaring that I wish to offer the people of this country an alternative direction. A third way. I offer myself as a candidate for president of the United States of America.'

Many of the 'neutral' ladies and gentlemen of the press burst into applause. Some shouted questions, while others pulled out mobile telephones.

Sinclair knew that no one could play an audience like Collins. It was one of the key reasons why he had chosen him. He watched the preacher confirm his judgement again. Collins's charm, energy, sincerity enveloped this audience of hardened reporters. He began to quieten them but several were still shouting into mobile phones. He said, almost ruefully, 'So this is what Babel was like.'

His audience laughed. The phone users soon realized they were the butt of the laughter and pocketed their phones except the man from the *Washington Post*, who, oblivious to everything, carried on. 'It's too early yet to say whether this hat will stay in the ring for long. There are too many questions unanswered about the Collins candidacy . . .'

Collins gestured, silently indicating his desire to talk directly to the reporter. The journalist next to the man gave him a dig that brought him up short. He realized for the first time that everyone else in the room was looking at him.

'Does your editor have a hearing problem, sir?' Collins asked.

It was said without malice, and again the room rocked. Collins never took his eyes from the *Post* reporter.

'Tell you what. Put that thing away and who knows? You might get some of the answers to those questions you haven't asked yet.'

The reporter blushed. 'I'm sorry, Mr Collins.'

'That's fine. In answer to the question that was implied by the copy you were filing, my hat will be staying in the ring until election day. I'd like you to meet my running-mate. The fact that I'm alive and standing here today talking to you is entirely due to him. In my opinion he will make a great vice-president. Ladies and gentlemen, John Reilly.'

As Reilly wheeled out his chair to centre stage, the man from the *Washington Post* had found his second wind. When the applause died, he called out, 'Mr Reilly, what qualifies you for the office of vice-president?'

Reilly beamed. 'Wasn't aware I needed any qualifications for the job. I'm chief executive of an organization that *Fortune* magazine has rated as one of the most efficiently run corporations in the United States of America. Will that do?'

The laughter and applause pushed the *Post* reporter over the edge. 'You're paralysed from the waist down, Mr Reilly. Will that prevent you from carrying out the duties of your office?'

'I can give you my answer to that question in just three words. Franklin Delano Roosevelt.'

Collins reached out and gripped Reilly's shoulder. 'Now,' he said to the press, 'let me introduce to you four men who need no introduction.' He brought out on to the stage his corporate cabinet of Paul McCall, Rupert Turner, Rick Forrest and Edgar Lee Stratford.

The sight of four doyens of American industry as the men who had persuaded the preacher to run had the media leaping to their feet with questions.

Collins deflected them by then explaining how these four men had given him a million dollars apiece. The money had been his to use as he wished but obviously the group had hoped that it would be invested in such a manner as to give him the financial independence necessary if he was to mount a serious challenge for the presidency.

The senior reporter of the *Wall Street Journal* now had the answer she had been promised.

When the reporters learned that Collins intended to spend a hundred and fifty million dollars if necessary between May and November in his bid to be elected, any remaining cynicism about his nomination disappeared as most of the press rushed out of the doors to the telephones.

Sinclair had not been paraded on the podium, neither had there been any mention of the million dollars he had donated. He had no objection to his support becoming public knowledge but, as he had observed to Patrick Collins, 'I think I can be of a lot more use to your campaign if at least in the short term the media and the public hold their focus on you, your platform, and the executive cabinet.'

While the waiters got busy serving refreshments to the press corps, Sinclair, who had retreated to his command centre with Sam Barnes and Collins, punched up channel after TV channel on his master control. Collins was on every single screen.

Sinclair stared at the picture. 'This is but the beginning, Pat. In one press conference we have seized the hour and the most satisfying aspect for me is that today they are voting in six primaries in this country and tomorrow the results of those primaries will be relegated to page-two news.'

Barnes nodded. 'It will send a helluva message to both of the parties. Now, how are we going to play this? I've got requests for one-on-one interviews from all the networks, from the *Times*, the *Post*, the *Tribune*, the *Globe* and more coming in every moment.'

Over the weekend and on into the following week, Adam Fraser got a taste of what it felt like to be on the wrong end of the camera.

'Look, Adam, we'd like to come in on a co-production basis. We'll sit in on the shooting as consultants. What do you say?'

What Adam said to that was not very polite. The next TV channel tried a little harder.

'OK, you get director's cut, but we cannot give you fine–cut approval. It's simply never been done.'

In between coping with an increasingly voracious and desperate television media, he was now enjoying profiles in the newsprint. They were summed up by *Variety*'s offering: 'Brit Heads For Boffo Pay Day'.

'Hello, is this a good time?'

'Always a good time to hear your voice, Laura. How's my favourite wife?'

Her laugh came gurgling down the phone, an almost shocking reminder of his other life, which suddenly he wanted to envelop him and take him away from this madness made in the USA.

'Thought you should know that the *Sunday Times* and the *Independent* both ran big pieces on you. Very positive stuff, acclaiming what they see as . . . what was it the *Sunday Times* called it? Ah, yes, here we are, "a very British coup". The answerphone tape is jammed with calls for you, mainly requests for interviews, but also from head of documentaries at the BBC, Mitch, and one I know you'll really enjoy from Bastard Bruce Clay. The Network Centre have reconsidered. They would like to do a deal.'

There was a silence on the line.

'Adam, are you there?'

'Oh, yes, I'm here all right. Just quietly savouring what you've told me. I'm going to enjoy telling the Bastard what to do with his offer.'

Laura cut in quickly, 'No, Adam. I don't think that's a good idea.'

'I think it's great idea. Laura, I've got American stations wanting to do co-production deals that I'm saying no to. I know what I've got hold of here. It's hot, I'm flavour of the month, so who needs Bruce Clay?'

'Adam, this is just one film. Maybe the biggest of your career, but still only one film. You'll need him for other productions. You move in a small world. The man you vowed never to work with last year is suddenly running a new channel next year. It happens all the time. By all means say no, but do it nicely.'

211

'Do it nicely' was a typical Laura phrase, thought Adam. She'd been 'doing it nicely' most of her life.

They chatted for a while, but Adam's mind slipped back to other concerns. Lost in thought, it was some time before he realized he was listening to a dialling tone. He had wanted to tell her of his plans, particularly a trip he was going to make, but the moment had not seemed quite right. He knew, deep down, that the moment was never going to seem quite right to discuss Mónica and Carla.

'She advised you to stay cool with Bastard Bruce Clay, didn't she?'

The question from Susanna brought him out of reverie. 'Yes, but how—'

'Did I know? My feeling is to tell Clay to go and fuck himself, so I'd bet serious money that Laura's advice would be, "Now, don't forget you'll have to work with him and the rest of these people in the future."'

Adam grinned. 'You know her well. She's right, of course.'

'Of course. Wives usually are in the right. Ham salad on rye, wasn't it?'

'Please.'

The phone rang again. The caller had Adam's undivided attention immediately.

'I've been locked up in an editing suite. That's why you couldn't find me. Go on. I'm listening.' He turned to Susanna, indicating that she should write something down. She grabbed a pen and paper. Looking directly at her, Adam said, 'You're prepared to offer me total editorial control? Hm. Hm.'

Susanna's hand had frozen over her pad. Adam indicated she should write.

'It will be transmitted over the network at peak-viewing time. Prime-time. When? The week of the presidential elections in November. Yes. Excuse me, Mr Phillips, is this offer predicated on Patrick Collins winning? I see. How much? Right. I'd like you to put all this in writing. As I'm sure you'll appreciate, I'm being deluged with offers, quite a number from your rivals. Will you? I suggest you put that in writing as well.

Yes, I'll put my PA, Susanna, on the line. She'll give you the details.'

Adam pressed the secrecy button on the receiver. 'Just give him the New York hotel address, phone and fax numbers, please.'

His mind whirling, he walked to the window and looked out at the view while Susanna spoke to Ralph Phillips.

'What on earth are you looking at?' Susanna asked.

Adam jumped. He had been staring at total blackness. Like many editing suites the world over, this one was below ground. He turned towards her.

'I'm looking at independence. Not just for one film or one project, but for the rest of my life.'

Susanna motioned him back to his chair. 'Now, sit down and start by telling me who Ralph Phillips is.'

'Phillips is the chief executive officer, the chairman of the board, of Network One. I guess you heard the rest.'

She picked up her can of Coke and moved her arm back as if to throw the contents over him.

'Whoa. He wants to buy the doco. I retain absolute control, make it exactly as I want to. It'll be put out on the prime-time slot in the same week as the presidential elections. He wants to buy world rights. One million dollars. If Mr Collins should happen to win that goes up to two million dollars. In any event they will pick up the production costs to one million dollars. He's offering me a ten-year exclusive contract, two hundred and fifty thousand dollars per year whether I make anything or not. Anything I want to make they get first look at, if they green-light the project they're offering to pay production costs of a million dollars per programme. If any rival network betters these terms he will better theirs. I think that's it. Susanna, you did get all that down, didn't you?'

Susanna was still holding her drink in a throwing position. Slowly she put the can on the desk. 'Since those recent mergers, Network One is the biggest TV network in the States, isn't it?'

'Yes.' They looked at each other, grinning foolishly.

Before that phone call, Adam had been planning to talk to

Susanna about Mónica and the unresolved problem of getting her daughter out of Colombia. Long before he had finished listening to the offer, all thoughts of the mule and her daughter had been pushed out of his mind.

CHAPTER THIRTEEN

PRE-EMPTION

BY SUNDAY THE TWENTY-EIGHTH OF MAY ADAM FRASER HAD brought his editing up to date and had accepted the offer from Network One. The contract was the size of a novella, with clauses that protected the network against every conceivable contingency. All editing had to be done at cutting rooms of their choice, all film had to be lodged with their security officers until the final edit was completed, but the bottom line was exactly the one Ralph Phillips had offered on the phone. Adam retained absolute control over what went in and what stayed out of the film, and the money gave him financial independence for the rest of his life. All he had to do now was make the film.

Like all modern political campaigns, the Collins team had developed the habit of working breakfasts. John Reilly, who was proving an invaluable asset to the film-crew, had tipped off Susanna to get on to the patio of the Collins residence in time for the team briefing.

Sam Barnes scuttled in just as the morning prayer was

finishing. He froze, waited for the 'amen', then moved into the empty space between Collins and John Reilly.

Collins looked at his press secretary inquiringly.

'The Christian Coalition are claiming you as one of their own. I've had the editors of the *Washington Post*, the *New York Times*, CBS and CNN on the line already.'

The group took the news calmly, far more calmly than Adam Fraser would have thought possible.

'The Christian Coalition called a press conference forty-five minutes ago,' said Barnes. 'A verbatim copy of their statement and the questions and answers are being run off now. Ah, right on cue. Thanks, Lisa. Hand them around, please.'

Sinclair took a copy from the young woman but his eyes were still fastened on Barnes.

'Anything in the Coalition's statement or the subsequent interchanges that we didn't cover, Sam?'

'Nothing.'

The team exchanged congratulatory grins and a few high fives. Sinclair rubbed his hands together.

'Excellent. I'd like to be a fly on the wall at the next closed-door meeting of the Christian Coalition state directors. All commercial slots confirmed, Sam?'

'Yesterday.'

Collins raised his eyebrows. 'Yesterday, Sam? And how long have you been able to look into the future?'

'One of my sources, Pat. Tipped me off about the press conference.'

Reilly was still working his way through a mental checklist. 'On-line communications?'

Sinclair checked his watch. 'Will be up and running within the next ten minutes.'

As the campaign team reacted to the implications of the news, Adam was quietly directing his crew. 'Close-up here, a sustained two-shot there, pull out when they break into group discussion, go tighter on Sinclair, he's the chairman of this campaign team, follow the money.'

In the documentary, the meeting would serve as an excellent

anatomy of a campaign team responding to a major event. It was now obvious to Adam that one of those private meetings on Beaver Island, from which Sinclair had so politely excluded the film-crew, had prepared a rapid-response strategy against any attempt by the Christian right wing to paint the Collins candidacy into their corner.

Now Sinclair was going through his own checklist. 'The statement from Pat is going via satellite to the seventy-five thousand downlink centres. Our fifty state directors have been fully briefed. And D.C., Guam and Puerto Rico.' (Adam smiled: as always Sinclair had forgotten nothing.) 'The statement's already on our website. The Florida command centre has pressed the button on the whole rack of commercials, TV, newspaper, radio. The fax, phone and modem juggernaut is already rolling.'

As John Reilly explained later the same day to Adam 'We predicted that they would want to claim Pat as one of them. He ain't. We had to wait until they committed themselves by going public. We're not going to put them on the defensive. We're going to kill them.'

Adam was puzzled. 'Surely Pat would have no problem endorsing everything that the Christian Coalition stands for? Pro-life, anti-abortion, pro-family, school prayers, the whole package.'

Reilly gripped his arm. 'Adam, sit in with the monitoring team in the media section of the command centre. Apart from getting some good footage for your documentary I think you'll get the answers you're looking for.'

He spent the rest of the day watching and listening as a *tsunami* swept over the United States. A tidal wave of Patrick Collins in the form of radio and television commercials. He read the on-line statements that had gone out to churches, the updates from the fifty state campaign directors, the advertising that had been placed in every major newspaper in the country. He wandered down to the banks of telephones and sat in on the outgoing and incoming calls. He read the faxes. He watched pre-recorded and live TV interviews, and then finally that

217

evening he watched *The Larry King Show*, devoted entirely to an interview with Collins.

Over the years King's style had not altered. He was, as ever, his avuncular, charming self, a non-threatening host. But this was an illusion, part of a formidable technique that believed you get more from the interview by friendly questioning. It relaxes the subject, tempting them to become expansive, a variation on Adam's own style of waiting for them to fill the silence that follows an answer.

Larry King swung his chair away from the TV monitor to face Collins over a desk. 'Good evening, Pat.'

'Good evening, Larry.'

He leaned forward towards Collins, hands together just below his chin.

'You haven't forgotten that Marine training, have you, Pat? Hit the ground running. You certainly did that today, sir. How on earth did you mount that reaction to the Christian Coalition so quickly?'

'My campaign team are first-class people with the capacity for quick response. Before I declared, we anticipated that the Christian Coalition might attempt something like this and we planned accordingly. To judge from the response that's flooding in from all over the country it would seem that we were right to do so.'

'We've got a crew in your Florida offices. Could we see some of that response?'

'Of course. My pleasure.'

King turned to camera. 'And joining us in Florida is the Reverend's running-mate, John Reilly.'

The command centre in Florida came on to the screen. Reilly was at the centre of a huge room in which there were row upon row of people on phones, others moving along the ranks. In a computer terminal room, messages from the phone operators were coming on screen. In a vast postroom, messages from the computer room were being dealt with and yet more people formed a production line that packed piles of leaflets, booklets and other material. The shot cut back to Reilly. Larry King spoke to his image on the screen. 'John, good evening. It's looking very busy.'

'The word is frantic, Larry. Apart from the calls that our operators are processing, our website is deluged. The phones are attempting to deal with some of the overflow, every available computer is in constant use and there has been no let-up all day. I'm bringing in an additional five thousand volunteer helpers here and at our other command centres. The phone companies have advised me that the telecommunications networks for the states of Florida, New York, Illinois, California and Texas have gone into meltdown as people try to contact our campaign offices. AT & T and Bell have got emergency crews working through the night putting in extra lines. I'd just like to say to anyone trying to get through, please be patient, we will get to you.'

'Thanks for joining us, John. When you get a chance to quantify this response, could you let me have the figures?'

'Sure, Larry.'

'Thank you. In the meantime, it looks like a case of praise the Lord and post the campaign material.'

He turned back to Collins. 'Are you surprised by this level of response?'

'No, but I'm very gratified. There were many reasons why I decided to run for president, but basically I believe I have something to offer the American people and I also believe that a multitude of people might want what I have to offer. Just what size of multitude we'll find out in November, but this response for information is most encouraging.'

King reflected. 'I understand that the Christian Coalition are overwhelmed by your tactics. I can't get any of their executives to go on the record, but I'm told they're walking around shell-shocked. Want to comment on that?'

'Yes. Let's begin with the name they've given themselves. Christian Coalition. Christian Omission might be more accurate. I don't see any blacks. I don't see many Jews. I don't see many single mothers or solo fathers or homosexuals. We're all equal in the eyes of God, but perhaps to the Christian Coalition some are more equal than others. I am not, never have been and never will be a member of their group. They had no right to claim me as one of their own.'

As Collins developed his attack, King sat silently across the desk, transfixed. 'You know, Larry, it's possible to be pro-life *and* pro-choice *and* pro-family *and* pro-school prayers *and* pro-single parents *and* pro-tolerance. As for being in favour of tax cuts, come on, now, next thing we'll hear is that the Christian Coalition is in favour of apple-pie and mother-love.'

As the discussion developed, Collins effortlessly quoted facts and figures to justify his views. He reminded King of how the Coalition's 1.6 million membership was almost entirely made up of white evangelical Protestants and traditionalist Catholics, and that although it was supposed to be non-partisan, it was exclusively locked into the Republican Party.

Larry King was clearly delighted: this show was going to be the most talked about and discussed in the United States.

Patrick Collins had saved one of his most perceptive observations until near the end of the programme. 'I was brought up in a Boston Catholic home in the nineteen fifties at a time when Senator Joseph McCarthy was considered by many, including my parents, to be a wonderful man. It was only years later that I saw how effectively McCarthy had used fear as a weapon in the political arena. I see echoes of that in the entire so-called religious right. What appals me is the way that these organizations, the Christian Coalition, the Family Research Council, Focus on Family, the Free Congress Foundation, apply a scorched-earth policy. Scorching the common ground between the two extremes. Attempting by coercion and moral blackmail to eliminate all the moderates. That's what I really abhor.'

On Beaver Island many had doubted the wisdom of such a direct attack on the powerful Coalition – including the candidate . . .

'Are you really sure about this, Teresa?'

'Patrick, I've never been more certain of anything in my entire life.'

They were in their Boston home organizing his packing a few

days before the conference was due to begin on Beaver Island.

'But these people in the Christian Coalition – in many respects it's my natural home, I share so many of their aspirations. And as for attacking Joe McCarthy, my father would turn in his grave.'

'We went right through this the day Sinclair came to see you in Florida. Remember? Out on the patio with John?'

Collins remembered only too well – and the paralysing anxiety he had experienced when Sinclair had mentioned casually that Fraser's film-crew had inadvertently recorded their conversation. He and Reilly had returned to the patio with Teresa to discuss Sinclair's proposal. In the initial excitement they had given full rein to a shared vision.

'What is needed is a country that is once again ruled and governed by Christians with Christian values. The liberals who made a pact with the devil are responsible for America's ills. God is angry with America. I think He's sent these Friday Bombers to punish the nation. To purge the country.'

The passion with which Collins spoke aroused not only Teresa and John. He himself was pacing the large patio, face flushed, arms in constant movement.

Reilly slapped the side of his wheelchair. 'Pat, we've been handed two great gifts. The Friday Bombers have produced a climate of fear. They've driven people back to the churches in millions. That has to be good. Now Sinclair is offering you the chance to address that fear. He's right. Cometh the hour, cometh the man.'

Collins had stood still, transfixed. 'If I stand and if I win we must hunt out this enemy within and not just the white-trash militia. We must look for the enemy in the ghettos of our cities. Reactivate the unAmerican Committee. We don't just need Neighbourhood Watch schemes. We need Neighbour-Watching schemes.'

Teresa tried to speak but her husband swept on. 'And we must reactivate the Internal Security Committee. Alien elements are attacking the host body. They've got to be eradicated. We have winked at sin and God is very angry with us.

Homosexuals . . . Let us forgive these sinners, but let us make sure that they sin no more.'

Teresa Collins held up her hand. 'And if you were to run and murmur just one of these sentiments, Patrick, you'd be stone dead in the water. You'd be labelled a right-wing reactionary and they'd probably throw in "Fascist" as well. If you do decide to run – and I said if – then I want you to win. You'll change nothing by losing. If you stand you're going to have to steal votes from the right and the left. You're going to have to suppress anything and everything that won't play to a left-of-centre electorate. Right-wingers can't win. Pat Buchanan proves that every four years.'

The three of them had gone over tactics for hours. If Fraser had got any of that on tape Collins knew that he would indeed have been dead in the water.

Now, as he and Teresa checklisted the contents of his various suitcases, he listened carefully to the woman whom so many people, including Andrew Sinclair and Adam Fraser, had misread.

'Patrick, in a couple of days you're going to be surrounded by advisers. Each with a point of view, each with some ideas about your campaign and each, possibly, with their own private agenda.'

'I wish you were coming. Please change your mind.'

'No, that first conference is no place for a candidate's wife. Relationships have to be formed. Trust has to be built. Each of these strong-minded individuals has to learn how to shake down and work as a team. I'd only be in the way. Later, perhaps, but this is one you have to do without me.'

Teresa leaned forward, closing the gap between them, and looked into his eyes.

'You will never win the White House by espousing what the Pat Buchanans and Christian Coalitions of this world believe in. You've got to stay left of centre. *You've got to*. That way you'll attract maximum support. After the election? That's another story.'

*   *   *

In the ideological battle Teresa Collins had an unknown ally.

'I'm delighted at the initial response to the strategy. We must never lose an opportunity to place our candidate in a non-religious moderate position. The advertisements with world leaders are satisfactory, but kindly arrange for the inclusion of Mandela.'

'How would you like that signed, Mr Rodriguez?'

'No name, Carlotta. He'll know who it's from. Just use the fax number I've given you, and let me have the American dailies as soon as you can.'

In the weeks following Collins's appearance on *The Larry King Show* the preacher's lingering doubts were put to flight.

Not only the traditional liberal media but the more conservative elements applauded Collins for the stance he had taken. Perhaps the most significant support came secretly from two Republicans still in the running for their party's nomination. Both expressed their gratitude and the hope that the Coalition's grip on their party had been permanently loosened.

The public reaction was even more extraordinary. Day after day, by phone, letter, fax and e-mail, the campaign headquarters of the Collins-for-President movement around the country was overwhelmed not only with requests for the information package but with pledges of support and money. Pat Collins was obliged to take to the airwaves to tell the public that not only was he not seeking donations for his campaign but, in view of his pledge that it would not cost them a single cent, he would refuse their money. Though this was a time-consuming and costly exercise, it was worthwhile: it offered the public a refreshingly new political position.

'I am deeply humbled and grateful for this outpouring, but I am carrying no one's tabs. All I want from you, the American people, is your vote.'

It was the third factor above all others that permanently silenced those in his campaign team who had doubted the wisdom of a pre-emptive strike on the Christian Coalition.

The first indication came on the day after Collins had

appeared on *The Larry King Show*. *USA Today* carried a poll showing that Collins had 35 per cent support. His nearest rival, the incumbent vice-president, had only 31 per cent, and the remaining potential vote dissipated between several Republican candidates and the don't knows. Later polls showed the Collins share moving towards 40 per cent. Within a month of his declaration Collins had moved from a novelty candidate to the hottest ticket in the country.

The political establishment moved from wrong foot to wrong foot as it attempted to deal with his candidacy.

The Republicans and Democrats announced, through a joint commission, that Collins would be barred from the autumn's presidential debates. The ten-member commission based its unanimous ruling on the advice of an 'independent' advisory committee which said, without supporting evidence, that Patrick Collins had no realistic chance of winning the White House. The commission added that candidates could not be included in the TV debates 'simply because they were interesting or entertaining'.

Asked to respond to the freeze-out, Collins was calm. 'I'm going to think about this for a while. I'll give you my response during the second half of August.'

The reporters who had besieged his Florida headquarters looked at each other knowingly. The second half of August was when the Republicans and the Democrats held their national conventions.

No one ever knew – not even those members of the campaign team who were closest to him – how Andrew Sinclair orchestrated it. What favours he called in remained a secret. The result was there for all to see: row upon row of empty seats – and this on the final day of the Republican National Convention. The day that the party's candidate would be paraded before the party faithful. Apparently a goodly number of the faithful were praying at a different church.

The stadium was packed to capacity. The audience had been treated to and had joined in with the thousand-voice choir and the support speakers. Now it was time for the main event. It was no accident that as Patrick Collins was picked up by the searchlights standing on stage, dusk had just turned to night. Timing was everything on a Collins crusade.

By the fourth of July Collins was leading the Democrat candidate Al Gore 43 per cent to 35 per cent, with the Republican front-runner Trent Lott trailing badly in third place. Keeping the momentum going, the campaign team had announced on Independence Day that there would be a series of rallies around the country. These were not designed to open the people's hearts to the Almighty and the words of the Bible; but to open their minds to Patrick Collins and the message of his manifesto.

The searchlights settled on the preacher.

'In June the Democrats and the Republicans announced that I would be excluded from any candidate debates on television. I was asked for my response. I said I would give it in mid-August.' He fell silent. He lifted his arms and slowly stretched them wide, then brought them slightly together, cupping his hands as if attempting to hold the hundred thousand people gathered in front of him in his embrace.

'This is my answer.'

The stadium erupted into sustained applause and cheering. Collins gestured for silence. 'I will continue to give this answer between now and Election Day.'

Again the stadium exploded with a sustained ovation.

'There are those in this country who wish to keep religion and politics separate. Seems to me that this is one of the central reasons why this country is in its current condition. Religion is not a Sunday-morning-only activity, nor a Friday-evening or Saturday-afternoon activity. It's not something you put back in the closet when the weekend is over, along with your suit or your dress.'

Adam Fraser marvelled once more at the preacher's control. Now nothing could be heard in the RFK Stadium in Washington except the voice of Patrick Collins rising and falling. He gestured to Leon to pan wide across the sea of faces.

Once more Adam recognized the suppressed excitement

focused on the solitary figure who stood centre stage. Yet again he felt the energy that radiated from this man. The potential for change that had moved the small group of sixteen on Beaver Island was clearly affecting the packed Washington stadium. The number of converts was growing.

'We live in strange times, when some among us see life in black and white. No shades of grey, no doubts, no uncertainties. Some want a ban on abortion, some want all restrictions on gun ownership removed, all gun controls abolished, and some want capital punishment for everyone found guilty of murder, no degrees, no extenuating circumstances. A few days ago I received a letter from a lady in Chicago. Twenty years ago she had been the victim of a rape attack. She became pregnant as a result of that attack and she wanted to have an abortion. She was persuaded by her local priest that this would be an unforgivable mortal sin in the eyes of God. She had the baby, a boy. No father, no support, no one to share her burden with. Two years ago, the boy, now eighteen years old, walked into a gun-store in Chicago and bought an AK-47 assault rifle, no questions asked, cash. He went out and held up a liquor store, shot the owner, got caught. They executed him last month. Pro-life? Pro-death? I don't pretend to have such moral certainty on these issues. But, then, I am not part of the Beltway, of the political machine, and I am not part of the religious right.'

The stadium erupted again. Collins silenced them after a while, only to arouse them again. 'I just wish, oh, God, how I wish that all of the problems that ail this great country of ours could be reduced to school prayer, gays and the abortion issue. Do you believe, do you believe, do you believe that? Do you? Do you?'

A great shout of 'No. No. No. No, we don't' rolled across the arena.

Collins stretched out his right arm and pointed from one side of the stadium to the other. 'Are we going to get full employment in this nation by making homosexuality illegal? Are we? Are we? Are we?'

Again came a roaring response. 'No.'

'Are we going to get a balanced budget by getting every child in this country to pray for one in their classrooms?'

Again a mass unified response. 'No.'

Such a curious mix, such a potent combination, thought Adam. Nuremberg and Nazareth.

'Are we going to get good decent housing for everyone, reduce taxes, eliminate crime, protect the environment, help business and ensure world peace by banning all abortions?'

Virtually everyone in the stadium picked up the chant this time. 'No.'

Collins grinned. 'Too right we're not. I can't see the sense of clearing up the backyard, pruning the roses and ignoring the fact that the house is on fire.'

The religious quality of what was a political rally was affecting many sections of the audience. There were frequent shouts of 'God be praised', 'Amen to that', and 'Yes, oh, Lord. Yes.' Adam felt a force pulling him forward as others were now moving forward to bear witness that they believed, that they had in a variety of ways strayed from a multitude of paths. The evening was cool, but he was sweating.

He was consumed with an overpowering desire to un-burden, to cleanse, to witness. Then, quite suddenly, he had the answer to his personal struggle. So simple, something that he had put to one side. In the excitement of the offer he had accepted from Network One and the daily buzz at the heart of the Collins campaign it had been so easy to forget a child in Colombia, whom he had promised to bring to her mother.

He had forgotten more than Mónica's daughter Carla. He had also forgotten the direction of his film since he had done the deal with the Network. He had always believed that he could never be bought, could never be deflected from a chosen path. The reality was that, since the Network deal, he had been filming the bland, the non-controversial. Take the money, take the power and the prestige. Forget the dark side, the cartel members who came to dinner, the bugging, the high-level security checks, all of it. Just make a pleasant safe piece of entertainment and thank you, sir, have a nice day. Susanna's anger on New Year's Day had been justified.

Suddenly he became aware that Leon, Barry and Susanna were standing directly in front of him.

'Adam, I said, "Are you all right?" ' Leon shook his arm vigorously.

'Yes, I'm fine. Why have you stopped shooting?'

The crew looked at each other. Then Barry eyed him keenly. 'You been smoking that wacky baccy again, Adam?'

Adam realized that he was no longer standing on the stage near the choir but had wandered off down one of the inner corridors of the stadium.

Susanna moved closer to him. 'Are you all right? You look dreadful and you're sweating. Come on, let's get you back to Laura at the hotel. I think you're coming down with something.'

The rally had finished some time ago. Apparently the others, who had been busy filming, had not seen him leave and had been looking for him. It was curious, like being preoccupied while driving and then having no memory of the roundabouts and turnings. A short-term memory lapse. He'd even forgotten that Laura had flown in from New York.

Now he had an excellent opportunity to address some of the issues he had recently been ignoring.

'I said to him, "Look, before you cast Dustin, just do me one favour. Talk to some of the directors that he's previously worked with. That's all I want to say." '

Laura was casting a big-budget movie and had flown to the States for a conference with the director and the producers. Adam listened as his wife elaborated on the intrigues and games that were played in the world in which she moved. Normally he found such stories a welcome relief from his own problems, but not this evening.

They were having dinner at the Hay-Adams Hotel. Having received his first-stage payment from the Network, Adam had upgraded the accommodation for himself and his crew while filming the Collins rally at the RFK stadium. After so many years of cutting corners and counting pennies on the road, the idea of wallowing in unashamed elegance had great appeal. Now, after the catharsis of the Collins rally Adam felt ashamed to be in the legendary restaurant. He began to tell Laura about the things he had kept hidden. He told her of the cartel men who had come to the Thanksgiving dinner, of Mónica and her daughter Carla. She sat silently until he had finished. 'Susanna said something about you being ill at the stadium. You've been overdoing it, Adam.' She struggled to remain calm and lost the struggle. 'You're suffering some kind of mid-life crisis. These messages you got during the Collins rally. Voices, were they?'

'Laura, I promised this woman that I would go to Cali and try to get her child out of the country.'

She stabbed her chest repeatedly with a finger.

'And you promised *this* woman you wouldn't do anything stupid. Anything like going after a couple of cartel members. It's no use building a house in the country for a widow. And just suppose you stay lucky, that you get the child out of Colombia, where are you going to keep her until her mother gets out of prison in – how long is it?'

'About four years, maybe less.'

Laura gave a grim laugh. 'Great. What were you planning to do with her?'

Adam took a deep breath. 'In the short-term, just until I finish this doco, I thought we could look after her.'

Laura screwed up her eyes as she stared intently at him. It seemed that she was hoping this would prove to be one of his jokes. Just a tease. His troubled expression looking back at her across the table confirmed that it was not.

'Adam.' For once her voice was steely. 'I gave up our children years ago for your career. I built a career of my own, without children. Now your career wants a child, someone else's child. I am sorry, but I do not. You're free and over eighteen. You want to go into Colombia and get yourself killed, I can't stop you, but don't leave me this problem in your will.'

*　　*　　*

'Are you telling me that you encouraged him to go after these people?'

'Yes,' said Susanna. 'I did.'

Laura had found Susanna in her room.

The two women stared at each other. To fill the uncomfortable silence, Susanna poured two whiskies, which neither wanted. At last, Laura spoke, controlled, remembering her timing and her breathing. 'Susanna, you've woken up in the morning with Adam as often as I have in the last fifteen years. Probably more often.' Susanna tried to speak, but Laura was in control. 'You know Adam's body. Now I want you to imagine it maimed and tortured. Like the people in his documentaries. Your documentaries. Now put that body in a coffin.' Again Susanna tried to speak and again Laura pushed on. 'I don't think that really troubles you. Not as much as it troubles me. You don't love the real Adam, the one that wakes up in the morning. You love Adam the ideal, Adam the fearless hero, maybe Adam the daddy you didn't have. But not Adam your husband. You have no right—' But now Laura had lost control. She swept out of the room before the other woman could see it.

John Reilly produced a bottle of bourbon from a drawer in his desk while Adam went to a nearby shelf and returned with two glasses.

'Medicinal, you understand, Adam. I keep it tucked away out of Pat's sight.'

'Thanks. Your health, Johnny. Any particular reason for Pat's attitude about drink?'

Reilly shrugged. 'It's a drug. Ever since 'Nam he's been very anti-drugs – mind-altering drugs anyway. Cheers.'

'It's good of you to give me a little of your time, Johnny. I know how stretched you must be.'

'Everything's under control. Sinclair's running an efficient campaign. This is a phoney peace period anyway. It won't start heating up again until the Democratic convention in two weeks' time.'

'I was hoping to get from you a little background research on some of the material we've already shot. I'm not sure who to ask.'

Reilly leaned back into his wheelchair, cupping his glass. 'Fire away.'

'Just a little info for a voice-over I'll be putting on the film we shot of that Thanksgiving dinner last year. Some biographical details on a couple of the guests. I've got plenty on most of the people at the table. The Colombians, how did they come to be there?'

'Yes, of course, you were banished before the turkey.' Reilly paused, sipped his drink, then went on unprompted. 'Drugs. Narcotics. That's why they were there. Part of the reason anyhow.'

Adam did not trust himself to speak. He took refuge in a slow drink of the bourbon.

Fortunately Reilly continued. 'Must be, oh, four years ago. Victor Rodriguez, Ricardo and Alberto started making huge donations to the Collins Foundation. Hundreds of thousands of dollars. Naturally donors of that significance are handled personally either by Pat or me, or one of the board of directors. We established that these three men, particularly Victor, have been committed for a long time to fighting the cartels in their country. They saw Pat as an outspoken force for good. Someone who was standing on the same side of the barricades as they were. We've seen quite a bit of them over the years.'

Adam kept his tone almost casual. 'So Pat invited them to the dinner?'

Reilly frowned. 'No, the suggestion came from Andrew Sinclair. He knew how committed Pat was to making the war against narcotics one of the major issues of the campaign. Seemed like a good idea to have them along to dinner. There was another reason that Sinclair wanted them there.'

'What was it?'

'The Hispanic vote. It could swing three states – Florida, Texas and California. That's one hundred and eleven electoral votes, Adam. Those three men have enormous influence on those voters.'

'Ah, I see. I'd thought that perhaps Victor hadn't met the two others before that night.'

Reilly laughed. 'I don't know what gave you that idea. They're bosom friends.'

'Are they contributing to the campaign?'

Reilly smiled. 'Now, now, Adam. You know no one's contributing.'

'Of course. Thanks for the info, John. When's the next poll due out?'

Reilly held up crossed fingers. 'Tomorrow.'

None of Barry's electronic sweeps had picked up any bugs in the guest bungalows since the previous summer, but Adam was more alert to danger than at any time since the documentary had begun. He drove to Naples and, locating a send-and-receive e-mail service, silently thanked good old American know-how and can-do, and sent an encoded message to Oscar. He drove to the Edgewater Hotel and just as before, a quiet conversation and ten dollars later, sat in a small room off the main reception and picked up a phone. 'Olaf, it's Adam. Look, just say no if this is impossible, but I need help.'

The computer on the far side of the room activated. Oscar, who had been rereading William Colby's obituaries and alternating between cursing and laughing, walked over to his Internet line terminal. On the screen a meaningless series of letters in blocks of five appeared. Oscar made a mock bow to the screen. 'Ah, the prodigal son returns.'

As the screen continued to fill with blocks and columns of random letters, Oscar strolled back to his desk, unlocked a drawer and took out a book. There were only two copies in the world. He had one and its co-author, Adam Fraser, the other.

Twenty minutes later, he replaced the code book in the drawer and began to pace. He had been highly trained to analyse intelligence information, to run through every conceivable strategy, to weigh all implications. The more he considered Adam's message, the more concerned he became. The film-maker had embarked on a dangerous, high-risk strategy. Oscar's anxiety triggered violent heartburn. As he rummaged for medication, he shouted, 'You stupid English bastard! You want to get yourself killed in Cali, that's your affair, but if you get out of there alive, I'm going to give you hell for the stomach-ache you're causing me.'

CHAPTER FOURTEEN

PIMPERNEL

LAURA HAD RETURNED TO NEW YORK. ADAM HAD HALF HOPED that there would be a phone message waiting from her when he and the crew flew back to Florida. Now, though, he had to put all thoughts of his wife out of his head. He would be landing in Cali in forty minutes.

The film-crew had been fully briefed. He planned to be back in a day, two at the most. If anyone asked, he was researching in New York or Washington. They knew what to film while he was away, all of the nuts and bolts of documentary-making had been attended to. Meanwhile the nuts and bolts of his life with Laura had come loose, but they would have to wait.

As far as he could tell, no one had been tracking him from Naples to Miami, no one observing his departure to Colombia. With luck he ought to be back before anyone noticed he had gone.

Over a gin and tonic, Adam worked his way through the problems he was flying towards. If nothing else, it helped him forget the ones he was flying away from.

*   *   *

Since Adam's e-mail message had arrived Oscar had confined himself to black coffee. He read and reread the decoded message, as though constant reading would put new words, fresh explanations on the page. He murmured, 'Riddles of death Thebes never knew.' Then, picking up his mug, he said aloud, 'Lucky Thebes.'

He turned to another puzzle that was stubbornly refusing to yield its secrets. On Adam's advice he had fed every conceivable fact on Patrick Collins into the computer. He had then fed in a large number of disks with details of his own life and set the computer on a programmed search seeking common denominators. Either the search program was malfunctioning or he was wasting time on a fool's errand. All that he appeared to have in common with the evangelist was that they had both served in Vietnam.

As the American Airlines plane touched down, Adam's eyes were drawn to a private executive jet that had touched down just in front of them and was taxiing to the main buildings. It was one of the trappings of the rich that he envied most – all that airport hassle eliminated – not least, his own problem of how to leave Colombia à deux.

He glanced again at the now stationary white executive plane. A large Mercedes had pulled up alongside it. Adam started, suddenly transfixed. Coming down the steps of the jet was Andrew Sinclair and the man who had emerged from the back seat of the Mercedes to shake his hand was Victor Rodriguez. Adam's view was obscured suddenly by a passenger behind dropping a pile of clothes on him as the plane suddenly braked.

When he next had a clear, uninterrupted view the car had gone.

He wondered why the man the campaign team called the Puppetmaster had come to see Victor Rodriguez. He wanted to phone his crew in Florida to see if anything had happened but he dismissed the idea at once. He did not intend to share any conversation with El Gordo and the Cali cartel.

*   *   *

'And the reason for your visit, Señor Ormond?'

'On my holidays.' Adam remembered in the nick of time to put on an Australian accent to match the passport Oscar had given him as a birthday present. He wondered if either would get past the man.

The customs official tapped in details from the passport to his computer terminal and waited for a response. 'How long will you be in the country?'

'Twenty-one days.'

The official yawned. He stamped the passport and handed it back to Adam. 'Enjoy your holiday, Señor.'

As Mr Ormond Adam had gained a few hours at most. He stepped out of the airport and headed across a small road towards the cab rank. A gleaming Land Rover driven at high speed came straight at him. If he had been carrying more than the one small case he would have been killed. He just made it to the other side as the huge vehicle swept by. The cab driver on the rank had seen the incident. His face reminded Adam of a deeply sad walrus.

'You did well to get out of the way, Señor. If you'd scratched it he'd have demanded a new one.'

Adam checked to see if the driver was joking. He was not.

'Inter-Continental, please.'

The driver lapsed into silence. Adam gazed out of the windows, aware that the man was staring at him through his rear-view mirror.

'You need a good safe driver while you're in town?'

'I might. Give me a card when we get to the hotel.'

The walrus relaxed into his spiel. 'Very wise, Señor. Always take a cab in this town. They shoot pedestrians.'

'That's one way of keeping the streets empty. *Who* shoots pedestrians?'

'The *traquetos*. That was one in the Land Rover. Nothing personal, you understand. Just target practice. Look.'

The driver was moving very slowly through heavy traffic. He pointed at a couple of plaster policemen with inane smiles on their faces, positioned to warn drivers of potholes and other road hazards. Riddled with bullet-holes, they still smiled.

The hotel was the normal Inter-Continental monument to bad taste – an excess of chrome and marble set in a foyer the size of a football stadium.

'I'd like to hire a car and I would be grateful if you could confirm my flight tomorrow to Bogotá. There will be two of us travelling. Here are my tickets.' A ten-dollar bill concentrated the mind of the concierge wonderfully.

Alone in his room Adam rechecked the address that Mónica had given him. It was in the working-class Obrero district. Timing was going to be crucial. Carla's relatives were not expecting him, and he had no idea how they would receive him. Then there was Carla.

The concierge phoned. The flight had been confirmed, his hire car was downstairs, all that was required was for him to come to the desk and sign the necessary papers.

When the day shift had gone and the night porter was on duty, Adam approached the desk again.

'I'm going to drive to San Agustín tomorrow. I'd be most grateful for a map and directions.'

Again a ten-dollar bill located a veritable spring of helpfulness.

At six the next morning Adam was parked outside a concrete block in the Obrero district. It had probably looked squalid before the cement had dried. The section was no better than the *barrios*, hovels half buried in rubbish, huts drowning in mud and effluent. He had brought with him, courtesy of the night porter, a large flask of coffee, a precaution against the likelihood of dysentery if he drank anything in the house of Flores.

Irene Flores was a sister of Mónica's. Neither she nor her husband Miguel was inclined to make their early morning visitor welcome. When he told them that he was a friend of Mónica's, the elderly couple erupted. A whore! A criminal! A disgrace to their family name! Miguel punctuated his diatribe with rhythmic spitting. Panic began to seize Adam. He felt sure that if the child had been there the oaths being heaped on her mother's head would have provoked her into appearing. He asked where she was and, to his relief, Miguel dragged her out of an inner room.

Carla crouched in a corner as Miguel launched into another impassioned attack on her mother. With each new insult she winced as if struck.

Adam moved quickly to the purpose of his visit. 'I want to take Carla away. Her mother wishes her to come and stay with me until she has finished her prison sentence. She realizes what a burden the child must be to you. That's why I'm here. To relieve you of that burden.'

He produced Mónica's letter confirming his story. Suddenly the burden was no more. Yes, it was true that they had to struggle, but to part with the girl would be a great loss to both of them.

Looking at Carla, wearing only a ragged slip, Adam's face was expressionless. 'Yes, it's clear to me that you care very much for the child. I would, of course, like to compensate you for the cost of looking after her. What would you say to fifty dollars?'

Irene's eyes glinted, like a magpie attracted to a glittering object. 'To tell the truth there's someone else who has taken an interest in her. An uncle who is fond of her. It would upset him if he came to see her and she was gone.'

'But, Señora, her mother wishes this. You've read the letter. Look, let's say a hundred dollars.' He held out the notes in the palm of his hand and let her focus on them.

Ten minutes later Carla was in the back of the car, and Adam was driving out of the Obrero district like a man pursued by demons. He was anxious in case they changed their minds and came after him. Eventually he reached the Avenue Colombia and stopped. He thought over his visit – he had taken back Mónica's letter and deliberately neglected to tell the Flores where he could be found. He had covered every contingency. Reassured, he was about to turn and look at the girl when he felt something sharp being held across his throat. It was Carla. In the driving mirror he saw the knife in her hand. He began to speak to her, slowly, calmly. He talked of Mónica and saw something behind the dark brown eyes respond. He reassured her that he was not like her uncle. She flinched at the mention and he felt the knife pressed harder. He told her that he meant her no harm. Still she did not move. Then Adam remembered. Very slowly, with great care, he reached into his pocket. 'Your mother gave me this. She said I was to give it to you. That it would help you understand.'

He held out the golden chain with the small crucifix dangling. Carla stared at it, hypnotized, then stretched out a shaking hand. Adam dropped the chain into it. Her small fist closed fiercely around it. Removing the knife, she retreated back to the far corner of the rear, to the little corinthia she had created for herself, and spoke for the first time.

'*Madre.*'

'It might be a freak poll, of course, Andrew, but to drop nine points at this time concerns me greatly.'

They had talked well into the night and now, as he sipped his first glass of Rodriguez's orange juice, Sinclair was immediately focused.

'It was inevitable, Victor. High bounce had to be followed by the ball dropping back a little.'

'Have the campaign team identified any specifics yet?'

'Possible combination of factors,' said Sinclair. 'The main parties have been throwing heavy armaments at Collins for the past two weeks – maybe that's beginning to do some damage.'

'I found his responses satisfactory. But did the public? Are the crusades hurting him? Is his faith getting between him and the voters?'

Adam had never acted as a fashion consultant to a twelve-year-old girl before. He had checked out of his hotel before driving to the hovel in Obrero, but had held on to the piece of plastic that opened his bedroom door. Careful use of the rear entrance and the service lift had got them up to his room, but when they had gone into the suite, and Carla had seen the large bed, she had turned and attempted to run away. Adam had been forced to grab her and hold her while again and again he told her that he meant her no harm, would not hurt her, was a friend of her mother, not some 'uncle'. Eventually she had calmed and he explained a little of his plan. He was tempted to make a game of it, but that seemed inappropriate. He sensed that she had long ago put away childish things. While she bathed, he slipped out of the hotel again, and returned with an armful of parcels – dresses, knickers, socks, shoes, sandwiches and a Coke.

Carla tried on each item in the bathroom, emerging from time to time for Adam to see and talked of the 'uncle' who had made so many visits to her since her mother had gone away. He had called her 'his little toy'. Mónica's worst fears had been realized: since just after her arrest the man had raped the child regularly. Carla talked of it in a detached way, almost as if it had happened to someone else, a close friend perhaps. She was a mixture of stoicism and *naïveté*.

It was while she was admiring the ill-fitting clothes in the mirror that she unwittingly sent a spasm of absolute terror through him. 'He said to me that, if I was very good, in a little while he would help me to see my mother again.'

'How was he going to do that, Carla?'

'By getting me to take some things to England. Just like he got Mother to do.'

'Are you sure?'

'Oh, yes. I watched him make Mother swallow all these balloons. That's when I first met him.'

Adam tried hard to stop his voice from trembling. 'This man, do you know his name?'

'Of course. Uncle Fernando. Fernando Salazar.'

'The attacks on the Christian Coalition did us nothing but good and I'm convinced that the attacks on corruption in Washington, the whole hogs-in-the-trough stuff, should not only continue but be stepped up.'

Rodriguez stood up and moved to the verandah rail.

'Of course. And, Andrew, I'd like to see him attacking the narco trade the next time he speaks on the crime issue. Which reminds me. Your recommendation that our fundamentalists should be given more of the New York banking business to handle has been acted upon. Hezbollah are now handling sixty per cent of our East Coast inter-bank transfers – excuse me.' Rodriguez broke off as a servant appeared on the balcony.

When Rodriguez returned to the verandah he was preoccupied. Sinclair, always attuned to the chairman's moods, waited silently.

'That was a phone call from Fernando Salazar. We have a problem, Andrew, a serious problem.'

Adam and Carla emerged from the multi-storey car park in the centre of Cali and waited for a passing cab. He felt vulnerable and exposed until they were safely on their way to the airport. Carla had not asked why they had parked the car in the middle of the city. She had learned young that curiosity was no help to survival in Cali. At the airport they joined the check-in queue for the flight to Bogotá.

Fernando Salazar had told Rodriguez a curious tale of an Englishman with excellent Spanish who had gone calling in the early morning and bought himself a mule's daughter. Rodriguez did not ask why Salazar had also gone calling on such people. He did not need to. He had known Fernando for many years, knew of his liking for 'little toys'. When Salazar learned the identity of the man who had bought his 'toy' – the documentary-maker he had met at the Collins Thanksgiving dinner, the man he had planned to send to his grave via Catia prison – he raged at the terrified couple, but despite his threats neither Irene nor Miguel could tell him where Fraser had gone with the girl. Now, an hour later, Rodriguez had the answer to that.

He had moved a telephone out on to the verandah. Now he replaced the receiver and drummed his fingers on the table.

Sinclair looked at him questioningly.

'Andrew, this man Fraser. Do not underestimate him.'

Sinclair remained silent.

'A clever trick, if he can pull it off, it merits our admiration. To fly north while simultaneously driving south. The information I have is that he is both driving to San Agustín, close to the Ecuadorean border, and flying with the girl to Bogotá.'

'One is obviously a diversion, Victor. He's anticipated a fast response.'

'The question is, which is the false trail and which the real one?'

'I'd put my money on Bogotá. He'd be planning to connect with an international flight.'

'But what is he using for papers for the girl? ID. Passport. Taking cocaine out of this country is easy. Taking a child out without the proper papers is more difficult.'

Rodriguez betrayed no panic. He trained his binoculars on a small bird in his garden.

The phone rang again. Rodriguez answered it, '*Si*', listened, eventually said, '*Gracias*', then hung up. 'He has booked two rooms in the Hotel Yalconia in San Agustín. He also checked in with the girl for the flight to Bogotá. A resourceful man. We will cover both eventualities.'

'And then?'

'Andrew, you are my counsellor. Counsel me.'

'The one unresolved question is, has the mule already made a statement to Fraser or was the deal "Get my daughter out, then I'll testify"?'

'We'll know the answer to that in due course. Meanwhile, we have only a few hours, whether it is Bogotá or San Agustín.'

Sinclair stood up and stretched, arching away the pain from sitting too long in one position.

'So ironic. Has Fernando said, "I told you so" yet?'

'Several times.'

'If we had allowed him to arrange Fraser's death in Venezuela it would probably have been linked to narcotics because of his friend Olaf, but under the present circumstances it would be a highly desirable solution.'

'If they are located on Colombian soil, it should be made to look like an accident. I'll arrange for some off-the-record briefings to be fed to the American media indicating that Fraser liked under-age sexual partners. If he gets out of Colombia we'll re-evaluate. This couple who had been looking after the girl? Irene and Miguel Flores.'

'Yes. They require immediate attention.'

'And, Victor, Salazar should play a leading role in all of this.'

'An excellent idea.'

The two men exchanged expressions of pleasure in a private joke. Then Sinclair went to telephone his children.

On the plane they made a disparate couple. He was coiled tightly. She was a young girl full of wonder. Everything had magic for Carla, the reclining seats, the little table, even the snack. Adam, his mouth dry from fear, drank the proffered can of lemonade and called for another. He thought of Laura, her indifference to Carla's fate. A surge of anger welled in him dominating his fear. He checked the time yet again, willing the aircraft to fly faster.

'Victor, about Fraser.'

'Yes?'

'He's still a film-maker. That is his craft, his first love.'

'So?'

'So, let's assume that somehow he's stumbled on what Salazar does. And that he's struck a deal with the mother in London. All right, he gets his statement. What's he going to do? Rush to the police? I think not. First, the British will be largely indifferent unless there's a stronger Brit connection than a Colombian mule rotting in one of their jails. Second, this man is right in the middle of making the most important documentary of his life. No doubt about that, Victor, and he knows it. Now, what would you do?'

Rodriguez considered for a moment, then turned full face to Sinclair. 'I'd put the evidence in my documentary.'

Sinclair smiled at him. 'Of course you would. That doesn't mean we don't resolve this problem today if we get the chance.'

The Cali to Bogotá flight landed exactly on time and taxied along the runway towards the arrivals lounge. Among those waiting were seven men located in various parts of the lounge. They watched casually as the plane came to a halt and the mobile stairs were trundled towards it. They showed no reaction as a police car followed the ground crew. The vehicle came to a halt, then two police officers climbed the steps and disappeared into the plane.

No one emerged for some time, until eventually the two policemen reappeared and gestured towards the main lounge. The seven men stared hard at the image for a moment, then one moved outside the lounge, pulled out a mobile phone and dialled a number.

Oscar, now in the second day of trying to make sense of the senseless, had cast a wider net. 'Follow the money' was a rule of investigation that he had invented decades earlier when probing the activities of the Vatican Bank. In this case he had neglected the rule far too long. Hitting computer keys with furious speed he began to hack into the confidential accounts of merchant banks and brokers, to trace the movement of share acquisition linked to the flotation of Cybersafe. He then began to identify the buyers of the shares, the people who had unwittingly made Collins so rich that he could now run a full-scale presidential campaign entirely self-financed. It might not lead anywhere, but one should always follow the money.

No one had been seen arriving or departing. It was as if wraiths had visited the house of Flores. The men who accompanied Fernando Salazar when he paid his second call of the day to Irene and Miguel had apparently done nothing to disturb the tranquillity of the neighbourhood. Seemingly not a sound had come from Miguel as first one ear and then the other was bitten off by Salazar. Miguel had apparently been equally stoical as his fingers were sliced off. Based on her neighbours' statements to the investigating police officers, Irene had presumably shown similar calmness, for not a murmur had been heard as the drill went through her knee-caps and then through the palms of her hands. When Miguel had been castrated he had demonstrated an unusually high pain threshold, for no sound had reached through the paper-thin walls. When confronted with appalling torture, the Flores had demonstrated forbearance, calmness and fatalism . . . The police estimated that the torture must have lasted the best part of an hour before the couple were beyond all pain. Whatever the motive, it had not been robbery. They found fifty dollars on Irene and fifty more on Miguel. Irene's money was stapled to her breasts, Miguel's to his penis.

Rodriguez replaced the telephone yet again and delivered an epitaph for two. 'The Flores had nothing of interest to say and Fraser was not on the Bogotá flight, Andrew.'

'San Agustín?'

Rodriguez shook his head. 'I think not. My people would have picked up the car long ago. He'd never have got halfway there.'

He picked up a list of the flights that had been scheduled to leave Cali that morning. 'So many destinations. We spend much of our waking life organizing product out of Colombia. If anyone should know how to move an illegal item across one of our borders, it should be me and yet—'

He broke off as something on the list caught his eye. Then he smacked the table hard with the palm of his hand, grabbed the phone and began to punch in a number. Simultaneously he checked the time. 'Damn. Let us hope that the flight is late.'

'Which one, Victor?'

'Cali to Cúcuta.'

'Cúcuta? Why would Fraser go there?'

'For much the same reason that we hold our annual meetings there. So near the border with Venezuela. So near . . .'

He began to speak rapidly on the phone.

The Cali flight to Cúcuta disgorged its passengers close to the small main terminal building. Like the flight to Bogotá, this too attracted particular interest but from just one man. He watched as the passengers came down the steps. His eyes fastened on two people in particular – a tall blond *gringo* and his companion, a young girl. The man moved towards the door where the passengers would enter. As Adam Fraser and Carla entered the hall the man moved forward. 'Welcome to Cúcuta.'

'Olaf. Thank God. We've only our hand luggage.'

On the outskirts of Cúcuta, Olaf stopped the car. 'Did you take the photos?'

Adam handed him two passport-sized photographs of Carla from the set taken at the automatic dispenser at Cali airport. Olaf began expertly to fasten one into a Venezuelan passport and the other on to a Venezuelan ID card. He produced a government seal from the glove compartment and over-stamped both photographs, then he handed the documents to Carla. 'You are now Carla Nilsson, my thirteen-year-old daughter,' he said.

Carla opened the passport and looked at her image staring up at her. 'Is this because of Uncle Fernando?'

Adam turned in the passenger seat to look at her. 'Yes, Carla. These papers mean you will never have to go back to Cali.'

The girl's face showed delight and she snuggled down in the back seat still staring at her image. Adam gripped his friend's arm. 'How long will those documents stay good?'

'As long as she needs them. Come on, let's get out of town. We're only a few miles from the border.'

Olaf headed towards Venezuela. The spot where he had chosen quite randomly to park was directly by the entrance to the Brothers of Mercy seminary. By the time Rodriguez had alerted those within and they had come roaring through the high double gates in pursuit, Olaf was over the Colombian border and heading for San Cristobal.

Rodriguez and Sinclair were deeply involved in planning appropriate strategies for the presidential campaign when the negative report came through from Cúcuta.

'You can't touch him on American soil, Victor. Far too dangerous, too close to home. It would only want the *Washington Post* or someone from the *New York Times* digging around—'

'Of course, Andrew. That leaves this mule in a British prison.'

'What are you planning?'

'First to find out exactly what the state of play is between her and this Pimpernel. Then appropriate action will be taken.'

Oscar scratched, stretched, rubbed his eyes, then sat up. He had lain down on his bed near the bank of computer screens for just a few minutes, a quick cat-nap. He checked his watch. He had slept for six hours. One advantage of a solitary lifestyle was the opportunity to keep anti-social hours and develop anti-social habits. He really had to have a shower and a shave. It had been more than four days since Adam's message had provoked him into a frenzy of activity at the computer terminal. He had deeply wanted the Englishman to be wrong. He did not want to believe that Victor Rodriguez was in bed with the drug cartels. It was this challenge that had motivated him for hour after hour as he had hacked into system after system and surfed his way countless times around the world of the Internet.

He rolled off the bed and padded over to the last pile of material that he had downloaded and printed. He picked up the pieces of paper and reread them.

The jury was still out on Victor Rodriguez. Oscar had found nothing that linked him with any criminal activity. His extended search had established, however, that there had indeed been a third person at that Thanksgiving dinner who was up to his armpits in the narcotics business – three narco men at the table of Patrick Collins, a man who seemed to be within touching distance of the White House.

Even without anything to link Rodriguez it represented an enigma. What were these three doing breaking bread with Collins? A man who had vowed an unremitting war against the cartels if he won the election.

CHAPTER FIFTEEN

POLLS

IT WAS KICK-ASS TIME ON THE COLLINS CAMPAIGN TRAIL. Sinclair was doing the kicking and some thirty asses were feeling it. Pollsters, media directors, marketing and advertising people, researchers, speech-writers, strategists: he held each one personally responsible for the 10 per cent drop in the Collins poll.

'As neither Pat nor Johnny will be joining us this morning we'll dispense with the opening prayer. No supplications. Just answers.'

As the campaign team shuffled their papers, he moved across to the film-crew. 'Good morning, Susanna. I think you'll get some very interesting footage today. Where's Adam?'

'Good morning, Mr Sinclair.' He was charmed by her English formality, still retained after so many months. She looked earnestly at him. 'It would be a great help if you could give me some indication of the order of speaking.'

'No problem.'

He was intrigued by her evasion of his question. 'He hasn't

gone to Washington already, has he? For the second rally?'
Sinclair stared at her as she seemed to struggle for an answer.

'I haven't gone anywhere yet, Andrew, but I'm about to.'
Adam handed Susanna some sheets of paper. 'I picked these up
from the press office – the running order for today's session. By
the look of it, it's going to be a long one.'

'The longest yet,' said Sinclair. 'Could go on for most of the
day. Where are you off to?'

'Some second-unit filming in Paris is giving me headaches.
Flying over to sort out the French.'

'It's about time someone sorted out the French.'

Sinclair moved back across the patio and a moment later had
gone.

'Perfect timing, Adam,' said Susanna. 'Don't worry about us.
We know what to film. Want a ride to the airport?'

'You've got enough to do. I'll be back in three days at the
most.'

'On his way to Paris apparently, something to do with his
filming, but that may be just a cover story. Perhaps he's taking
the girl to his friend Oscar?'

During his most recent visit to Colombia Sinclair had
received from Rodriguez a sealed pack of mobile phones. Each
was electronically linked to a twin receiver. 'For emergency use.
Once. Then discard,' Rodriguez had advised.

Sinclair had moved some distance from the Collins residence
and strolled to the gazebo before calling Bogotá.

Rodriguez stared down into the central dealing room of
Andino Incorporated. 'I think the answer to this problem will
be found in London as well as Paris. Call me later.'

Back at his desk he buzzed his secretary. As she entered and
approached he reached out and handed her a mobile phone.
'Ah, Carlotta. I'd like the flight times of all planes flying
Miami–Paris today. Oh, and have that incinerated, please.'

The young girl's high voice resounded around the prison
visiting room. 'So, dearest Mother, do not worry about me.

I am safe. I am well and I am happy, and I hope to see you again soon. All my love, your daughter Carla.'

The tape continued to spin silently then clicked and stopped. Tears had been running down Mónica's face since Francesca had slipped on the tape cassette. It had arrived by air courier that morning and Francesca had lost no time in bringing it into the prison. In a few minutes of unconfined childish joy, Carla had told her mother how Adam had come to Cali for her, of her new clothes, her plane journey and her new home, though not where it was. Of her experiences at the hands of Fernando Salazar there was no hint. It was a message of the present, not of the past. Adam had written a short covering note.

> Dear Fran. So far, so good. By the time you get this I will be on my way to see both you and Mónica. I have arranged a safe haven for Carla until all the paperwork is completed. As you will hear on the tape she is well and happy. Tell Mónica I will give her all the details when I see her this week. Will phone you to make arrangements. Adam.

'Fran. You must tell Adam when he calls of my gratitude. He has kept his word. I wish to keep mine. When he comes this week. I will make a full statement about Salazar.'

Francesca gripped her arm as if further to strengthen the other woman's resolve. 'Keep the cassette, Mónica. A small present until you can enjoy the big one.'

Francesca had never seen Mónica smile before. By the end of the visit she was laughing and giggling like a young girl.

They kissed on both cheeks and before Francesca was across the prison courtyard Mónica was back in her cell replaying Carla's message.

As Francesca swung out of the prison gates and turned into the main road she did not see the large black car parked nearby. She headed towards Archway and northwards out of London. The black car slipped out into the traffic behind and began to track her.

*   *   *

The campaign meeting on the Collins patio had moved from an analysis of the focus groups through a study of dial groups to media image, TV commercials and editorial perception. They considered how his performance was playing to big business, small business and the man in the street. How each ethnic group, each colour of the American rainbow, felt about their candidate.

As lunch-time approached they had begun to consider the Collins effect on farmers, military veterans, working mothers and dog and cat owners.

The last few miles from the motorway to her cottage on the edge of the village never failed to relax her. For Francesca it was as if the city stopped at the exit from the A1. The undulating countryside seemed a world away from the aggression, stress and increasing alienation that were part of everyday London life. Francesca never stopped rejoicing in her discovery of a corner of England that still retained echoes of a gentler age. She became aware of a car close behind her and edged over to let it go past. She laughed at the black sedan speeding away. Foreigners taking a short-cut. Locals never drove that fast. Five minutes later she stopped outside her cottage, picked up her briefcase and walked towards the front door. She had not noticed the black car parked off the road between the trees. It was unoccupied.

The post-lunch session on the patio had got to the stage where the team was attempting to reach tentative conclusions.

The media consultants had concluded that GOTV no longer meant Get Out The Vote, but Get On TV. They wanted to see the candidate on *Good Morning America*, CBS *This Morning*, the *Today* show, *Arsenio Hall*, every networked chat-show and ideally *The Larry King Show* at least twice weekly until November. They had no strong feelings about the subjects he addressed as long as he looked the interviewer directly in the eyes, kept his hands away from his mouth when talking and smiled a great deal.

*   *   *

The back door, left unlatched by visitors long gone, was banging softly in the gentle summer breeze. Francesca's cat, entering from the garden, trotted briskly through the beamed kitchen into the living room. She stopped and stared unblinkingly at what remained of her mistress, then, edging slowly forward, sniffed at the pool of partly congealed blood.

Many hours earlier the departed visitors had phoned a contact in Amsterdam, the owner of a fashionable art gallery on Spuistraat. It was the first of a series of relay stations that led eventually to Victor Rodriguez.

It had been pathetically little to kill an attractive fifty-year-old Colombian widow for, but before she had died she had told them all she knew. People always did.

For the second time that day Rodriguez stared unseeingly down on his trading room. Then he turned, opened the door and beckoned to Carlotta. He was gratified to note that she cleared her monitor screen before joining him. Such a discreet employee.

'I need to speak to Fernando Salazar. Is he in Bogotá at present?'

'I believe he is in Cali.'

'Then please contact him. Tell him to phone me on one of the secure lines. He should have details of his London-based workforce near to hand.'

Rodriguez closed his office door and began to pace. The mule was going to make a statement indicting Salazar some time this week. As always this film-maker was such a busy man. If the surveillance team in London had fulfilled their work tasks, the Paris team had failed abysmally for the second time. Fraser had arrived alone at Charles de Gaulle and had then vanished. What a pity, Rodriguez thought, that we did not catch up with him in Cúcuta. He felt sure that his people would have slowed the man down considerably. 'Some time this week,' Francesca had said. It was now late Monday afternoon in London. The white telephone on his desk rang once.

'Fernando? There is a small problem I wish you to deal with.'

*   *   *

Sinclair had confined each campaign executive to two minutes, allowing himself five minutes to summarize. Their audience of three had remained silent throughout the presentation. He reached his concluding remarks.

'We have tried to counter the poll slippage. We do not believe that there is anything profoundly flawed in our campaign, but we do feel that the suggested changes should ensure we recapture and hold the momentum.'

Collins rubbed his chin thoughtfully. 'Johnny?'

Reilly turned his wheelchair to look directly at Collins.

'These guys are the professionals, Pat, but I can't help thinking we just might be in danger of overreacting to what might be a rogue poll.'

'Exactly, Johnny.'

It had come from Teresa Collins. She reached over and touched Reilly on the arm. He stopped dead. Teresa folded her hands in her lap, a simple gesture that turned every eye on her.

'I think that campaigns should drive polls not the other way around. A poll is no more than a snapshot of the electorate. Perhaps the camera caught them frowning when a split second later they might have been smiling. I also think that with all this talk of "focus groups", "dial groups" and "advertising strategies" we are in danger of catching the disease that the public wants Pat to cure. The voters are sick of leading the politicians. They want someone to lead them, not someone who spends a fortune on a consultant to teach him to say things they agree with.'

Sinclair's face betrayed nothing, but his mind raced. He had badly misjudged Teresa Collins. His initial assessment of the perfect, unthreatening candidate's wife had not established a single ounce of the steel that was now on display. The leadership qualities that had largely created America's favourite preacher had been instilled in him by Teresa Collins. Sinclair made a mental note. He would prefer that the documentary should not contain any footage from this session.

Warning glances were flashing from the pollsters to the media executives, from the strategists to the spin managers.

Teresa Collins caught the glances and a tight smile passed across her face. Then she continued, 'I think you all want campaign changes that will make Pat and Johnny more like conventional politicians. If the public wanted that in this election then Pat would never have got anywhere near thirty-nine per cent of the poll. Putting him on prime-time television is an excellent idea, but what he actually says when he gets on there is just as important as being seen on there.

'The American people want solutions, not saxophones. They want someone to attack unemployment, poverty and crime, and I mean attack. They want someone to make the economy grow, to give their children a better standard of life than they have. God damn it!' No one even blinked at the expletive. 'That was America's birthright and now it's gone. Pat can give it back – but not if you make him a man for all seasons, if you book him on prime-time TV to say nothing at all.'

Teresa paused and looked round the room. 'Now, I've one or two modest proposals to make and then I'll go and organize some refreshments.'

Patrick Collins came hurrying down the path towards the departing film-crew.

'Did you get that? All of it?'

Leon lowered the camera from his shoulder. 'Yes, Mr Collins. We got it all.'

Collins beamed. 'Wonderful. My God, wasn't she stunning? Wasn't she just brilliant?'

Susanna nodded. 'I hope Adam uses every word.'

Collins gripped her arm enthusiastically. 'So do I, Susanna. By the way, where is Adam?'

Quite a few people were asking that question. When Susanna entered her bungalow the phone was ringing. It was Laura.

The only sound was from the birds at the bottom of the garden and the soft rustle as Adam finished another page and placed it on the pile of already read printouts. Occasionally he would stop, annotate a page and make a note on his writing-pad.

Eventually he had worked his way through the pile of paper. He turned to Oscar, sitting across the small patio. 'Putting it simply . . .'

Oscar gestured encouragingly.

'Edgar Lee Stratford owns a laundry. He's been washing hundreds of millions of dollars of narco money for years and a large part of the frenetic share buying of Cybersafe was narco money moving out of Venezuela into a Stratford boutique bank in Belize and then on into his Mill Valley Bank headquarters in San Francisco.'

'You understand correctly, young sir. Award yourself a glass of this excellent Californian Cabernet Sauvignon, harvested from grapes not a mile from Stratford's home.'

Adam began to pour wine into a glass but almost immediately stopped. 'That means that at least five members of Collins's corporate cabinet are cartel, that cartel money pushed up the share price and that cartel money is therefore financing the Collins campaign.' He shook his head, yet again trying to clear an appalling image.

Oscar obviously relished the vision. 'It gets better. Stratford is one of America's richest men. An all-American hero. Self-made billionaire. Presidential counsellor. Living proof of what you can do in the can-do society.'

He held up his glass and studied it as the dark red liquid sparkled in the setting sun.

'Are you absolutely sure about all this, Oscar?'

'I'm sure. The key is the Venezuelan bank, Banco Latino Groupa. I've traced thousands of smurf wires sending just below the maximum amount of ten thousand dollars. Sure sign of narco money. Lots of little guys filtering drug money back to the big guy. This Latino Groupa has correspondent accounts with at least three of the major American banks and, of course, with Stratford's little bank in Belize. It's all there. I managed to hack into the Belize bank and Latino Groupa. El Dorado!'

They sipped their wine and contemplated the swifts tracing figures of eight above the trees.

'That was a neat idea. Throwing Sinclair the line about going to Paris.'

'Give yourself credit for it, then. You suggested in January that I should take the surveillance team that was following me for a little tour of Paris before losing them.'

'Be careful, my young friend. If you keep taking the piss out of the French cartel members they might forget that their job is to follow you until you lead them to me.'

'At least we now know for sure that Sinclair is cartel. He must have been straight on the phone to them. Their people in Miami followed me virtually to the steps of the plane.'

'Call me self-centred, but I'm still interested in learning exactly why the cartel want me dead.'

'Are you absolutely sure you fed everything into that computer comparison, Oscar?'

'I'm sure. Look, what would you expect to find? We both served in Vietnam. That's it. Nothing else.'

'Get your friends in Langley to take another look at his war record. Maybe the answer's there.'

'If it was there, Adam, someone's destroyed it – but OK, I'll pull out our respective war records. Worth another try. Talking of computer searches reminds me. Ever heard anyone at the Collins residence talk about the Colombia Project?'

'Not that I can remember, but the world is full of Colombia Projects. What's this one for?'

'I've no idea. It's a file title I came on when trying to hack into Sinclair's company in New York. A file I can't yet get into. They're always the sexy ones. There'll be a password hand-picked by Sinclair. I'll keep on trying. I've nothing on Victor Rodriguez yet either.'

'Have you hacked into Andino Incorporated?'

'Hey, is Clinton horny? Of course I have. Nothing. But there wouldn't be, would there?'

Adam leaned towards Oscar. 'The seating at that meal. You went on and on about it. Rodriguez wasn't sat away from the action so that he could be set up some time in the future. He placed himself there to ensure that Collins would be photographed surrounded by cartel people – Salazar, Pastrana and Stratford – but *not* Rodriguez or Sinclair.'

'And this set-up? The purpose?'

Adam drank some wine. 'It doesn't make sense. Presumably part of their plan is to compromise Collins. The paradox is that one of the reasons he's so highly electable is because he's violently anti-drugs. It's a key part of his platform.'

Oscar threaded his fingers together and cuddled his stomach. 'Just imagine that the cartels could control such a president. A man with such an unblemished record, a devout Christian, a war hero. A man who represents all that is good about America. What a front man!'

'There's just one flaw in that, Oscar. So they have him breaking bread with the cartel, they finance his entire campaign with laundered money. He gets elected and Sinclair arranges a happy-snaps evening and talks about his public duty to reveal the truth, unless the war on drugs is reduced largely to a PR exercise. What is to stop America's only living saint going public and exposing the whole conspiracy? It just doesn't add up.'

'No, my friend, it doesn't. Unless they're hoping to soften up Collins just like the current president was softened up.'

Adam choked on his drink as Oscar continued agreeably. 'If the cartel is hoping to compromise Collins they have to start somewhere. Bankrolling the Collins Evangelical Mission for four years is a start.'

Oscar held up a finger, more to check himself than to keep his companion silent. 'Four years. Now is that significant? 'Bout the time that the current president got elected. Three men – two of them certainly, the third probably, major players in the Colombian drugs cartels – start donating millions of dollars to Collins's evangelical movement. Curious thing for three apparently devout Roman Catholics to do.'

'Even more curious to give as a reason their admiration of the preacher's condemnation of the narcotics industry.'

The wine was forgotten.

Oscar pointed a finger at Adam. 'You a betting man?'

'Only with unimportant things like my life.'

'I'll bet you an even hundred that if you can track the first donation from these three men it will be after the last presidential election. That's when these motherfuckers began. They knew that they had this administration by the balls for four more years. They were looking beyond that. I've got to get into that computer file of Sinclair's.'

'Yeah, but wait a minute. Consider the current president. Governor of a state that had become a centre for international drug-smuggling and gun-running. People like Greg Rochford and his cargo plane – what was it?'

'A C-123K.'

'Right. In and out of Fisher airport as regular as a Greyhound bus, carrying narcotics by the ton.'

'To be precise,' said Oscar, 'at least thirty-six metric tonnes of cocaine, three tonnes of heroin and a hundred and four tonnes of marijuana. OK, so what's your point?'

'You didn't need cartel smurfs in Fisher when the President was in the governor's mansion. If you wanted to cash transfer ten grand, twenty grand, a hundred grand, no problem. No official report. Grand juries never got convened unless the governor said so. He had premier-division cocaine dealers like Dan Hunt as a close friend and generous fund-giver. He had brother Alan dealing in cocaine as well as shoving it up his nose.'

Oscar chuckled. He was eager to get a stir of the pot. 'Often joined by the governor and a roomful of ladies, don't forget.'

'Oscar, who's telling this story?'

'I'm sorry. Go on, Adam.'

'The President's rise to political power can be linked in part at least to narco money donations to his political campaigns right back to the Medellin cartel. You know, I've always been amazed that he was so dumb that he kept turning up at that little airport near the state border line. My point is, Oscar, when you look at that lot, I think it's very reasonable to assume that the cartels broke open the champagne when he was elected, but why try to replace a man like that with the nearest thing America has to a living saint?'

Oscar stared at the nuthatches dining upside down from the hanging bird-feeders. 'Get me that password and I'll tell you.'

'I'll give it a go,' Adam said. 'I'll ask if we can film in his New York offices. The real nerve centre of the campaign, that sort of thing. This stuff on Stratford. I want to sit on it. Use it in the documentary with everything else, including Mónica's statement. The lot.'

Oscar spread his hands. 'Fine by me. It's your party. When are you going to see this lady?'

'Tomorrow. Soon as I fly into London.'

Not until he reached the airport did Adam remember someone else in London waiting to hear from him.

'I'm in Hamburg about to catch a plane to London. Laura, I'm sorry I haven't been in touch. I've been on the move most of the time.'

'What time does your flight get in?'

'Oh, about midday.'

'I'll come out to Heathrow.'

'No need for that.'

'Yes, there is. Every need.'

As he came through Arrivals, she engulfed him in her arms. Her anxiety and needs were so desperate he staggered to keep his balance. 'Whoa, easy, Laura. You'll get us arrested.' He tried to pull free, but Laura clung to him. 'Laura. We're going to have them backing up to the runway if we keep blocking the exit.'

'Sorry. Let's find a table in that café.'

'Are you sure about that? I seem to remember the last time we sat down for a meal, it ended up with you going into orbit. Mónica and her daughter – remember?'

It had been said lightly, but the effect on his wife alarmed him. She began to weep.

He tucked her away in a corner of the cafeteria and was about to hurry off to the service counter when she restrained him.

'It's all right. I'm sorry. I don't want anything. Just sit.'

Laura laid the newspapers she had been carrying on the table. 'I don't know how to tell you this. I don't know what are right words or what are wrong ones. Typical me. I'm taking the coward's way.'

He stared at her uncomprehendingly. She gestured towards the front pages of the newspapers. Staring up at him with those dark brown Spanish eyes was Francesca. The text varied from paper to paper, but all gave precisely the same basic information. Fran was dead. Murdered. Her injuries, reduced to tabloidese, were described as 'appalling', 'horrific', 'gruesome' or 'dreadful'.

There was press speculation that she had come home unexpectedly and surprised burglars, mention of some valuable pieces of native Colombian art being a likely target for a 'robbery that went wrong'.

Adam realized suddenly that in some papers he was now staring at a second photograph, not of Francesca but of Mónica. She had been discovered hanging in her Holloway cell in the late evening. Francesca, the prison authorities confirmed, had visited her earlier the same day. There was a press suggestion that the prisoner's suicide had been triggered by news of Francesca's murder. 'Her only friend's death, too much to bear', ran one headline. The *Sun* newspaper, claiming an exclusive, revealed that Mónica had hanged herself with her brassiere from the bars over the window.

Adam buried his face in his hands.

'Darling, I'm so sorry. So sorry.'

'The bastards.'

Laura reached over and gripped his hands. 'Who?'

'The cartels, Laura. The men who ordered these murders.'

'But this woman in prison, Mónica. She wasn't murdered.'

'Oh, but she was, Laura. I'm sure of it.'

He told her of the tape he had sent that Francesca must have taken into the prison on the last morning of her life. Would a woman who had suddenly been given so much to live for choose that moment to kill herself? He told her of his covering note that either the Colombians had found or been given by Francesca as she begged for her life.

'They silenced Mónica because she was going to testify against a senior member of the Cali cartel. I was due to see her later today. Let's go, Laura. I need to think this through. I'll drive.'

He checked regularly in the rear-view mirror. At least they were not being followed.

The journey home was difficult, so much to say that each took refuge in silence. He had almost reached Camden before he spoke again. He looked at her wryly.

'One of the two men I need to speak to is the guy I've just left in Germany.'

'Ah, your friend Oscar. Who's the other?'

'Olaf.'

'Oh, shit.'

'What's the matter?'

'I'm sorry, love. It went right out of my head with all this. Olaf has been trying to get hold of you for a couple of days. He said you'd know the number.'

Once home he made no attempt initially to phone either friend, but sat hunched in an armchair. When he thought he had worked out a coherent strategy, he picked up the phone to call Olaf at his Miami home, then replaced the receiver.

Laura looked at him enquiringly.

'Just going for a stroll. Back soon.'

'Like me to come?'

'I wouldn't be very good company at the moment. Need to think things through.'

She crossed the room and kissed him gently. 'I'll be here when you get back.'

Adam crossed by Camden underground and headed towards a number of public telephones. With his credit cards in his hand, he entered one of the booths. The possibility that his home phones might be tapped had occurred to him just in time. If these people were capable of murdering Fran and Mónica, arranging to have a telephone bugged would be a moment's work. Before he could give Olaf the grim news, he listened to details of what had happened after his visit to the Flores.

'Combination of rage at finding the girl gone and a desire to send a message to her mother, a warning. Typical cartel tactic.'

As Olaf described what had happened in the house of Flores, Adam instantly transferred the horror to a thatched cottage in Hertfordshire and cried out in anguish, an involuntary lament for a dead friend. He told Olaf what had happened, not only in the imagined sanctuary of an English village but in the supposed security of an English prison. Olaf's voice broke as he said, 'How do I tell Carla?'

'You don't. When she has to be told I'll do it. What purpose would it serve to tell her now? Look, Olaf, can you look after her until November?'

'Of course, Adam. She's one of the family already. Poor Mónica. What a wretched life.'

They talked for a long time, attempting to build from the wreckage. Then Adam spoke to Oscar. He asked him for his view on contacting the British police.

'Sure, great idea to talk to Scotland Yard. I can just imagine their reaction when you talk about Colombian cartels. They won't need any cocaine to make their eyes glaze. Forget it, my young friend. All you've got in your corner is a little fat man, his hands and his talent on a keyboard. You wanna get even with these people? Don't get mad, get me a certain password. And, Adam, you don't need to hear this, you already know it, but I'm gonna say it. Be very careful. You're not dealing with the Mafia. These people like killing and they like hurting before they kill. With them killing isn't just taking care of business, it's taking care of business *and* pleasure.'

When Adam got home he sat as if huddling against a strong wind. Laura came into the living room. 'Come and have some lunch. I know you're not hungry, but you must eat.'

He followed her out into the kitchen. They sat opposite each other at the breakfast bar. Laura watched him as he stared at a plate of food. 'Can I help?'

He looked at her for the first time since they had met at the airport. He seemed so vulnerable that she instinctively reached out a hand and caressed his face. He kissed her palm very gently. 'You always help. Just by being there, you help.'

'Put it into your film, Adam.'

'Put what in?'

'The fact that all of these people have been murdered. And tell the audience why.'

'I can't prove that Mónica was murdered.'

'You don't have to. Just put it together the way you told me. The tape from her daughter . . . what's happened to that by the way? Interesting line of inquiry. The fact that you were coming to London to take a statement from her that would have indicted a cartel member. The fact that virtually as you were flying here she conveniently obliges the cartel by hanging herself.'

'Aren't you the lady who told me not to go down that path? Didn't you say, just give the Network an entertaining film on the Collins campaign?'

'That was then. This is now. This little girl Carla. I'm going to be in Los Angeles until mid-November, but if you want to bring her to London then, Adam . . .'

Her voice trailed away as she failed to work her way through the maze that such a change in their lifestyle would create. He squeezed her hand, then shook his head. 'She's safer where she is. Thanks all the same. God, what a world.'

He stood up, walked to the window and stared out blankly. Then he turned suddenly and looked at her. 'Did you say mid-November?'

'Yes. Don't you remember? We talked about it in Washington. You said that as you were going to be tied up making your Collins film at least until the election in November it wouldn't be a problem. Is it?'

'No, no. Sorry, love, I'd forgotten. Sorry.'

Laura laughed. 'Don't be silly, you're always the same when you're in the middle of a piece of work.'

'Meaning?'

'Meaning that whatever you're working on becomes the

centre of your universe until it's in the can and transmitted.' She moved to him and put her arms around him. 'That's how it's always been. It's one of the reasons that you're so bloody good. Now, come on and eat some lunch.'

He had not forgotten that she would be working in California for several months. He had wanted to make sure that he had remembered correctly. Had wanted to be certain that she would be out of London until after his film was finished and broadcast. He had a particular reason. The black Mercedes he had seen in the street. The one with what looked like a surveillance team in it. He had rationalized not telling Laura about it. No need to alarm her. What good would it achieve for her to know that nowhere was safe from the cartels? There was another reason for his discretion: he wanted nothing to stop him making what was going to be the most sensational film of his career. He hungered for the acclamation that would follow the broadcast every bit as much as the very large cheque from the Network that would be his when he delivered it.

The last words Mónica had heard in this life had been those of her daughter Carla. The tape was now on its way to Victor Rodriguez. Nothing else of any significance had been found in her cell. The appropriate action had been taken and Rodriguez hoped that the matter was now closed.

It had not been too difficult for Fernando Salazar to organize. A call to the public telephone in Holloway prison, a conversation with one of the other mules. All that Salazar had told the woman was what had happened at the house of Flores. He had then told her that it would happen to every member of her family in Cali, all sixteen of them, unless she did just this one thing for him. Confronted with that threat the woman had been pathetically eager to squeeze the last drop of life from Mónica. Carla's tape had continued to play while the woman had first garrotted her, then, hanging her from the window bar, had pulled and pulled on her legs to ensure that this threat to her own family was removed, permanently. The woman had chosen her moment well – the free-association period when the prisoners gossip together or watch television.

'I've had round-the-clock surveillance on him. No police activity.' Fernando Salazar sat across the desk from Rodriguez.

'The mother is beyond helping Mr Fraser. The daughter?'

Rodriguez watched Salazar's knuckles on his right hand whiten as he responded. 'Carla has vanished without trace.'

Rodriguez stood and crossed to his observation window above the trading floor. He was gratified to see the various wheels of Andino Incorporated running so smoothly. 'I want you to go to Miami, Fernando. Our colleagues in the DEA will introduce you to a gentleman from Jamaica, Winston Thomas.'

Rodriguez crossed back to his desk and handed him a slim file. 'This will give you some of his background. He's a senior member of the Yardies currently being run by Miami DEA as an undercover agent infiltrating the Medellin cartel.'

Salazar's eyebrows rose slightly. Rodriguez continued, 'I want your personal assessment of his potential to carry out a job for us.'

'What kind of job?'

'The assassination of Patrick Collins.'

CHAPTER SIXTEEN

POSITIONS

RESPONDING TO TERESA'S ADVICE, COLLINS HAD REFUSED TO reposition himself, had declined to bend to the whims of focus groups, dial groups and advertising strategies. Instead of giving the electorate less religion, he had given them more. He had told them where he stood on the important issues; he had made no attempt to hide his political inexperience, rather he revelled in it. The professionals in his team had winced, held their heads and feared wipe-out. A Gallup poll revealed that Collins had bounced back even higher. He now had 43 per cent. Sinclair drafted Teresa Collins to all the morning strategy meetings.

Adam listened to her overcome the professionals again. She refused to plant stooges and soft questions in Collins's live rallies. When the meeting was over, he made his way across to Sinclair. 'Andrew, have you had a chance to consider my filming request?'

'Into the very heart of the campaign nerve centre, yes?'

'Something like that, but to a degree that's just background to my interview with you. Seems to me you're very much the nerve centre.'

Sinclair bowed slightly. 'You're far too kind, Adam. Look, why not film a piece in the World Trade? Then we'll take the boat up-river to my place in Hamilton. You'll love it. Great locations, and Mary would like to meet the crew. Lunch and film the rest of the interview in my home?'

Adam hid his disappointment well. 'Excellent idea.'

'Good. Give me a couple of days and I'll offer you a date.'

'Thank you.'

Sinclair looked thoughtfully after him. To have flatly refused his request might have aroused further suspicions. The sooner he got the crew out of his office and up-river to Hamilton the better.

Fernando Salazar had chosen the location for his first meeting with the man from Jamaica with care and attention to detail, a small, discreet restaurant in the Coconut Grove district, not far from Miami airport. Salazar and Winston Thomas took an instant liking to each other. They had so much in common: narcotics, organized crime, murder, under-age girls and guns. Particularly guns. The field testing would come later, at this stage Salazar was merely establishing Thomas's level of technical knowledge. He rapidly established that the man knew the tools of his trade exceedingly well. After that they exchanged opinions like two men discussing wine.

'For me, Fernando, the Beretta model 12 ranks with the Skorpion as one of the most efficient automatic weapons. It is simple, elegant, has two safety systems and, with a forty-round magazine, it gives a wonderfully heavy concentration of firepower in an urban situation.'

Outside the restaurant, in a carefully positioned car, Roberto and a colleague waited. They had obtained a number of excellent photographs of Salazar and Thomas entering. A similar number of the pair emerging, and they would then have fulfilled the assignment that Roberto had been given by his briefing contact in Washington.

Roberto was no longer bemused at the tasks he was being given. Breaking into garage workshops to conduct some industrial espionage, climbing on roof-tops to photograph a dinner party and long-lens work outside a restaurant – he viewed it all with tranquillity. He had realized long before the public flotation that Cybersafe would be an excellent investment. He had followed subsequent events with great interest, and increasing job satisfaction.

Several hours later, Roberto had all the photographs he needed. His car eased into the traffic, then sped away. If he had stayed he would have been able to take some additional shots that would have greatly interested Rodriguez. Having waited while Winston Thomas caught a cab, Salazar decided to take a stroll. The area had an interesting mixture of art galleries and boutiques. He was looking in the window of a gallery near the Coconut Grove theatre when he first saw her. Carla, one hand in Olaf's, the other in Isabella's, in newly bought clothes and with her hair recently styled, was totally transformed. The Colombian flower had bloomed. Three hours later when the group emerged from the theatre, Salazar followed them back to the apartment block where the Nilssons lived. The gold teeth gleamed as he noted down the number. He would be in Miami working with Winston Thomas for quite a few days. With luck he would catch up with Carla when she ventured out on her own.

Again on Teresa's advice, and over the heads of the professionals, Collins embarked on a series of 'electronic town halls': open meetings, on live television, in towns and cities coast to coast. The professionals objected to copying the Clinton campaign of 1992. 'Clinton won in 1992.' Meeting closed. The town-hall sessions were edited into successful half-hour 'informercials'.

The location for the first town hall was chosen carefully – Collins's home town of Boston. So were the issues.

'OK. Now, before I open up to you all, here are just a few more facts that we as a nation have to face. Medical science is on the verge of identifying the specific genes that determine just how long each of us is going to live. When they do, every insurance company in this country is going to be demanding genetic testing on potential customers. Think about that. Think about the implications.'

Collins got up from behind his desk in the studio and began to move towards the audience as he continued. 'The people here are a representative cross-section of American society. During their lives one in four will need long-term care. Let's assume that all of you have the gene apolipoprotein E, or apro E. That means you are four times more likely to live for a hundred years.'

The audience clapped and whooped at their good fortune.

Collins beamed back at them and raised a hand. 'A studio full of centenarians. Wonderful.'

Then he became serious. 'Ten per cent, maybe more, will suffer from Alzheimer's some time after their sixty-fifth birthday. Still feeling lucky? Fifty-five per cent, more than half of all people over the age of sixty-five, will suffer from sustained illnesses that will limit their activities. Within the next fifteen years, at least a quarter of the population of this country will be over sixty-five years of age. Now when we discuss affordable health care for all, these are some of the facts we should be examining.'

He worked the studio audience just as he worked the throngs that gathered in the stadium, as he worked the TV viewers for his weekly church service. He created a new TV format, a visual problems page with an in-house charismatic wise man. Although he met Teresa's demand for straight talking, he managed to fit in plenty of soundbites. 'Oh, I'm in favour of downsizing. I want to downsize the budget deficit. I want to downsize crime, poverty, unemployment and the need for food stamps.'

That brought the audience to its feet, clapping and cheering. In the final moments he brought two chairs downstage and, placing one on either side of him, he said, 'One of those was for a Republican, the other for a Democrat. Heck, if I'd been as responsible for the mess we're in as those two are, I guess I wouldn't want to debate Pat Collins either. Goodnight, America, and God bless you.'

It was not merely the studio audience who loved it. The next major opinion poll showed Collins moving to 47 per cent; neither of the main party candidates attracted even 25 per cent of the vote. Yet again the professionals were confounded.

Without consciously trying, Collins managed to please all the 'dial groups', 'voter segments' and 'focus groups'. He seemed to find a personal relationship with each voter. One of his passages brought a tear to the hardened eye of Andrew Sinclair. 'I ask you who are parents: do you love your children? Of course you do, truly, deeply, utterly. But sometimes you have to hurt your children. Put something that stings on to the cut knee. Take them to the doctor for a shot. And it's so easy to say, "Don't worry, it won't hurt." But then your children get something that hurts much more that the sting or the needle. They get a parent who lies to them. So can we learn something from our children? I think so. Let us choose not the lie that soothes but the truth that stings.'

Each day Fernando Salazar worked with Winston Thomas on a variety of tests. They worked their way through a range of rifles with Salazar marking him for speed and accuracy.

'Remember, Winston, it's to be done with just one shot through the heart.'

'The head would be better. Greater guarantee of fatality.'

'I agree, but who are we to argue with the client? Now try a series of single shots with this Armalite AK-18, maximum rate of single shot fire is forty rounds per minute, see how close you can get to that figure. The target is set at the maximum effective range of five hundred yards. In three. One, two, three.'

At the end of the daily session when he had safe-housed all of the weapons, Salazar would take a cab to the apartment block where the Nilssons lived, pay off the driver and stand in the shadows on the other side of the street. Waiting. Near the block was a small park, an ideal place for a child to play. He saw the woman on several occasions, entering or leaving, but of Carla there was no sign. What Salazar had no way of knowing was that he was directly responsible for her non-appearance outside the apartment.

The morning after the family expedition to the theatre, Carla had been playing with Isabella's makeup. Her young face showed intense concentration as she strained to put on lipstick. Her eyes screwed half closed, she leaned into the mirror and the small gold crucifix round her neck tapped gently on the glass. She caught at it, then turned to Olaf, who had been watching her. 'When will I see Mama?'

Olaf gathered himself to lie, then found he was struggling against the look in the dark brown eyes that stared at him. He moved and sat in a chair close to the dressing table.

'Carla, your mother has been ill for some time in London. Last week, her condition became much worse. She was taken to hospital, but there was nothing that could be done. I'm sorry, Carla, but Mama is dead.'

Carla considered this thoughtfully. 'Does that mean she is now in heaven?'

'Yes, my dear.'

It was as if she had known already or sensed it at least. Olaf had expected her to become distraught, but as he and Isabella comforted her, she was calmer than they were.

Suddenly a thought occurred to Carla. 'Does this mean I'll have to go away? That I can't stay with you any longer?'

Isabella put an arm around her. 'You can stay with us for as long as you like.'

'For ever?'

Isabella looked at Olaf.

'Yes,' said Olaf. 'For ever, Carla.'

'But what about Uncle Adam?'

'I'm sure he'll have no objections. I'll phone him. Now why not go out and play in the park for a while? Isabella will come with you.'

'No, I want to stay here.'

It seemed that she feared that if she went outdoors, they

might change their minds. Might refuse to let her back in. Even her extraordinary stoicism had a limit.

Ignorant of the drama that he had caused to be played out in the Nilsson apartment, Salazar sipped from a brandy flask to pass the time while he waited for the chance to intercept his little friend.

'You're a hard man to keep up with, Adam.'

It was Olaf phoning from Miami. 'The Collins residence in Florida gave me your Boston hotel number. The Boston hotel gave me the New York hotel. Life in the fast lane?'

'Sorry, Olaf. I need a thirty-hour day at the moment. How is Carla?'

Olaf told him of her response to the news of her mother's death. 'Adam, she wants to stay with us, with Isabella and the kids. I mean permanently. How do you feel about that?'

'Point is, Olaf, how do you feel about it?'

'It's fine by us. She's a delightful child. Gets on real well with everyone. We'd be very happy, and, don't forget, according to her Venezuelan passport, she's already my daughter.'

'You've got my blessing. Tell Carla that once this country has itself a new president and the dust settles I'll come and see all of you.'

'Now if I'm a very good boy will you buy me one of these, please?'

The request came from Leon. The 'one of these' was the Sinclair residence complete with rolling lawns and river frontage. It was two weeks into the campaign proper, and Adam had been permitted to film and interview in the campaign nerve centre on the hundredth floor of the World Trade Center. Adam's discreet search for anything that might indicate the password into the mysterious Colombia Project had proved fruitless. Sinclair and his staff had been very relaxed about the filming. The crew had been allowed to wander all over the extensive suite of offices, but Adam had invariably been accompanied by Sinclair's personal assistant, Clare. It had always been long odds against finding the information that Oscar needed. The man in Hamburg would just have to keep on hacking.

Sinclair was in a state of suppressed excitement as the boat approached his home. Adam sensed that here, if anywhere on earth, was the gap in the man's emotional defences.

Adam disembarked and stood on the small quay to gaze up the immaculately kept gardens. He started to frame a compliment, but was cut off by Sinclair's two children, squealing with delight at Daddy's return. They were introduced, then flooded the crew with questions, Kathy eagerly, Peter shyly.

'Wonderful kids, Andrew,' said Adam.

For a moment his host glowed, and then slipped back into control. 'You can shoot wherever you like, Adam. Perhaps you and the team would like to start with a drink, have a look around to see where would be best. And meet Mary.' Adam caught the split-second pause which turned the last three words into a sentence.

Mary Sinclair was the perfect hostess. She had arranged for lunch to be served on a side lawn, she was charming, witty and apparently thrilled that a film-crew was about to disrupt her home life. She posed only one problem. When they returned to the lawn after a tour of the house with Mary, Leon whispered, 'I think you've cracked it there, Adam.'

'Oh, come on. She's just being sociable.'

'Absolutely. That's why she hasn't taken her eyes off you.'

'Perhaps she's having trouble with her contacts.'

'Yes, and perhaps I'm the man in the moon.'

Mary Sinclair advanced across the lawn towards them. 'Have you made up your mind where you want to do it, Adam?'

Leon stared towards the Hudson river, stifling a burst of laughter.

'What about the library?'

Leon had been right about Mary Sinclair. She had not meant to make it so obvious, but she wanted Adam the moment she met him.

She did not regret her marriage to Andrew; after all, it had been her idea. But she had not realized how little of his energy and passion would go to her. She had found that energy elsewhere, but never enough passion to make her want to leave Sinclair's house and his money. She wondered if he noticed that all the teachers of her many classes were young men. Probably not. He might even be glad not to be bothered as often as he had been in the early days of their marriage.

But Adam suggested another possibility altogether, a dangerous life, without compromise or arrangement. She smiled as she watched Susanna arrange everything for shooting in the library. Perhaps we should swap partners, she thought. Andrew would be so well suited by Little Miss Perfect, and Adam would get a woman instead of a daughter . . .

'Is there anything you would like moved?' she asked him, so close that she blocked his view of the room, but before he could reply Andrew Sinclair strode in.

'This chair?' He followed Susanna's gesture and sat down. Adam moved to the facing chair, and began. 'Andrew, most presidential candidates use one basic speech. I've been following this campaign from day one. I have yet to hear your candidate make the same speech twice. Does this demonstrate a refreshing innovation or a confused mind?'

Sinclair's body language was impeccable. Slight nod. Good smile. Shoulders moving forward slightly towards the interviewer, an aura of agreeability. He did not even hint at the words 'You son of a bitch' as he responded.

'I think it demonstrates how unique this candidate is. The idea that a politician, any politician, can explore every major problem in this country during the course of one speech is dangerously simplistic. It carries the soundbite age we live in a little further down the road to the funny farm.'

'Yet, although the words differ, there are certain themes that emerge more often than others, Andrew. Crime. Drugs. Fortress America. These warnings Collins gives – the enemy within, for example. Do you agree with him? Take last night's electronic town hall from Orange County. The Reverend Collins painted a bleak future. To compare the United States to former Yugoslavia and to talk of the risk of America disintegrating to a pre-Civil War condition could almost have been taken straight out of the Book of Revelation. Terrorists at war with the state. Militia groups transforming their collective paranoia into suburban violence. It's been five months since the last attack by the Friday Bombers—'

The phone on Sinclair's desk rang, startling everyone in the room. Sinclair was apologetic. 'I thought they were all unplugged. Excuse me a moment. Hello? Yes, speaking.' He listened. 'Thank you.' He looked across the desk at Adam. 'It sounds as though someone else has answered your question before I could. A bomb exploded a short while ago in Miami.'

Adam stared at him in shocked disbelief. Mary, who had been sitting quietly at the back of the room, screamed. The television soon confirmed the accuracy of the phone call. Right in the heart of the restored art-deco district in Miami a bomb had exploded. The images on the TV showed all too well the fear, the trauma and emotional mayhem.

Leon looked across the room to Adam, who nodded almost imperceptibly. The look had said, 'Shall I carry on filming?' He responded like a documentary-maker. They panned with the blood. Time for tears later.

Sinclair had missed the mute interchange. He looked at Adam. 'I must call Pat. Alert him to this dreadful thing.'

He reached for the phone and began hitting numbers. Adam leaned a restraining arm across the desk and pointed to the television. Collins was on screen, he seemed to be covered in blood. 'I was at home in Collinsville when I heard a news flash,' he was saying to a reporter. 'I've just flown over to see if I can help in any way.'

'There are reports that a militia group is responsible. Do you think we should retaliate?'

'What we should do is avoid making a rush to judgement. First let us bury the dead, attend to the injured and comfort the survivors.'

'Last night, Mr Collins, you predicted the likelihood of attacks like this. Do you think there will be others?'

'Young lady, this is neither the time nor the place for such speculation. I am trying to comfort grieving relatives. If you can't lend a hand, then get out of the way.'

The news team swung the camera on to a partially demolished building as Collins clambered back inside past firemen, police and emergency services.

As the death toll mounted, the visual image of a blood-spattered Collins rounding angrily on a journalist caught perfectly the mood of America. It was another defining moment. The image of Collins in Miami fused with his words of the previous evening in Orange County to achieve symbiosis with the mood of America.

The Orange County broadcast was run in its entirety as a news item on radio and television. Newspapers quoted and requoted it. The *New York Times* ran an editorial headed 'A Prophet In His Own Country'.

Patrick Collins warned us to beware the enemy within. He talked of the evil forces that have foregathered in parts of this country. While others had reassured the public that the Friday Bombers had stopped indulging in their acts of inhumanity, Collins warned the nation of the dangers ahead. Less than twenty-four hours after he had talked so eloquently of the alienation, viciousness and godlessness he saw within our land, eighteen – many of them young children – lay dead, a further seventy-three have sustained injury and a great American city has been most horribly violated.

That Collins responded so quickly and with such compassion speaks profoundly of the man who would be president.

The fact that none of the other candidates saw fit to fly to Miami and that the President himself made only a TV appearance from his vacation home in California was not commented on by the *New York Times*. Other newspapers were not so discreet. When it was established that a home-made pipe bomb had yet again been responsible for the carnage and that this pointed directly to the involvement of one of the private armies, the militias, the self-proclaimed paranoiac defenders of the free, media demands for interviews with Collins flooded in.

When Sinclair reported these developments privately to Victor Rodriguez, he received a terse reply. 'Satisfactory. But why the switch to Miami from the Magic Kingdom in Disney World?'

'The Magic Kingdom would have upset my children.'

By early October the issues of concern in the presidential election had virtually all become internal. Iran, Libya, even China had been sidelined. Voters wanted to discuss only the evil from within.

'Look, if you want to do an interview with Mr Collins and Mr Fraser wants to film you conducting that interview, then that's the deal.'

Sam Barnes put the phone down with the élan and confidence of a press secretary whose candidate was showing at 52 per cent in the latest Gallup poll.

'Thanks, Sam.'

Adam had been waiting in the campaign press office for the day's schedule.

'They accepted, of course. You'll enjoy filming this one. It's for the BBC.'

'Sam, they'll tie Pat up for a couple of hours, then use just a couple of minutes.'

'I know that, Adam. But we want to target the overseas vote. They'll sell the interview on throughout Europe.'

'There are just three weeks to election day. I need to have a one-on-one with Pat Collins. This change in the campaign. The national preoccupation with domestic issues. I want to get into it. Ask *my* questions instead. I'm going out of my mind listening to people putting questions he's answered a hundred times. I want to take a walk through the American interior with Pat Collins as my guide.'

Barnes consulted his schedule and rubbed his chin. 'Can you make it a fairly brisk walk? Say about an hour?'

'Sure.'

'On Thursday, October nineteenth, Pat and John will be at a strategy campaign meeting at Andrew Sinclair's home. If Mary Sinclair doesn't mind, when the meeting breaks mid-afternoon I'll give you an hour with Pat. Subject to that not causing any problems for anyone, I'll slate it in.'

'I think we should make a start by bombing the sub-human scumbags in Libya and the worms, weasels and trash in Teheran. Let's do it Texas style. A good hanging followed by a fair trial.'

Susanna punched another button on the car radio.

'. . . Yes, I know all about turning the other cheek. I also know all about an eye for an eye and a tooth for a tooth. We're dealing with fanatics. Islam doesn't have a monopoly on bigotry. When they catch the slime that's bombed Miami let's have no probation reports and prison sentences. Let's just kill them. If you—'

Adam put a hand on Susanna's arm. 'Su, you're not going to find a station talking about anything else. Just imagine, clear across the country, over a thousand radio talk-shows all pressing the hate pedal.'

They were on their way to the editing suite on West 43rd Street. With the presidential race now moving into the final mile, Adam had elected for New York editing facilities to work on the rough-cut assembly of the film.

Susanna, hoping to lighten the mood, pressed the radio on in search of some music. The voice of Patrick Collins filled the air. 'I wholly refute the idea that these atrocities have any link to a vast international conspiracy. The answer is within this country and within ourselves.'

'Reverend Collins, do you think these could be the Last Days?'

'Only God can answer that question. No one knows how long we have. Meanwhile we should start addressing the whole host of problems that confront this country. We should rediscover self-belief, replace hate with love. I tell you Nietzsche was wrong. God is not dead. Nietzsche is dead, but God is very much alive. Let Him in. I'm talking long-term salvation.'

'Fine, Reverend. And what about short-term preservation?'

'We are at war. Make no mistake about that. This is no far off enemy from a foreign land of which we know little. It's pointless looking for an alien scapegoat. This time the barbarians are not at the gate. They are inside the walls. And these barbarians have American accents. For the first time since the Declaration of Independence a hostile army intent on evil stalks our villages, towns and cities. We must behave as citizens of an occupied country should always behave. With vigilance. The terrorist is the worst kind of enemy. No morality. No ethics. No courage. They are not only nature's cowards, but nature's failures.'

With a start Susanna realized that they were at their destination and that Adam was waiting for her. He switched off the ignition. She looked across. 'He's going to win, isn't he?'

Adam shrugged. 'A lot can happen in three weeks.'

The casually tossed-off remark came back to haunt him before the end of the day. Mark, the editor with whom he always worked, had flown in from London where he had been putting together a rough-cut assemblage. Now he, Adam and Susanna had grafted throughout the day without taking a break. Eventually, tired but satisfied that progress had been made on the final edit, they locked the basement suite and emerged into the now dark New York streets.

'Bit like moving from a small editing suite to a big one,' said Adam. 'Come on, I'll shout you dinner.'

The three of them ran exuberantly across the road in search of a restaurant. New York, mid-evening, is a maelstrom of sound, but even by the city's normal standards of noise pollution the mixture of sirens, alarms, bells, wailing was deafening. They passed a middle-aged woman sobbing. She could have been one of the hundreds of crazies who walked the streets. Mark, lacking New York street wisdom, approached her. 'What is it? Are you all right? Can we help?'

The woman turned and gazed unseeingly at him. 'Don't you know? They've blown up Grand Central.'

This time there were forty-seven dead and over two hundred injured. The same technique. A pipe bomb in a trash can. There had been no warning and no group accepted responsibility. No demands were made.

Two nights after the rush-hour carnage in New York, the Collins electronic town hall was in Greensboro, North Carolina. A sombre Patrick Collins spoke directly to camera.

'Before the enemy attack on Grand Central, I had planned to discuss, with the audience here tonight, the economy. Seems to me the economy will have to wait for another day. This situation is too urgent, too dangerous to be left until another day.'

Instead of the normal thirty minutes the programme ran for an hour.

'This is our America, my friends. Fortress America. Every home a fortress, every screen in every home a fortress, but inside each fortress a fifth column of fantasies and filth . . .' Collins talked of enemies visible and enemies invisible, secret armies, unknown generals, pollution, pornography, poison . . .

Adam walked thoughtfully to join his film-crew, who were standing by his car. 'The interview is confirmed for this afternoon. We'll take a leisurely drive up to Hamilton, have lunch, then interview Collins at the Sinclair residence. Don't fret if we get separated, Leon, just stay on Broadway.'

'What, all the way?'

'Sure. It becomes Highway Nine. Just outside Hamilton there's Janson's Fish Restaurant. You can't miss it.'

Barry picked up a large tape-recorder. 'Just watch him. Now, Leon, you'll know we've gone too far when you hit Canada.'

Still verbally sparring they picked up the equipment and went back to their own car. Susanna was about to join them when Adam restrained her.

'Like to keep me company?'

'Of course.'

Preoccupied, Adam opened the passenger door for her. As he

got in, Susanna saw him stare hard in the direction of Park Avenue and Grand Central station. He caught her looking at him. 'We were working so close to that bomb. People lost their lives, others lost arms, or a leg, or an eye. Just ordinary people trying to catch a train, and we just carried on working.'

She leaned over and gripped his shoulder. 'Adam, love, we never heard a thing. Of course we were working.'

'Something like that, Su, makes all this so meaningless. Totally worthless. You know, when that bomb went off, I was probably agonizing about whether to cut out of the Collins crusade rally a few frames earlier? Whether to drop in more voice-over during the Boston College sequence? Something like that. At the end of the day it doesn't amount to a bale of hay.'

Susanna made to respond, but he went on, 'No, Su. It's not a fishing expedition. I'm not seeking any kind of reassurance about my place in the scheme of things. Right now I'd drop it all in that river if I thought it would stop the bombings.'

They drove out of the city in silence. They were well into Yonkers before she ventured to speak.

'It's bizarre. One moment we're in upmarket millionaire's row, the next it's virtually a ghetto, then it's back to the money again.'

Adam glanced out of the window. 'Yeah. It settles down in a few miles. The further north we go towards Sinclair the more you'll see those Fortress Americas that Collins is always talking about.'

She reached out a hand, gingerly touching his arm. 'Can we stop on the way?'

At Hastings-on-Hudson they parked outside the village, parking close to the river. 'Come on, then,' said Adam. 'Let's find a café.'

Susanna held up a take-out bag. 'Got this before we left. It's still hot. Good old American know-how. Polystyrene and all.'

In a moment they had a picnic by the water's edge, coffee and bagels for two.

'You're wrong about your work, Adam. It does count. It *is* important. Because they blow up a railway station, that doesn't invalidate the rest of life. If it did, then the bombers have won.'

He studied her carefully. 'That sugar on the tip of your nose really suits you.'

'Oh, good. I thought you'd never notice,' she said, and brushed it off.

He put his cup on the grass and turned slightly towards her. They were sitting close to each other. 'Su, I think it would be better if I finished the editing with Mark on my own.'

'You really know how to give a girl a good time at a picnic, don't you?'

'I don't want to expose you to any more risks on this film. There are certain things I want to add to the fine cut, extra material.'

'So?'

'There might be reaction when it's transmitted. I mean, a violent reaction. If you're still here in New York you might be at risk.'

'And what about Mark and the crew?'

'They'll all be back in London before transmission.'

'Fine. I'll fly back with them then.'

'But—'

'Adam, I'm staying. Save your energy for the film. Now, have another bagel.'

There was a curious mood of suppressed excitement in the air when the film-crew arrived at the Sinclair home. It seemed to Adam to be singularly out of touch with the times. Many of the dead from the Grand Central bombing had yet to be buried. The source of the mood was the campaign team. While the crew began to set up for the Collins interview, Sam Barnes sought him out. 'Two pieces of information that you might like to use when you interview Pat. Three polls coming out tomorrow. We've just been tipped off. Harris, Gallup and Time all showing Pat on sixty-three per cent. That's proved last-straw time for the Democrats and the Republicans. They've caved in. Agreed to three TV debates. One for the potential vice-presidents, two for the presidential candidates.'

Sam punched Adam's shoulder and went out to rejoin the others in the garden. Adam stood for a moment deep in thought.

'Adam, you look so lost. Anything you need?'

'Is there somewhere I can change, Mary? Put on a clean shirt for the interview?'

'Of course. Come on, I'll show you.'

They moved through the house towards the stairs.

'What were you thinking about just then? You seemed to be in another world.'

'I was thinking about the bombings in New York and Miami. I'm going to the requiem mass at St Patrick's tomorrow.'

'Really? You're filming it?'

'No, no. Just to pay my respects.'

'Oh, of course. Dreadful business. Truly dreadful. You know Jed, our gardener, he lives in Dobbs Ferry. He knew one of the victims. Used to give him advice on his shrubbery. Lived just two blocks away from Jed. Dreadful. Here you are. I'll be just across the corridor if you need anything.'

Adam glanced around the guest suite, then placed his fresh shirt on the bed. He unbuttoned the one he was wearing, tossed it to one side and went into the bathroom. As the water ran in the wash-basin he stared at himself in the mirror. He was supposed to be the uncaring, hard bastard. At least, that's what people often told him on location. He was the one who would ask the grieving father in Gaza, the shocked family in Tel Aviv, the policeman's widow, the suicide-bomber's mother, he was the one who would ask them to do it just one more time, just one more take. To get it right. To get it perfect. To ensure that the watching audience got the full power/horror/shock, delete where non-applicable. Perhaps it was all finally catching up with him. He talked aloud to his mirror image. 'Alas, poor Jed's neighbour. I knew him, Horatio; a fellow of infinite jest, of most excellent fancy – his shrubbery, however, left something to be desired.'

'Who *are* you talking to?'

Adam spun round. Mary Sinclair was standing in the bedroom, holding one dress in front of her and a second in her other hand.

'Er, oh, just myself. Sorry if I disturbed you.'

'Adam, you have no idea how much you disturb me. Now, which is it to be? Should I wear this? Or this?' Mary held the second dress in front of the first.

'They both look very nice.'

'*Nice?* One does not shop at Valentino for "nice" clothes. Now come on, is it to be the yellow or the blue?'

She held her arms far apart displaying both dresses. She was naked.

'Mary, you've got a houseful of people downstairs. Someone might walk in at any moment.'

Mary laughed. 'Perhaps you'll help me solve the problem another day, then?'

'Yes, of course.'

'You'll call me?'

'Yes, yes.'

'Soon?'

'Yes, soon, Mary. Now please go and put on one of those dresses.'

He washed, dressed and sat on the bed until he heard her going back downstairs. What Sinclair might have asked his colleague Victor Rodriguez to arrange if he had chanced to come upstairs did not bear thinking about.

Adam came away from his latest interview with Patrick Collins with the overriding impression that he had indeed been talking to a president-in-waiting. He could not detect in the preacher even a flicker of uncertainty or insecurity. Two weeks before the election, Patrick Collins's impossible dream had turned into his manifest destiny.

'Where I differ from the religious right is that I believe in the freedom of choice, but – and this must never be forgotten – that choice should always be exercised by a well-formed conscience.'

That takes care of the homosexuals, the pro-abortionists, the radicals and the liberals, thought Adam. No wonder he's showing sixty-three per cent in the polls.

'Your position on illegal drugs, has it changed at all during this campaign?'

Those hypnotic green eyes fastened on Adam. 'Yes, Adam. I think I can say that my position has moved.'

Adam could not stop himself leaning forward. Were the cartel about to receive a payback on their four-year investment?

'The facts, the figures, the statistics that have been made available to me during the past nine months have convinced me that I had previously underestimated the enormity of the problem.'

'You had underestimated it?'

'Oh, yes, very seriously underestimated the narcotics problem in this country. I will be making a major speech on this issue in my final campaign rally on the third of November. If elected to the presidency I shall apply a policy of zero tolerance to those who are destroying the fabric of the American way of life. At the moment crime pays. That's going to stop.'

'Are you sure that phone you're talking on is clean?'

'You tell me, Oscar. Have the cartel got the Lincoln Center bugged? Your fax said call immediately. I didn't think that gave me too much time to be picky about which phone I used. You were right about the donations to the Collins Evangelical Mission. First contributions were two weeks after the last presidential election. One hundred thousand dollars each from Rodriguez, Salazar and Pastrana. 'Fraid I'm not any nearer the entry word you need for that file if that's what you're calling about.'

'You may not need it. I've struck gold. Collins was a member of the CIA in Vietnam. A special operations unit that functioned undercover with regular Marines.'

Adam listened spellbound as Oscar talked of how he had analysed yet again the one common denominator he appeared to have with Patrick Collins: their Vietnam service.

'There's something unusual about this whole episode which

ended with Collins and Reilly wounded and the rest of the patrol wiped out. The size of the patrol is odd. Three times the usual number. The only account on record is that given by the two survivors. There's no corroborating evidence from any independent sources and the recommendation that their bravery should be acknowledged with the highest possible awards, and that they should be given by President Johnson, is strange.'

'What's unusual about that? Johnson decorated lots of soldiers.'

'The recommendation doesn't come from their commanding officer or Westmorland. It comes from Ambassador William Colby, who as you know was not only our top diplomat in Vietnam, he was also running the CIA.'

Oscar knew from previous trawls through the files that someone had been there before him.

'They'd been through every damn file. It was picking up my mail from the States that did it. There was my pay slip from the company. Now the one government department that no one fucks with is the IRS – the Revenue. I had a discreet search made through the accounts department at Langley. Bullseye.'

'What were his duties?'

'Hey, come on, Adam. We're talking accounts departments. He was seconded in September nineteen sixty-seven and ceased being an operative on March twenty-first, nineteen sixty-eight. Immediately after that intelligence-gathering patrol.'

'It's fascinating, Oscar, but how much further does it take us? No dark secrets.'

'Listen, my friend, the CIA were not in Vietnam for the fishing.'

An idea was forming in Adam's mind. 'Oscar, there are just two weeks to the election. I can't be in two places at the same time. I've got plenty of contacts in Hanoi. There's every chance that the Vietcong have got intelligence reports on that patrol in their records, but someone is going to have to go there and ask the right people, and if that someone gets lucky they should get something on film. Tell me, Oscar, have you ever handled a Hi8 camera?'

*　　*　　*

When the potential vice-presidents TV-debated, the calmest person, not only in the studio but probably in the country, was John Reilly. He had deliberately maintained a low profile during the months of campaigning: now he could not avoid the spotlight. Again and again he demonstrated a grasp of the issues that appeared to elude his two rivals. Eventually, exasperated with the obvious evasions from both Democrat and Republican, Reilly uttered what was to become the most quoted remark of the year.

'Pat got more sense out of those two chairs than I'm getting out of you.'

'Some talk of building a wall two thousand miles across, cutting the country off from Mexico. I remember Buchanan talking about that. Again, just half measures. First thing to do is ban all immigration for ten years. Give us a little breathing space. Next thing is voluntary repatriation to home country, offer cash inducements, it'll be cheaper in the long run. By all means build a wall across the South, but a shoot-to-kill policy would be a damn sight cheaper. Look at Florida, no better than a Third World country. Cuba's given us Castro's dregs, Venezuela and Colombia have given us embezzlers, drug barons and moral degenerates.'

Collins stood up and stretched. He had been reading through his notes as he prepared for the forthcoming presidential debates when Teresa had begun to discuss with him the problem of illegal immigration. She smiled at her husband. 'And if the issue gets raised during the first debate?'

Collins returned her smile. 'I shall criticize the current administration for its failure to solve the problem, and promise to make greater funds available to the relevant government agencies, new legislation with tighter controls, a total review of all existing policies, etc., etc.'

When the presidential debates took place, the consensus was that Collins won by being the only one of the three candidates to remain polite, charming and coherent. It also helped that as the third candidate he could move in and out of the wrangling created by the other two as if he was in some way above their squabbling. By the morning of the third of November, the day of Collins's final campaign rally, the preacher stood at 65 per cent in the polls and his rivals were fighting for second place.

By that same morning Fernando Salazar had completed an exhaustive series of field tests with Winston Thomas. In Salazar's opinion, Victor Rodriguez had made an excellent choice. The logistics had been finalized. Thomas had been supplied with a detailed plan of the layout of Madison Square Garden, been given details of a New York safe-house and precise instructions concerning every aspect of the operation. They parted at Miami airport, Thomas to catch a plane to New York, Salazar to while away the hours until his flight to Cali.

Olaf, Isabella and Carla peered up at the departure board. 'Ah, there it is. Delayed three hours! After all that hurrying we've plenty of time. Isn't it always the way?'

It had been a sudden impulse. Carla had been withdrawn since Olaf had broken the news of her mother's fatal 'illness'. He had discussed the problem with a child psychologist who, after an hour of platitudes, had come up with the one useful suggestion of giving the child a holiday.

'There's a cartoon cinema on level two. Can I go?'

Olaf pulled a face. 'I'd rather get something to eat.'

'That's fine. You take Isabella for a meal, I'll go to the movies. It'll help my English lessons.'

Isabella laughed at the idea of Tom and Jerry conducting a language class. 'Come on, then, I'll buy you some candy.'

Isabella watched as, clutching her small handbag and a king-size carton of popcorn, Carla moved through the doors to the interior of the cinema. She walked back to a waiting Olaf. 'She'll be fine. It's a two-hour show. I've arranged to meet her outside. Now, where shall we eat?'

Someone else had been watching as Carla had vanished inside the cartoon cinema. Now he rose from his seat and slowly made his way to the pay desk.

In the dark Carla settled down in her seat. Her eyes never left the screen as she fumbled with the lid of the popcorn carton.

'Hello, Carla. How good it is to see you.'

She froze. Immobile with terror. She had no need to turn to seek his identity. She would hear that voice in her mind on her death-bed.

'Hello, Uncle Fernando.'

Salazar grinned as he leaned over from the row behind and looked down at the child.

'OK, now let's try that sequence on Stratford and his Caribbean laundry with those edits and the new voice-over intro.'

It was seven in the morning and the editing session had been underway for over an hour. The film-crew were already setting up in Madison Square Garden, the location for Collins's final rally. Adam had ten hours of editing in front of him, followed at four in the afternoon with the Collins rally, which was not scheduled to finish until ten in the evening. He planned then to return to the editing suite for two more hours, then be back there again at six the following morning. His colleagues would be working identical hours.

'And roll.'

'As these flow charts make clear, much of the money invested in Cybersafe was from the Colombian drug cartels. The money moved out of Venezuela into the National Trust Bank in Belize, the majority shareholder of which is Edgar Lee Stratford. From there the narco millions moved to Stratford's Mill Valley Bank in San Francisco where they were used to push the share price of Cybersafe ever higher. A majority shareholder in Cybersafe who benefited to the tune of two hundred and seventeen million dollars was Patrick Collins. It was this money that has exclusively financed his campaign for the presidency.'

'Good. Mark and hold on that freeze frame of Collins preaching in his church. For two seconds. Give the viewers time to realize where Collins is. Now spin back to that Thanksgiving dinner and let me see the additional sequence.'

Susanna looked up from the desk where she was working out running times. 'What additional sequence, Adam?'

'The one that comes after we've begun to identify Salazar and Pastrana as cartel members.'

'I can't see the Network lawyers letting you get away with that. "Unnamed intelligence sources" is not going to convince them.'

'You're right, Su. I wonder if this will convince the lawyers. Roll it, Mark.'

'I was sitting by the fountain in the Central Square in Cali. This was during the summer. It was a Sunday—'

'Just a minute, Adam. Hold it.' Susanna had her hand in the air. Mark had hit the pause button before she could speak.

'Who the hell is that? We didn't film that interview.'

'No, I did it on my own. Visiting room, Holloway Prison.'

Susanna stared hard at the frozen image of a beautiful young Colombian woman.

'Is that Mónica?'

'Yes, it is.'

'But she's dead. She died before you could get her on film.'

'No, Su. When I flew to London to see her the second time I took a Hi8 into the prison. Hid it under my overcoat. I got her to tell me her story again before I said I'd try to pull Carla out of Cali. Just taking out some insurance in case she reneged after her daughter was out of Colombia. People do renege, so don't look at me like that.'

'But you've had that interview all this time and not told me.'

'For God's sake, I haven't told anyone. These people we're trying to expose, they'd slice you so thin you'd be transparent.' He gestured at the screen. 'They had Mónica murdered inside prison. They've murdered four people to stop her testifying in this film. I don't want to go to your funeral. Come to that, I don't want to go to my own for a while. *This* is why I wanted to put you on a plane and get you back to London.'

Susanna was quieter now. 'I'm sorry. It just shocked the hell out of me when I realized who it was.'

'Just imagine what it's going to do to Sinclair and his friends, then. Roll it, Mark.'

Given that Adam had been filming secretly, the framing and technical quality were excellent. The content was compelling. With the occasional gentle question from Adam, Mónica had unknowingly created her own epitaph, complete with three drawings of the rings on Fernando Salazar's fingers and a fourth drawing, a pencil sketch of Salazar himself. Mark had re-edited this last drawing a second time so that it finished the interview. The close-up shot mixed through to Salazar sitting next to Patrick Collins. As the dinner sequence was replayed the commentary came in.

'There are many questions that Patrick Collins must answer concerning the curious collection of people at his dinner table, and the huge donations that his Church had been receiving from cartel members. Which, as this document confirms, started within weeks of the last presidential election. Then there are the questions concerning Victor Rodriguez and the photographer on the roof—'

'Yeah, that's fine, Mark. Let's spin through the material that came back from the lab this morning. I want to use some of the second Andrew Sinclair interview, the one we did on the day of the bombing at Miami.'

While the second machine was searching the rough-cut material for the required sequence, Adam glanced over at Susanna. 'You OK?'

'I'm fine. The shit's really going to hit the fan when this goes out. And how are you going to get it out? The Network will have a roomful of lawyers crawling all over it.'

'That's why it has to be one hundred per cent kosher. One bridge at a time, Su. First we finish the doco. That'll be in the small hours of next Wednesday when we have the concessions and the acceptance. They'll be the last segment. Later on Wednesday I'll show it to the Network and argue they should clear their evening schedule and put it out that evening. Just a minute, Mark. Stop. Let it roll forward, normal speed. Hold it there. Well, I'm damned.'

On the screen was the scene in Sinclair's study just after the phone had rung to tell Sinclair of the bombing at Miami. All eyes in Sinclair's study were fixed on the TV screen as they saw the horrific images and a blood-spattered Collins. All eyes except those of the camera Leon had kept running. What it had caught was Andrew Sinclair smiling.

When he had finished using her, he had drunk himself into a stupor. Carla lay quite still until she was sure that Salazar was fast asleep.

'Now you're going to come with me, Carla. Don't shout or scream or draw attention to us. If you do, I'll kill you right here and now. I'll also kill that nice lady and gentleman sitting on the other side of the concourse.'

Carla knew only too well that Salazar was capable of carrying out his threat. Knew from what he had told her in the past in Cali, when he had come visiting to the house of Flores. She could not, would not, put the lives of Olaf and Isabella at risk. They had given her so much. Salazar gripped her hand tightly and hurried her out of the cinema, out of the airport. There was plenty of time before his flight.

Terrified, she had waited while he booked a nearby motel room. As he used her, he boasted how she would never escape him, never get away from him. He had already found her passport in her little handbag.

'How thoughtful of you, my little one. This means you can fly to Cali with me. You can come home. Not to the house of Flores. They now rest in their graves. You can come and live with me.'

He had tucked her passport and her room key in his case. What a wonderful gift, his little girl returned to him. For his pleasure. Eventually he drifted into a deep drunken stupor. Quietly, gently, she eased her body away from his. She stood up slowly and stared down at him. Carla wondered if she could get his case open without waking him. Whatever happened, she was not going to Cali. Not going back to that. With great care she opened the case. There was the key to the room and her passport. She removed them and was about to close the lid when she realized that there was something missing. His gun. He had threatened to use it on her, on Olaf and Isabella, on anyone that might try to stop him abducting her. Quickly she searched inside the case. There was no gun. She looked down on the naked Salazar. Rapidly she searched the suit that he had thrown on the floor in his anxiety to lose no time. Plenty of money, but no gun. Of course, he was flying to Cali, he wouldn't have risked carrying a gun through the airport security checks. She thought of what she had just endured because of his threat to kill. She thought of what awaited her in Cali. Her eyes went to the bedside table, on it a copy of the Gideon Bible, a note-pad and two complimentary metal biro pens.

Rage and fear welled up within her simultaneously. She seized the pens and rapidly inserting one up each of Salazar's nostrils, slammed them up into his brain with the Gideon Bible. He died instantly without making another sound.

Carla was about to unlock the room when an alternative occurred to her. She replaced the key in the case and closed the lid. The room was on the ground floor. Opening the window, she climbed out and closed it behind her.

In a few minutes she was back at Miami airport and had re-entered the cinema. She was calm, determined that nothing was going to jeopardize her new life. She settled down and re-entered once more a world where appalling injuries are magically healed thirty frames later.

'How incongruous, Victor.'

Sinclair had come hurrying from his World Trade Center suite to an impromptu meeting with Rodriguez.

Rodriguez leaned on the railing and looked out across the Hudson. 'Miami Homicide are baffled. Such a bizarre way to die inside a locked room. Fernando had many enemies, of course.'

Although they were alone on the river promenade, Sinclair still glanced around before he spoke. 'We go to all that trouble to use Salazar. Sit him next to Collins at the Thanksgiving dinner. Get him secretly photographed breaking bread with the next president. Protect him from premature exposure by sanctioning murders in England and Cali. All of this to compromise Collins, and the stupid bastard goes and gets himself murdered.'

'Don't worry, Andrew. He's just as useful to us dead as alive, and there is still Pastrana. Then there's the banker. And the other data from the files . . . We still have a very full hand of cards to play if we need to keep Collins in line.'

'Frankly I don't think we're going to need any of the blue chip insurance we've placed around the Reverend. You know, Victor, these past few months have been a revelation to me. Collins is just like the clientele who buy our product. He's addicted too.'

Rodriguez had been gazing at the spectacle of a small boat-owner making a hash of mooring. Sinclair's remark so startled him that he appeared to jump slightly into the air as he whipped round and stared at his counsellor.

'No, I don't mean on one of our products. Collins mainlines on manipulation, control. He gets off on exercising control over huge audiences. He adores it. When he walks into the White House he will never contemplate giving up the opportunity to control and manipulate that goes with that particular pulpit. When he realizes that he can only remain in the White House if he keeps you happy, he will reach the necessary compromise with his conscience. We might help him, Victor, perhaps reduce the supply of product, perhaps deliver him some of our less reliable members. He enjoys his successes and we enjoy a higher price structure . . .' He glanced at his watch. 'I must be away, Victor. I have an appointment with America's only living saint.'

CHAPTER SEVENTEEN

PUNISHMENT

'IF ANY SON OF A BITCH OFFERS ME NOODLES AS MY MAIN COURSE again, so help me, I'll take him out.' Oscar had not travelled well. 'Have you any idea how it feels for me to be sitting in this city?'

Freshly showered and dressed, and surrounded by the American way of life, Adam conceded that he could not imagine Oscar coping with Vietnam.

'Listen, I have never, but never, before set foot in this country without firepower. Right now all I have is this god-damn Panasonic DVC Pro camera and a laptop. This is no way to fight the enemy.'

'Oscar, the war is over. Don't you remember? Your side lost.' He held the phone and a stream of expletives away from his ear. When Oscar had subsided he asked, 'What time are you meeting the general?'

'Tomorrow morning outside the Army Museum at nine.'

'You'll enjoy that, Oscar. Get him to show you the tank they drove through the gates of the presidential palace. When are you seeing Professor Nguyen?'

'Still trying to pin him down.'

'Good luck, and remember to hold focus and keep the mike near the general.'

It looked as though the entire contents of his store at the Collins Association in Florida had been shipped up to New York and spread around the Garden. Although that was, indeed, the source of some of the religious material available, the Collins ministry did not have an exclusive on the location. God was for sale on a non-monopoly basis. Alternatives to abortion, accountants, air-conditioning, antiques, architects and auto-repair: each company, each individual, came with the Shepherd's Guide trademark. This indicated that the owner had signed the following statement of faith: 'I have received Jesus Christ as my personal Saviour. I pledge to hold the highest biblical code of ethics in my business transactions.'

Some had managed to interweave words from the Good Book into their placards. The appropriately named 'Galilee Marine Service. Engine Repairs – Gas & Diesel' drew inspiration and, hopefully, customers from Psalm 107: 23–4. 'They that go down to the sea in ships and do business in great waters; These see the works of the Lord and His wonders in the deep.'

There were Christian radio-station broadcasters conducting vox-pop interviews and a mass of Christian TV stations. Television monitors were sited throughout the corridors and walkways outside the main arena. This enabled the overflow audience to join in the hymns, the words appearing in large script on the screens.

In one annexe a fundamentalist preacher from Texas and his followers had erected a mobile swimming pool. The sign above it read, 'Instant Salvation. Get Baptized Today. Hot Towels Available.' The noisiest of the fringe attractions was a placard-waving group chanting about the unborn child or shouting for greater use of the death penalty. They were called the Silent Majority.

Then there was the Main Event.

In the central area the final rally in the presidential campaign for Patrick Collins had been warming up since midday. A mixture of the sacred and the profane, it had been building in tempo as it approached the scheduled appearance of the candidate at eight in the evening. The movers and shakers had followed each other on to the podium and in their various ways all had made the same plea: 'Vote for Collins.'

At exactly four minutes to the appointed hour the lights dimmed except for those trained on the thousand-strong choir who sang an unaccompanied version of 'Amazing Grace'. As the singing died away the lights gradually went out until there was only one, a spotlight on the lead soprano. She spoke quietly, but the radio mike she was wearing carried her voice to the furthest corners of Madison Square Garden. 'Please, dear Lord, walk with your servant Patrick Collins on this last stage of his journey to the mountain-top.'

In that moment her spotlight went out and a second came on to reveal the preacher standing, Bible in hand, centre stage.

As the arena went back to full-house lighting virtually every member of the capacity audience stood up, clapped and cheered. The cheering grew even louder as Collins moved a few paces towards the choir and gestured for John Reilly to join him.

He used neither notes nor autocue nor any prompts, yet he spoke with great fluency. Adam stood still in admiration: he had never seen the preacher stumble or hesitate.

'We hold these Truths to be self-evident, that all men are created equal, that they are endowed by their Creator with certain unalienable rights, that among these are life, liberty and the pursuit of happiness . . .'

Collins paused. His hands, though not touching, had been close to each other, now they began to separate. They stopped in mid-air three feet apart.

The preacher's reference to truths struck a chord in Adam's memory. Dinner at the Collins residence on that first evening after he and the crew had arrived from England. Adam remembered the strange moment when both Collins and Reilly had been reduced to silence at his quotation from the Bible. Now he understood why. 'And ye shall know the truth and the truth shall make ye free' was not only written in the Bible. It was carved in the marble hallway of the CIA headquarters at Langley.

'I say to you people of America, those truths are no longer self-evident. Many in this land have been denied, are being denied, those unalienable rights. The victims at Miami suffered that denial. The victims at Grand Central Station suffered that denial.

'I tell you, my fellow Americans, we are a long way from God. Evil stalks this land. Rampages through it. The devil's most brilliant trick and oh, he has so many. The devil's greatest trick . . .' Collins paused, then continued slowly. 'The devil's most brilliant trick has been to convince so many of our people that he does not exist. For evil to flourish, all that is required is that good men do nothing. If we do nothing, more planes will be blown out of the skies. There will be more bombs, more bodies, more burials.

'It's time to go to war. We've beaten the Communists. It's time we went after the new enemy. The enemy within. This evil comes in many forms and guises, some more tangible than others. If we still have to come to terms with the paranoiacs and their bombs and guns, if we still struggle to understand what drives such people to such deeds, there are other manifestations of evil in this country that are only too easily understood. The narcotics industry. The Unholy Trinity. Marijuana, cocaine, heroin. There the enemy is easily identifiable. There we can take immediate punitive action. There *we* can go on the attack.'

A loud crack of rifle fire resounded in the Garden and Patrick Collins was flung backwards. The first person to react was the man closest to the preacher. Almost simultaneously with the rifle shot there was a second shot as John Reilly pulled out a gun from his wheelchair pouch and fired a rapid burst high into the lighting gantry area to the rear of the Garden.

Leon looked at the security men rushing on to the podium.

Squinting into the eyepiece, he continued to film the group around the prone body of Patrick Collins. He caught a glimpse of blood coming from the right temple. A team of paramedics lifted the unconscious man on to a stretcher and rushed off the stage. Millions throughout the country were watching the rally on TV, others closer to the centre of the tragedy stood around television screens within Madison Square Garden transfixed by the screen images while, within a few feet of them, they could have observed the events happening in the flesh.

Andrew Sinclair and his entire executive cabinet had been waiting in a nearby reception room. Collins had planned to bring them all on stage, had planned to tell the audience how if elected it would be men like these to whom he would be turning when selecting his cabinet. When Collins had fallen to the floor of the stage, all colour had drained from Sinclair's face. He sat frozen to his seat while confusion swirled around him.

Then he became aware that someone was talking to him. He turned in his seat. It was Teresa Collins. 'Andrew, let's get to the hospital.'

Sinclair's reflex actions obeyed the request as he stood and began to shepherd Teresa towards the door. For the first time for many years he was engulfed in a situation that he could not control. Back in the main arena, John Reilly restored a semblance of calm. 'We will achieve nothing by panic. Let us try to achieve something by prayer. First I would ask the choir to sing and I would ask that each and every one of you joins in. Let our voices be heard. Let our heads be held high.'

The choir began 'Amazing Grace' with John Reilly urging the audience to join in. By the end of the second line everyone in the audience was singing.

Through much of the bedlam Adam had not taken his eyes off the lighting gantry at the far end of the arena. His vigilance was rewarded halfway through the hymn. He tapped Leon on the shoulder and pointed. Leon swung the camera round and filmed uniformed officers carrying a stretcher from the gantry.

Adam and his crew made their way to the nearest exit and ran through the corridors. They were in time to film the police officers descending to ground level. The assassin's identity and his background details were not going to be volunteered by the man they had on the stretcher: John Reilly's burst of firing from his Heckler Koch had taken off the top of the gunman's head. The crew continued to film as the dead man was rushed towards the main entrance and the waiting ambulances. They were about to return inside when another ambulance came wailing to a halt. Out of it stepped Patrick Collins, a large plaster over part of his forehead. Adam and the crew got to him before anyone else.

'Pat, are you all right?'

Collins turned and recognized them. 'I'm fine. We'll talk later. I've got an audience that's been kept waiting far too long.'

Collins hurried inside. Again the film-crew began to move in the same direction. Again they were halted, this time by a police car depositing Andrew Sinclair and Teresa Collins.

'O Lord, hear our prayer and let our cry come unto you. Watch over your servant Patrick Collins. We beg—'

John Reilly was interrupted by a deafening roar. The next moment he was being held in an embrace by the man he had feared dead. 'Pat! What happened? Are you OK?'

'I'm fine, Johnny. Just fine. Thank God Andrew insisted I wear this bulletproof vest.'

'But the blood?'

'Guess the impact of the bullet knocked me flying. I caught my head on the side of the choir rostrum. It's nothing, just a scratch.'

They were close, faces almost touching, but still they were forced to shout over the maelstrom of sound rising up from the audience. Collins straightened and moved to the podium. In his right hand he still held his Bible. He raised it high. Many were openly weeping, convinced that they were seeing the first miracle of the Patrick Collins era.

Collins dropped his hand, but this time the audience kept on cheering, clapping and shouting. He grinned. It was a novel experience. It had been many years since he had lost control of an audience. Eventually he moved to the choir who, with John

Reilly, had heroically calmed and comforted a shocked and distressed stadium. The lead soprano threw her arms around him, almost as if fearing that unless she held him he would slip away again. Collins held her for a few seconds then murmured to her. A moment later she began to sing. Collins had requested the one piece of music that he knew would silence them. He stood back at the speaker's rostrum, right hand still holding the Bible by his heart, as the words of 'God Bless America' rang out pure and clear through the arena.

As the audience settled at the end of the singing Collins looked out across the sea of faces. 'As I was saying.'

It broke the tension. They hollered and whooped, and eventually fell silent then listened as Patrick Collins delivered a blistering attack on the illegal narcotics industry in America.

Later that evening Adam and the crew attended a reception given by Patrick and Teresa Collins. With Teresa on his arm the preacher offered a short prayer and a gracious thank-you. Among those personally thanked were Adam Fraser and his crew. 'Although perhaps I should reserve that thank-you until we've seen the finished programme.'

As Adam moved around the party he caught sight of the press secretary, Sam Barnes. Characteristically, he held a mobile phone in one hand and a drink in the other.

'What's the latest on the would-be assassin, Sam?'

'He is, or rather was, Winston Thomas, a leading light in the Yardies.'

'The Yardies. As in West Indian Yardies? Drugs? Organized crime?'

'The same. The narco-barons obviously wanted to stop Pat before he got elected and stopped them. It's an absolute miracle.'

'It certainly is, Sam. I was certain he'd killed Pat.'

'That too, of course, Adam, but I was talking about Johnny getting him. The son of a bitch had enough weaponry up there to take out a lot of people. He'd obviously planned a massacre.'

'But where was the security? Not only Pat's normal security team, but the government security. CIA or whatever.'

Sam grabbed his arm vigorously. 'You better believe it, Adam, there's been a fuck-up somewhere. It'll take time to find out where. Hey, excuse me, I must grab Johnny Reilly.' He plunged into the crowd and across the room.

'You were going to call me.'

It was Mary Sinclair. Whoever she had consulted this time about the dress she was wearing had done an excellent job. Provocative was the word that came to Adam's mind.

'Mary, I'm working a sixteen-hour day.'

'Such a waste. I'm going to be all alone up at Hamilton this weekend.'

Susanna had been trying to attract his attention for some time. He motioned for her to join him.

'Sorry, I've got the laboratory on the phone. They're rushing the negs of tonight's filming through. Do you want the film couriered to the editing suite?'

'I'll have a word with them. I'm sorry, Mary, I'll phone as soon as I can.'

As he hurried towards the phone, he muttered to Susanna. 'Thank you for that, Su.'

'For what?'

'Never mind. Where's the phone?'

The journey from his hotel to the Army Museum on Dien Bein Phu Street by cyclo stirred yet more phantoms within Oscar. During the war the cyclos had been used extensively by the Vietcong but often with time-bombs rather than passengers. He stopped a short distance from the museum. Pure habit asserted itself. Survey the meeting-place, check alternative exits. Within a few steps the humidity caused him to perspire freely as he struggled with the pieces of equipment. The general was waiting.

'Good morning, Mr Lear. What a pleasure to meet you.'

After the attempt on his life in Amsterdam, Oscar had been obliged to create a further false identity for his overseas travels. Yet again he had borrowed from Shakespeare. The general and Adam had known each other for many years, since Adam had first come to Hanoi with his crew. Adam worked assiduously at maintaining his contacts, many of whom – like the general – had become a friend. He had contacted just two men in Hanoi and opened the doors for Oscar's visit. Notwithstanding his friendship with Adam, though, the general had initially been circumspect. Oscar approved of such caution. It probably explained why the man had risen to his present position within the Ministry of Defence. He had questioned Oscar closely during a number of telephone conversations. He appeared to want every detail, no matter how trivial, that dealt with the last mission Collins had led during the war. He strolled with Oscar through the museum and, without prompting, showed the American the tank that had pushed the gates of the presidential palace in Saigon as it had entered and brought the war to an end.

'Our records are not on computer yet. One day perhaps, but for the present we are confined to more traditional filing methods, therefore the more detail the more chance of ident-ifying the particular intelligence files.'

They paused by a B52 bomber, on top of it a MIG 21.

'And was your search successful, General?'

The general responded with a wide grin. 'Yes, it was.'

Oscar waited for the general to elaborate. Instead he con-tinued to act as an enthusiastic guide as they toured through the rest of the museum. After they had considered every item, the general beamed again. 'I would be honoured if you would be my guest for breakfast.'

Oscar duly accepted the invitation. This was the Vietnamese way, when they were ready and not before. He suppressed a groan as they headed for a noodles stall and the general, having selected a table on the edge of the area, turned to him. 'A bowl of *phô* and a Hanoi beer?'

'Just what I need.'

Oscar's bulk descended on to a stool less than two feet high.

Eventually with the bowls emptied and removed, the general leaned back. 'I have located a number of reports that deal specifically with the incident that is of interest to you.'

'Excellent. May I have copies?'

'No, I am afraid that will not be possible.'

'Then will you go on the record and give me a briefing based on those reports?'

'No, I am afraid that will not be possible either.'

'Off the record. Come on, General, this is important to Adam Fraser.'

'I realize that, but I'm sorry, not even off the record.'

'You have the American version of these events. Do your reports confirm or contradict that version?'

The general looked up and down the street. Satisfied that they were not being observed, he leaned towards Oscar. 'They contradict the American version. That is off the record.'

Oscar was exasperated.

'Look, General, not long ago my country was fighting Vietnam. We were the Yankee imperialist enemy, remember? I would have thought that you would have been delighted to have yet another opportunity to show what bad people we were.'

'Again, off the record, it is not in the interest of our future relationship with the United States that this information is made public.'

Oscar stared hard at the General. 'The Waldheim gambit. That's it, isn't it?'

The general looked genuinely bemused. 'Waldheim gambit? I'm sorry, I don't play chess.'

'Oh, but you do, General, you do.'

As Adam showered he listened to the five a.m. newscasts. The President was expressing relief at the miraculous escape of the man who was within a few days of being elected his successor.

'Extraordinary news just in. The Miami DEA have confirmed that Winston Thomas was under their control and acting as an undercover narcotics agent. A DEA spokesman said that the department was fully aware that before recruiting Thomas he had murdered at least ten people in the West Indies and that he was also involved in the illegal drugs trade in the

Caribbean.' The TV news reporter speculated on the would-be assassin's likely motive. As Thomas had also been a major player in the sale of cocaine in Detroit, he may have regarded Collins's war on drugs as a personal threat.

Adam was still considering the implications of this development when his cab dropped him on West 43rd. He hurried out of the early-morning chill into the building where his editing suite was located. Mark, his editor, and Susanna were waiting at the security point near Reception.

'Hey, come on, you two, I thought you'd have the film up and running by now.'

Susanna moved quickly to meet him. 'We've been locked out. The security guard has been instructed by the owners of the building that we are to be denied access to our suite.'

The security guard was Himmler without the charm. 'You Adam Fraser?'

'As I've been coming in here every day for the past month for at least sixteen hours a day and every time I come in you say, "Good morning, Mr Fraser," you tell me who I am.'

The security guard eyed him keenly. 'You being a smartass?'

'Would you recognize one?'

The security guard thrust a clipboard into Adam's hand. 'Sign opposite your name.'

Adam obliged and was handed a bulky envelope. He ripped it open and read the first page of a long letter. He looked up at Susanna and Mark. 'Let's go and find somewhere quiet and have breakfast while I read this little lot.'

Mark glanced at his watch. 'Adam, we've no time for breakfast. We're behind schedule for the day's work already.'

'We won't be working today, Mark. Come to that, we won't be working tomorrow or any other day. Not on this doco anyway.'

Susanna gripped his arm. 'What do you mean?'

Adam read aloud from the letter. ' "Network One has therefore decided not to proceed with this project and we confirm that it will not be transmitted." '

'The bastards! They can't do that.' Susanna's raised voice caused the security guard to get to his feet.

Adam looked at her. Suddenly he felt completely exhausted. 'Oh, Su. I'm afraid they can and these nice New York lawyers have sent me a copy of my own contract all marked up to demonstrate that they are acting entirely and absolutely within their legal rights. Come on, let's get out of here.'

By the time they were having breakfast, Susanna and Mark were showing an advanced state of shock. It helped Adam and gave him a focus. 'They go out of their way to say how highly my work is regarded by everyone at the Network. However, "Recent changes on the board have caused Network One to review a number of its long-term commitments . . ." ' Anger began to rise up within him. ' "Major sponsors have indicated considerable unease at the possibility of a critical examination of a new president so close to his election . . . Possible negative public reaction . . ." They've covered themselves totally, I'm afraid. That'll teach me to sell world rights to one company, won't it?'

Mark was continuing to shake his head in disbelief. 'And that's it? Just like that? You've been working on this project for over two years and now there's nothing to show for it.'

Adam held up some pieces of paper. 'Oh, I wouldn't say nothing. Apart from not showing the film, they're honouring all aspects of my contract with them. Being terribly generous, even paying the escalator that only becomes due if Collins wins the presidency. I've got cheques here to the value of four million dollars. That also covers the ten-year exclusivity clause and assumes that Collins has already won. All paid up and I can offer anything I make in the future to anyone I like. The downside? No way does the Collins doco ever see the light of day and if I cash these cheques it will be deemed that I accept their offer in full, no legal recourse, etc., etc., and there's a long letter to that effect for me to sign and return by hand to their bank when I present these cheques for payment. That's about it.'

Susanna looked at Adam across the breakfast table. 'What are you going to do?'

Adam looked back at her, holding her gaze. 'I'm going back

to my hotel room to study all of this paper. I don't think they've left me a loophole, but I'm going to look for one. If I can find a way to resurrect the film we'll still need a couple of editing sessions. I want my doco up there on the screen. I want America to know what it's getting by electing Collins. I'd be grateful for a call first if either of you decide to go out just in case by some miracle I can get this show back on the road.'

'World Trade Center, please.'

Adam sat coiled in the back of the yellow cab planning what he would say to Andrew Sinclair, then he'd cab over to the campaign office near Central Park and find Collins and Reilly, then . . . He checked himself. His obsession with this particular project was, had been, so great that he had forgotten one of his basic rules of survival: don't let the bastards have unknown victories.

There would be no Sinclair at the World Trade Center. Not on a Saturday morning. Particularly with the election so close. With the last rally over, there would certainly be no Collins or Reilly at the New York campaign office. Running all over town hunting bogeymen was pointless.

He had to calm down. There was no time to indulge emotions. Just sit on the phone and ring round. Give nothing away. Act as if it was an everyday event to see so much hard work thrown in the bin.

'Driver, I've changed my mind. Take me to Broadway at 48th. The Renaissance.'

It was quite remarkable, the number of people who had now apparently vanished. Certainly they were uncontactable at every number.

Adam sat in his hotel bedroom creating an ever-growing list of the missing. He flicked on the wildtrack tape that Barry had recorded a lifetime ago on the Collins patio in Florida. The day that Sinclair had come calling and dangled dreams of the White House in front of the preacher. He had taken to playing it a great deal over the past month. The sounds of the mockingbirds, mourning doves and northern cardinals effortlessly evoked a perfect summer's day. He added the name of Sam Barnes to the list of uncontactables. It was always possible that the campaign team were having yet another of those off-the-record briefings so beloved by Sinclair. Andrew Sinclair, now where was he? Not at home, Mary had said she'd be alone this weekend. Sinclair would be wherever Collins was. Where was Collins? It was becoming circular. He picked up the pile of correspondence from Network One's lawyers and, crossing to the desk, began to study it yet again.

If only he hadn't been so eager to sign the contract but, then, no matter how long he had negotiated he would never have anticipated this. It didn't make sense. The phone rang. It was Susanna. 'I've been busy.'

'And?'

'I got hold of a contact on the *Wall Street Journal*. It was that remark in the lawyer's letter about recent changes on the board at Network One.'

'Oh, yes? I'm having trouble getting Ralph Phillips, the man I did the deal with.'

'You won't get him. He was moved sideways six months ago.'

'You sure, Su? I think someone on the Network One board would have been in touch earlier if that was so.'

'I'm sure. No publicity. Confidentiality clause. Part of the sweetener package. All recommended by the management consultants who advise Network One. Sinclair's company. Corporate America. They were brought in by the new majority shareholder nearly a year ago. The new majority shareholder is a company called Mill Valley Holdings, a subsidiary of Global Systems. Hello, Adam? Adam, are you still there?'

He was fighting yet again to control rage. 'Oh yes, I'm here. Beautiful. So Edgar Lee Stratford owned the bloody Network before I was signed up to it. That's why they were so insistent that all the footage had to be stored in a bonded area. They never intended to put the piece out. I have to hand it to Mr Andrew Sinclair. He has comprehensively screwed me—'

'Adam? Hello?'

'It's all right, Su. Still here. That takes care of the documentary. It's not going to happen. No way. Hey, if you want to go back to London early, that's fine. I don't think I'll be doing any more filming. No point, really.'

'I think I'd like to wait until Wednesday, if you don't mind.'

'OK. I may be uncontactable for a while. Don't worry. And, Su . . .'

'What, Adam?'

'Thanks for the information. You always were the best researcher in the business. Take care.'

With the birds of Florida still singing happily in the background, Adam sat running through his options. He picked up the phone. 'Hello, Mary. How are you? Yes. I've decided to play hookey for the day. Still want to see me? I'll be with you before midday.'

Having run the lines through his mind, he shook his head. Sinclair was far too bright to have left anything incriminating lying around at his home. He replaced the telephone on the hook. It rang immediately.

Oscar listened quietly for longer than he ever had before.

'So you see, Oscar, the Network owns the copyright on everything that is in the documentary as it stands today, plus of course all the out-takes. Leaving everything else aside, no media outlet is going to risk being bankrupted in a multi-million dollar breach of copyright action. I've got a second copy of my interview with Mónica in London, but on its own what does it prove? That a cartel member now dead had a meal with Collins. He'll plead ignorance.'

'How much of what we've got hold of is in your film?'

'All of it, Oscar. They've waited until almost the last minute to make sure of just that.'

'Your day is not about to get better.'

It was Adam's turn to listen while Oscar struggled to keep his temper as he recounted the details of his meeting. 'I was so close to it, Adam. So near, I could smell it. The government out here have struck gold. Our gold. Goddammit, we've led them to something that they'll parley with the next administration for favourable trade terms, huge interest-free loans or something equally significant. I was tempted to grab him by the throat and shake it out of him.'

'What about Professor Nguyen?'

'He seems to be permanently uncontactable. I'll keep trying. I'm going back to my hotel. Anything breaks, I'll phone you or raise you on the Internet.'

Adam began to pace the hotel room trying to find a way through what now seemed a series of impenetrable obstacles. All of the evidence that he had so painstakingly assembled now lay in a bonded area controlled by the Network. Working in a dictatorship he would have exercised greater prudence, particularly with regard to duplicate copies. But this was the United States of America. Citadel of the Free World. One Nation Under God.

That evidence, now permanently out of his reach, pointed to a conspiracy to seize ultimate power in America, but this was no bloody coup or insurrection. It was to be done through the ballot box. He had been thinking of a direct approach to Patrick Collins, but after listening to Oscar's account of his meeting with the general that was ruled out. What was the truth of the last mission that Collins had carried out in early 1968? If the general was to be believed, asking Collins for help was out of the question. And someone had been through his files before Oscar and Adam got there. The someone was likely to have been Sinclair. If anything had been found it had been removed. The Vietnamese were not the only ones playing the Waldheim gambit.

Suddenly Oscar's last remark about the Internet came back to him. If he had not been so caught up with his own anger, he would have remembered before. Professor Nguyen was on the Internet. Adam switched on his laptop, and checking the number on his index went through to the professor's website. 'I need to talk to you very urgently,' he tapped in, followed by his identification and number.

He had barely finished ordering food from room service

when the laptop activated. The professor had been collecting his e-mail when Adam's message came through.

'He wants you to take on what appointment?'

Victor Rodriguez had halted dead in his tracks. He had been on his way to the bar in his Boston hotel suite when Sinclair had stopped him.

'Collins wants to appoint me as his national security adviser with a special secondary role as – and these were his exact words – "narcotics overlord".'

The chairman broke into one of his rare paroxysms of laughter. Finally he brought himself under control and said, 'Highly satisfactory.'

A phone rang in the suite. Rodriguez yet again demonstrated an economy of language when obliged to answer it. 'Yes. Thank you.' He replaced the receiver and turned back to Sinclair.

'Our Mr Ruby has returned safely to the bosom of his family.'

'I must tell you, Victor, that was as near as I've come to dying of shock. When I saw Collins hurtling backwards, then the blood. I thought Thomas had shot him in the head or that the bulletproof vest had been penetrated. I thought he was dead.'

'So did the rest of the world, until he made the greatest comeback since Lazarus. Thomas was a first class marksman, that was one of the reasons he was selected. The vest? Let me tell you, my friend, we tested it thoroughly. One volunteer who was wearing it was hit by an RPG 7 anti-tank rocket. The rocket didn't explode but the impact sent the volunteer through a wall. He survived the test without injury.'

Sinclair's eyebrows rose. 'Volunteer?'

Rodriguez shrugged. 'I think you'll find Thomas's links with our industry useful when you take up your government position.'

'Oh, yes, very useful. The fact that he was working for the DEA is an exquisite bonus. I'll be able to make them jump through any hoop. Now, Mr Adam Fraser.'

'You have news of our film-maker?'

'He banked his cheques at ten this morning and paid for them to be priority cleared. Those clauses you suggested putting into his contract appear to have served their purpose.'

'Not the clauses, Andrew, the money. Everyone has a price, it's just a matter of establishing it. His documentary?'

'Having viewed it, Victor, I recommend that when you've done the same, you have every scrap of material destroyed. That contract was the best investment you ever made.'

'So, my friend, all we have left to do is to wait just three more days to celebrate the successful conclusion of the Colombia Project. Please join me for dinner this evening in the Harvard Club. Say eight?'

Professor Nguyen was head of the history department at Hanoi University, but it was his expertise during the war that Adam sought. Military intelligence. After an extended conversation with him, Adam had then phoned Oscar at the Metropole Hotel. 'He will be expecting you within the hour.'

'Is he going to play?'

'Can't say yet, Oscar. He's going to pull the files out of the archives and study them. I've hired an editing suite complete with computer facilities. Let me give you the Internet number. And, Oscar, I'm going to wait by that computer until I hear from you.'

Clutching his equipment, Oscar moved through the archway into the central courtyard of the university, a yellow ochre relic of the French colonial period. Professor Nguyen occupied a large, high-ceilinged room, but any impression of power and influence offered by the size of the room was contradicted by the central fan, which had not worked for many years, and the latticed bookcases and walls that were in desperate need of a carpenter and a painter. Books were piled high over much of the desk. The occupant, like much around him, was also in need of renovation. The professor was by far the tallest Vietnamese that Oscar had ever seen, at least six feet. His shoes were badly scuffed, his trousers far too short and, like the jacket, the black material gleamed in the light. It was so shiny and had worn so thin that it lay on its owner's body like delicate silk. As Oscar was shown into the room he rose and shook his visitor's hand. Showing him to a chair, he displayed a directness that was in refreshing contrast to the general.

'I have studied the details carefully. I find the discrepancies fascinating.'

'The discrepancies?'

'Yes, between the version that Adam sent to me on the Internet, the US Army version, that is, and the reports from the Vietcong.' He began to count off points on his fingers. 'The American report talks of a six-man patrol and an incident that occurred ten miles south of Khe Sanh on March twenty-first, nineteen sixty-eight. Four members of the patrol were killed. The two surviving members killed at least eighteen members of the Vietcong before being rescued by helicopter. Our reports agree on just two facts. The date and the number of Americans who survived.'

The professor stood up, moved to the windows and closed them, reducing the sound of constant car horns to a bearable level. Oscar's eyes followed him back to his desk. As he sat, he began to tick off points on his fingers again. 'The American patrol numbered twenty-two. No Vietcong were killed and the incident did not take place ten miles south of Khe Sanh but forty miles west of there. Not in Vietnam, but in Laos, on the Ho Chi Minh trail.'

'In Laos? What were they doing there?'

The professor put his elbows on the large desk and leaned towards Oscar.

'Tell me. Have you ever heard of a CIA operation called the Long Silver Train?'

No matter how hard he tried, Adam found himself looking again at the clock on the wall of the editing suite. Oscar must have been with the professor for nearly two hours. Sitting by the waiting computer were his film-crew and Mark, his editor.

The five had created the best documentary that Adam had ever made. They were all aware that it was a film that would never be seen. The master print, the out-takes, Susanna's files – everything, as per the contract, was in the hands of the Network.

He had no qualms about taking the Network's four million. There was no compromise. You do not compromise with the cartels. They do not negotiate. Four million was generous: Adam might have settled for a full set of bodily organs.

The computer activated. 'Adam. Are you there?'

'Yes.'

'Give check words.'

'The truth will set you free.'

'Good. I have what we're looking for and will begin sending to you shortly. There are two sections. Use both. I repeat. Use both.'

'Understood.'

'I shall leave this place as soon as I finish sending.'

'Understood.'

Moments later the computer emitted a high-pitched tone, indicating that it had begun to receive.

Susanna looked anxiously at the others. 'There's nothing coming through. Have we lost the connection with Hanoi?'

'It's coming through digitally, Su. Whatever Oscar's recorded is being sent from his laptop via the prof's computer on the Internet through to a computer program here, which will interpret the sound and pictures. We won't see anything until he's finished sending. Then Adam will be able to play it back.'

The explanation had come from Barry. The soundman and the others began to elaborate for Susanna's benefit, like surgeons breaking off an operation to describe their techniques.

Eventually the tone stopped and a one-line message came across the screen. 'That's it. Go for it, my young friend.'

Adam looked at the others. 'Let's see what the man's sent us, then. We'll just watch it right through the first time, then we'll rerun looking to clean it up, edit points, maybe move material around, check picture and sound quality. Roll it, Mark.'

Suddenly a medium close-up of Professor Nguyen Tran Minh was on the screen. He was talking calmly and clearly in perfect English. The technical quality was excellent. 'Contrary to the version that the Pentagon released at the time, this patrol led by Major Patrick Collins was not on an intelligence-gathering mission south of Khe Sanh. It was meeting a group of Meo tribesmen in Laos, near the town of Ban Nabo. The purpose was not to obtain information but to exchange a large quantity of Kalashnikov rifles for five hundred kilos of heroin.'

Adam let out a long, loud yell of exultation.

The professor's calm, almost matter-of-fact manner added great power to what was already an extraordinary story. Adam began to realize just what Oscar and the professor had been doing while he had sat waiting and wondering in the editing suite. It was beautifully presented. A close-up of a document here, the dog-tag of one of the dead servicemen there. Translated intercepts of messages from John Reilly, who had been the radio man on the patrol. Photographs of a large pile of Kalashnikovs and an equally large pile of refined heroin. The story that Adam had listened to in a Hamburg restaurant, of the Long Silver Train, was gradually laid before the audience of five. Oscar had not only persuaded the professor to raid government archives, he had also rehearsed the interview – it flowed so seamlessly from one aspect to the next. The horror of using the dead bodies of GIs to smuggle heroin into the United States and the part that missions like Collins's played in the operation was followed by another devastating revelation.

Professor Nguyen had explained how the meeting between the CIA team and the tribesmen had been ambushed by a platoon from the Vietcong 514th Regional Battalion.

'As the Vietcong opened fire, Major Collins and his radio man, Lieutenant John Reilly, dropped the heroin they were carrying and deserted their comrades. They ran into the jungle and headed south. This information was given to the Vietcong platoon by two wounded Americans, John Drummond and Paul Taylor. Drummond died before the medics arrived, and Paul Taylor died three days later in a Hanoi hospital that was bombed by a B52. Members of the platoon subsequently gave chase and caught up with Collins and Reilly two miles south and running towards their helicopter. One of the Americans was shot in the back as the helicopter began to climb. I now know that to have been John Reilly.'

Again the allegations were substantiated by transcripts of intercept radio messages from Reilly to the search helicopter. The call sign of the Collins patrol was 'Pilgrim'.

Oscar had hardly asked a question throughout, but now he did. 'Professor, why have you decided to go on record with the information?'

The academic considered the question. 'Before today I did not know of its existence. Why go public? At the end of the war this country, like your own, had many, many drug addicts. Over two hundred thousand in Saigon alone. Over the past two decades we had thought the problem was cured, the number of addicts dropped to a few hundred in the entire country. Now because Vietnam is a major trade route out of the Golden Triangle to the United States, some of the heroin inevitably falls off on the way, just as straw falls from a cart as it makes its journey to market. I fight this industry wherever I find it. It is right that the people of the United States should know about the single greatest reason for the drugs problem they face.'

Suddenly Professor Nguyen was replaced on the screen by Oscar. 'I can't verify the details you have just been given about that mission led by Patrick Collins. But I can verify the accuracy of all that you have heard about the operation known as the Long Silver Train.'

As Oscar began to outline his own involvement he held up to camera a whole range of passports and documents that established him as a CIA agent. Susanna murmured to Adam, 'You can't use that. He's signing his own death warrant.'

'Oscar knows that as well as we do. That's why he said at the start about using both sections. By the time we get this out, Oscar will be safe at home.'

'But for how long?'

'I don't know, Su. Let's just make sure that the risk he took was worthwhile.'

Adam and the crew worked quickly, editing, cutting, refining the picture, enhancing the sound. As finished copies were completed and delivered to selected media targets, others were being compiled. By midday a hundred video-tapes had been sent out. In just three days' time the nation would elect a new president.

Adam was working on the principle that most would balk at playing it on air until someone, somewhere, opened the flood-gates. The man who obliged was a shock-jock called Big Al, previously one of Collins's greatest fans. Once the media had a cable station breaking ranks they elbowed and jostled to be next out with the news.

'. . . The purpose was not to obtain information but to exchange a large quantity of Kalashnikov rifles for five hundred kilos of heroin.'

The newsroom of the *New York Times* had never been so silent during a weekday mid-afternoon. On the deputy editor's terminal an unfinished editorial for the following day advised the paper's readers to vote for Collins. The terminal asked, 'Save?' The deputy editor wiped the text, permanently.

In supermarkets, malls, stores, bars, lifts, restaurants throughout the country activity stopped, everywhere people were listening and watching.

'As the Vietcong opened fire, Major Collins and his radio man Lieutenant John Reilly dropped the heroin they were carrying and deserted their comrades. They ran into the jungle and headed south . . .'

The Collins campaign team had gone into overdrive attempting to halt the tidal wave rushing across the country. They issued denials and threats, they prevaricated, they blustered, but the broadcasts kept coming.

'I can confirm that the Reverend Collins had been seconded to the CIA and had been working for them for the last eight months of his tour of duty in South East Asia. I can also confirm the details of operation Long Silver Train that the professor has given are absolutely accurate. I was also part of that operation. My duties covered every aspect, including packing the heroin into the bodies of dead American servicemen.'

In his palatial Boston residence Collins had been entertaining Edgar Lee Stratford and the other members of his corporate cabinet when the first wave of reporters hit the phones seeking a response from the candidate. The cabinet sat transfixed, watching TV.

Sinclair sat in his command centre on the hundredth floor at the World Trade Center. In May he had sat here shortly after Patrick Collins had declared his candidacy. Then, as now, every screen in the room had shown the words of the preacher being carried across the United States.

Clare entered carrying a sheaf of messages. 'The switchboard is going into meltdown with the calls, Andrew. Are you still unavailable?'

'To everyone except Victor Rodriguez.'

She was about to leave the room when she realized that no sound was coming from any of the screens. 'Shall I turn up the volume?'

'No, thank you, Clare. They're just fine as they are.'

She closed the door quietly.

Sinclair gazed at the silent images for a moment longer, then, hitting a master control button, turned them off and walked back into his office. For the first time in many years he was aware of the skyline across the Hudson. The November sun was already beginning to slip away, throwing the skyscrapers on the far bank into dark relief. Shafts of blood orange hung on the New York skyline. Sinclair smiled. He had been mentally seeking the up-side, the positive. As always, he had found it. They had come so close, so very close, to seizing the heart of democratic power, to getting the best president that money could buy. If that fat old CIA agent had been eliminated the project would have achieved all of its objectives. Oscar had shared with the nation what Sinclair had caused to be removed from the preacher's security files.

The phone rang.

'Victor? I've prepared a statement for the media. Wanted to run it past you before I release it.'

Collins strode to the large TV set and turned it off. Stratford studied him for a moment. It was difficult to know what the preacher was thinking. He seemed deeply preoccupied.

'Pat, we've got to issue a statement. We must refute these allegations. It's obviously some kind of smear tactic to de-stabilize the country on the eve of your election. No one's going to believe a Communist professor and a CIA agent. No one's going to take their word against yours.'

'I've done nothing to be ashamed of, Edgar. Nothing. I served my country to the best of my abilities. I did my duty.'

The phone rang and Teresa Collins picked it up.

'Hello? What statement? No, he has nothing to say.' She slammed down the receiver and turned the TV back on. A newscaster was reading from a single sheet of paper.

'. . . I therefore do not think under the present circum-stances we can continue to offer ourselves as candidates in this election. I will not stand idly by while the highest office in the land is subjected to such controversy. I have sought at all times, both in my civilian life and during my service in the United States Army, to serve the people of this country. This I and John Reilly will continue to do. Thank you, and God bless America.'

No one in the drawing room moved or stirred, except Teresa, who switched off the set. 'He's boxed you in, Patrick.'

'Who?'

'Andrew Sinclair. He's just announced your withdrawal from the race.'

'Then I'll deny I'm withdrawing. I'll insist on a retraction. We were only obeying orders. No more than that. In war, different standards, different values apply. We were fighting godless Communism. LBJ understood that, so did Nixon. The cover-up was the government's idea, not mine. The public will understand. They won't condemn me.'

320

Teresa moved to him and gently took his hands. 'No, Patrick. Sinclair was right to withdraw you. Imagine the accusations going on day after day. Central government would cease to function. It would be Watergate all over again. Remember what they did to Richard Nixon. Month after month. A political crucifixion that went on for two years before he resigned rather than be impeached. I'm not going to let you suffer something like that. If you're not elected, Patrick. If you stand aside. Now. Today. Then we may be able to contain the damage.'

Still in his New York office, Andrew Sinclair was feeling more positive. It was a temporary setback, no more than that. The American voters would do no more than win themselves a four-year respite. Nothing had happened to prevent another assault on the democratic process. The blueprint that Sinclair had worked on for the Colombia Project was intact. He mentally ticked off the other names on his shortlist, those who had been also-rans for this election. Fortuitously his entire corporate cabinet were in Boston where, in a few hours, he would be having dinner. When Victor Rodriguez called he would suggest that instead of dinner for two they should make it dinner for six.

Oscar sat in the heart of the Dolls' House. He had every television set and every radio tuned to American wavelengths. A cacophony of sound that to his ear was more beautiful than anything he had ever heard. Like a proud parent he lit a Cuban cigar, opened a bottle of special wine and strolled around his domain. He stopped to address a photograph of Collins, yet again on the cover of *Time* magazine. The headline read 'Destiny Beckons?'

'Destiny has just screwed you, preacher man. Do you know, I think maybe later I might just take a little stroll down the Reeperbahn.'

At JFK airport a huge group had gathered around the television set in the departure bar. To one side, sipping their drinks and waiting for their flight to London to be called, Adam and his film-crew watched and listened. Adam turned to Susanna. 'When I began this, I remember saying, when I pitched the idea for a doco on Collins to Mitch, that everyone has a dark side, even someone like Patrick Collins. We looked so hard for it, didn't we? All that research. All those questions. Remember on the plane from Florida to Boston? I got Collins talking about his gospel according to Elmer Gantry. About the three most important traps any would-be evangelist must avoid. Money, sex, and hubris, or pride. Elmer Gantry was also an appalling hypocrite. We've just nailed Collins to the wall by exposing his pride and his hypocrisy. Now the entire nation, the entire world, knows about the preacher's dark side.'

'Does it feel very sweet?'

'No, Su. Very sour. Very bitter. I feel angry. Cheated.'

'Because we never got to transmit the documentary?'

'I suppose that colours my feelings, but it goes deeper. Over the months, until very recently, I'd become convinced that Collins was the exception to the rule. That the outer truth was the inner truth. But he wasn't. He's just like everyone, a prisoner of the enemy within.'

EPILOGUE

POST MORTEM

'ONE YEAR AGO, ALMOST TO THE DAY, WE EMBARKED ON A project to purchase the United States of America. What occurred shortly before the presidential election should not in any way obscure the successes of that enterprise. There are, of course, lessons to be learned, but I believe we should also acknowledge our achievements.'

The annual general meeting of the board, the Cartel of Cartels, was considering the first item on the agenda. The Colombia Project. Andrew Sinclair had the floor.

'Our selection of candidate was perfect. Collins had everything, including one fatal flaw in his history. Given that the flaw remained secret, he presented an ideal subject to compromise and manipulate and but for the actions of a renegade member of the CIA, we would now be referring to the Reverend as President Collins.

'The flaw in question also conveniently applied to the

intended vice-president, John Reilly. Had it become necessary to depose both men simultaneously, their constitutional successor, the Speaker of the House of Representatives, was even more compromised in a different way.

'The trail of cocaine that we laid right to the door of the Oval Office; the donations from cartel members to the Collins religious foundation, the photographs of Collins at dinner with those same members, the Stratford laundry supplying traceable funds for the Cybersafe takeover and flotation, the linkage of the late Fernando Salazar with the would-be assassin Winston Thomas, each and every tentacle was perfectly placed. Your various contributions to the entire exercise were – with the exception of our French colleagues – flawless. Their inability to fulfil a contract in Amsterdam or to identify the target's base in Paris resulted in something less than a complete success. I believe, however, that the entire operation should be regarded as a rehearsal for the *next* presidential election in four years' time. All of the entrapment techniques that I have just mentioned can be used again.

'Another element that can be reactivated is the concept of the strategy of tension. The mid-air destruction of Cola One, the Chicago bank, the Miami bombing and the attack on Grand Central dramatically demonstrated how even a country as powerful as America can be unnerved. It created the perfect climate for our candidate. I am convinced that the large lead Collins enjoyed in polls throughout the campaign can be traced to public perception that he was the man to lead the nation at this hour of peril and that he would find the answer to this threat from within.

'I am aware that the decision to arrange an apparent assassination attempt on Collins had its critics among you. While it is true that Collins appeared to have an unassailable lead at that stage of the election, one can never have too much insurance and in selecting Winston Thomas our chairman gave the enterprise the added bonus of simultaneously compromising the DEA while inflaming public opinion against our industry. We must never forget, gentlemen, that the success of our business depends crucially on our products remaining illicit. If they were ever made legally available to the public, we would become history. That is precisely why we chose Collins, a president whose religious convictions would never have allowed him to take this logical step.

'I cannot say it too many times. Remember what happened when the Volstead Act was repealed and alcohol became legally available again in the United States.'

Because over many years Victor Rodriguez had carefully cultivated the image and reputation of a man in the front line of the war against narcotics, he was privy to a wealth of information on the illegal narcotics industry: top-secret government reports, the most sensitive DEA files, even those identifying CIs – confidential informants – reports from Mossad, the CIA, Interpol, British Intelligence. The list of top agencies that kept Rodriguez regularly updated covered almost every country in the world.

Oscar's hacking had failed to reach one section in particular that deals with the Cartel of Cartels' greatest fear. There is a National Security Agency global analysis of 'The Lobby to Legalize'. The lists of names are given country by country. The head of Interpol, senior British judges, police officers and Home Office officials, the former Secretary of State George Shultz, the former US Surgeon General Jocelyn Elders, leading medical specialists in many countries including the British Medical Association, opinion-makers like the *New York Times*, the *Independent* and *The Economist*, Colombia's chief prosecutor Gustavo de Greiff, billionaire financier George Soros, Milton Friedman, judges from the USA and a dozen more countries, the Ford and MacArthur Foundations. The full list numbers over three hundred. Most worrying, from the Cartel of Cartels' point of view, were the identities of prime ministers, heads of state and high-ranking officials of the very agencies committed to fighting the illegal narcotics industry. It was an extremely well-funded lobby. Billionaire Soros and multi-millionaire Richard Dennis, the analysis revealed, had donated many millions of dollars in the fight to decriminalize drugs. They saw their use as a 'human-rights issue'. The report concludes: 'Already California and Arizona have introduced legislation that legalizes marijuana and decriminalizes cocaine and heroin. Where California leads the rest of the country invariably follows.'

There are extracts from an FBI report. The front page showing the distribution and title is missing, but it is clearly an attempt to quantify and to cost some aspects of the illegal-drugs problem in the United States. 'Office of Management and Budget estimate that drug abuse is costing the nation $350 billion annually.' Much on the appalling cost to that nation follows.

> Drug prohibition is the reason why America has 1.6 million people in prisons. Sixty-three per cent of all inmates in federal prisons are drug offenders. Most have never committed a violent crime, but under 'mandatory minimum sentences' passed by Congress in 1986 their average sentence is longer than those convicted of murder or rape. Imprisonment for drug offences is now the biggest single cause of single-parent families and family break-up among the black population. Apart from the financial cost of this policy the zero-tolerance approach is an overwhelming failure. Drug abuse is now higher than in the 1960s. Marijuana use among teenagers, for example, has doubled during the past four years. It is clear that approaching 70 per cent of global crime would be eliminated by the legalization of marijuana, cocaine and heroin.

The author of the report, still dealing only with the fiscal implications of the problem, then moves into the up-side of legalizing what the report called 'the big three'.

> Legalized drugs would provide a major new source of public revenue. This has been estimated as a potential yield of a minimum of $12 billion annually in new taxes.

The writer also examines what happened to the street price of cocaine when there was a government crackdown:

> New York officials report that within three weeks of the Colombian government's increased drive against the cartels, the wholesale price rose by nearly a half and retail prices by three-fifths. Prices in New York have moved from $18,000 per kilo to $26,000 at this time of writing.

In Rodriguez's computer files there are extracts from a State Department document. Entitled 'Real Politics in the Real World' it gives details of the 'deep involvement at high government levels' of an array of countries in the illegal-narcotics industry. Syria, Burma, Iran, Italy, Germany, Pakistan . . . A United Nations of narcotics. The report discusses the impossibility of ever winning the war against drugs without destroying foreign relations with these countries. It cites the dependence these nations place on the industry:

> Twenty-nine per cent of Pakistan's GDP is derived from the illegal narcotics industry . . . Syria's continuing occupation of Lebanon is entirely financed by the production and sale of illegal narcotics . . . The building industry in Italy . . . The tourist industry in the Caribbean . . . Narco money is underpinning so many nations that to stop the flow of this revenue would have catastrophic implications.

'The secret study that this board authorized on certain aspects of President Clinton's two terms of office is nearly complete. The chairman would like to share some preliminary observations and findings with you.'

'Thank you, Andrew.'

Unlike his Stanford University-trained adviser, Rodriguez had not had the benefit of any lessons in public speaking. He was always unsure whether to stand or sit. On this occasion with printed-out pages spread before him, he elected to remain sitting.

'I think just a few fragments of this report will help concentrate our minds as we consider the future.

'Item. There was not a serious attempt during Clinton's two terms to utilize satellite intelligence. If the USA is sincere when the administration states it has declared war on drugs, then they have the technical capacity to precisely pinpoint every field of marijuana, coca bush and poppy in the world. This they have not done.

'Item. In Great Britain not one case of money-laundering has ever been brought by the government, this although a minimum of one hundred billion dollars a year is laundered in London.

'Item. Major tobacco companies in the United States are positioning themselves to take over officially the distribution of marijuana. One of the ways that I believe we should combat that particular threat is to position ourselves to take over the distribution of tobacco when its sale is inevitably declared illegal. I'm gratified to report that the happy day when we start to reap huge profits from the sale of tobacco has come much closer since the Vatican called for it to be banned and compared its addictive qualities with heroin.

'All of the prophecies made by our consultants in their last report have come true. Some examples – the President has waged war against nicotine, but not against our products. Eighty per cent of the staff of the office of National Drug Control in the executive branch have been eliminated during the past four years. During the same period US Customs has lost nearly sixty million dollars of its drug interdiction budget, five hundred and thirty-three positions have been eliminated from the DEA, the Coastguard's interdiction budget has been cut by nearly fifteen million dollars. The Pentagon has had its drug-related budget slashed by three hundred million dollars. Conclusion: the way has been prepared for the next administration to legalize marijuana, cocaine and heroin.'

Rodriguez collected his various notes and papers and tapped them into a neat pile. 'It is, of course, true that many government agencies worldwide still contain individuals who believe we can be beaten if the war against us is continued. Long may they live. It is also true that it is in the interests of certain sections of the CIA, British Intelligence and other government agencies to ensure that our product continues to remain illegal. This ensures that they are able to finance their "off-the-books" activities with the profits they make from drug sales. I do not believe we should rely on such elements to ensure that the present situation of illegality continues.'

Rodriguez paused and looked thoughtfully around the table at his fellow board members.

'We came within touching distance of buying the United States. Just as in the past it is, indeed, for sale. The Louisiana Purchase, Florida, Alaska, even New York are powerful historical precedents, but we require just the seat of supreme power. During the 1992 presidential campaign hundreds of thousands of dollars were donated by drug cartels to the Clinton campaign. Four years later large sums of money were again donated to President Clinton's campaign. Subsequently these donations have been traced back to the donors. The real beauty of what we so nearly achieved twelve months ago is that every cent raised was entirely clean, was legal. What we have done once, we can do again.

'I propose that we apply Andrew's solution to this problem and that we begin to plan now for the next presidential election. All those in favour please raise their right hand.'

APPENDIX A

'ON PAGE TWENTY-SEVEN OF THE ANNUAL REPORT YOU WILL find details of the highly successful meetings held in Miami and London between board members and a group of Russian bankers and businessmen. Agreement was reached with the Russian consortium on two crucial problems. First, trade routes: after Chechnya was neutralized by central government and therefore ceased being a centre for our business activities your board urgently sought a viable alternative. This they have now established at Azerbaijan and the Baltic States, particularly Estonia. These routes have been guaranteed by senior officers in the Federal Security Service and the Main Security Directorate. Second, banking: agreement was reached with the Russian consortium to channel three billion dollars through their services. This money will then be extended as a credit line to the Russian government and your board is delighted to confirm that Anton Markov has added three new members to his divisional group: Minister Shulov, Minister Akayev and the former head of the FSB, Filipp Bobkov. As a result of this we will soon be acquiring two Russian navy submarines complete with their full complement of crew. These diesel-driven Kilo submarines will operate between Colombian and Baltic Sea ports. They will be very welcome additions to the forty-three Russian helicopters that the company already owns.'

APPENDIX B

'AS MOST OF YOU ARE FULLY AWARE, YOUR BOARD IS CONSTANTLY preaching the value of long-term planning as opposed to crisis management. Our activities in Mexico, particularly with regard to the problems on the US/Mexican border, underline the value of patient long-term strategy. Consequently, as truck traffic over the border increases, product seizures decrease. Three years ago there were seven thousand seven hundred and eight seizures. The following year this had been reduced to one thousand seven hundred and sixty-five. I am still awaiting confirmation of last year's figures from our personnel working within the DEA, but the indications are excellent. Those contacts have advised us that the percentage of our various products used in the United States that have come via Mexico during the last financial year are as follows. Product one, seventy-five per cent. Product two, twenty per cent. Product three, sixty per cent. Which of course is precisely why Mexico is invariably described as "the trampoline".'